D1738697

Books of Merit

A Good Man

CYNTHIA HOLZ

A GOOD MAN

A Novel

Thomas Allen Publishers

Toronto

National Library of Canada Cataloguing in Publication Data

Holz, Cynthia, 1950–
A good man / Cynthia Holz.

ISBN 0-88762-118-X

I. Title.

PS8565.O649G66   2003   C813'.6   C2002-906153-9

PR9199.3.H584G66   2003

Jacket and text design: Gordon Robertson
Editor: Patrick Crean
An early version of chapter 1 appeared in *Parchment:
    Contemporary Canadian Jewish Writing, 2000–2001*

Published by Thomas Allen Publishers,
A division of Thomas Allen & Son Limited,
145 Front Street East, Suite 209,
Toronto, Ontario M5A 1E3 Canada

www.thomas-allen.com

ONTARIO ARTS COUNCIL
CONSEIL DES ARTS DE L'ONTARIO

The publisher gratefully acknowledges the support of
the Ontario Arts Council for its publishing program

07 06 05 04 03   1 2 3 4 5

Printed and bound in Canada

For Paul
and in memory of my father

Acknowledgements

For their advice and enthusiasm, thanks to Bill Grouchy, Lesley Krueger, Deborah Levine, Helen McLean, Peter Munk, Yerme Shain, and especially to Patrick Crean and Colleen Mohyde.

Part One

1

SUCH A CROWD AT HIS FUNERAL! There were three, maybe four hundred, Izzy thought. He lost count. One son, two ex-wives, employees, acquaintances, reporters, the curious . . . They sat in pews, on folding chairs, every seat in the room full, and some were even standing at the back nodding and whispering. Not so many would come to bury Izzy when it was his turn, but if he died in his own bed, he wouldn't mind that so much. Better to have a quiet death, an ordinary service, than to be shot like an animal on the steps of your own factory—even if you get your picture in the papers after.

Not a heart attack, not a stroke, but *murdered*. A man like Phil. How can a man like that be gunned down in the open, in daylight, in full view? How could a life like his end in such a terrible way?

Not a business rival or a worker with a grudge—but the boyfriend of someone he was *shtupping* in Florida. The name was in the papers, only Izzy can't remember now, he's not so good with names anymore. Probably a loser in a cheap suit and white socks, the gun shaking in his hands. Probably he tripped on his shoelaces running away and that's why he got caught. Why would Phil have anything to do with a man like that?

His daughter squeezed his shoulder and Izzy shifted to face front. The rabbi was already speaking into the microphone, chanting in Hebrew, the casket big and glossy beside him like a parked car. He was clean shaven, pink-cheeked—not like the pasty one Izzy used to know in the Bronx, a beard down to his *pupik*. The rabbi seemed a little tense, pushing his glasses up his nose, and every once in a while he turned and squinted at the casket like he was expecting the lid to pop open any moment and the dead man to sit up and join in the service. Izzy was thinking the same thing: Phil Lewis wasn't one to miss his own funeral.

Then there was a clarinetist playing something slow and sad. The music stirred his feelings and Izzy wanted to cry out the wrongness of such a death. Phil was only sixty-six, still spry enough to have a new lover half his age. Izzy had known him forty-two years—since 1947—the only one he spoke to openly about the war; the only one who understood escape, survival, loss, and guilt. Phil listened, Phil knew... even though they were unalike. Phil had been a partisan fighting in the Polish woods, a fearless man who rescued Jews hiding from the Nazis. A man who knew nothing of weakness. He was a hero and Izzy was not.

Next to him his daughter Eva squirmed a little in her seat, and Izzy sat up straighter. The clarinetist had disappeared and Phil's son was at the mike. Eva stared down at her lap, picking at a thread on her dress while Sam, sitting on her left, put a hand on his mother's knee.

Roger hunched over the mike, waiting for people to settle down. There was murmuring at the back of the room, a few creaking chairs, and the rustle of cloth. Finally he spoke up. "My father," he started off fine, "my father was... my dad was—" and then his voice cracked like a dropped plate. He shouldn't be giving the eulogy, but if not him, who then? Izzy might've done worse.

Roger coughed and began again. "My father was an amazing— a most extraordinary man," he read from a notebook. "Many of you knew him as a generous employer who greeted his workers personally and took an interest in their lives; others, as a philan-thropist, a genius who built and ran a highly successful business. And many will remember him best for his heroism in the war..."

A good thing to be a hero, Izzy was thinking. Women adore you and men give you business, they trust you like a brother. War heroes triumph. Men like Izzy wind up working for men like Phil.

"There are those here today who owe their lives to my father—to his courage and compassion. He never turned away anyone who found his camp in the forest, and helped many Jewish men and women survive the war..."

Beside him on the cold bench Izzy felt his daughter shake, and one seat over Sam leaned forward with his hands clenched. Eva covered her mouth with her fingers, making little choked sounds. It bothered him that she should be as broken up as she clearly was; that Phil meant so much to her.

Roger's voice rose and fell—"*doting* grandfather, dear and *devoted* dad"—catching Izzy's attention again. Dear and devoted! He had to laugh. Izzy remembered days at the plant when Roger and his father would holler and throw things in Phil's upper-level office, glass-walled on two sides. Books would fly, sheets of paper, pencils, a picture frame, a stapler, an ashtray... while every worker on the floor paused to watch and listen. The clatter of machines would dull as if it were the lunch hour, and even Izzy cocked an ear to overhear a few lines: "...invest in new technology and stream-line the business..." or "Don't tell me what to do!"

Now Roger would get the chance to run things the way he liked.

Finally Roger took his seat and the rabbi stepped up to the mike to lead them in Kaddish. "*Yisgadal v'yiskadash...*" Izzy muttered with the rest. He knew the Mourner's Prayer well, had said it for his father in 1941, then for his mother and sister and her two boys (even though there were no bodies, no coffins, or funerals); years later for his wife. Now he would say it for his friend.

Yisgadal v'yiskadash... he recites the words when he can't sleep. Some people count sheep; Izzy counts dead souls.

He stared out the high narrow window past the end of the bench. It was drizzling outside and the panes were scored with wavy lines. In a few hours the dirt they threw on the coffin would be heavy and wet.

The casket was carried out and the crowd moved steadily from chapel to foyer and onto the street. Eva hooked arms with Izzy and Sam and held them back a moment as several people passed by, Roger talking to someone, then a short-haired shiksa with a purple mouth and dark glasses. "Something the matter?" Izzy asked.

"No, no. It's all right."

Eva led them to the car, skipped in front of her father, and beat him to the driver's seat. "Let me," he said.

"I'll drive. It takes my mind off things."

"There's nothing wrong with my driving."

"Who said there's anything wrong?"

"I just got my license renewed and can't drive at night, that's all."

From the backseat Sam said, "Can we go already?" He was sixteen, impossibly tall, and when he spoke at all, he had a fresh mouth.

"Sure, Mr. Wiseguy," Izzy said. "Whatever you say."

Eva pulled away from the curb and drove north. There were cars in front, cars behind as far back as they could see, all with little signs poking up from the side of their hoods: FUNERAL.

Sam was staring out the window. "Look at all the guys with medals."

"Veterans," Eva explained. "Phil was a soldier too—a partisan, I told you. That's like a guerrilla."

"I don't know many people and who I know I don't know well, so promise me you'll both come to my funeral," Izzy said. "At least there'll be the two of you."

"Don't be silly," Eva said. "There'll be lots of people."

"Yeah, a guerrilla," Sam said, "killing Nazis in the woods."

"I'm sure he killed a few, but mostly he was a saboteur blowing up trains and telegraph poles."

Sam stretched out on the backseat and made several explosive sounds, his lips pursed and vibrating. Then he said rapidly, "What if the killer was really a Nazi looking for revenge and pretending to be someone else?"

"Anything's possible," Izzy said.

"What if he was really a pro and this was like, you know, a hit?"

"A hit? What're you talking about? Phil wasn't Al Capone. He made shirts, for God's sake."

Murdered by a Nazi, a hit man, or jealous beau: any way you looked at it Phil's death was dramatic. If ever a bullet was shot at Izzy, it would be meant for someone standing close behind him, no doubt. A man of more importance.

The cemetery was far away, north of Highway 401. Between the tick of the wipers and the hiss of wheels against the wet pavement he felt drowsy. As Izzy closed his eyes and sank deeper into the bucket seat, his mind filled with pictures of his wife in her coffin, a plain pine box with a Star of David on top. When they opened it briefly for him in the funeral home and he saw her expressionless face, he wished the lid had stayed shut. Smaller in death than ever before, Hilda looked like a ten-year-old. No one he recognized. How could he say goodbye to this pale child, this stranger? Only after midnight, when he saw her through his shut eyelids putting on her flannel gown and slipping into the hollow where the mattress had long since curved to her exact shape, did he understand how much he'd lost.

Eva touched his arm and he sat up. "We're here," she said. "You want an umbrella? I've got two." He shook his head, straightened his glasses, squinted through the side window, and saw dark sticks of people standing in clusters on the grass like stalks of asparagus in a field. He put a hat on over his yarmulke, opened the door, and stepped out. Sam and Eva came up beside him under black umbrellas, even though it was just sprinkling. As they walked toward the grave site she dipped her umbrella in front of her face, her cheeks wet with drizzle or more tears.

They huddled near the back of the group, behind a plastic canopy with rows of chairs underneath, and caught only a glimpse of the casket, sheets of artificial grass, and the top of the rabbi's head. Speaking without a mike now, the poor man could hardly be heard. Eva told her son to take a seat up front where he could see, but the boy wouldn't budge.

Sam turned to Izzy. "Where's the guy who caught the killer?"

Izzy pointed at the crowd. "The one with the long hair."

"He doesn't look big but he must be really strong, the way he got him down and held him."

"Maybe the murderer's a ninety-pound weakling."

Sam cocked his thumb and finger, aimed at the roof of his umbrella and fired twice. "Two bullets in the brain. He knew what he was doing."

Izzy winced, recalling what he'd read in the papers: two bullets, eight a.m., the gun fired at close range; then the plant manager, just coming on the scene, tackled the accused while another worker phoned the police.

Eva said, "Let's go. Everybody's lining up to throw dirt on the casket."

He never saw it being lowered, but when he got to the grave site the coffin was in its hole. Izzy balled dirt in his hand and lobbed it into the open grave, where it smacked the lid and spattered. Was there to be nothing more than this? No rose petals on top? No grateful Jews who owed him their lives keening and beating their chests? No salutes or medals or a sword buried alongside to honor such a leader?

Eva gave him a nudge and he moved forward, away from the grave, as someone poured water from a pitcher over his muddy hands. Roger was standing to one side. Izzy narrowed his eyes at him but Roger only nodded, then he stepped in front of Eva, making her gasp. "Are you coming back to the house?" he said. Eva said she wasn't.

"Sam's coming, isn't he?"

"Why don't you ask him?"

Leaning on his closed umbrella, Sam was gazing into the grave. He was too young to appreciate death but fascinated, no doubt, by the morbid rites of burial: a body locked in a wooden box, the box under a mountain of earth. When Izzy was his grandson's age, the worst he could imagine was to be kidnapped and buried alive—clawing against the shut lid, screaming into the blackness till the air ran out and his lungs burst. Years later he learned there were even more horrible ways to die.

Roger called his son away from the grave and said, "Come with us, we're going back to the house now for something to eat." Sam said he was feeling sick, he thought he was going to throw up, but his dad wasn't moved. "Go vomit behind a tree, then come back, I'll be waiting."

"If he doesn't feel good . . ." Eva said.

"He looks a little green," said Izzy.

A woman in high heels that were sinking into the soggy lawn was suddenly behind Roger, tugging his sleeve and whispering. He turned quickly and walked off. Izzy couldn't help but notice the way her *tochis* filled her skirt and rolled slowly from side to side as she tiptoed across the grass, following Roger into the mist.

"That's his new wife," said Eva.

"He likes them meaty, like his father."

"Phil—" Eva broke off and started again. "Roger isn't like Phil."

Back in the car again, heading toward downtown in bumper-to-bumper traffic, Sam said he was feeling better—in fact he was starving, he hadn't eaten since breakfast and all he'd had then was toast—so Eva said all right, she'd look for a restaurant.

"There's McDonald's over there."

"No, not McDonald's."

"It's too late for lunch," said Izzy. "Why don't you wait awhile and then we can all sit down to a nice dinner."

"I'm hungry now," Sam said.

"Who gets hungry at a funeral? Me, I couldn't eat a thing."

"So have coffee or something."

"He should've gone back with Roger," Izzy said to his daughter, "then there wouldn't be a problem."

"No problem," Eva said. "We'll stop for a few minutes. There's too much traffic anyway." She turned the car into the driveway of a coffee shop.

"How long's he staying with us?" he heard Sam whisper to his mother as they walked in. Izzy's mouth tightened: he could show a little more respect. Eva should've taught him.

Sam and Eva went to the counter for drinks and a sandwich, then took seats by a window with a view of the street. The sky was gun-metal gray, only a shade lighter than the wet road, crawling cars, and square, boxy buildings beyond. Izzy thought the faces of his grandson and daughter were pale too, though whether because of mourning or another bleak Toronto winter, he couldn't say.

He took his time ordering. The woman behind the counter in her purple-and-white uniform put her hands on her hips and smiled; they weren't busy anyway so what did it matter? She had a small round face, red lipstick on her mouth that was shaped like a bagel, and overall reminded him a little of his wife Hilda. He asked her to name a few desserts—the ones with layers of whipped cream, the ones with chocolate curls on top—and also the doughnuts, which had tags under each row that were too tiny for him to read even with his glasses. The woman didn't seem to mind, she pointed and recited the names—"Honey cruller, maple dip, blueberry, lemon-filled . . ."—while Izzy frowned and shook his head. "I'm not very hungry," he said. "I just came from a funeral."

"My goodness. I hope it wasn't anyone close."

"Unfortunately, a close friend. My wife I buried years ago—a fine woman, a real gem, I still haven't recovered—and over there"—pointing at the table by the window—"you see the rest of my family."

"At least you've got them," she said. "It's no good to live alone."

Late forties, he decided, squinting at the gray roots in her hair as stiff as Florida grass. The young ones weren't patient and they never showed any sympathy. "Except I don't live with them, I'm only here for the funeral of my good friend Phil Lewis, shot to death recently—but maybe you heard, it made the news."

"No"—shaking her head slightly. "No, I don't think so."

"A wonderful man, my friend Phil. We go back many years. I'll never know a man like him again, it's such a tragedy. A war hero, a partisan—a Jewish avenger! Once"—pausing for effect—"he held a wounded comrade in his arms as he was dying, a man who cried for his mama like a baby though he was eighteen, and Phil stroked the man's hair, saying he was a brave boy, a son to make his mother proud, while he groaned and shook and bled and hugged his guts, which were half out. After the fighter died, my friend Phil took revenge on a pair of German soldiers. He and his men caught them and beat them till they begged for their lives . . . then he shot them, one-two."

"Oh my," the woman said.

Izzy stopped to remember how he'd listened to this story before, with his tongue loose and mouth ajar, his fingers pumping like a heart, squeezing the handle of an imaginary rifle. He himself could never shoot anyone, he was certain, no matter what the crime was, but Phil was impulsive, larger than life, a man of righteous anger. You couldn't judge his actions, you could only gulp at his daring.

"Later, when the war ended," Izzy hurried on, "he became a wealthy businessman. He took his uncle's clothing store and turned it into a plant with a hundred and thirty workers, then he made me the manager. Now I'm retired, so I live in Florida year-round. It's too hot in summer but in winter you can't complain."

"Aren't you the lucky one, away from the snow and cold. If I could afford it, I'd be there in a flash."

Izzy winked and said, "You can come down and visit me, there's plenty of room in my bungalow, I'm still living by myself. It's just a short drive to the beach." He watched her face closely to gauge her reaction.

Her red mouth puckered, then she leaned forward on her arms. "If only I could convince Ted—he never wants to go anywhere."

Izzy put some coins on the counter and stepped back. "Just coffee after all—with milk, no sugar," he said, "because I have to watch my weight."

Not counting Hilda, of course (and maybe one or two more who weren't so important), he'd never had luck with women. Phil had all the *mazel*. Phil the talker, Phil the *k'nocker*—big-shot war hero. At least until his luck ran out.

He carried his drink across the room and sat down next to Eva, opposite his grandson who was eating some kind of *chozzerai*, a ham sandwich on white bread. Eva asked what took so long and Izzy told her he'd had a nice chat with the server.

"You were flirting, weren't you?"

"Why shouldn't I flirt with her? I'm not dead yet," he said.

"You could be her *grandfather*."

"In my opinion she's not so young, she looks about your age."

"I think it's embarrassing the way you talk to strangers. What makes you think every Tom, Dick, and Harry you meet wants to hear your life story?"

"Just because you're not interested doesn't mean no one else is."

"I've heard your stories too many times."

Sam dripped a gob of mayonnaise on his fancy tie decorated with sea creatures. It landed on the back of a whale, and he flipped up the tie to look. "Will it come out?"

"Possibly."

"Don't worry," Izzy said. "I'll buy him a new one with something special on the front, palms trees with coconuts. Not just a tie with fish."

"Sam belongs to half a dozen wildlife protection groups. He loves whatever flies or dives—anything that doesn't speak or run around on two legs."

"I'm doing a science project," the boy said with food in his mouth, "about how pollution hurts oceans and animals."

"Very nice," said Izzy, who was thinking more about his own stories than about Sam's.

And suddenly—even more now than when he heard about the murder, more than at the funeral—Izzy felt his throat ache, his eyes burn, his chest squeezed: suddenly he was missing Phil. Who would listen to him now? Who would care like Phil cared?

Nights when Hilda was still alive but Phil had already lost the first of his three wives, they'd sit among the single- and double-needle sewing machines, long after the workers left and the factory floor was silent, to reminisce about the past—their easygoing boy-hoods and the unspeakable war years, and how they met while work-ing for *bubkes* in Manhattan, then shlepped across the border to Phil's uncle's store in Toronto, Canada. "Who'd guess we'd wind up mak-ing shirts," Phil would say, and Izzy would agree, though he really couldn't imagine anything else he might have done with his life.

Then they'd have a few beers or if it was Friday night, schnapps, still telling the old stories, the same sentences going round like ponies at a children's zoo. It didn't matter how many times each had heard the other's tales or if the stories didn't always come out the same way—maybe a little exaggerated, maybe with certain parts missing—they never got tired of listening. Sure they argued and complained ("That's not what happened—you forget"; "Tell it right or not at all!"), but it never got to the point where one of them covered his ears. That would've been the worst thing. For who was left to hear their stories? Who would not be merely amused, or irritated like Eva because she'd heard them so many times? Who would know exactly when to laugh, cry, or sit still? Only Izzy. Only Phil.

Quickly he slid a finger under his glasses and wiped his eyes, pretending he was scratching, ducking his head against the stern glare of the overhead lights. After he finished his coffee, he tore the paper cup into ragged strips.

"Can we go now?" Sam said.

Half an hour later they were back in Eva's neighborhood, driv-ing along St. Clair. A few minutes more and they parked under-ground, then got on an elevator that stopped at almost every floor,

Eva pushing the "Close" button like she was poking out an eye, until they reached her apartment, number fourteen-ten. Once inside, Izzy went straight to his bedroom (Sam's room really, but for now the boy was sleeping on the chesterfield in the living room) and lay down. He was not a young man anymore, just turned seventy-eight, and a day like this one—running around from breakfast to late afternoon—made him ache with weariness, his feet, hips, knees, neck. He only wanted to sink into sleep, except that his stomach was growling, and if he slept without eating, he'd wake up with a headache. So inch by inch he rolled up, then put on his slippers and left the room.

Eva was washing the breakfast dishes and Sam was sprawled on the sofa with the television near his feet. He was playing Nintendo, holding a controller while his thumbs mashed the buttons. Izzy called out, "You should read more often," but the boy didn't even pause.

In the small kitchen Izzy opened the fridge and said, "What's for supper?"

Eva dried her hands on a towel. "I'll go shopping tomorrow but tonight we have to eat out."

He clucked his tongue and screwed up his face. "Can't do it, I'm worn out. Maybe you could make something easy for me, eggs and toast."

"We finished the eggs this morning."

"A can of tuna?"

She shook her head.

"I thought you were a *baleboosteh*. You don't even have tuna fish?"

Eva shrugged and sat down at the tiny kitchen table, so small that when the three of them ate breakfast earlier they'd bumped knees. Izzy stood behind her with his hands on the back of her chair. "Your mother, may she rest in peace, never had an empty fridge. Stewed chicken, cheese blintzes, leftover kugel—there was always something good to eat, you never went hungry, day or night."

"My mother was home all day. She had time to cook and clean."

"I can't help thinking . . . if only you stayed with Roger, you wouldn't have to work so hard, you wouldn't be living like this."

She twisted around and turned up her face. "You *know* what he did to me."

"I know all about it. But men are like that sometimes, they don't act the way they should. I'm sure it had nothing to do with you."

"It had *everything* to do with me."

"If only you looked the other way. Now you have no one."

Her jaw swung for a moment like a screen door caught in a gust. "I have my son," she said at last. "I have myself." Then she turned her back to him and said that he should sit down and stop breathing down her neck.

This is how you talk to a father? As if he didn't have enough pain in his life already. As if he hadn't lost his family, lost his pride—everything! And what did he say that was so terrible any- way? Nothing she hadn't thought of herself. He was only con- cerned for her well-being.

After he was seated, Eva pulled a flyer from some papers on the table and announced what they were having for dinner: take-out chicken balls, fried rice, and mixed greens. Izzy didn't like greens but decided not to make a fuss. "Whatever you want," he told her. "After all, it's your apartment, I'm only a guest here."

She reached for the phone and dialed a number. Izzy sat with- out speaking, waiting for his supper, while his daughter glanced at a magazine, her mouth pulled down. Such a serious person, he thought. She almost never laughs or smiles. All he ever wanted was for Eva to be happy and give him some *naches*—to cheer him up and keep him from always looking backward—and this is how she turns out.

A while later she got up to answer the doorbell, then came back with a plastic bag of Styrofoam containers. She set the table with three plates, popped off the white lids, and stuck spoons in the cartons. Sam came in from the living room, declared that the cartons were environmentally harmful—"You know how many hundreds of years it takes this stuff to break down?"—then filled a plate with chicken balls and went back to the TV.

"He won't eat with us?" Izzy said.

"He's almost seventeen now. He does what he wants."

That's because the boy doesn't live with his father, Izzy was about to say, but Eva shot him a look like she knew what was coming, so he flattened his lips and kept still.

The chicken was *chaloshes*—breaded, greasy, and tasteless—and the green stalk he bit into was undercooked. "The broccoli isn't done right, it's hard like a rock," he said, coughing it into his napkin.

Eva rolled her eyes and said, "Here, have some more rice."

In Florida he could eat what he liked, five different entrées, soup, salad, dessert, and a bottomless cup of coffee, only $4.99 for the Early Bird Special at Mallory's Cafeteria on U.S. 19. Roast beef well done, with mashed potatoes and gravy, and maybe a few peas because they were soft and inoffensive. After that, apple pie with a scoop of ice cream on top and perked coffee served in the same thick white mugs Izzy used to drink from in the Automat in Manhattan. He ate at Mallory's once a week and more times than not he would find a person to talk to, someone who was interested in hearing about his life. "I was a Jew in Germany when the Nazis came to power," he'd say. Who can resist a story like that?

When Phil was in town they would often dine in a fish place—Phil loved fresh fish—some fancy-shmancy restaurant overlooking a river where fishing boats were tied up and men were cleaning their catch on the dock. Phil's choice, on Phil's card. A fine spot if you liked fish, which Izzy wasn't crazy about. (Sole he could tolerate, lightly breaded and pan-fried.) But anyway the view was nice, especially with the sun going down, the green lawns darkening, the water turning inky, and the sky like a fruit cup: slices of orange, purple, and pink.

Mostly they talked about old times, the same way they used to tell stories in the factory—before the war, during the war, and when they were greenhorns in New York—but now and then Phil would mention his son or an ex-wife. "I don't know where I went wrong with Roger," he might say; or, about his third wife, "I always knew it wouldn't work. She was too clingy." Deciding in the end that nothing was his fault, he had to do what he had to do because of his nature: that somehow they had let him down; they weren't enough.

"Tell me," he would ask Izzy, "how can you stay married to one woman forty years?" And Izzy would say he loved her, there was no more to it than that. Why eat out when you know you're well fed at home? Then Phil would cross his arms, lift his chin, and stare at the ceiling, a pose so full of annoyance that the waitress hurried over to ask if everything was all right, and Izzy would be left to wonder if Phil ever loved his wives.

"What was that?" said Eva.

He must have spoken out loud. "I was thinking about Phil," he said, "that maybe he was selfish. He did whatever he wanted, never mind who got hurt."

"Phil Lewis *selfish*? Do you know how many starving Jews he saved from the Nazis?"

Izzy pushed a chicken ball around on his plate. "Sometimes looking after yourself is all you can manage."

"I wasn't comparing the two of you. I only wanted to point out—"

"Anyway, we weren't there, we don't know how many he saved, we only know what he told us."

"Even if he saved one, he'd still be a hero."

"Once I saved a man from drowning. He gave me a silver cigarette case to thank me—"

"You told me about that already," Eva interrupted, "and that was a different thing. It had nothing to do with the war."

"If Phil was so wonderful, why is he dead? Who runs off with somebody young enough to be his child? Who gets mixed up with a girl with a crazy-jealous boyfriend?" Izzy leaned back in his chair. "I always thought a man like that could get away with anything... but I was wrong."

And just like that, out of the blue, Eva started crying. Softly at first, but soon she was making bubbly noises over her dinner plate, a few grains of fried rice stuck to her lower lip. "I don't know—" she tried to speak. "Don't know why anyone... He had such a big heart."

"Sure he had his good points. Why else would I have been his friend?"

"He was good to me right from the start." She blew her nose and wiped her eyes. "Even after I split with Roger... even then. He didn't have to do anything—no one was twisting his arm—but he stopped by, stayed in touch, sent little gifts, and remembered Sam's birthdays."

"I always send a card and a check."

"He promised to leave me money. He said he put it in his will..."

"For you? He left money for *you*?"

"So I could buy a condo apartment or a townhouse. Something for my old age."

"When I die you'll inherit everything, my whole estate. You don't need his money!"

"But that's just the way he was. He looked after people. He cared about their problems and wanted to help out."

So okay, he was generous. A man like that, with money to burn... why wouldn't Phil give gifts to his grandson and the boy's single mother? Izzy would've done the same if he had gold in his pockets and didn't have to watch what he spent.

"I'll say one thing," Izzy said, "after all he went through, after all the horrors he survived, he didn't deserve to be murdered on the streets of Toronto."

"I loved him dearly," Eva said. "He was a very special man."

Her words flew into his head and out, like bullets shooting through his brain. How could she say that? Was it true? It wasn't right for her to love a father-in-law so much—an *ex*-father-in-law at that. There was only so much love in the world, and the more his daughter felt for Phil, the less she'd have to give him.

God forgive him, Izzy thought, but he wasn't altogether sorry Phil was gone. God should forgive him, he was jealous enough himself to have wished him dead.

2

EVA LEFT THE CAR and took the subway to the library, Sam was on his way to school, so finally there was peace and quiet for Izzy to relax and read. Later he could go for a drive. He picked up the paper and looked around the apartment. The living room was upside down, Sam's pillow, blanket, and sheets half on the sofa, half on the rug; an armchair buried in clothes, another one cluttered with tapes and unfamiliar gadgets; the coffee table hidden under magazines, candy wrappers, crumpled tissues, and dirty cups—like the place had been blitzed. Izzy decided to stay where he was, at the kitchen table suited for dwarves.

The oil spill was big news: 240,000 barrels of crude leaked in the sea since the tanker *Exxon Valdez* hit a reef. (Here was something Sam should know about for his project.) Bad weather foiling the cleanup off the Alaskan coast; the spill spreading. Local fishermen angry and worried about their livelihood. Environmentalists trying to rescue otters, seals, and sea birds caught in the huge slick. Meanwhile the captain, nowhere near the bridge when the huge tanker ran aground, was given a blood-alcohol test...

So where was he? Sleeping in? Snoring in his cabin after a night of drinking and *shtupping* the cook? A fine model for his crew! What can you expect of the rest if the boss is a *shikker*? At Phil Lewis and Sons you arrived early and stayed late, sober, responsible, hard-working: management set an example. Phil swore he needed only four hours of sleep a night, and God knows he spent the rest of his time in his office. He was always doing paperwork, phoning manufacturers, contacts, and customers, talking loudly, waving his arm or fist behind the glass walls. The man never tired out. Ten hours a day they worked, sometimes even longer, and on Saturdays if need be. Izzy would be there by eight to check the plumbing and heating, the compressors and boilers; to order trims, threads, pins, buttons, bags, and whatnot; to oversee the cutting room, important deliveries, and the output of the workers; to keep production steady through the day and on schedule; to hire and fire personnel and handle emergencies. If needed, he could fill in for anybody in the plant: there wasn't a machine on the floor he couldn't operate. Not that he was properly thanked. Not that he was shown the appreciation he deserved for practically running the operation single-handedly. But at least he was well paid, a five-figure salary and two percent of profits. Couldn't complain about that.

Sometimes he would skip lunch, grab a sandwich for supper, then drive home and fall into bed, Hilda stroking his hair and sighing, "Look what they're doing, they're killing you, they don't give you a moment's rest." So he'd offer to buy her something nice, whatever she wanted, to make up for his time away. Jewels, furs, a dishwasher—"Name it and it's yours," he'd say, "anything your heart desires." But she never asked for so much as a hat pin, she was that good.

Izzy put the paper down, got up, and boiled water for tea. If he wasn't thinking about Phil, he was thinking about his wife. Always returning to that hard fist of loneliness. Bending over the kettle and stove he rubbed his hands in the heat of the red-hot element, but still felt cold in his bones. Surely it would help to get away from Eva's apartment with its drafty windows, cluttered rooms, and not enough light to grow even a snake plant. Surely it would help to find a person to talk to instead of the four walls. "Only a stone should be alone," his mother used to tell him.

The half a lemon he found in the fridge was dried up and turning green, so he had his tea with sugar and milk, emptying the container. There was never enough milk here, never enough of anything—just two more tea bags in the box, as a matter of fact. Not that Eva didn't try, but she was too distracted. If she made a list and picked up groceries on her way from work, she wouldn't run out so often. Maybe he'd suggest it, though she might not like him advising her to change her ways. That he could understand, they were both alike in that respect. Izzy got along with Phil and Roger at the factory because they let him do his job, they didn't interfere or make him do things differently. But of course he'd done his work well: output was high, they were always on schedule and never short of anything. "Keep doing what you're doing," Phil used to say with a hand on Izzy's shoulder. "Everything's going like clockwork."

You do a job, you do it right, Phil would agree with him—whether it's running a factory or keeping house.

Izzy poured water into the last cup in the cupboard and drank his tea without pleasure. He really didn't like it with milk, the way the goyim drank it, but what could he do? There was no coffee either.

In the bedroom he put on a blue-and-white thin-striped dress shirt and a bold tie, not that he expected to be going anywhere special, but he liked the stiff smoothness of fine cotton next to his skin. Button-down collar, box pleat, flat-felled seams, and French cuffs with gold cufflinks: Izzy loved a good shirt. Shoes, socks, pants, overcoat—everything else was just clothes.

After he dressed and cleaned his glasses, he combed the strands on his pink scalp and frowned at his face in the mirror. Thin hair he didn't like: the mark of an *alter kocker*.

Izzy took the elevator down to the underground lot and climbed into Eva's car. The garage door opened automatically as he drove up. Sunlight splashed the windshield when he turned left, onto the street, and he felt better right away.

But such a *tummel* out there! Streetcars, buses, ambulances, and everywhere construction with backhoes, dump trucks, rollers, and drills—everything honking, beeping, thumping, and coughing fumes. Not to mention jaywalkers who jumped out in front of you and banged your hood when you stopped short and cyclists you couldn't see passing on the right side, and naturally cars and more cars braking and turning and cutting you off so that you moved about as fast as dough rising in a pan. His heart pounding so hard he thought it would *plotz*, he pressed the horn and screamed curses at anyone who crossed his path, wishing on this one a black year, on that one the plague—"*A shvartz yor oif dir! A choleria oif dir!*"—and for the driver who sped up, then squealed to a halt for a yellow light, making Izzy hit the brakes and bounce off the steering wheel, he prayed that the stupid putz should lose all his teeth but one and that one should ache forever!

In this manner Izzy made his way south, street by street, and crossed the city to the west end. If you asked him, he couldn't say just where he was going, but the car seemed to know the way, and suddenly he was parked on a narrow strip of asphalt outside a one-story yellow brick building with tinted windows at the front. After all these years he was still excited to see the plant.

He locked the car, strode ahead, then paused to examine the factory steps. Five long concrete slabs. He bent over to touch them, a tremor in his fingers as if he were actually feeling flesh. How had Phil fallen, he wondered, and where did he lie? Was there no stain, no scratch, no chalk outline to mark the exact spot? Had no one even left flowers? He straightened up, his back hurting. The scene was too ordinary, the steps too white and clean. As if all proof of the shooting had been removed. As if no one cared to remember the crime.

He walked through the front doors and stopped at Reception, where a girl was typing behind a desk, cradling a phone receiver between her head and shoulder. While she was busy he looked around, surprised to see that nothing had apparently changed. To his left was the conference room, its long table buried under a jumble of shirts and fabric samples, but no one ever did much business there anyway. Everything important was decided in Phil's office.

He veered right and wandered down a hallway to the offices, Roger's, the manager's, and one for the sales rep, each of them with dark-tinged picture windows facing the street. No one seemed to be around. Across the aisle a large room, the glassed-in office that was once Phil's, overlooked the shop on a lower level and the warehouse beyond. Someone had tidied up, cleared out personal things, arranged all the desk paraphernalia in straight rows, emptied the IN box, and pulled several books from the shelves so that they looked like mountain ranges with unexpected valleys. Was Roger going to move in? Of course he'd want the biggest office now that his father was out of the way.

"Hey there! Come back here!"

Izzy turned to see the receptionist leaning over her desk and motioning him closer. He took his time walking over, opening his coat so that his silk tie and high-quality shirt were conspicuous, so that she wouldn't think he was a schmo who didn't belong here. "Yes? What's the problem?"

"Who did you want to see?" she asked in a sharp voice.

"Tony."

"Is he expecting you?"

"Tell him it's Izzy. He'll know."

She pressed some buttons on her phone. "Tony's on the floor right now, I can't reach him. You'll have to wait in his office."

"Don't worry, I'll find him." Izzy headed toward the stairs leading to the shop but the *meshuggeneh* came after him, her heels clattering on the floor like a handful of dropped stones.

"You can't just walk in. I don't even know who you are."

"Izzy Schneider, that's who—and I was running this shop when your parents were still in high school."

"Never heard of you. Anyway, the way it works around here, I have to get permission—"

But Izzy was already on the stairs and moments later Tony saw him, rushed over, and pumped his hand. "It's okay," he told the girl, who was dancing up and down the steps like a chicken without a head.

"Izzy, Izzy," Tony said. "Good to see you, old man, though I wish it was under better circumstances."

"Naturally."

"No one can believe what happened. We thought he was Superman and bullets would bounce off him."

"You were very brave," Izzy said, "throwing the murderer to the ground. You could've got yourself killed."

"Anyone would've done the same."

"Not anyone," Izzy said. "It takes courage."

"I only wish I got there a few minutes sooner."

"Tell me, was he a big man?"

"About average," Tony said. "It must've happened suddenly or Phil would've knocked him down himself."

"What was his expression?"

"His what? I don't know . . . mad. His face was all twisted."

"Naturally he'd be upset—Phil stole his girlfriend. Such a *meshugge* thing to do! What was he thinking?"

Tony stared down at his feet, then peered over Izzy's head. "I'm still expecting any minute Phil's going to walk in and ask what kind of day we're having—'Everything on schedule or not? No problems with the machines?' We're all going to miss him."

Izzy nodded, looked around. He glanced up at the long rows of bright fluorescent ceiling lights, then beyond Tony to where dark-haired operators were bent over whirring machines. He wanted to move among them, examining their work, and remember what it was like to be part of this beehive.

He fixed his eyes on Tony again. "I'm going to miss him too. Phil and I go back a long way, we were very close"—pressing his palms together. "As close as two leaves on a branch."

"He was one in a million," Tony said.

Then he asked about Sam and Eva, and Izzy said they were doing fine. "And your family?" Izzy asked. Tony said they were just great.

He had a wife and four children (whose names Izzy always forgot), every one of them born since the young man came to the plant. Boy or girl, Tony used to pass out Cuban cigars, and sometimes Izzy would smoke with him in the grassy lot behind the building, littered with butts and paper cups, and tell stories about his life.

"You know what I did when I got to New York?" he'd poke him with a finger. "I was a peddler on the streets, I sold ice cream in the summer, shoelaces, razor blades, and all kinds of *chozzerai*—you know that word? It means 'junk'—that's what I hawked the rest of the year. In Berlin I sold expensive clothes, I owned a car and traveled, but here I was a nebbish . . . Anyway, I learned English, I found a job as a polisher in a jewelry factory where Phil was the foreman. One time he got so mad at someone who called me a kike he picked up the loudmouth and dumped him in a trash can! Soon we became good friends. Then Phil decided to work for his uncle in Canada who paid better wages. He invited me to come too, his uncle needed reliable men. So as it turned out, Phil decided my future."

Tony was always a good listener, not to mention a hard worker, as hard a worker as Izzy himself. Also he never gave you trouble. Whatever you told him to do, he did without any back talk. For the longest time he called him "Sir," until Izzy assured him it was fine to use his first name. Except for the difference in age and status, they could've been friends.

One of the sewers shouted for Tony, something happened to her machine, and he told Izzy over his shoulder not to leave, he'd be right back, why didn't he look around in the meantime and see what was changed.

Not much, Izzy hoped. He hated how nothing stayed the same, the world was always changing—people, cities, history. When you look at something familiar but also a little different, it's hard to remember how it was, the past as wrong as the present. What actually took place? Was it like this or like that? Wondering and unsure, till most of your memories are ruined, falling from the walls of your brain like so many paint chips. The stories you tell wind up being more real to you than what might've happened. What remains of life itself are muddy images, severed words: *mother, hero, coward, death*. What remains are shocks of pain.

Izzy slapped his head and counted backward from sixty. When his mind became quieter he went to the cutting room, where a stocky man he didn't know was rolling a bolt of cloth loaded onto a spreading machine along the length of a table. The man moved from one end of the table to the other, then back again to start over, layer after layer. Izzy walked up to him, stuck out his hand, and promptly introduced himself, but the man had his hands full with scissors and a yardstick and didn't return the gesture.

Izzy asked him his name and the man muttered, "Carlos."

"Let me tell you something, Carlos, I was a cutter once too. I started in 1950, before you were even born, and a few years later I became plant manager."

The man glanced at him sidelong.

"First in the factory downtown and after that in this one—you can ask Tony if you doubt what I'm saying. I taught him everything he knows. Now I'm retired of course, retired eleven years ago when my wife Hilda got sick, so I could take care of her. But she passed away a year later and then I moved to Florida, where I still live. I came back for Phil's funeral. Naturally, while I'm in town, I wanted to see the shop."

Carlos went about his business, cutting and smoothing fabric on the long metal table. The man kept his eyes on the cloth while Izzy paused to recollect the time he nearly lost a finger, early on in his career when he knew to slide his left hand over the pattern as he cut but didn't remember to move it back faster than he pushed the electric knife forward, even though he'd been warned plenty— "Don't get your hand in the way!"—and so the vertical blade caught his left hand in the *V* between his index finger and thumb. The wound needed several stitches, then he required surgery to fix a nerve and tendon but still had no feeling in his finger for months. Even now it tingled a bit and went numb sometimes, although he never complained because the sensation reminded him of busier and happier days.

"Phil used to say I was born to be a cutter, I was some kind of genius. I never ruined a single piece. It takes skill and training to do a job like this well. Cut wrong and you can spoil a thousand shirts, maybe more."

"He said the same thing to me."

"He said you were a genius?"

"He told me I was going places."

"Sure, sure," Izzy grumbled. "Everyone's a genius."

Carlos walked up and down, pulling the spreader, laying plies, checking for flaws in the fabric, while Izzy kept pace alongside, relieved to see that little had changed. Everything the man did was perfectly familiar, as if Izzy himself had been a cutter only last week. Except for a few small details—a motorized spreading machine instead of a manual one, a motorized cutter at the end of the table—all was as he remembered. If he wanted to, he could lend a hand without looking foolish, he could easily impress the little genius with his know-how.

"I used to make markers too." Izzy moved his hand in the air to imitate tracing pattern pieces. "The art is in arranging the pieces on the paper so finally you only use the least amount of yardage— like putting together a puzzle. A tough job but I was good at it— talented, you might say. A perfectionist."

Carlos moved around the table, eyeing the fabric, and Izzy followed close behind. "We don't do it like that anymore," the man said gruffly. "It's done by computer now."

Izzy stepped back from the table as if he'd been shoved, feeling pressure on his head like the push of a giant hand. No pieces, no paper? Done by computer instead? But how is that possible? He couldn't even imagine.

"Done a lot better too," the man said for good measure.

Izzy's brain was all in knots. Carlos thought he was obsolete. Carlos thought he was worthless, an antique pile of junk fit for the scrap heap! And maybe he was . . . maybe so. But silently he cursed the *farshtinkener* cutter anyway, wishing he should grow like an onion—head in the ground and his feet in the air!

Then he pulled in his breath and said, "Everything now is high-tech, no one has to be skilled anymore, it's quantity over quality. We used to turn out beautiful shirts, not so much as a missed stitch, but they don't make shirts like that today—you probably don't even know what I mean."

The cutter peered at him sharply, his eyes beady, black with scorn.

Izzy wheeled away from him and headed toward an operator die-cutting collars and yokes, standing at a tall machine making such a *thunk-thunk* that Izzy put his hands on his ears. The man looked up, his face pinched, looked down. Nearby, a red-faced woman with a wrinkled brow was heat-fusing interlining to collars and cuffs. She scowled at Izzy for no apparent reason as he passed by. What had been going on in the years since he was manager and all his workers got along, a big happy family?

Quickly he moved past a large newfangled device—eyes straight ahead so he wouldn't see it directly—and on to something he recognized, a cluster of sewing machines. Hilda worked as a sewer in New York before Eva was born in 1942, hour after hour in a crowded, noisy, stuffy room, hunched over, making uniforms, neck hurting, eyes burning, but what could she do, they needed the money. Izzy was earning no more than she was in those days. It wasn't till he started working for Phil years later that he made enough to support them.

He stopped behind an olive-skinned woman sitting up straight, her hair down to her shoulders like Hilda used to wear it, her bare neck as smooth as a pole. There were always a few operators like this one working in the plant, pretty young girls who could make you dizzy and *farmisht*. When Izzy became manager he used to encourage them to tell him about themselves, he took a fatherly interest. He figured it was good business, the girls would work harder in a friendly family atmosphere. But *oy!* the things they told him. Behind the building, on their breaks, he'd light their trembling cigarettes, touch their hands, and hear their secrets: violent lovers, faithless husbands, unwanted pregnancies. "Uncle Izzy," they called him, with their eyes like berries, mouths like plums. Who could blame him if he went a little further sometimes than he meant to? He kept it quiet—unlike Phil, who got away with more foolishness than he had a right to, even if he was the boss.

"You know," he said now to the sewer with the lovely neck, "you remind me of my wife. She used to do this same work back in the thirties and forties, but not in such a nice place. She wasn't yet sixty when she died—a real tragedy—and in my opinion she would've lived to be a hundred and twenty if she never worked in a sweatshop."

The woman didn't look up but kept feeding pieces of fabric to the needle. She was topstitching, her fingers as slender as the prongs of a fork.

"Whatever else you say about Phil—the wives and the girl-friends—he was a mensch when it came to the plant. A union shop, decent wages, an hour for lunch and two breaks, the building in good shape, the floor airy and well lit—who can complain about that? Except for noise"—he cupped his ear and listened for a moment to the whine-click-clang of machines, something he never got used to and which made him partly deaf after almost three decades—"but what can you do about noise? After a while you hardly hear it. All things considered, it's a good place, you have to admit. I'm sure all the operators went to his funeral."

The woman didn't smile or speak, just kept stitching cloth, and Izzy had a sudden thought: she wasn't at the service. A good-looking girl like that, what if Phil came on to her and she turned him down, furious? What if he wouldn't stop and even threatened to fire her? Certainly he'd done it before. There was always provocation when you managed so many females—cleavage showing, naked arms, long legs, and wet lips—but whereas Izzy fought temptation for the most part, Phil didn't even try. This sewer with her delicate neck wouldn't have been the first one, although she might have been the last.

Izzy bent low so his lips were close to the woman's ear (those curved ridges and plump lobe!), the long strands of hair across his scalp falling forward. "You didn't like him, did you, so you didn't go to the funeral. Maybe he took advantage of his position, if you know what I mean, and you wanted nothing to do with him."

She swung her head sharply and her loose hair swatted his face. He straightened up abruptly as a hand clamped his shoulder. "Don't talk to her when she's working," Tony said. "Time is money for these girls."

"She looked so unhappy, I was just trying to cheer her up."

"Nobody's unhappy, they're just focused on their work. They don't want to fall behind, they have to meet their quotas."

Tony steered him away from the sewers. "Here, let me show you some of our latest technology"—gently pushing Izzy from contraption to contraption, which he didn't want to know about. But Tony told him anyway: a pocket setter with one worker that could do the job of four; a pair of sleeve-placket machines and only two operators to do what ten did before; buttonhole and button machines and then the unit production line, where shirt pieces clipped to hangers traveling on overhead rails were assembled, pressed, folded, and bagged by operators along the course.

It made him queasy in his *kishkas*. How was everything done before? Izzy could hardly remember. He shut his eyes but saw only a long-necked beauty, her fingers like the spokes of a wheel going round and round and round . . .

His legs were like rubber. He leaned against a handy table, worried that he might fall. Tony's voice was loud in his ears: "Thirty people were let go when we automated and bought computers—and still we make as many as a thousand shirts daily."

In Izzy's time the best they could do was a thousand a week.

He steadied himself by flattening his hands on the table. Izzy's time was over: he didn't belong here anymore. Not that things were better now . . . only a lot faster. Not that people were happier.

"This is progress," Tony said, sweeping his arm across the room.

Progress-shmogress, Izzy thought. Tell that to the workers you fired, the ones you never heard from again. Tell that to the ones who are left, not a smile among them. In Izzy's day there were fewer shirts—there's no denying that—but always time for a joke and a grin. Now, lucky to still have jobs, the workers keep their eyes lowered, mouths shut.

Izzy needed to leave the floor and sit down. Words crashed between his ears—*pocketsplacketsbuttonholes*—and his forehead hurt like an open wound. He started walking slowly toward the steps to the upper level, Tony chattering at his heels.

"Roger's taking us even further—more machines, competitiveness, expansion into bigger markets . . ."

"Phil wouldn't have liked that, he hated letting workers go. Roger put him up to it—he said you had to modernize or go under."

"Phil was getting old, Izzy. Old men have old ideas. Roger and me are more in tune."

Getting old and useless: even a big cheese like Phil. Half remembering bygone years nobody cares about; telling the same tired stories nobody wants to hear. But what else is there to do? What's left to an old man except the patchwork of his mind, the scraps of another time?

Izzy sat down on the stairs and Tony stood over him, his foot on a step. Izzy aimed a finger at him and pictures blinked before his eyes. "Remember twenty years ago you came in to see me, a *boychik* with long hair, a spotty beard, and blue jeans with so many holes in them I thought they were polka dots?"

"You told me to shave, get a haircut, and borrow my father's good suit."

"And when you did I hired you, trained you, promoted you. I pulled you out of the cutting room and made you my assistant, then it wasn't long before you were the manager, not me."

"Roger started the same time. We learned the business together."

"You were like a son to me, a hard worker, same as me. I never lost my temper with you, I never had to raise my voice. Not like the *gantse macher*." Izzy watched Tony's face, and when he nodded, Izzy winked, pleased to think that after all these years he still remembered the Yiddish Izzy taught him.

"Phil had a temper, all right." He ran his fingers through his hair (which was almost as long as it once was, down to his collar, and if he asked for a job today, Izzy would tell him the same thing, *Go home first and clean up*).

"Once I told him about my plan to reorganize the floor—the clicker next to the cutting room, the fuser next to collars and cuffs, a sleeve department, front department, a section for backs and yokes. Hell, it was a great idea! But Phil cursed me under his breath, he chewed me out in front of everyone—'Forty years I been calling the shots . . . !'"

"Then along comes a *pisher* like you and threatens his authority."

"If Roger hadn't stepped in, I swear I would've flattened him, to hell with the job."

"No one would've blamed you."

"Don't get me wrong," said Tony, glancing toward Phil's office as if the boss were still behind the glass wall listening. "I liked him as much as anyone. I would've done my best to save his life if I had the chance."

"You're a good person," Izzy said.

Tony looked at his watch and said he had to get back to work now. Izzy squeezed his arm goodbye. "Maybe we can talk again, I'm here for another week. You can reach me at Eva's place. Roger's got the number."

He was no longer in such a hurry to leave the plant. He got up and climbed the rest of the steps slowly, not looking back, trying to pretend it was still the early seventies, before Hilda got sick and Izzy was thinking he would work till he was seventy-five. Those were good years, though he didn't know it at the time: when people respected him and every morning he woke up knowing what to do with himself.

At the top of the stairs he turned right. A man in a helmet and leather jacket was talking to the receptionist, who was pointing in Izzy's direction. The man nodded, took off his helmet, gripped it under his left arm, strode down the hall like a soldier in his black boots, and shook Izzy's hand. "What are you doing here?" he asked.

The man in the motorcycle getup was Roger. His face was flushed, his lips chapped, his eyes like tablets, small and flat, his cheeks so smooth and downy you'd think he had never shaved. Wearing a sweet cologne that smelled like cotton candy. Who could guess he was old enough to run a business, bury his father, marry for the second time? Izzy bobbed his head and smiled. He came to say hello, he explained, to look around and see what's new.

A phone rang and Roger said, "Excuse me a minute, have a seat," sweeping Izzy into his office, a messy room opposite Phil's with files and papers on the desk and furniture, even the rug. Izzy had to kick a stained coffee mug out of the way and clear swatches of fabric from a chair before he could sit on it. Roger put the phone down, scribbled something on a pad, crossed and uncrossed his legs, rocked in his swivel chair, and rolled a pen in his fingers. The gestures made Izzy tense: they reminded him of a Nazi bureaucrat in an airless room examining his papers. *You are no longer a citizen of the Reich*, he half expected to hear.

Roger leaned back and grinned, his teeth small and pointy like Phil's. "What did you think of the funeral?"

"A good turnout," Izzy said.

"Hundreds of people showed up."

"Such a beautiful service . . . but I saw how upset you were, I didn't expect you to finish your speech. To watch a father put into his grave is a sad thing."

But not to watch is even worse: how well Izzy knew that. If not for the Third Reich, he would've seen his own father buried properly, he surely would have been at his side as he lay dying. He might've touched his father's hand and heard his final whisper: *Take care of your mother, Izzy. Izzy, be a good son.*

"I was thinking about my mother," Roger said, "when I was up there. That's why I choked up."

Izzy raised an eyebrow. "Your mother was a fine woman, there's no denying that."

"She was always talking about Dad, that he was such a hero. She used to show me letters he got from Jews he rescued during the war, people who wrote that they owed their lives to his hideout in the forest. They sent pictures of who they married, photos of their homes and gardens, children and grandkids, everyone smiling and grateful."

"He took care of his people like nobody else did. He led a band of Jewish fighters and looked after a camp of a hundred helpless fugitives. One day they gave him a horse—a beautiful brown stallion with a white mark on his head like a crown . . ."

"I heard that one," Roger said.

"But maybe you don't know this . . . how one time he stole a coat from a dead Nazi officer—with epaulettes and a leather belt!—then rode in the saddle with his coat spread like the robes of a prince . . ."

"I heard that too," he said. "I know all his stories. I grew up believing the world was a scary place but Dad would protect me, the way he defended Jews hiding from the fascists. I thought he was a great man. I used to think no one held a candle to my father."

Izzy ducked his chin and gazed at Roger over his glasses. "Is that what you think now?"

He swung his chair completely around, then stopped to face the window. "It's true that he was fearless—fearless and relentless. A hard-nosed businessman . . . some say he was cutthroat. He cared about his workers, but in the end he did whatever he had to do to stay on top."

"He wasn't easy to work with."

"We had our disagreements, as I'm sure you know." Roger turned around again. "My mother taught me to love and respect him and I did my best."

"Your mother was a jewel," said Izzy.

"She only saw the good in people."

"Hilda never had another friend like Rachel." He joined the middle and index fingers of one hand. "They were that close."

They'd meet for coffee every day, watch the children, go to movies, eat together when Phil and Izzy worked late at the factory, share gossip and secrets as only two women can. A few times he'd walk in the door and hear them kibitzing, their laughter like the tinkly bell on a tricycle, and Izzy would pause, suddenly shy, feeling like a lost boy who'd entered the wrong house, not daring to interrupt the circuit of their friendship. His love for Hilda, great as it was, could never be as big as that.

Because of Hilda and Rachel there was a second Mr. and Mrs. Lewis. Hilda told him how they hoped for the wedding of their children—how they imagined the number of guests, the color of the tablecloths, and what they'd write on the matchbooks—referring to each other throughout as in-laws, "my *machetayneste*"; how Rachel sealed the youngsters' fate by making their union her dying wish. Phil objected to the match because he said Eva was too old for Roger—but Izzy suspected the real reason was that an employee's daughter shouldn't marry the boss's son. Sure Izzy was his friend, but not quite his equal.

So after his wife died, Phil tried to louse things up. He flew his son to vulgar cities like Vegas and L.A. and sent hookers to his rooms; he introduced him to pretty girls younger than Eva, from well-off families; finally he simply forbade him to see her. But Roger couldn't be swayed: he would do his mother's bidding and marry his childhood friend. He didn't count on Eva being hard to win over. It took several years to convince her that he loved her and was good husband material, by which time his father had already remarried and Eva was pushing thirty, afraid of being an old maid perhaps and not so choosy.

The marriage lasted twelve years, a good stretch by today's standards. The young no longer stay together, they don't have patience anymore, they don't understand that love changes, grows deeper with the years, you only have to give it time. Eva didn't wait things out: she wouldn't look the other way. Not every wife was as forgiving as Hilda.

Izzy pulled his chair close to Roger's desk. "Hilda's dead, your mother's dead, Phil's dead too now, but some things don't change. We're still *mishpocheh*, aren't we? You'll always be my son-in-law, even after what went on between you and Eva."

Roger pulled his boots off, then took off his jacket and dropped it on the cluttered desk. His shirt looked expensive: black silk, reversible collar, concealed-button placket, and barrel cuffs. He paced in front of the tinted window, patting his thighs. "Whatever Eva told you about what happened to us, she didn't tell you everything."

"She told me enough, believe me. She wasn't going to close her eyes while you fooled around with someone else."

"My marriage was already over when I met Loreen."

"Not according to Eva."

His phone buzzed but he didn't pick up. "Eva was no angel," he said. "Something was going on, but I never figured out what."

"Exactly what are you saying?"

He shook his head. In his black shirt and stockinged feet, framed by the big window, he looked small. His eyes had shrunk to buttonholes and his chest was visibly heaving. He looked like Phil the week that he sat shiva for Rachel, slumped on a low bench, his eyes squeezed to pinpoints: Roger looked as sorry as that.

Izzy knew his daughter. She was serious and secretive, also a good liar. As a girl she was quiet and shy, cowed by children half her size, and kept to herself, a bookworm. Maybe it was his fault for saying too much about the war—although he tried to protect her and keep things from her till she was old enough to hear them. Still, she might've learned from him that life was very dangerous and people couldn't be trusted, it was better not to get involved.

And yet she was capable of furious acts. She'd set fire to caterpillars, pull the legs off grasshoppers, keep warring ants in a jar. "How can you hurt little innocent creatures?" Izzy would say. "Isn't there enough pain and cruelty in the world already?" Then she would start to cry, "Sorry, sorry, sorry," but he never knew for certain if she was or not.

Sometimes things would vanish from the apartment, never to reappear—Hilda's favorite necklace or a tie pin, a gold ring, a pair of mules, a pillbox—and though she swore she didn't do it, Izzy recognized Eva's work. Although he never understood her *meshuggeneh* behavior.

But Roger was no bargain either: Phil had told him stories that were just as alarming as the ones he told about Eva. A willful boy— explosive—and the way he liked to bully other children was disgraceful. Nevertheless, he learned good manners when he was older. He always treated Izzy fairly in the shop, for instance; he was never disrespectful. But business was one thing, your life at home another. Who knew what kind of husband Roger had once been— or what secrets Eva hadn't told about her marriage.

"Anyway," Izzy said, "it's not important who did what, it's all water under the bridge. What's important now is for you and me to keep in touch. I knew your parents, I know you . . . I want us to stay friends."

Of course they were never buddies—not like Izzy and Phil were—but still they have a history together, which counts for something. Twenty-one years ago when Roger joined the company, Izzy taught him all he knew. Three years later he became

Izzy's son-in-law, but nothing changed between them. They remained polite and distant, as they were in the factory, not very interested in each other's lives. Even though Izzy and Hilda visited the newlyweds, phoned often, and sent gifts, he and Roger weren't close. They had so little in common. The boy was pampered, spoon-fed, overprotected, and though he knew about making shirts, he knew *bubkes* about life. After his wife died and Izzy moved to Florida, Roger became nothing more than the person who picked up when Izzy phoned his daughter.

"Anything's bothering you, I want to be the first to know. Now that your father's gone I feel a responsibility."

"Sure. I'll call you sometime."

"But right now," Izzy said, "there's something bothering me."

Roger stepped away from the window. "What's that?"

"The man who shot your father—did you know much about him?"

"I only knew that Dad had a girlfriend in Florida who was living with her boyfriend—that she was supposed to leave and move in with Dad instead."

"They were going to live together in his new house in Port Chase, your father told me, but I knew there'd be *tsuris*. With so many available women, why chase a girl like that? How could he be so stupid?"

"I told him it was crazy, but he didn't care what I thought. He went after anyone or anything he wanted, no matter what."

"The same way he ran the business."

"He wasn't doing much of that after he met her." Roger half sat on his desk, one leg swinging, one straight. "Things'll be different now."

Izzy wrinkled his forehead.

"We're making changes around here, cutting costs overall and finding new markets—especially in the U.S., where we're selling more aggressively. First off we'll be importing more finished goods and expanding into other lines—boxer shorts, casual wear, high-end ladies' shirts. I want to double annual sales."

"Your father's turning in his grave."

"I don't need his approval anymore."

Izzy pursed his lips. "Must be nice being in charge, no one to answer to. Finally the company's yours."

Roger slid onto his feet. "I'm not happy he was killed, if that's what you're thinking."

"I wasn't thinking anything . . . except how things turned out."

The receptionist was in the doorway. "Harv Butler's waiting for you. I buzzed but you didn't answer."

"Give me a minute." To Izzy he said, "I'll see you out."

"Don't bother"—motioning for Roger to stay put. Izzy got up slowly—"Remember to stay in touch"—and walked out.

He paused for the last time in front of Phil's office door. He stuck in his head and looked hard, searching for an object that would bring his lost friend to mind, but the place had been picked over, wiped clean of traces of Phil. Anyway, he walked in and sat in a chair beside the desk, the same place he used to sit when Phil told him stories. Izzy shut his eyes a moment and heard him again.

Did I tell you about the time we attacked a police station? At night in a snowstorm, in sub-zero temperature . . . no one expecting us. There were seven of us, all Jews, my very best fighters, every one with ten good reasons to wring a German neck. We stabbed the guard who was out front, then four of us hid by the entrance, two by the back door, one on the roof. The main room was lit up. Through the window we saw a dozen Nazis and local police drinking and playing cards. When I gave the signal we broke in and shot the bastards where they sat—they didn't have time to draw their guns. The walls, the floor were thick with blood. A few who were still alive we dragged outside in the snow and finished them off with punches, kicks, and jabs from our rifle butts, to save on bullets . . . and one I strangled with my hands. Later, when we tallied up, I scored the most dead. I always killed more than my share—I liked to set an example.

Izzy was barely breathing now, his mouth round with astonishment as if he were hearing the story for the first time. He could feel Phil's superhuman strength in his own hands: his own curled and wrinkled fingers suddenly rigid, fever-pink. But he also felt his throat being squeezed in a vise-grip, his neck stretched and shrinking... the way he felt when Phil had actually sat across from him, talking; when Izzy suddenly started to choke and Phil had to get up and slap him across the back, reminding him to take a breath. Then they were laughing about it, sitting together face to face. Everything normal. Perfectly safe.

He left the office quickly. He would never hear that voice again, feel that big hand on his back. Another terrible loss for Izzy: his heart becoming a dried fruit.

The receptionist was at her desk, fluffing her hair and giggling with a young man in a loose suit, when Izzy passed without a word. As he pushed open the front door Roger called after him, "Take care!" He imagined the three of them snickering as he shuffled through the glass entrance, fumbled the keys to Eva's car, and climbed in. Then, he imagined, they wouldn't give him another thought.

He drove back as fast as he could in stop-and-go traffic, speeding up, hitting the brakes, yelling a chain of curses at cars ahead of him, cars behind, and anything on either side: "You should swell up like a mountain! You should break a left hand and a right foot! May your stomach *drey* round and round like a music box! Like a treasure, you should be buried with care!"

At last he reached St. Clair and put the car in the underground lot of Eva's apartment house. He waited till his breathing slowed, then he took an elevator up to the fourteenth floor. In the hallway he caught the scent of meat and potatoes and thought of where he lived as a boy... a building that had always smelled of boiled beef and cabbage. Where women sat in the courtyard, crowded into a sunny nook, and everybody knew he was Chana and David's son; where Mutti stuck her head out the window at suppertime and cried, "Izzeleh, come inside!"—while other mothers did the same, calling children to dinner. But what the women looked like and what their boys and girls were named, he can't quite remember. What he knows now is the smell of beef and vegetables... the sting of things missing that will never return.

Sam was home when he walked into Eva's apartment, slouched in his usual pose in front of the deafening TV. Izzy hung up his overcoat and pulled off his oxfords. "You'll hurt your ears," he said, but the boy was oblivious. When Izzy asked him about school, Sam grunted, eyes on the screen.

"Turn that off and talk to me, I'm only here another week."

Sam lowered the volume and sat up straighter, still watching the picture from the corner of one eye. "Yeah, what?"

"What's with 'what'?" He turned off the TV, cleared a spot on the littered couch, and sat down an arm's length away from his grandson. "We should get to know each other while I'm in Canada, it's easier than talking long distance once in a blue moon."

Sam hunched forward with his elbows on his thighs and his hands dropped between his knees. He stared at the floor.

"I was reading about the *Exxon Valdez*," said Izzy. "Do you know that story? You could use it for your project."

Sam looked up. "It's real bad. Thousands of birds and otters, hundreds of seals are going to die. Prince William Sound used to be totally unpolluted."

"It's terrible what happens in the world," said Izzy. "I can tell you worse things."

Sam became silent again. "Tell me something else," Izzy encouraged him.

"Like what?"

"Something I don't know."

The boy looked thoughtful. "I'm doing okay in science... but I'm failing English."

"English! How can you fail English, you were born speaking it. What's the matter with your *kop*?"

"I haven't told Mom yet."

"Because you don't read enough. You play games and watch that"—pointing at the blank screen—"so how can you expect to learn? Me, I know three languages, German, Yiddish, and English, and also I understand French from when I lived there. German and Yiddish we spoke at home, and English I studied at the gymnasium when I was young, that was my best subject."

"Too bad I didn't inherit your talent for languages," Sam said, his voice mocking, but sad too.

Izzy made space on the coffee table and put up his feet. The boy needed discipline, someone to keep an eye on him. How could he be successful with a mother who never stayed home and a part-time father? If Izzy lived in Toronto . . . but he didn't, it was too cold.

"So tell me something you like to do. Something you're very good at."

"Volleyball." He perked up. "You should see my serve, Grampa. No one can return my serve."

"You hit the ball over a net?"

"A high net. Two teams. Six players on a team."

Izzy wrinkled his nose up. "Volleyball-shmolleyball, what kind of game is that? You should play soccer like we used to play in Germany—now *that's* a game."

Sam pulled his knees up, swung toward the TV, and rounded his body like a fist. "There's something on I have to watch." He touched the remote and the screen came alive.

"We're having a conversation and you turn on the TV? That's how you treat your *zayde*, with no consideration?" But the boy only shrugged at the screen.

Izzy sighed as he got up. He went to his bedroom, shut the door behind him, and lay down. No use trying to talk to young people who hardly spoke, and when they did it was all *bubbe mayseh*.

When he closed his eyes he saw Phil. They were walking on the beach together under a clear Florida sky so bright it made them squint, Phil in a tiny bathing suit showing off his *shlong* and his oversized muscles that he worked out in a gym to maintain, Izzy in shorts and a knit shirt. They were speaking Yiddish, telling jokes; then Izzy was swirling his hands, explaining how it was when he first came to New York.

When I was peddling in the Bronx, I saved up my pennies for a hot meal on Shabbes. I went to a little restaurant and ordered a nice steak and a few boiled potatoes. The meat was like a burnt log, but I was still a greenhorn and couldn't explain with my broken English what was the matter. "Meat bad," I said, but the waiter only laughed at me and walked away. I was so hungry I chewed the wooden steak till my teeth hurt, swallowing tears with every bite...

Izzy dozed and woke angry. The lunatic who shot Phil took from him the last person he knew how to talk to.

Eva came home grumpy and late. He heard her in the living room growling at Sam. He got up, smoothed his hair, fixed his glasses, and left the room. The coffee table, he noticed, had been swept clean. Books, papers, magazines, assorted trash, this and that, were in a pileup on the rug. Eva put her hands on her hips and stabbed the mess with the toe of her shoe—"I'm a librarian, I like order"—and Sam said, "Okay already, I heard you."

Izzy's stomach was groaning but he decided to wait for a better time before he mentioned supper. Instead he asked her why she was late and Eva talked about unexplained delays on the subway: she was sorry she didn't take the car. It was no fun standing for an hour hanging onto a bar, squeezed so tight between overheated passengers she couldn't open her paper. From now on he'd have to take public transit to get around, she hoped he wouldn't mind that. As long as he avoided rush hours he'd be fine.

He spread his fingers on his gut and pressed in to stop the noise. She said, "You must be hungry."

"Naturally. It's after six."

She went to the kitchen and soon after Izzy heard a clatter of dishes, the crash of pots. He poked his head in the doorway. "It doesn't have to be fancy."

"I never have enough time." She was boiling water in one pot, pouring a jar of tomato sauce into another. She tore open a bag of pasta, emptied it into the water, stirred the sauce. He didn't have high hopes for the meal they were about to eat.

When everything was finally ready Eva called Sam in and the three of them sat down together, bumping knees, slurping food. It wasn't meat and potatoes, but it satisfied his hunger so he didn't complain. Sam got tomato sauce on his sweatshirt and said, "Shit!" Eva told him not to swear and Sam asked her to pass the cheese. To stimulate the conversation Izzy asked about her day, but Eva only held up her hand like a traffic cop. "Don't get me started. All I'm going to say is this: Anyone who thinks that librarians have it easy has never worked with the public."

What could be so terrible? Someone dropped a book on her foot or put it on the wrong shelf? Someone asked for useless information she couldn't find? She was always getting bothered over nothing important. Life was always weighing her down. If Eva had to go through what Mutti and Rosa went through, she wouldn't mind the small stuff. What Izzy longed to see in her were hope and happiness reborn, an end to suffering once and for all . . . but Eva was a disappointment in that way, he had to admit.

Sam finished eating first, jumped up without even excusing himself, and left the room. Eva didn't say a word about his dishes or bad manners but only sat quietly, elbows on the table and her chin in her hands.

As soon as Sam was back on the couch Izzy said to his daughter, "I went to the plant today and talked to Tony and Roger."

"I knew you couldn't stay away."

"Roger's got big plans."

"He's a very good businessman." She went to the stove for seconds and filled her plate. "You want more?"

"Listen to me. Come sit down." She came back to the table and Izzy leaned forward so their heads were almost touching. "He likes being the man in charge—I think he likes it more than he should. He's not sorry his father's dead."

"What a lousy thing to say." She jabbed spaghetti with her fork. "Roger loved and admired Phil."

"You never know what people are really thinking deep down. It doesn't matter how nice they seem on the surface."

"I know about Roger." Eva stopped eating for a moment, her fork in the air. "I hope you didn't say that to him."

"Not in those exact words."

"You accused him of wanting his father dead?"

"I told him it must be nice running the business by himself."

"You're lucky he didn't slug you."

"Something else was on his mind . . . about when you were married."

"Oh?" Eva lowered her eyes.

"Something he wouldn't talk about—that you were no angel either."

"What's that supposed to mean?"

"Think back," Izzy said. "What can you remember?"

"There's nothing to think about. I told you what he did to me—dirty panties under the bed, hair in the bathroom! What more do you need to know?"

In the next room the TV was suddenly turned up loud. Izzy heard gun shots, screaming, and sirens, though the noise might well have been real, blowing in from outside. "Maybe something else happened you forgot to mention."

"Nothing else happened." She stood up, eyes wide. "Believe Roger if you want—a cheat and a liar! Or else"—her voice wavering—"believe me, your daughter." Her mouth twisted, her eyes shrank. "Why don't you ever believe *me*?" Then she turned on her heel and ran. Her bedroom door banged shut.

Izzy was puzzled, his head a block. Who was guilty, who was innocent, who was lying or telling the truth? Who remembered properly and who was spinning stories? How could anyone figure out anything as tangled as that? Better to give his brain a rest and leave it for the moment. Too much thinking's unhealthy, as his mother used to say. Tomorrow is another day.

He exchanged his empty dinner plate for Eva's full one, even though the mound of white pasta with its red cap like a snowman's hat was already cold. Not that he was hungry, but he felt suddenly hollow, his stomach a hole like an empty grave. He filled his mouth, chewed, and gulped . . . as if he could swallow all feelings, all losses, all thoughts. As if he weren't alone at the table, alone in Toronto, alone in the world. As if he were admired and loved.

3

SLOWLY IZZY CLIMBED THE STEPS to the biggest house on Riversee Lane. He was already out of breath. He'd taken the subway south and west, then traipsed through a park with a lazy river and up a path through bare trees. A month from now the trail would be a wonderland of buds and flowers, a scenic passage that justified the high price of real estate hereabouts, but now it was only a hard walk that left him hot and winded.

He paused on the top step of the house that was once Phil's and now belonged to his third wife. Izzy recalled the time he went inside to use the bathroom, which had two sinks, a sauna, and enough towels to wrap a mummy. The opulence was striking, even if it was overdone.

He loosened his tie and looked around. Riversee was a wide road, more a boulevard than a lane, with stern brick or stone buildings set off by tall windows, four-columned porticos, archways, and gabled roofs. Despite the naked trees there was no view of the water below, yet all the streets had fancy names like Rivercrest, Riverside, Riverfront. His own address in Florida was 720 Muddy Creek Road, a reference to a dry bed in a patch of moss-laden oaks at the far end of Izzy's street—though after a heavy rain the creek would indeed come to life as a dirty stream.

When his breathing was normal again he banged the brass knocker on the paneled door. He heard nothing from inside. Maybe he should've phoned first and got a proper invitation—but what if she refused to see him? Surprise was a better strategy, except if she wasn't home—in which case he was wasting his morning. He knocked again, and another time, and the door swung open at last.

A woman looked him up and down and Izzy was glad he'd decided on the formality of a dark suit, striped tie, and white-on-white twill shirt: there was no mistaking him for a bum looking for a handout or a salesman down on his luck. Her bleached hair was pulled back, tight and unmoving; her eyes were like fragments of shrapnel when she peered at his face.

"Yvonne?" He wasn't certain. Izzy had met her just once, as far as he knew, and only remembered her as someone blonde and zaftig.

"What do you want?" she said.

"Yvonne, don't you know me? Izzy Schneider, Phil's friend who used to run the factory?"

"Why should I know you? I never went near the place."

"Once I came here with Phil, it was two or three years ago. Don't ask where we were going—dinner maybe, out for a walk, or just to drive around and talk. We only stayed a few minutes but still he introduced us, you were wearing a sweater, I think—gray like your eyes—and a black shawl on top."

"It's a drafty house," Yvonne said, her voice a little softer. Izzy knew to keep talking.

"I came for the funeral, I'm staying with my daughter. You must remember Eva—she was married to Roger twelve years, they have a boy named Sam, he's almost seventeen now and taller than his father. Anyway, in a few days I'm flying back to Florida, but meanwhile I can't stop thinking about my friend Phil, the places he went to, people he met, the things I know, the things I don't. So last week I drove to the plant, I spoke to Roger and Tony—the man who caught the murderer—and now I'd like to talk to you . . . to stir up some memories."

"About Phil?"

"What else?"

"You're not writing a book or something?"

"Me? I don't even write letters."

"A lot of people want to speak to me all of a sudden so I have to be careful."

"You don't have to worry with me, an old man who only wants to talk about an old friend with anyone who knew him. That's how it is when someone dies—you need to remember him, you can't just let go. You want to hear other people's stories too."

From within the house a woman hollered, "Who is it? Who's there?" and Yvonne glanced over her shoulder, said something he couldn't make out, then motioned him in. "I remember you now," she said. "You went to use the bathroom and complained there were too many towels."

Izzy looked down at his shoes, polished to a high gloss. There *were* too many towels, he would say the same thing today. How can you tell what's for using, what's for show?

He followed her through a foyer that was lit by a chandelier; then past the living room, past a dining-room table and severe-looking straight-backed chairs. The hall led to a sunny kitchen with glass doors overlooking a deck and muddy garden, a few crocuses poking through. The kitchen had a counter and stools, and on one of these sat a woman Izzy thought he recognized: Irene, Phil's second wife.

"I know you!" she called out, making him start and bump the fridge. "That's Izzy," she said to Yvonne. "He worked for Phil, he managed the plant. I used to run into him all the time. I saw you at the funeral"—talking to him again—"and wanted to say hello, but I was crying so hard I couldn't get a word out."

"A very sad day," he said. "To think that a man like Phil was murdered in cold blood . . . and all because of a woman."

The ex-wives exchanged looks but didn't speak. Yvonne had a hard-looking *punim*, he decided: thin nose, pale skin, stone-colored eyes, and a mouth as straight as the blade of a knife; a face that spoke of *tsuris*. Why was Phil attracted to that? Didn't he have enough trouble in his life already? Irene you could understand—a face as sweet and colorful as an ice-cream sundae: rosy cheeks, blue eyelids, yellow hair. At first glance they seemed alike, a pair of big-bosomed blondes, but up close the two were as different as water and stone.

Yvonne started pacing. First she circled the counter, then stopped at the doors to the garden. "So, I guess you two have known each other a long time."

"I went to her wedding," Izzy said, climbing onto a high stool. "Such a celebration! There were five hundred guests and a cake up to the ceiling."

"My God, my wedding!" Irene said. "I remember it like it was yesterday—the yarmulkes embroidered in gold, *Mr. and Mrs. Phil Lewis*, filet mignon and champagne, a thousand tiny beads on my gown, and a white limo to drive us away."

"I was there with my wife and daughter—who, as a matter of fact, would stand under the *chuppah* with Roger only months later."

"Eva—such a sweetheart—and their little boy Sammy . . . I meant to stay in touch, but you know how it is."

"Roger and Eva had a nice wedding too, only not such a big deal."

"No one ever tops Phil." Yvonne was leaning against a glass door with her arms crossed.

"You could've had a big wedding too if you wanted."

"I didn't want," Yvonne said.

"They snuck off to city hall," Irene told Izzy, "which I think was a big mistake. Why miss out on a good party?"

"I'm surprised to see you here," he said. "I didn't know you were friends. Who would think, the ex-wives . . . How did that happen?"

"When Phil and I divorced I got a very nice settlement, so when it was Yvonne's turn she phoned me for my lawyer's name. That's how it started."

"A friendly divorce, I remember it well. Nineteen seventy-nine, the same year my wife died. I was already retired but not living in Florida yet."

"Mine was friendly, hers wasn't."

"He doesn't want to hear about that." Yvonne scowled. She tapped the glass sliding door and frightened a squirrel off the deck. She could frighten a boulder, Izzy thought.

There was coffee on the stove and a cup in the dish rack. He got up and helped himself. Irene pointed out the cream and sugar on the counter but Yvonne just ignored him. A woman like that you can't expect to be a good hostess. He sat down again, lightened his drink, and raised his cup toward Irene. "Twenty-eight years I worked for Phil and all day long it was coffee, coffee, coffee. You'd think I'd hate the stuff by now, you'd think there was nothing left of my *kishkas*."

"Phil loved his coffee, all right. He said it made him sociable. There was nothing he liked better, he said, than conversation and coffee."

"Not counting wine, women, and real estate," Yvonne said.

"She didn't know him like I did," Irene spoke to Izzy. "Sure he had his faults, but he did so much good in the world you had to forgive him certain things."

"Like drinking and screwing around and spending money he didn't have."

"He needed love," Irene went on, "to help him forget the past. He took care of people, but in return he wanted them to love him completely."

"The man was insatiable."

"He had trouble getting close. I guess he was afraid of losing anyone he loved too much. His whole family died in the Vilna ghetto—an awful place. We can only imagine what it was like, the horrors he lived through."

But Izzy could picture it very well. "The ghetto was in old Vilna," Phil used to tell him, "separated from the rest of the city by a big gate. There were schools in there and factories, an orchestra and library, even a choir. But also we had overcrowding, no fuel or running water, beatings and executions, people dying in the streets from dysentery, starvation, typhus, and heart attacks."

"How did you manage?" Izzy said.

"I was able to lay my hands on a *Schein*—a yellow permit—and get a job in a workshop. With that I could help my mother, sister, and brother," Phil said, "at least for a while. In the end they were murdered anyway."

"What about your father?"

"They took him right away to a forced-labor camp, and I never saw my father again."

Phil always stopped there, his eyes half closed and his lips pressed together, and Izzy would be left to think about his own mother and sister, who met the same fate as Phil's. He never felt so close to his friend as when they were speaking about death.

"The man was amazing," Irene was saying. "After he escaped the ghetto he fought with Soviet partisans and fed and protected hundreds of Jews."

"*One* hundred," Izzy said.

"After an airdrop he'd ride through camp on a white horse—"

"Brown," he corrected.

"—giving out boxes of food, and everyone would call his name and touch him as he passed by."

How easy it was to imagine himself in the camp too, a skinny tailor mending clothes. He saw himself rush forward along with the others to stroke Phil's boot as he rode among his people; to cheer him and praise God for sending a deliverer.

"Years later," Irene said, "a few of them even came to the plant—a whole family one time—to shake his hand and thank him and tell him what they'd done with their lives. Two or three he gave jobs because they were out of work. You have to admire that."

"I was there," said Izzy. "I remember the family. Some of us cried to see them."

But he wasn't always as helpful as that, Izzy didn't say aloud. When a small manufacturer he put out of business by undercutting his prices came begging for a job, Phil turned the man away.

"A lot of people owe him their lives and their livelihood. You can't judge Phil like other men."

"Someone judged him," Izzy said. "Somebody wanted him dead."

Yvonne came up to the counter and flattened her palms on the surface. "Because he was greedy and took what he had no right to. He ruined more lives than he saved."

"You have to understand something," Irene told Izzy. "Phil hurt her very much. They divorced only last year and Yvonne isn't over it yet. For me it's a different story. I can look back and remember the good times, the trips we took to Paris and Rome—evening walks along the river, breakfasts in roof gardens—the jewelry, clothes, and souvenirs . . . He liked giving people gifts, and not just to those he loved but anyone, for no reason, just to make them happy."

"Selma must be overjoyed rattling around in her big house."

Izzy straightened on his stool. "The new house in Florida?"

"She moved in before he died."

"She even came to the funeral. Maybe you saw her, Selma Gold. A skinny thing with short hair. Looks like a boy."

"A baby chick."

"Not exactly Phil's type." Izzy looked from one ex-wife to the other. "I can't understand it."

"Any girl was Phil's type—the younger the better."

"I never thought she'd show," said Irene. "That took chutzpah."

"The house is all hers now." Yvonne's cheeks were flaming and her eyes too suddenly bright. "Maybe you should ask Selma what Phil saw in her—that's if she'll talk to you, if she's not too busy decorating nine rooms!"

To Izzy's astonishment Yvonne slumped across the counter, sending a plate flying. The dish landed with a crack and splintered into pieces. Irene was at her side at once, struggling to lift her as she slid to the floor. "Help me," she commanded Izzy.

Hooking her arms over their shoulders, they half dragged, half carried Yvonne to the living room and laid her on a sofa. Irene ran to the kitchen and returned with a glass of water and something in her hand which she popped into her friend's mouth. Then she made Yvonne drink and covered her with an afghan. The woman closed her eyes and was soon snoring lightly.

"This has been hard on her," said Irene. "Reporters, cops, and now you, everyone talking about Phil and how he ruined their marriage. Her blood pressure skyrockets whenever she hears Selma's name. She didn't sleep a wink last night. All she wants is a quiet life."

Izzy backed away from the couch. "He cheated on her with Selma? He was still married to Yvonne . . . ?"

She pulled off Yvonne's shoes and sat down close to her feet. "They were married only a short time when Phil started messing around. It broke her heart to find out about him and Selma, but she got her revenge in court."

"Revenge is a tasty morsel, as my mother liked to say."

"He wasn't a one-woman guy. All you had to do was see him nodding and winking at his female employees—those pretty Italians and Portuguese—to know what was on his mind." Irene sighed, looked away. "Even when he was married to me I knew he was seeing someone else. He leaned on me, needed me . . . but that didn't stop him."

Izzy made a clucking sound and winced. "Such things . . ." he said.

Irene smoothed Yvonne's skirt and tucked the afghan around her legs. "He divorced me to set me free so I could find a better man—and you know what? I never did. I married again but it didn't last. And then I lost interest."

He moved to an armchair alongside the piano and stretched out his stiff legs. Phil the philanderer, Phil the cheat: Izzy had never thought that before. It was one thing to toy with the girls in the factory, another thing to have an affair big enough to end your marriage.

Irene stood up, crossed the room, pulled something from a drawer, and dropped it on Izzy's lap. "Open it." She perched on the arm of his chair. "It tells a story—a love story. I think you'll find it interesting."

A photo album, quite slim, the binding loose. He started at the beginning, where the snapshots were in black and white: a woman wearing a dark cloche, flat curls on her forehead; a man in a dress shirt opening the hood of a car with headlights like the eyes of a frog. After that some pictures of the woman with a baby; then the little girl herself, with dimples and chubby legs, riding a tricycle, digging in sand, posing with a boy on a beach. Throughout, while he studied the pages, Irene spoke quietly: "Her parents and brother... That's Yvonne."

There was a jump of many years, then a color photo of Yvonne at her brother's wedding, pretty in a mauve gown. Then nothing— no more shots—until the ones of her own wedding, dated 1984. As if she'd been in hiding all the long years in between. As if Phil had woken her like Sleeping Beauty from a deep, mysterious slumber. And suddenly, at the turn of a page, Yvonne and Phil at city hall: grinning on the long marble stairs of the lobby; signing a register; greeting friends; holding hands on a loveseat in a wood-paneled alcove; standing before the judge, Yvonne's face redder than the crimson bow of her corsage; the newlyweds enjoying a kiss.

"They look very much in love."

"She was crazy about him."

On the following pages there were portraits of Phil. A close-up of his round face, his eyes squeezed to half-moons, teeth small and pointy, and his chin riding the folds of his neck. Bare-chested, in blue jeans, a pineapple palm in the background, somewhere in Florida. Squatting in front of a chalky stuccoed building with balconies like dashes on a sheet of paper: home of Phil's condo apartment, bought the same year Izzy moved into a bungalow. A shot of him on the deck of a boat in a windbreaker and plaid shorts, arms crossed under his head, eyes closed and his mouth set in a gentle, smug, or happy grin, depending on how you saw it. After that the album was blank, a collection of smooth, white, plastic-covered pages, like the sides of an empty bathtub. Not so much as a pressed flower.

"You could say," Irene said, "that everything started and stopped with Phil. Unlike me, she relied on him completely. He was the earth and she was his moon." She twirled a finger in the air and Izzy's brain flashed to a picture of Phil and Irene waltzing at their wedding, bobbing in a circle like creatures on a merry-go-round.

"And now what? Look at her now—fighting to hold herself together."

"It makes you wonder about him."

"I have to keep reminding myself how much he suffered—the death of his family, the years of cold and hunger . . . He even had to eat his horse."

"Phil ate the stallion?"

"One winter they ran out of food, they shot it and cooked it. He said that it didn't taste bad, they had worse meals than that."

"He *ate* it?" Izzy repeated.

"It's true that what he went through scarred him forever; he couldn't help himself when it came to his love life. But when I look at poor Yvonne . . ."

Irene put the album away. Then she returned to her friend and sat down beside her again, stroking a piece of the afghan. Yvonne's hair had come undone and hung like pale roots over the end of a cushion.

"I should go," said Izzy.

But still he sat there, suddenly tired. The light in the room was soft, dulled by the drapery, the only noise the steady tick-tocking of a mantel clock like the drip of a leaky faucet. When Hilda was alive they would sit together in such a room with dark furniture, thick curtains, upholstered chairs, and a plump couch. Hilda would be reading a book or doing her needlepoint while Izzy skipped through the paper, the crackle of pages the only sound. They were conscious of each other but also apart in the quiet of the evening: stillness brushing against you like a cat rubbing its back on the leg of your trousers.

The silence wasn't always easy. Sometimes they were distant, each locked in private thoughts, an impenetrable solitude. In the end, as she was dying, Hilda withdrew more and more into her sphere of illness in which he imagined she was looking back, reliving her youth, remembering when her body was strong and could be depended on. Those nights he understood he was already losing her little by little, invisibly, and though he didn't cry till later, when she was dead and in the ground, the mourning should have started sooner, much sooner than it did.

Yvonne stirred on the sofa. He thought he heard her sigh his name—"Izzeleh," he thought she said—which is what Mutti used to say, and also what his sister called him ("*Izzeleh, mein kleiner Bruder...*"), at least when they were getting along. When Rosa wasn't scolding him for breaking their mother's heart because he dated shiksas. "*Oy*, he's killing me!" Mutti would cry and Rosa would chime in, "Look what you're doing, you're killing her"— though it didn't change anything, he paid no attention; he liked girls with tiny noses, fair hair, and pale skin. If it wasn't for Hitler and his gang, he might have eloped with his Aryan girlfriend, Charlotte.

He didn't like to think of Rosa. Couldn't help but think of her now. Slim and elegant, long-nosed, her eyes bright with intelligence, she was nothing like the ex-wives, and yet... the piano and curtains, the big sofa, Yvonne's voice, so like his sister's when she hummed along to something she was playing on the piano.

He pushed himself out of his chair and went to sit on the piano stool, spreading his fingers on the keys. Irene asked if he played and he said no, not him, he was unmusical. He lacked the sensitivity, patience, and interest to master an instrument, and though his mother nagged him to keep up his lessons, he never did. Years later Eva would stop taking lessons too, showing little promise, and he would feel the same disappointment Mutti had felt in him.

But Rosa played. Played well. Chopin, Schubert, Mozart, Liszt. Unlike Izzy, neither scholar nor musician, Rosa made her parents proud. She might have been a concert pianist, she was that good—or her sons, Kurt and Martin, who were also very talented.

She had a photo album too, Izzy remembered, with postcards of movie stars and snapshots of family and friends, a thick book with extra pictures slipped under the covers. By 1935 she had packed the album away for good, hidden it for safekeeping. Things were bad that year: "Jews Not Welcome" signs in cinemas, theaters, cafés, and Rosa's beloved concert halls; her husband Arnold fired from his job at the university. "We have to get out," Izzy had said, "before it gets impossible!" But Rosa thought they'd seen the worst, the Nazis would be overthrown, it was easier to weather the storm than start again in a new place.

Izzy pressed the piano keys, making a doleful sound. If only she had listened to him! If only he had tried a little harder to convince her. *Think of the boys and not yourself*, he might've argued. *Don't you want your sons to grow up unafraid?*

In fact it was calmer in 1936, the year of the Olympics, the year he fled Germany. Once he was gone they wrote often, letters between Berlin and Lyon, then between Berlin and the Bronx (of which there are only a few left, the rest were lost or damaged). Though Rosa's letters were indirect because of mail surveillance and the fear of reprisals, he knew that things were getting much worse, as he'd predicted.

In New York he spoke to refugees and read articles, heard rumors. Jews were being beaten on the streets of Berlin, he understood, arrested and murdered; and other changes had taken place. "We have now adopted the Biblical names Israel and Sara," Rosa wrote, "because they are such fine names . . . The children have decided they will not go to school anymore. They prefer to study at home."

In coded messages she alluded to the deportation of thousands of Polish-born Jews—including their own parents—to a refugee camp in Poland in October 1938: "The autumn is a lovely time for a trip across the border. They left at night, however, so I was unable to say goodbye and cannot be certain when I will see them again. Papa forgot his wallet and now I am worried they will not have money to eat well. I worry that they may not be having a good time. You know what a worrier I am. I cannot sleep with worrying."

After Kristallnacht she wrote, "The synagogues are very old and need a great deal of repair, now more than ever . . . Our neighbors the Nussbaums have unexpectedly closed their store. The Habers sold their business to a young Aryan couple . . . Many people are taking trips."

She hinted that she and Arnold could no longer go for drives or move about freely and mentioned the loss of all their property, the start of war. He knew when she got the money he sent; that Arnold moved from Kraków early in 1941 to Brzesko, Poland, where Mutti finally wound up, to take care of her after Papa died of a heart attack; that Martin was bar mitzvahed in a rabbi's apartment in July of that same year; that Rosa moved to another place—a *Judenhaus*, Izzy guessed—probably in the fall. But how she managed day to day, her fear and grief and heavy heart, all that he didn't know, though once or twice she wrote about a "breakdown" and "damaged nerves."

Everything stopped by the end of 1941; his letters returned. He never knew for certain what happened next and could only imagine her final months: toiling in a factory for starvation wages; the yellow star on the front of her coat; the roundup in the dead of night and deportation to a ghetto in Poland; Rosa and her frightened boys in a cattle car to Auschwitz.

Were they shot, bludgeoned, tortured in experiments, or simply starved? Was she separated from her sons? Did they die alone in terror, or climbing over each other in a pyramid of choking bodies under a shower of Zyklon B?

And what of Mutti and Arnold? The last card arrived in October 1941, then nothing. Nothing more. His letters to Poland returned as well. He never heard from them again or found out anything and could only assume they died too. Died most horribly.

Hunched on the piano stool, he felt himself flatten like a leaky tire. What more could he have done? Mutti asked for money and he gave as much as he could spare. To Rosa he mailed an affidavit, but the waiting list for visas to America was so long, years long. And even after she got a visa there was the problem of passage. Without ship tickets she could not apply for a passport and would never be allowed out—and she didn't have the money. She begged him to find a way—if not for her, at least for the boys—and God knows Izzy knocked on every available door, sent what he could, and pleaded for more, but no committee, no organization he spoke to came through. It was too late, years late, everybody told him, there were too many desperate Jews frantic to leave Germany.

Rosa was angry and scared but what more could he possibly do? Pick pockets? Rob a bank? Deal with a loan shark? His life with Hilda was hard enough, and still he sent every extra dime he had to Europe. His sister didn't understand. "Try harder," she wrote him. "There must be something else you can do!"

What? *In God's name, what?*

In the fall of 1941, when Izzy was finally able to make certain arrangements, Jewish emigration was banned and Rosa and her children were trapped for good. Regardless of his scheming, he couldn't save them in the end. He couldn't get them out of Berlin or help them survive the war: his sister and nephews gone to smoke. Izzy let his family die.

Yisgadal v'yiskadash sh'may rabbo . . .

"You're crying," Irene said.

Phil would say the war's over, let it be, enough already, why torture yourself when you did all you possibly could? Yes, he'd answer, yes, you're right, and sometimes even now he believes he tried everything, he left no stone unturned . . . But still Izzy can't sleep. At night, when he tries to sleep, terrible pictures play in his mind over and over until at last his brain sizzles, his thoughts collide in a roar of grief, his throat closes, he can't breathe, he claws at the sheet and waits. He only waits for morning.

"What is it?" Irene said.

His eyes were wet and burning. He looked up, looked around. Slowly he became aware of the room, the women, the piano, and the year, 1989. He wiped his face with the back of his hand and stood up, his legs weak. "I have to go."

"I'll get you a glass of water first."

Izzy shook his head no. "I can't stay any longer."

On his way out of the big house he stopped in the bathroom to empty his old man's bladder before the ride home. There were dozens of towels in the room, just as he remembered, folded and stacked on shelves, draped on different gold rails, pulled through rings or arranged on trays next to the twin sinks. After using the toilet he washed his hands in the left sink, washed them again in the right sink, and dried them finger by finger on every towel he could reach. Exactly why he did that he couldn't say. What makes people write their names in spray paint on brick walls? What makes them pay money to get their names on brass plaques in churches and synagogues? Why do lovers carve their initials in tree trunks and children scribble in wet cement? To be remembered, naturally—but Izzy's mark was fleeting. Why bother leaving a sign knowing that an hour from now the proof of your existence would have dried up?

This much he knew at least: the wet towels linked him to the women in some way. Because of the towels they would not forget him right away. They'd think about him after he left, call him in Florida, his phone ringing at all hours: first Roger, then the wives.

How are you doing? We were just talking about you . . . Like Phil, he'd be part of their lives.

Izzy closed the front door quietly behind him and started the long hike back to the subway. At least it was downhill. Across the broad neighborhood streets, along the steep path and its guard of tall trees like so many pickets on a fence, through the park with its slow river, and finally into the station. He bought a paper, paid his fare, rode an escalator down, found a place on the platform overlooking the eastbound tracks, and waited for the train to arrive. It was still early afternoon and the platform wasn't crowded, a clutch of people on one side, a few on the other. He opened his paper.

The oil spill was still in the news, the captain of the tanker facing charges of drunkenness . . . Oil-drenched sea otters, birds, and other wildlife: an environmental disaster. One catastrophe after the next, that's how the world proceeds—that's what he should've told Sam. *It makes you sick what goes on, but what can you do to stop it?*

Hitler wasn't Izzy's fault. He couldn't have stopped the murder of Jews any more than he could have prevented the war itself. He was forced to leave Berlin—to run from city to city, a step beyond the Gestapo's reach—lucky to escape when he did. Lucky to know nothing of hunger, lice, and typhus, the weight of a gun, the smell of blood. He was blameless. An innocent! So enough already. *Stop this!*

A splash of light in the tunnel: the train approaching from the right. Izzy folded his paper and stepped to the edge of the platform. Something was happening on his left, something moving swiftly in the corner of his eye. A package maybe, thrown on the tracks. A knapsack. A bundled coat.

The train entered the station with a gust of wind, a screech of steel, and lurched to a stop as the thing on the track disappeared under the front car. Voices rose in a single howl. Someone shouted, "Oh my God! Sweet Jesus! Get help!"

People were moving crazily, like flies in a bottle. The train was dark, frozen in place, as transit workers ran to the scene. Everyone was crowding the platform, straining to see.

"What happened?" "Do something!" "Move aside! Out of the way!"

Izzy didn't want to see. Don't look, he told himself. *Enough blood. Enough dead.* He didn't want to know what happened, whether someone fell, was pushed, or jumped under the wheels of the train. He didn't want to help either. What could an old man like him do anyway? Hop down and drag the pinned body out from under the car? No, no, he had to get away from the squeezing crowd. *Go quickly! While you can!* He pushed his way to an escalator, rode to the surface, burst through a turnstile and onto the street.

He was wheezing for breath. He felt lightheaded and collapsed on a bench by the doors to the station. Why did he have to witness such a terrible thing? Wasn't Phil's murder enough—not to mention all the other deaths he has had to endure? He was only in town a few more days, then back to Bay Point where you never see such goings-on. A car accident maybe . . . but nothing as bad as this.

All the years he lived in Toronto he never rode the subway—and look what happens when he does! If only his daughter had left him the car. If only she didn't insist it was perfectly safe to take the train. The best transit system in North America, Eva said, nothing at all to worry about. Shows you what she knows.

As Izzy collected himself on the bench, sirens rang in his ears, then along came fire engines, police cars, an ambulance. Uniformed men with bulky equipment dashed into the station while subway passengers staggered out. A man sat on the curb with his head in his hands and started to moan. A woman was wailing. In minutes the pavement was packed with frenzied people. Some raced from the station, while others got in taxis and sped away. By the time his legs were steady again and Izzy rose to hail a cab, the cars were gone. He waited by the edge of the sidewalk but none appeared. Sure he could phone, but the line at the booth by the station doors was ten people deep now, his legs would never hold up . . . and anyway, where did he want a taxi to take him? No one would be home at Eva's apartment at this hour, and after what he just went through, Izzy needed to talk.

Without thinking further, he headed back to the lifeless park, the sleepy river and tall trees. If the going was hard before, now it was painful. At every step his feet stung, his knees creaked, his hips hurt. His neck and shoulders had welded into one solid, aching mass so that he couldn't turn his head to see the trees on either side as he crept up the steep hill. Several times he had to stop and slap his chest, gasp for breath, and once, feeling dizzy again, he looped his arms around a trunk and clung to it for balance. If a stranger had happened by, he might have taken Izzy for a poor *tsedrayter* kissing a tree, but at his age you couldn't avoid appearing ridiculous now and then. An old body was unpredictable, often embarrassing, a letdown, a bitter pill, and you had to make allowances. Compared to wetting your trousers or farting in a crowded room, hugging a tree was a small thing.

He finished the climb and made his way slowly, pausing frequently, one street after the next, to the big house on Riversee Lane. As he rapped on the front door, Izzy imagined what he'd say: *Standing on the platform and the train was just pulling in . . . A box, I thought, an overcoat . . .* Yvonne wouldn't care but Irene would be horrified. She'd ask him in and offer him a sandwich, a cup of tea. She'd turn on the radio and listen for the news while he lay on the sofa with the afghan across his legs and told her what he saw and heard and felt, what it meant to him—murder and suicide. He'd say even more than he might've said to Eva, who always interrupted him when Izzy told stories and tried her best to cut him off.

In Berlin, he'd confide to Irene, many Jews took pills, they drowned in the Spree, or they jumped from their apartments. In the camps there were prisoners who threw themselves gladly against the high-voltage fences: Izzy had seen pictures and heard tales. Maybe his mother or sister had been lucky enough to die like that.

But how much should he disclose to a woman he hardly knew? How could he trust her with his grief, the way he had trusted Phil? Better just to say little, rest a minute, have a glass of cold water, call a cab . . .

No one answered his knocking. He peered through the side-lights framing the door but saw only darkness. He crossed the porch to a window with paneled shutters on either side, fifteen panes high at least, banged on the glass, and looked in, cupping his hands around his eyes. The living room was empty. Maybe the women were sleeping or had gone out. Maybe they saw him coming and were hiding somewhere upstairs. He tried the door once more, then sat down on the porch steps.

Now what? He couldn't walk to the station again, he wouldn't make it ten feet, but how could he stay here in the damp, chilly afternoon? Besides, he was hungry. He pushed up his sleeve and glanced at his watch. All he'd had for breakfast was an English muffin and cream cheese and now it was after two. Another trick the body plays: first it runs out of steam when you need it to go to another place, then it insists on being fed no matter where you happen to be or what else is on your mind.

In the ghetto as in the camps, Phil used to say, there was nothing more important than food. People were skeletons, their bones clearly visible through the papery sheet that was their skin. As if they were dressed up in scary skeleton costumes like children on Halloween. "Every day in the Vilna ghetto," Phil said, "was Halloween."

They were eating in a nice restaurant, someplace Phil had chosen. "We were always hungry," he continued, picking at the pricey fish and vegetables on his dinner plate. (Izzy had already finished his meal and was reading the menu, wondering whether to have pie or something fancier for dessert.) "All we talked about was food—what we needed, how to get it, what could be traded for a piece of bread, a carrot, a beet. What we could remember of the taste of meat, a cup of coffee, layer cake with whipped cream . . ."

Phil had lost his appetite, but Izzy ordered chocolate mousse. Maybe it wasn't right, but hearing stories of deprivation made him want to eat more—as if he were getting away with something, doing something his friend couldn't.

By then Phil was relating his escape through the sewer pipes— wet and shaking, inching forward, hour after panicky hour, squeezed by the tunnel walls. "You can't imagine what it was like— the stink of shit and piss and fear! I had to remind myself to breathe, praying that I wouldn't cry or vomit or pass out. And you know what I was thinking of while staring at the feet of the man crawling ahead of me? My next meal, that's what. When would I get it and what would it be? Wheezing and gagging, I was dreaming of fried potatoes and bread."

Izzy put his spoon down. "But you survived everything. You got out and got revenge! Me, I missed the whole war. What do I know about killing Nazis? What do I know about saving Jews— including my own family?"

"Listen, Izzy. Hear me out . . . The day after I escaped they wiped out the ghetto. I stayed there as long as I could, but in the end I left behind everyone I held dear—aunts, uncles, nieces, nephews, my mother, brother, and sister . . . I still see them in my dreams. They went to Sobibor . . . but I went into the forest."

"You did what was necessary—no one would disagree. You went on to save others."

"I saved my own neck," said Phil. "And now they call me a hero."

Izzy paused to consider this, then pushed aside his dish in an act of solidarity: they had things in common. Both men had saved themselves. Both married and fathered children—thereby advancing the survival of the Jewish race. Who could deny the rightness of that? They foiled Hitler by staying alive! What would've been gained if they had perished with their families?

Yet neither truly escaped the war: both stuck in an orbit of re-playing images, no more alive than the ghosts of their nightmares.

The dead never leave you alone.

"So you suffer too," he said.

"I suffer," Phil replied.

Imagine that! Izzy had thought. Even a man like Phil, a warrior and avenger, felt the same squeezing of his *kishkas* that Izzy did. Even Phil could be accused of abandoning his family—regardless of how many Jews he rescued after. Not everyone would call him brave; not everyone would thank him. And if Phil wasn't such a lion, Izzy wasn't such a mouse.

But now, as he waited on Riversee Lane, he tried to pull his thoughts forward and figure out what to do next. He couldn't think straight anymore, the past always gobbling the present. Plus it didn't help that his stomach was still kvetching.

"When the stomach is empty, the brain is also empty," Mutti used to say, coaxing him to eat more supper than he wanted. "When I was your age," Hilda scolded Eva years later, "all I had for lunch was a pickle and a slice of bread. The food you're leaving on your plate is more than I got in a day."

In the Vilna ghetto, he might have explained to his wife and child, a piece of bread was a banquet, a pickle was a miracle. But by then Izzy no longer repeated Phil's stories. They would only frighten Hilda, and Eva used to cover her ears.

He sat on the porch steps and stared into the distance. After a short while a taxi appeared across the street and a couple got out and walked into a neighboring house. Izzy stood, waving his arms, and moved as fast as he could to the curb. The driver finished a three-point turn, spotted him, and pulled over. Izzy got into the backseat and the cabbie said, "Where to?"

"Somewhere with a lot of people. Somewhere I can get food."

The driver turned to peer at him, his eyebrows peaked and meeting in the middle like the letter *M*. "I'm supposed to guess where?"

"Take me to a busy place, a tourist attraction."

The man winked at the rearview mirror, shifted gears, and took off. He needed a shave, Izzy thought. He was not in the habit of trusting men who neglected their personal hygiene, and as they headed downtown and the meter clicked off dollar after dollar, he knew he'd made a mistake. "The Eaton Centre," he decided. "That's where I want to go."

It was almost three when they got there. He paid the cabbie the huge fare, adding a meager tip, and the man scowled and drove off. Izzy entered the gaping mall, took a pair of escalators down to the lowest level, and hobbled to the food court. Even so late in the afternoon the place was packed. He lined up at the nearest counter, bought a chicken salad sandwich, coffee, and a bran muffin, then carried his tray around the tables grouped together like building blocks, looking for an empty seat.

The only available chair was across from a well-dressed middle-aged woman who was eating from a small tub of low-fat yogurt. Pretty in a goyishe way, in a beige jacket with padded shoulders, beige skirt slit at the side, her hair in a stiff bubble leaning a little to one side. Her skin was heavily powdered and her lipstick carelessly smeared, so that her mouth seemed to be frozen in a clownish grin. He stood over her, waiting for her to remove a lumpy canvas bag from the table to make room. She yanked it to the floor with such a thump that his arms jerked, his tray shook, and coffee splashed out of his cup. A few drops hit the table. She goggled her eyes at him as if this were his fault and wiped the spill with a napkin. Izzy sat there anyway.

After a bite into his sandwich he said to her, "Let me tell you something that you may find interesting—what I saw on the subway today, an honest-to-goodness tragedy. But maybe you already heard about it on the news?"

"I don't talk to strangers," she said.

"Izzy Schneider—how do you do?" He stuck out his hand but she wouldn't shake. "I live in Florida normally, but came to

Toronto for the unexpected funeral of my old friend Phil Lewis—
well-known partisan and shirt manufacturer—shot by a lunatic
outside his own plant." He paused to let that sink in. "We were as
close as this"—interlacing his fingers.

The woman pulled at her bottom lip, plump as a pincushion.

"Now that you know who I am, I'm not such a stranger," he
said. "Now we can sit and talk."

The woman gave her hairdo a shove, centering it on top of her
head.

"So there I was standing on the subway platform . . . and all of a
sudden I saw something that looked like an animal or maybe a suitcase falling across the tracks. It could've been anything"—his voice
getting louder. "I didn't know what to think! Then everyone was
screaming and pushing, such a commotion you wouldn't believe."

The woman folded her hands on the table, spinning her
thumbs. "Someone jumped."

"How do you know someone jumped? Maybe the person fell."

"People get pushed too, but mostly it's suicides that hold up
the subway. I've been stuck many times. You have to get out and
take a bus. It's gotten so you can't expect to get anywhere on time."

"Doesn't it upset you?"

"I don't like being late."

"I mean that someone died like that—that someone was in such
pain and didn't want to live so much he threw himself in front of a
train."

"If someone doesn't want to live, that's his business. But why
ruin my day by killing himself in public? Let him put his head in an
oven or cut his wrists in the bathtub."

The woman jiggled her hand in her purse and pulled out a
lipstick. She retouched her lips without benefit of a mirror, so
naturally the line was wrong. Something wasn't altogether right
with her, he decided.

But how could she be so indifferent to suffering? Izzy finished
his sandwich and used his crumpled napkin to wipe sweat from

his forehead. How could she sit there, smacking her lips, as if another person's pain had nothing whatever to do with her? As if she weren't a human being like Izzy was, like *he* was, that poor soul broken under the steel belly of a train.

He drank some coffee, already cold, had a bite of his bran muffin, already turning stale, dropped it on his tray, and pulled his chair up even closer. He fixed his eyes on the woman's face, determined to get through. "Listen a minute"—leaning forward. "Try and understand what I'm saying."

"I understand you perfectly."

"Someone *died*, I'm telling you—he died in a terrible way—and you act like it doesn't matter. Death matters! Every death. I know what I'm talking about, I know something about loss—most of my family died in the war and recently I lost my friend, before that I lost my wife. So here's what you should understand—we're all part of the same tribe. What hurts one of us hurts us all."

"What do you expect me to do? Run down to the station and give the transit men a hand?"

"You should do something—" His voice broke. Why wasn't she sympathetic? Why didn't she shed a tear? He sipped coffee, spoke again. "You shouldn't be so heartless."

"And what exactly did you do?"

"I'm an old man. What could I do?"

"Hold a flashlight, manage the crowd. There's always something to do if you want. You could've jumped down to see if the man was still breathing. If he was alive, you could've talked to him or held his hand."

"You know nothing," Izzy said. His cheeks were hot, his eyes burning. "I thought you were someone I could talk to, but I was wrong."

"You didn't do anything, did you? Just ran away and tried to get home."

"You don't understand a thing. Enough already!"—striking the table. "Be quiet. *Zol zein shtill!*"

"There's nothing wrong with leaving the scene. I would've done the same myself."

He jumped to his feet. "I'm not like you! I care what happens to people."

"Big hero," the woman said. "I'll hear about you on the news."

Izzy was shaking. He fled the table and elbowed his way through the food court, bumping people, staggering, wandering through the mall, until he turned by chance into an uncrowded corridor. He didn't stop till he reached the end, where an escalator climbed up steeply to another level. He stayed at the bottom, in the empty hall, and looked around. On either side of the moving stairs a booming waterfall tumbled into a shallow pool of agitated water and bright coins. There was no one in sight.

He sat down on a corner of the low wall containing the pool and leaned over as far as he could so that the spray washed his face. He was panting and overheated: water thundered in his brain. He couldn't get enough air. He was going to faint—*Don't faint!*—the pool a sea of swirling dots. He was going to land face down, splayed in the tepid water, no one here to rescue him. Going to drown in a pool in a mall, plastic straws and bits of paper floating on the surface—a humiliating end to his life.

Gottenyu! Not like that!

He sucked in his breath, let it go . . . breathing, breathing deep breaths . . . Eventually his chest relaxed, his pulse slowed, vision cleared. He focused on the churning water, twinkling coins. What did people wish for, he wondered, as they tossed pennies? Long life? A million bucks? Izzy wanted none of that. He jingled change in his pants pocket, fished out a quarter, and pitched it across the pool. It landed with a decisive plop.

I wish for a brave death.

If that wasn't possible, he'd settle for a quick one. And, God willing, it should happen soon.

4

HIS LAST SUNDAY IN TORONTO he woke early
and dressed quickly in simple, yet respectful
clothes: a sport shirt and cotton pants, those
nice Italian loafers, and a zippered jacket on
top. Izzy shuffled in and out of pools of golden light as he circled
the bedroom getting ready. The sky behind his window was
dabbed with clouds like cotton balls. A fine day to spend at the
cemetery with Hilda and Phil.

His daughter was at the table with a glass of juice and a box of
tissues when Izzy entered the kitchen. Her eyes were watery, nose
swollen; red tracks ran from her nostrils to her upper lip. He told
her to get dressed, he wanted to get an early start, but Eva said she
had a bad cold and was going back to bed. No, no, she had to come
along, he insisted, there was no one else. Sam was at Roger's and
Izzy wouldn't go alone, it was too much for one person. "To grieve
alone is to suffer most," he quoted dear Mutti.

How well he knew the truth of that! This time at least he would
share his pain with his daughter. Here was a pain she could understand—not like what he held inside because of his dead kin, people Eva didn't know, murdered in countries she'd never seen. At
last they would cry together, standing over Hilda and Phil.

"But not today," she pleaded. "I feel awful."

"So you'll feel a little worse."

To speed things up he suggested that they eat on the road. He
waited by the apartment door while Eva put some clothes on, then

led the way to the elevator, through the underground parking, and up to her car.

"Who's driving?"

"I am."

"You always drive."

"It's my car."

She slid into the driver's seat and Izzy got in on the other side, crossed his arms, and pouted. He liked it better when Eva was young and always rode in the backseat while Hilda, who didn't drive, sat up front beside him. She never had to learn how, he drove her anywhere she asked, but Eva got her learner's permit the day she turned sixteen. Freedom and power, his daughter said, that's what it meant to drive. He didn't understand her then, doesn't understand now. What kind of woman thinks like that?

They drove to a pancake house, where Izzy ordered Number Four and Eva had some more juice. When his breakfast arrived he poured syrup over everything and gulped it down. "It's not real, it's imitation," he said with his mouth full of pancakes and sausages. "Tastes like motor oil."

"Nothing's real anymore."

"That goes for people too." Still chewing, he shook his fork. "The world is full of phonies. You think someone's like this, but deep down they're like that. You never know what's what."

"You don't trust anyone."

"From the start I trusted Phil, I believed he was a mensch. But after listening to Irene, after seeing poor Yvonne . . . now I don't know what to think. Maybe I'll understand him better when I talk to Selma Gold."

"It's really none of your business."

"Did you see her at the funeral? I heard she was there."

Eva stared at her orange juice. "I don't know what she looks like. We never met."

"What do you know about her?"

"Only as much as you do. They bought the house jointly and Phil paid for it in full—a gift for his girlfriend."

"Irene said he liked giving gifts."

"He was generous."

"When I die—" A piece of something lodged in his throat and Izzy started coughing.

"You're eating too fast," she said. "Slow down. Where's the fire?"

"When I'm dead, the bungalow—"

"Have some water. Don't rush. It doesn't matter what time you get to a graveyard."

When I die. When I'm dead . . . He drank water, his thoughts veering. If she buries him in Toronto, will Eva feel the same way about visiting his grave: why hurry? No big deal? Will he lie in the ground year after year with no one coming to see him? Izzy couldn't live with himself if he flew back to Bay Point without seeing Hilda and Phil, but his daughter was different. She did what she wanted to soon enough, but put off everything else. She didn't care like he did about doing the right thing.

A few minutes later they were back in the car, heading north. The cemetery was forty minutes from downtown if the roads were clear. Eva sneezed and sniffled as she drove with one hand on the wheel, the other wiping her nose with a balled-up tissue. Why she insisted on driving with a cold was a mystery. She'd be better off lying down in the backseat while Izzy drove, but if he told her that, she would probably take it the wrong way. *You only want to drive,* she'd say. *You don't care about me.*

Which absolutely wasn't true. Sure he liked driving, but his daughter's health came first. Why didn't she know that? How frightened he had been whenever she coughed or sneezed as a little girl. He could never have borne the loss of his child, who carried within her the spirit of those who died before; who looked so much like Rosa he would stare sometimes until he cried.

Didn't he watch her all night when she tossed and turned with fever? Didn't he *shmeer* her with VapoRub, wipe her face with a cool rag; feed her children's aspirin, spoonfuls of cough syrup and homemade chicken soup? Didn't she throw her arms around his neck when she felt better and tell him that she loved him? He can still remember her arms like sticks, the scent and smoothness of her skin, the press of her cheek against his. If only they could've stayed like that, in each other's arms.

He half turned in the passenger seat, listened to her wet snuffling, studied the tendons in her neck. She was looking skinny these days, her face a little washed out. An unhealthy look, as if she weren't eating or sleeping well, there was too much on her mind. All he'd ever wanted was for her to grow up happy and strong, and this is how she turns out.

They drove past industrial parks, housing developments, a farm or two, and open fields. The entrance to the cemetery, marked by a small sign, was camouflaged by tall trees. If you didn't know where you were going, you would probably miss it. Eva slowed down and they turned onto the main road, followed a long loop to an older part of the graveyard, and drove to the section where Hilda was buried. Izzy was out of the car as soon as Eva came to a full stop.

The ground was squishy under the dormant grass. There were still disks of snow in a few hollows in the earth, like milk left in saucers for prowling cats. He made shallow footprints as he climbed up a bare slope, moisture creeping into his socks. Her grave was at the top of a hill overlooking the road and a row of trees.

Like all the neighboring tombstones, Hilda's was only as high as his hip, even though it was set on a thick marble pedestal. The site itself was shorter and narrower than he recalled, the plots on either side so close he had to shuffle sideways to get to her monument. The gray stone was cool to his touch as he traced the words with a finger: IN MEMORY OF HILDA SCHNEIDER, BELOVED

WIFE AND MOTHER, JUNE 12, 1919—FEBRUARY 14, 1979.

Valentine's Day. In the morning he had brought expensive chocolates to her hospital bed, not that she could eat them, but he wanted her to see the box wrapped in red with gold ribbon, shaped like a huge heart. She was only fifty-nine and he still loved her dearly.

Izzy closed his eyes now and saw Hilda young again, in a belted coat to mid-calf, high heels with ankle straps, a flat hat with a curved brim worn at an angle. A Sunday afternoon: they were arm in arm on the deck of a Staten Island ferry, eating hot dogs in the salty breeze—or was it shoulder to shoulder on the boardwalk at Coney Island, Nathan's hot dogs in their mouths? Either way there were hot dogs—that's the important part. And what he'll never forget is how he dripped mustard on his sleeve and she flicked it off with her finger, then shockingly, seductively, licked the yellow fingertip clean, her head lowered, eyes up, as blue-white and sparkling as water churning under a boat or waves breaking on the beach. It was only their third or fourth date and already he was weak with love.

Life was sweet and precious then, though thoughts of death were always near (by accident, disease, or design), and so his tender fluttering heart would sometimes freeze in panic. What if something horrible happened to one of them just when he was feverish with unheard-of happiness? How could he bear it! Only a few years earlier, stateless, unemployable, stalked by the Gestapo, dying didn't matter to him, it was one more thing to be endured. But Hilda shook the dust from his soul, opened it to air and light. Even after forty years of marriage he was angry—is angry still!— that God took her so soon. An old man deserves peace and comfort in his final years, not to stand at his wife's grave and feel hollow as a pipe, his *kishkas* turned to ashes.

When he opened his eyes he saw Eva standing by the tombstone. She said, "Why didn't you reserve a plot next to hers? Now they're all filled up."

"The soul matters, not the flesh. You can put me anywhere—Florida, Canada—it won't make a difference, I'll still be with Hilda and the rest of my family."

"You should leave instructions so I'll know what to do when the time comes."

"Did anyone bury your grandmother? Did anyone bury Arnold and Rosa and their children? Do you think I remember them less because I can't visit their graves?"

"Don't start with that again. We're talking about you now. I want to know what *you* want."

"What I want . . ." He bobbed his head. "You can bury me anywhere—a backyard, a flower bed."

"There are laws against that sort of thing. You have to be in a graveyard."

He leaned over the monument and narrowed his eyes. "I could outlive you, it's not so impossible. My mother's grandparents died in their nineties and maybe I take after them. Maybe *you*"—aiming a finger at Eva's nose—"should write down instructions for me."

He picked up a small rock and put it on the gravestone to mark his visit. Eva did likewise, then started sneezing again. She was wearing pumps and stockings and probably her feet were wet. She hugged herself in her car coat: probably she was shivering. The sky had clouded over and a cool wind blew unchecked across the treeless hill. This outing wouldn't help her cold. "Go wait in the car," he said. "I'll be there in a minute."

Eva hurried away from the site. It bothered him that she hadn't cried a little at her mother's grave. Hilda deserved a tear at least, a moment of silence. Even if they weren't close, a mother is a mother.

But she was always Daddy's girl. The older Eva got, the more she grumbled about her mom. She didn't like that Hilda never argued or lost her temper; that she didn't work, didn't drive, get involved in politics, or follow her own pursuits—all the things Izzy thought made her a good wife. She was no one his teenage daughter could look up to.

For her part, Hilda was embarrassed by her grown child. She disapproved of her smoking, her tight sweaters and dyed hair, and nagged her with worried questions. *Why do you dress like that? Why do you smoke like a chimney?* By the time Eva married they had more or less reconciled, and when Sam was born she was proud of her daughter—though she didn't like that Eva put him in daycare and returned to work. Hilda offered to mind the baby but Eva wouldn't hear of it, she wanted her son in a "stimulating environment." Hilda was offended and Izzy had to step in and smooth things out as best he could. Finally he had to admit his wife and daughter were mismatched, they'd never see eye to eye on anything, big or small. They'd never share recipes or tell each other secrets ... and years later Eva wouldn't weep at her mother's grave.

"I'm so sorry," he whispered.

He stooped beside the headstone and scooped up a ball of earth. It was moist in his palm and he mashed it in his fist until it squeezed through his fingers. How do you say goodbye to something as inert as this? What did a lump of mud have to do with Hilda, their life together, their love that endured the bumps of a marriage? Was it really so necessary to come here after all when she lived in his mind day and night?

This time, he'd thought, maybe this time he could let go, leave his heavy heart on the tombstone, like another rock. What he can't do for Mutti and Rosa and the little boys, who have no markers, no plots: let go.

But he felt nothing, didn't cry. His mind bulged with images and jumbled strings of words said in three different languages, one phrase butting the next ... and still his heart was unchanged. Like all the other times, there was no relief in being here, only the satisfaction of having done the right thing. He shook dirt from his fingers, then pulled a handkerchief out of his pocket and wiped his hand.

With that he turned and walked slowly back to the car. When he opened the passenger door warm air rushed out: Eva had the heater on. He said, "When you're ready," and she drove around the loop again, turning onto a narrower road shaded by red pines. Soon after, she pulled over, stopped the car. He recognized the area. Here the graves were farther apart, the tombstones higher, the landscape transformed by juniper bushes, evergreens, and wooden benches with wrought-iron legs. In the background, beyond the graves, the silhouettes of maple and oak.

"I'll wait in the car," said Eva.

"What's with the 'wait in the car'? Don't you want to see him again?" He scrunched up his face as if he'd chewed something bitter. "You don't have to stay long."

"You go. Take your time."

"You're feeling worse?"

"I just can't."

There were pine needles underfoot as he walked toward the grave site, but not a single snow-whitened dimple in the soft ground. He passed several recent graves, a few mounded high with dirt, others level or sunken; some topped with sand or clay, some with cracked lumps of earth. Each of the plots was marked with a stake and a card on top that named the deceased and noted the date of death. Izzy paused to read the tags—Gruber, Grossman, Berkowitz, Klein, Wittenberg, Shapiro—all of whom had died in the last few months.

He didn't look up right away but when he did, turning in the direction of Phil's grave, he saw someone already there. Izzy moved closer, stepping quickly and quietly. Soon he was able to make out the white hair and nice-looking suit of a small man. At first Izzy thought the man was standing at the foot of the plot, but when he got to the site he saw the man was actually *on* the grave, moving his feet up and down as if he were mashing grapes in a barrel. As if he were dancing on Phil's chest.

"Get off there!" Izzy cried. "Have you no respect for the dead?"

The man swung his head and squinted, his face thin and deeply lined; moles on his forehead and chin. He seemed to be older than Izzy by several years. "Respect for Lubinsky? Hah!"

Izzy pulled the man's sleeve. "Lewis," he said. "Phil Lewis. You don't even have the right grave."

He plucked Izzy's fingers off his jacket with surprising strength. "It's the right one, all right. All these years I kept track. In 1946 he became Phil Lewis—but in 1943 he was Fishel Lubinsky."

Izzy's arms dropped to his sides. "You mean you knew him during the war?"

"I knew him, all right."

"In the ghetto?"

"In the woods."

The man stared at the metal stake and plastic nameplate. His eyes were slots, his jaw tight; the moles on his face blackened. Suddenly he yanked the stake, drawing it out with both hands, and smacked the tag against the dirt over and over until Izzy grabbed the post in mid-air and pulled it away. "Why are you doing this? What did Phil ever do to you?"

The man slouched and seemed to sink deeper into the black earth. "Lubinsky killed my daughter in the Rudniki Forest."

"He *killed* her? He killed your daughter? Phil Lewis did that?"

The old man starting crying, rocking slightly back and forth as if he were davening. "She was all I had left—the only one who hadn't died. A beautiful girl—beautiful hair . . . beautiful eyes, like spoons of honey."

Izzy gave him his handkerchief, apologizing for the dirt, then he put the stake back, cleaned the tag with his finger, and reached for the man's arm. "Get out of there, come with me"—helping him off the grave. "Look what you did to your trousers."

There were slurping sounds when the old man lifted his legs. There were deep footprints left behind. His shoes were lumpy, swollen with muck. "Let's sit down and talk," said Izzy, leading him carefully to a bench. The man hobbled at Izzy's side, dragging his muddy feet as if they were encased in cement; a spot of *shmutz* on his left cheek.

It took forever to reach the bench. "Now," Izzy said when they were seated, "tell me about it."

The man drew a noisy breath. "My name is Tanenbaum"—exhaling with a long sigh. "All I ever wanted was to outlive Lubinsky—to walk on his fresh grave—and that much the Almighty finally granted me."

"Go on," said Izzy.

"Why should I? Who are you anyway?"

Izzy introduced himself. "I met Phil in 1947 in New York. One day I followed him to his uncle's shop in Canada, then Phil took over the business and I wound up working for him. I know a lot about his life, including the war years, but you're the first I ever met who actually knew him back then."

"What do you know about his time in the forest?"

"I know he was a partisan, I know some of his stories ... how he couldn't join the Russian unit without a rifle, so he stole one from a farmer and twelve rounds of ammo ..."

Tanenbaum nodded. "Later some of us killed a few soldiers in a stalled truck, then all the Jews had weapons."

"And how he wore a grenade on his belt when he went on a mission, so the Nazis wouldn't take him alive ..."

"All the Jews did that, whether they attacked trains and bridges or the fascists."

"The best, he said, was when they blew up a bridge in front of a train that was carrying German soldiers. He set off the charge himself, and the cars fell into a river like an avalanche of boulders. No one got out alive."

"But what did he say about my daughter?"

"He said he loved a beautiful girl who died during a raid—that's as much as he told me. Nothing like what you said."

"You want to know more about the Jewish camp, I'll tell you."

"How long were you there?"

"About a year. I don't remember exactly."

"How many were you?"

"Fifty Jews."

"Only fifty? Phil told me a hundred."

"There were always people coming and going but never more than fifty of us, give or take a couple."

"Maybe you can't remember now."

"Things like that you don't forget. I knew every person, I can still see their faces. Some of them I buried myself . . . women, children, old men."

"What was it like? How did you live?"

"An island in the swamps, where the Germans didn't like to go. We worked for the Soviets. We cooked their food, sewed clothes, built huts, fixed guns, tanned hides to make boots, and took care of the wounded. In summer we were eaten alive by mosquitoes, in winter we nearly froze; the rest of the time we sank in mud. Always there was lice and disease, but the biggest worry we had was food. Some we got from villagers, some from the Russians, but mostly we were hungry." He spread his hands on his belly. "Every meal the same thing, a thin potato or cabbage soup—that was on a good day—and other times we ate grass. Once in a while we also had a bite of meat, a few berries, a sip of milk, a piece of bread. That was manna from heaven."

Tanenbaum paused and the men sat quietly. After a while Izzy said, "What else can you tell me about Phil?"

"Lubinsky was our leader. He fought with the partisans, but also he looked after us. He said if we were useful to the Russians, they'd protect us. One hand washes the other."

"What about your daughter?"

Tanenbaum struck the bench with his fist. "Rivke was fourteen—a child of fourteen!—when she moved into his bunker."

"Why didn't you stop her?"

"She said she loved him—what could I do? Lubinsky and his men had guns, they did whatever they wanted. It wasn't a democracy—we followed his orders. If I tried to stand in his way, he could throw me out of the camp or worse." He dropped his head and wrung his hands.

"Keep talking," Izzy said. "You'll feel better if you talk."

"You want to know? He called her his wife. And right away she got pregnant. A girl she was—fourteen! What do you think about that?"

"I think... what a terrible thing."

The men fell silent again. Tanenbaum began rolling forward and back like an empty rocker in the wind. Izzy placed a hand on his knee. "Tell me how your daughter died."

"There was a raid in the spring," he said, "policemen and peasants hunting for Jews. It was early, just dawn. The partisans were gone on a mission. Only a few of us were left to guard the families. We were outnumbered, so we ran." Tanenbaum put a hand over his mouth and spoke through his fingers. "Rivke, my Rivke... she was seven months pregnant and couldn't keep up with the rest of us. We ran into the woods but I didn't see her anywhere. Then I heard shooting." He stared straight ahead as if it were happening now. "The captured were rounded up and slaughtered in an open field. I knew the moment Rivke died. I felt the bullets entering my own flesh, my own heart. I felt like it was my blood watering the meadow..."

The old man was rocking again. Izzy put an arm around his shoulder to quiet him. "You don't have to say more."

"I want to talk," said Tanenbaum, his voice rising suddenly. "People should know what happened!" He cupped his hands as if he were offering Izzy a drink. "The partisans came back to the camp and scared off our attackers. When Lubinsky counted all the dead, and Rivke—when he found her... he and his buddies took revenge. They captured one of the leaders of the gang—a known collaborator—killed him and burned his house. When we saw Lubinsky again, he was covered in blood and smelled of smoke."

Izzy was still for a moment, then he said, "Why do you blame Phil? The raid wasn't his fault."

"Rivke was pregnant and couldn't run. That was because of him."

"Maybe he shouldn't have done what he did . . . but those were unnatural times. Such things happened. He was only a boy himself, no more than twenty. Who can judge him right or wrong?"

"*I* judged him. Damned him to hell! When I read he was murdered in Toronto, I was a happy man."

"If you hated him as much as that, why didn't you kill him yourself?"

Tanenbaum looked startled. "I was never big and strong. I was never daring. How could a man like me go after Lubinsky? All I could do was pray for his death . . . and not forget my daughter." Then he started whimpering. "Rivke, my Rivkele. My beautiful angel! I couldn't—there was nothing to be done. I couldn't save her."

"Go home, Mr. Tanenbaum. Go home now and have a rest. You must be tired."

The man blew his nose hard in Izzy's dirty hankie. Then he said, "Go ahead. Me, I want to sit awhile."

"You'll stay on the bench?"

"Where else?"

Izzy got up. Tanenbaum dangled the handkerchief but Izzy told him to keep it, he might need it later on. The men shook hands and Izzy left. Almost back to the car he turned and looked over his shoulder: Tanenbaum was heading back to Phil's grave.

Izzy kept walking. Why was he foolish enough to think the old man could forget the past? Who can! It stays with you, eats at you, darkens every moment of life. Let Tanenbaum have his anger, let him dance on his enemy's grave. Without that, what would be left to fuel his existence? Without rage there's only despair . . . and that can kill you just as sure as hunger or a bullet can.

Eva was half asleep in the car. She jumped in her seat when he opened the door. He said, "Someone was at the grave. Someone was *on* the grave—actually standing in the dirt—an old man who knew him, a Jew from the forest. He talked about his daughter Rivke, also from the camp, who was only fourteen but was carrying

Phil's baby. I knew Phil was in love . . . but I didn't know the whole story."

"Roger told me all about it." Eva revved the engine.

"Why didn't you say something? You didn't think I'd be interested?"

"Phil wanted to keep it quiet."

"I was his best friend! Why wouldn't he tell me?"

"He might've been embarrassed. It's not something a friend should know."

"But Tanenbaum knew! If he told me, he told others."

"Phil was giving him money."

"Tanenbaum a *blackmailer*? Phil paid him not to talk?"

"He gave him money to help out. Phil helped lots of Jews he'd known in the forest. They used to come to his home at night asking for handouts."

"Maybe they all knew something that could ruin his reputation."

Eva gave him a sharp look. "Why don't you stay out of it. It doesn't matter anymore."

"It matters to me what kind of person he really was."

She drove out of the cemetery, the car leaning and squealing through a left turn. The scenery blurred as she picked up speed: trees and fields, homes and malls became a stone-colored band. "You're driving too fast," he said. "I don't want to wind up with my nose in the windshield." But Eva didn't slow down. She said they were running late, she had to pick up Sam at Roger's before noon.

"Better you should take your time and get us there in one piece."

Eva said nothing. She was in one of her moods again, scowling at the empty road. It didn't take much to get her going. Just the mention of Phil's name—or Tanenbaum's or Roger's—would have been enough reason, never mind all three.

He angled his shoulders right and gazed out the window. As he stared at the smudged screen of the wavering landscape, Izzy pictured the family camp in the Rudniki Forest. He saw the starving, ragged Jews searching for berries, tanning hides, stirring pots of grass soup. He saw Phil in his bunker, which he'd once described as covered with dirt except for the entrance and a small window at the back—an underground dugout that was big enough for ten fighters. This was where he slept with Rivke, huddled on a straw bed.

My first love, skinny as a twig but still a beauty. I used to touch her hair at night and promise she'd survive this, I wouldn't let anything happen to her.

But something happened?

Rivke died.

One eye open, one eye closed, that was how Lubinsky slept: alert to every noise beyond the snoring of his comrades. Always aware—completely aware—that each breath could be his last, that suddenly a tossed grenade might explode in the bunker, that he could be shot or stabbed where he lay. That something could happen to Rivke. When death is always with you, is it wrong to snatch what pleasure you can? Would Izzy not have done the same in Phil's situation?

No. She was just a child. Frightened and desperate, she only wanted to feel safe. Lubinsky took advantage.

But wasn't a man who risked his life protecting others entitled to whatever warmth and comfort he could possibly find?

"You think it was right?" he asked Eva.

"What? Do I think what was right?"

"To sleep with a girl of fourteen. To make her pregnant at such a time, in such terrible circumstances?"

"Can't we talk about something else?" Eva's voice was crackling. "It was almost fifty years ago. Why is it still important?"

"All those stories he used to tell... maybe some of them weren't true. Maybe there were people besides Tanenbaum who hated him and thought he was no good."

"I'm sick of hearing about the past—you did this, Phil did that. No, he shouldn't have slept with the girl, but he's dead now—the man's dead! His putz is rotting in the ground!"

For a moment he was speechless. He rounded his back and hung his head. This is how she speaks to him, with no courtesy, no respect? "We're just talking," Izzy said. "Why are you getting so upset? Why do you have to carry on? You act like she was your child."

Eva hit the gas and he was whipped back hard in his seat. *Gevalt! Another lunatic!* He gripped the seat and pumped the air with his foot until she eased up. When he glanced at her he saw tears. Tears! What was that about? Why was she crying now and not before, at Hilda's grave? She looked awful when she cried, her face red and blotchy. He passed her a tissue and she patted her eyes.

"Sorry I yelled at you. It's just this lousy cold and all . . . I'll feel better tomorrow."

At twelve o'clock exactly they pulled into Roger's drive. A wide circular driveway; a two-story modern home with terraces and balconies, the front practically all glass, one window after the next. Eva let the car idle and honked the horn. That's no way to pick up Sam, Izzy thought to himself, then he said he needed to stretch his legs, got out, and walked to the house.

The front door was half glass, no curtains behind the panes, so Izzy (or a burglar) could peer into the living room and see racks of tapes and a hi-fi system, a TV with a giant screen. In Florida he kept the blinds closed and the curtains drawn on all his front windows, and his door was solid wood with a very strong lock—but if Roger liked to take chances, that was his business.

Izzy tapped the glass and Loreen came to the door at once, holding a container of something in one hand. She was wearing a sleeveless sweater and a short knit skirt and he grinned just to look at her: she was like a TV model selling floor wax or shampoo. "I'm Sam's grandfather."

"Yes, I know. I know who you are"—her voice as breathy as Marilyn Monroe's. "Sam will be here in a minute . . . Oh, here they come now."

Loreen withdrew to another room. Sam said hi and walked around him, straight to the waiting car. Roger said, "I thought you'd be in Florida by now," and Izzy smiled at him: "Tomorrow."

Roger moved to close the door but Izzy leaned against it. "A question before I go . . . Today I went to your father's grave and talked to an old man—a man by the name of Tanenbaum—who knew Phil during the war. Do you know who I mean?"

Roger looked past him, his eyes fixed on the distance. "I might've met him once or twice."

"Was he blackmailing your father?"

Roger flicked his head like a horse shaking off flies. "That's what he told you?"

"Never mind who said what. Is that what was going on? Was Phil paying money to protect his golden image—for the sake of the business, if nothing else? You must get lots of orders thanks to his fine reputation."

"He gave Tanenbaum money to keep him from starving."

"You knew about his daughter?"

"My father said he loved her. When she was killed he went berserk. He never got over it."

"What do you think about what he did—getting the girl pregnant?"

"Sometimes my father did things I didn't like much, in business and privately." Roger's eye was twitching. "But I don't blame him for anything that happened during wartime. He did what he had to do to survive. Anyone might've done the same."

He gave the door a sudden shove, but Izzy stopped it with his foot. "Anything else I should know?"

"Have a good flight, okay?" Roger toed Izzy's shoe out of the way and shut the door.

When Izzy got in the car again, Sam and Eva were bickering. She drove with one hand on the wheel, the other hand stirring the air. "When *I* buy you something," she said, "it's always the wrong thing—wrong fabric, wrong style, wrong color, wrong size. When *she* buys you anything, it's perfect."

Izzy swiveled in his seat and looked at his grandson. Sam was wearing a Blue Jays cap Izzy hadn't seen before, shaping the brim between his hands. "We went to a game," he said. "I had a really good time."

"When *I* want to take you to a game, you say no way, let's go to a movie. When *she* takes you, it's lots of fun."

"Your mother's jealous of Loreen, that's why she's all worked up. It's only natural," Izzy said, trying to calm things down.

"First she takes my husband and now she's trying to steal my son."

"She was being nice," Sam said.

"Don't tell me she was nice! Women like that are never nice. They go after what they want, it doesn't matter who they hurt or what they're destroying."

Sam took off the cap and shoved it under his thigh.

"Now look what you did with your big mouth," Izzy said. "Now he won't even wear it."

He stared at his daughter, who glowered back. Her long nose and strong chin were so much like his own, so much like Rosa's . . . but her eyes were no one else's. Wide with innocence, dark with knowledge: eyes that warmed or frightened you, invited you closer, kept you away. He thought he knew his own child but didn't know her really. She was like a stranger sometimes.

"Tell me something," Izzy said. "What did Loreen do? She bought your son a baseball cap, why is that so terrible? Better she should treat him bad?"

They were almost downtown now. The highway had narrowed, they were hemmed in by speeding cars, and on either side of the road there were high-rises with balconies that made him think of Eva's pouting bottom lip. As soon as they were back in her apartment he would start packing. One more night to get through and then he'd be flying home to hot weather, his own place.

When Eva spoke again her voice was almost gentle. "Put on the cap, Sam. I shouldn't have said anything. You're right, she was being nice."

But he left the hat where it was.

Once they were back home Izzy lost no time in heaving his luggage onto the bed. He went through the closet, emptied drawers, cleared the bathroom of everything except for what he'd need later on and tomorrow. He set aside a pressed shirt, clean socks, and underwear to put on in the morning, then he filled his suitcases, as well as a flight bag, and stacked them against a wall. When he finished and looked around, Sam was in the doorway.

The boy was holding his baseball cap in front of his groin like a codpiece. "Take this too," he said. "A souvenir."

"But Sam, it's yours, from Loreen. You can't just give it away."

"I don't look good in hats. I wouldn't use it anyway."

"Your mother's already calmed down. She won't mind if you wear it."

"I want you to have it." He held out the cap.

Izzy took it and put it on: a loose fit. Later he would fix the strap. For now, he turned the brim to the back and screwed up his face like a shlemiel. "So tell me, how do I look?"

"Cool."

They laughed a little too loud. Then Izzy stuck out his hand, but the boy sprang forward instead and grabbed him in a clumsy hug. Izzy wriggled, freeing his arms, patted him on the back, and said, "I'm going to miss you too"—the words sounding husky.

How long since he stood this close to someone? Not since the last time he saw Phil in Florida, and in the middle of saying goodbye, Phil pulled him against his chest and locked him in a bear hug.

Like Izzy's father used to hold him sometimes when he was a boy, lifting him up and squeezing him between the sleeves of his stiff shirt that smelled of starch and tobacco. With Phil he'd been embarrassed—they were grown men, after all—but no one was watching, so he didn't move. Feelings rose up in his throat and popped from his mouth like soap bubbles blown high by a happy child.

"I have something for you too," he said to his grandson.

From his flight bag he pulled out a silver cigarette case, which he always carried with him as a good-luck charm; a reminder of his daring youth. *"In Dankbarkeit meinem Lebensretter . . ."*

He handed the case to Sam. The boy opened it, read the inscription, asked what the words meant. "In gratitude to my life-saver Isidor Schneider, from Jakob Abrahamsohn, July 1930."

"What's the guy thanking you for?"

"When I was young I saved his life. He was drowning in a lake in Berlin and I pulled him out."

Sam looked down at the case. "I don't think I should have this. I wouldn't know what to do with it. Maybe you should give it to Mom."

"One gift deserves another. I want you to have it. Put it away somewhere safe, then one day after I'm gone you'll look at it and remember that I saved a man from drowning—that your *zayde* was once very brave."

Sam dropped the present into his pocket and left the room. At the dinner table later he behaved the same as usual, gobbling a plate of food, rushing off without a word to sit in front of the TV. This is who I trust with such a keepsake? Izzy thought.

Eva served a nice supper of meat loaf and mashed potatoes, peas for him, a salad for her. The conversation while they ate was mostly about arrangements: when he was getting up in the morning; what time the cab would be here; when his plane was taking off. She asked if he was coming back soon and he said no. He asked when she was coming to Bay Point and she didn't know, it was difficult to find time.

"You're so busy you can't manage a trip to see your father? I'm not getting younger," he said.

After the main dish she served slices of cantaloupe. The melon wasn't as sweet or fragrant as it might have been: probably she didn't know how to pick. Hilda used to sniff a melon and press her thumbs on either end to check for ripeness, but Eva didn't have the patience to learn about squeezing fruit. Her mind was always elsewhere when you asked for her attention; she was busy thinking her own thoughts.

Next there was coffee cake and tea in a fancy-shmancy pot. The cake was delicious, he had to admit. Eva didn't bake it herself, she wasn't talented that way (unlike her mother), but her heart was in the right place. She bought it to please him, the way she served tea with lemon and cooked some of his favorite foods. She meant for them to celebrate his last night in Toronto. She was trying to do right by him . . . and better late than never. "That was very nice"—patting his belly—"a wonderful meal."

She smiled like a schoolgirl and touched his hand across the table. Her fingernails were chewed to the quick. She'd always been a nail-biter, much as he discouraged her. He used to warn her about germs, but didn't scare her enough because apparently she never stopped. Something scratched at the back of his throat as he looked at her fingertips that seemed to be staring back at him, ten little red eyes.

She used to wear a white skirt with candy-red polka dots that flared like an umbrella when she danced through the living room. *Look, Daddy, look at me!*—and he'd watch till his eyes ran. She used to give him *naches*.

"Remember the time I had a make-believe tea party and you were my only guest?"

"Ach! I remember. It was all very serious. We talked about the weather and our plans for the weekend."

"We ate crackers and strawberry jam and drank water from paper cups."

"Tonight is even better," he said. "Real china, real tea."

"Maybe if you didn't live so far away," Eva said. "Maybe if you lived here..."

"At my age, Canadian winters are too hard."

She drank her tea and gazed unblinking into the empty cup. He asked if she was reading leaves, if she could see the future, and then he took her cup and studied the dregs at the bottom. "I see changes up ahead. I see travel... you're on a plane. Next year, a warm place, not one but two trips—two trips to Bay Point! And Sam will be going too, maybe not both times but at least once."

"I can't promise anything."

"Ach! we'll have a wonderful time. I'll take you to Busch Gardens, Weeki Wachee, Tarpon Springs—you never saw anything like it."

"We went two years ago. Remember? Phil was with us too."

"So then we'll go somewhere else, there's always something new to see. What about Clearwater Beach? You never went there before—a beautiful spot, very clean. You'll love swimming out there, the water's perfect, nice and warm."

"Phil was a great swimmer. I can do the dog-paddle and float on my back."

"Anything! We'll do what you want."

"We'll see what happens," Eva said.

Her last visit wasn't too successful, he had to admit. They drove around and looked at things—mangroves, flower gardens, shells, and flamingos—but mostly they argued. Phil was also in Florida, but not with his wife Yvonne, who stayed home for some reason. Though Eva was there to see Izzy, she often asked Phil to come along for the day or to meet them for dinner.

Once they all went out to a restaurant his daughter picked, with low lights, comfortable chairs, tiptoeing waiters, and a violinist playing tunes that sounded like a cat wailing. Not a bad spot if you were on a date. Eva sat beside Phil, and Izzy sat across from her, his elbows on the table. She was chewing on a crust of bread while

Phil talked real estate. "I want to buy a house here," he said, "and sell the condo."

"I thought you liked it," Eva said. "It's such a nice neighborhood and right near the water."

"All the buildings close together, one on top of the other..." He spread his arms. "What I want is a huge place with the ocean in my backyard. I could live there part-time, a few months in Florida, the rest in Toronto. After I retire I could even stay here year-round."

"What does Yvonne think?"

"We haven't talked about it yet."

Izzy leaned forward. "So maybe you can give me your apartment at a good price."

Phil laughed and Eva said, "What's wrong with the bungalow?"

"I want more rooms and a view. Phil's not the only one with big ideas."

"You can't afford it," Phil said. "Be happy with what you've got."

He moved closer to Eva, pointed with his finger, and brushed a crumb from the side of her mouth. He didn't lower his hand at once. "What are you doing?" Izzy said.

"Just a little something there."

"Eva doesn't like that. She can wipe her own mouth, she's not a child."

But Eva didn't seem to mind. She dipped her head toward Phil, grinning like a halfwit.

One night she even went to his condo apartment and didn't return till the next day. It was too late to drive back, is how she explained it, so she slept in the guest room. Izzy chose to believe her. Phil was his buddy, after all, and practically a newlywed in 1987—besides which he was older than Eva by almost twenty years. Never mind his money and his muscles, he was an old man!

Of her two weeks in Florida, Eva spent nearly half her time in Phil's company. That was too much, he said. Who was more important, he asked, a father or father-in-law (an *ex*-father-in-law by then)? His daughter refused to choose. "You're ruining my vacation," she said, "making such a fuss." Then she called him selfish and flew back home in a huff.

But now there was no reason they couldn't have a good time. "Come in the fall, when it's not too hot, not too cold. September's a perfect month."

"It's too soon," Eva said.

He grabbed the teapot, filled her cup. "It'll be different next time."

"Phil won't be there."

Izzy stiffened: Phil again. Even in death he was still here, a specter rising in the steam from their teacups. What was she trying to say—that things would be better now without Phil in the picture, or things would be worse? Izzy studied his daughter's face, her eyes the color of secrets. Like a stranger, he thought again. And as quickly as he'd moved closer only a minute before, that's how fast he drew back.

5

IT WAS SO HOT that when he left his air-conditioned bungalow to walk to the curb and check for mail, his eyeglasses fogged up. He groped in his mailbox and pulled out a glossy paper, slippery in his fingers. When his lenses cleared he saw that a realtor wanted to sell his house. The ad had photographs of places she had recently sold and a blowup of the woman herself, not bad looking except for a big mouth. There were no letters in the box, but who was he expecting to write? Izzy wrote to no one and nobody wrote back.

His neighbor Frank was approaching with his bull terrier on a leash. He seemed about to cross the street when Izzy waved and called out. Frank paused and Izzy raced along the sidewalk to greet him. "Hot enough?" he asked Frank, and the man nodded his long head, the same oval shape as the dog's. The same hair, short and white (though the terrier had more of it), and even their eyes were alike, dark, dull pebbles. Neither man nor animal was looking his way.

"Out for a walk in this heat? Well, what can you do about it, the dog needs his exercise. But why aren't you wearing a hat? You're bald on top and it's not good to get a burn."

The terrier lifted his back leg and peed on a strip of parched grass. "No manners," Izzy laughed. "Anyway, the grass can use the water, so who cares."

The dog was straining on his leash. "Can't stop," Frank said. "Snowball's getting impatient."

"Snowball! I always forget. I was thinking Snowbird—a much better name for an animal in Florida. Snowballs we never see, but snowbirds we get by the thousands."

Frank let the dog pull him away from the sidewalk, and Izzy followed them onto the road. "I used to ski in Switzerland when I was a young man," he said. "Ach, you never saw so much snow! In some places, up to our hips. But back at the lodge, out of the wind, the sun was so strong we would strip to our shirtsleeves. Hot like in Florida, if you can believe it. Those were wonderful days," he sighed, "before the start of the Third Reich..."

The dog barked and tugged at his leash and Frank blurted, "Got to go. Snowball can't wait anymore."

"The dog calls the shots, I see. Not that I have anything against pets. My daughter always wanted a dog and that was okay by me, but Hilda didn't like them, she said they made the house dirty—and one thing I learned is if you let your wife have her way on household matters, you can do what you want on everything else. So while she was living, no pets . . . but now's a different story. People say they're good companions—Eva tells me to get a dog, it'll give me something to do all day—but who says I have nothing to do? Who says I have the time to look after an animal? Who wants to shop for dog food, walk in the boiling sun, and clean up their droppings?"

A car appeared and honked at them, and Frank, instead of drawing back, darted across the street with his dog, leaving Izzy standing on the other side. Quickly they turned a corner and were out of sight. Izzy walked back to his house. When he got to his mailbox he checked inside again. Maybe he missed a little something the first time.

Next door, Pat was dragging an overstuffed garbage can slowly down her driveway. When she saw him she called him over. Dutifully he grabbed a handle and together they carried the can to the curb. Pat was a widow now for more than a year. Izzy had disliked her husband, a know-it-all *shvitzer*, red-faced, and big as a truck, and wasn't surprised to hear that he dropped dead one day while cleaning the pool in their backyard—which neither of them swam in but kept for their children, who came to visit less and less because they had such busy lives. After a decent interval Izzy started flirting with Pat, although it was quite innocent, a compliment now and again, an invitation to join him for dinner at Mallory's. God knows he wasn't in the market for another wife, for who could replace Hilda? He was just having a bit of fun, enjoying his own swaggering and whatever conversation they had. Also he was thinking she'd invite him to use the pool now that her disagreeable mate was out of the picture.

But Pat took it the wrong way. For weeks she avoided him, running into her house whenever she saw him coming. He began to feel insulted. Was he so unattractive that his banter had alarmed her? Sure, he was no longer the muscleman he once was—his eyes were bad, his hair thin, he had a few liver spots and was soft around the middle—but next to her one-time spouse he was Adonis. So maybe she was anti-Semitic. Even in this day and age you couldn't discount that. Jews were scarce in Bay Point and lack of contact led to wrongheaded assumptions.

But just as his resentment was building to fury, she brought him a homemade pie. It was lemon meringue, too sweet, but still he was touched. He asked her in and they ate pie and drank cups of coffee with the front door open (so the neighbors wouldn't talk, she said). All the while she ran off at the mouth about her dead mate— Rudy did this and Rudy did that, Rudy always used to say . . . So after that he avoided *her*: there was nothing worse than a woman who didn't know how to listen.

"What about you?" she said to him now. "Aren't you going to put out your can? The truck'll be here any minute."

"It's almost empty," Izzy said. "I'll wait for the next pickup. A man alone doesn't make a lot of trash."

"Rudy took care of the garbage, I never had to think about it. He used to change the filters on the furnace and clean the pool.

Now, of course, I have to do every little thing myself. It's amazing how much time you can spend doing nothing."

"The pool?" he said brightly. "Do you use it more often now?"

"Oh no, I can't swim. Rudy was going to show me how but never got around to it."

"I'm a good swimmer, I could teach you if you want to learn. It's a shame to let a pool sit unused in weather like this." He wiped his hand across his sweaty forehead for effect.

"I'd just as soon stay indoors and keep the pool for the children. If not for that, Rudy always said, they wouldn't visit at all."

Izzy started backing away. "Too hot to stand and talk. I'm going home to swim in the tub—a cold bath is the best I can do." He emphasized the word "swim," but clearly she couldn't take a hint. She advised him to drive to the beach—at which point Izzy simply turned on his heel and left.

Most of the blinds were closed in his house, the air conditioning turned on. Sometimes he shut it off at night and in the morning to save electricity, but not in a heat wave, when you had to run it constantly or the bungalow never cooled down. He fell into his La-Z-Boy and put up his feet. The heat plus talking to his neighbors had exhausted him. He stared up at the ceiling fan, the wide, brown blades clicking softly, turning sluggishly, barely stirring the cooled air.

His eyes half closed as he pictured the contents of his fridge—a package of English muffins, eggs, cheese, frozen dinners—enough to get him through the day. He didn't really have to go out before Thursday, which was when he did his grocery shopping for the week. Tuesday was banking day, but there was nothing so urgent it couldn't wait till tomorrow. He was happy enough to stay indoors.

Eva thought his life was dull. She thought he needed more friends, interests, and activity. Every time she phoned she would nag him to buy a dog or sign up for bingo and socials at the Jewish center. In fact, he had gone to a tea-and-cookies gathering one Sunday afternoon. He'd sat on a folding chair at a long metal table covered with a paper cloth, sipping weak tea and eating day-old Danishes. On either side and across from him were wrinkled grannies with blue hair combed and sprayed into helmets. They made him feel ancient. Here and there along the table sat a few old men, round-shouldered, vacuous, gobbling pastry, while the women filled their cups and said, "Take your time, don't *fress*," as if they were little boys. Izzy left early and never went back.

What Eva doesn't understand is how well you can fill a day all by yourself once you've set up a few routines.

Like right now, before lunch, was when he read the paper. It was folded on the coffee table, under his elbow. He picked it up and skimmed the news, stopping at an article about the Alaska oil spill, still making headlines. To date the *Exxon Valdez* had spilled millions of gallons of crude. Total bird kill, at least 50,000; estimated number of dead otters, 2,000; also dead were hundreds of seals. If his grandson knew the numbers, he would probably weep.

And how was the captain of the oil tanker feeling—the man charged with drunkenness, recklessness, and negligence? Was he able to sleep? Did he dream of oil-blackened birds and dying fish? Did the ghosts of the poor creatures squeal in his ears at night the way Izzy's own ghosts cried to him?

It didn't matter to what degree you were actually responsible for the suffering of others, blame was absolute. If you couldn't prevent a catastrophe, regardless of why not, the world called you gutless . . . and you called yourself even worse. Shame and guilt arrived whole, not in manageable pieces, so that you were flattened by their weight. Never the same man again. Cracked and chipped as an old plate, doing your best to hide the nicks. At one time staying alive was all Izzy could think of: he ran because his legs were pumping, his heart was screaming, *Live, live!* But now death—the splintering of all images, all thoughts—was even more attractive.

The pendulum clock struck the hour with twelve bongs. Now it was time for lunch. He put down the paper, went to the kitchen, poured a can of heat-and-serve vegetable soup into a pot, toasted an English muffin, put a slice of cheese on top. Eva hated the sound of that clock, he remembered while stirring soup, because it kept her up at night. On her last visit she took out the batteries without asking and left it to hang on the dining-room wall, as still as a painting. When Izzy stayed at her place he never touched anything.

After lunch he put on a record of German songs, polkas and waltzes, to lighten his mood, then stretched out in his recliner. *Oompah-pah, oompah-pah*, he tapped on the armrest, enjoying the brassy sound of trumpets, horns, and tubas. Choruses whistled, clapped, and yodeled; the soloists' voices were high and clear. Izzy started singing along, the words flying off his tongue easily: his native tongue. What a *mechaieh* to speak it! Ach! how different life would've been if only there were no Nazis, no need to flee Berlin.

As a young man he'd listened to jazz (which shocked his parents, who preferred classical music), but since his retirement his tastes had changed. It was *Volksmusik* he craved now, tunes that reminded him of beer halls and cabarets, of cream cakes and cafés, the brash happy days of his youth.

He had lived with his parents in the Kreuzberg district, close to an Orthodox synagogue. Their apartment house was five stories high, with an arched and pillared entrance, elaborate cornices, and pediments over the windows. Attached to similar buildings behind and on either side, it faced a wide, treeless street guarded by street lamps. The apartment itself was small and dark, a third-floor walk-up, with long curtains, stuffed chairs, heavy, waxed furniture, and a slender coat rack in the hall. It overlooked a courtyard of trash cans, wooden sheds, and an undernourished poplar, where he sometimes played as a boy—but he preferred the playground, to fly his kite in an open field, ride his bike on the sidewalk, or race along the banks of the canal with his family. He liked to visit his father in his nearby tailoring shop, which stood between a grocery store and a pharmacy, and watch him, a measuring tape dangling from his neck like an unknotted tie, while he measured his clients for suits. When Izzy grew up he would do the same.

But best of all was to take a jolting ride on a streetcar with its clanging bell, clatter, and sparks, to sit on the open top deck of a double-decker bus, or to hurtle across the city underground in the U-Bahn, his nose pressed to a window as stations rose out of the gloom and were just as suddenly swallowed up.

At fifteen he started an apprenticeship at Crohn and Company, sewing coats. Later he worked as a tailor, then as a salesman at Tietz's and other stores, finally at Ullendorff and Bieber, an exclusive house, selling custom-made clothes for elegant ladies and men. In winter he spent his free time skating on ice rinks, in summer he swam in nearby lakes, and nothing pleased him more than to spend an afternoon in Grunewald Forest walking among the birches and pines, listening to the racket of birds, or to drink cups of coffee on the terrace of a café, gazing into the blue eyes of a shiksa with bobbed hair. He was a young man of twenty-two in 1933, when Hitler became chancellor: the year his good life started to come apart.

Izzy got out of his La-Z-Boy and took off the record. It was Nazi music, after all—loud and aggressive, hard on the ears. How could he listen to songs that reminded him of all he'd lost—that made his fingers tremble as they danced on the armrest? How could he sing words that hurt his throat and stopped his heart? What was he thinking! He stumbled to a rear-facing window and shut the blind.

No one was safe anymore, he remembered. Jews were attacked in their homes, in the open; their businesses boycotted or turned over to Aryans. They were thrown out of the civil service and other professions. Anti-Jewish signs, speeches, and posters were everywhere. At the swim club he belonged to he was told all of a sudden that he couldn't use the pool anymore—"No dirty Jews allowed!" On a crowded street one morning, he saw a band of Brownshirts terrorizing a rabbi. First they cut his beard, then they clubbed him till he didn't move—and nobody interfered. Not even Izzy, who shuddered with anger, panic, and shame. If he tried to help the old man, they would've done worse to him.

From then on he tried his best to keep to himself and stay out of sight. Nevertheless, one day in 1935—even before the Nuremberg Laws—he was called to police headquarters on Alexanderplatz and his passport seized on the spot. The official behind the desk was someone he'd known in school, a sleek-haired boy who resembled an otter. "Horst, don't you remember me?" Izzy had said, but the man eyed him coldly. "I don't know foreigners or Jews," he replied, then told him he had to leave the country.

"But I was born here," Izzy said. "Look at my papers! I'm a German citizen. Why should I go?"

"Your father is a foreigner, so *you* are a foreigner. Your father is a *Judensau* and *you* are a *Judensau*!"

Soon after, a letter came: his citizenship had been revoked. He was no longer a German subject, no longer had any rights; from now on he was stateless. Later the Employment Office wrote to his employer, demanding that the "foreign worker" Isidor Schneider be let go. His boss appealed but was turned down. Izzy's application for a work permit was also refused.

Then two Gestapo officers arrived at his parents' door and told them their son was a dangerous enemy of the state. They searched Izzy's belongings for incriminating evidence but left empty-handed. When he came home that evening he found Mutti crying and Papa doubled over on a chair with his head in his hands. "They're picking up young Jewish men," said his father. "You must get out of Germany right away! While you can."

"And you?"

"We'll be fine," he said. "What do they want with us?"

He knew they weren't safe, but he left his parents anyway. Left them to their destiny. He was thinking, *Gestapo!*—arrest, torture, death. He was thinking of himself when he bought a ticket to France and escaped Berlin for good with a suitcase, his photo album, a few marks in his pocket, and a gold ring on his finger.

Instead of seeing his parents in the gloom of their apartment, he peered out the window of a speeding train. Instead of his father's worried voice, he heard the chug of wheels and the frantic clicking of his pulse. But his lips repeated silently, *Mutti! Papa!* His chest hurting so much he thought it would tear apart and his heart hit the glass like the dumb head of a jack-in-the-box. He didn't want to leave them behind—*God knows his suffering!*—but here he was, getting away. By himself.

While still on the German side the train slowed, squealed to a stop, and uniformed men got on board. Compartment by compartment, they checked everyone's ID. When they came to Izzy, a stateless Jew, they shook his suitcase upside down and spilled the contents onto the floor. Was he going to France to spread atrocity stories about the Reich? No, no, he stuttered, he was only going to see a friend—he was taking a holiday. They kicked his belongings out of the way, every jab of their boots like a paralyzing blow to his ribs. He sat breathless, still as a post. *Gott in Himmel, help me!*

There was a ruckus outside: an old man was pulled from the train. Izzy squinted at the window. He heard whacks and wallops and his lungs tightened, he wheezed for air. A Jew? he thought. *A Jew like me?* For just a moment the man seemed to float up higher than the heads of his attackers, then he collapsed like a pierced balloon. Quickly he was dragged away. The train began to move again. The whistle screamed, the wheels shrieked, *You're next, you're next...* but Izzy was left unharmed.

He tried to sleep that night on a park bench in Paris, but a policeman smacked his feet with a stick and told him to move on. Never before had he felt like a bum or wished so hard he had someone to talk to. *Papa, look what's going on! I'm nothing here— a piece of dreck! Something to kick aside.*

All night he walked the streets, shivering and mumbling. In the morning he caught a train for Lyon. There he met a fellow Jew who found him a low-paying job in a silk factory, operating a knitting machine. Izzy put in long hours and tried to keep his mind on his work: there was no point brooding about what was, what might have been.

The owner took a liking to him and invited him to breakfast with his family every morning in a house adjoining the factory. As it turned out he was trying to match him up with his daughter, a plain girl with big hips and a *punim* like a donkey's. Partly to sidestep an undesirable *shiddach*, but also because the mattress in his furnished room had bedbugs, and not least of all because he feared a German invasion, Izzy decided to leave France and travel to New York, where his father had a brother who could send an affidavit.

So he saved money, planned his escape. "Go quickly," his father wrote him. "Start a new life in the *goldeneh medina* and soon we will join you."

A year later he was ready. Smart enough to sail across the Atlantic on the *Aquitania* before the Germans invaded France, he was smart enough to save his own skin, if no one else's. He was lucky, shrewd, and gutsy . . . if not quite heroic.

He did what he was forced to do. Who wouldn't run with the Gestapo breathing down his neck? Who wouldn't try for a better life in America? A young man who schemed to stay alive—where's the shame in that? Half the time he didn't think, he acted out of instinct: the fundamental urge to go on living, no matter what. Didn't Phil do the same when he fled the ghetto for the woods? Didn't Izzy tell him he was blameless, there was no choice?

And yet he is ashamed. Still. Even now he wishes he had stayed with his parents and shared their fate. Every night he misses them. He cries in his bed where no one can see, hiding his face in a pillow.

Someone was at the front door: he turned away from the window. Izzy heard polite rapping, too slow for a meter reader, too firm for his neighbor Pat bringing him another pie. Salesmen, he thought, or the mailman; possibly the paperboy. Only for a second did he think the word *Gestapo*.

He undid the chain lock on the inside and opened the door. A short-haired man in a suit and tie, his jacket unbuttoned, smiled at him with expressionless eyes. His face was pink and shiny with sweat. "I bring you the word of God," he said.

"I don't have time to listen."

Izzy started to close the door but the man took a step forward, elbowing the door wide. "You don't have time for the word of our Savior, Jesus Christ?"

"He's your savior, not mine. I'm a Jew—I don't believe in Jesus, the Holy Ghost, or virgins having babies."

"Our Savior was born a Jew."

"Then he might've saved some more of us from the ovens, don't you think? For old time's sake."

The man winced and quickly reset his face in neutral. "I'd like to come inside," he said. "I've got something to show you."

"No one comes inside I haven't known for a lifetime."

The man pulled his shirt up and pointed at coins of purplish skin. "Bullet wounds," he announced.

That's terrific, Izzy thought. A *no-goodnik* they send making door-to-door conversions. He locked his hand on the doorknob.

The man hunched forward like a pink-faced animal. "I used to hang around with a bad crowd."

"Drug dealers?"

"That too. And one day I couldn't pay a man the money I owed him, so he came after me with a gun."

"I have a friend who was shot for less."

"Someone called an ambulance. They drove me to a hospital but didn't think I'd make it, I was bleeding like a slaughtered lamb. And as I was lying there, barely conscious, near death, I had a vision . . ."

"Naturally."

"I saw Jesus over me in a halo of golden light, his face almost touching mine. I smelled his breath, like orange blossoms, felt his beard on my lips like a kiss. 'I will save you,' Jesus said. 'I will forgive your sins if you believe in God the Father and His Only Begotten Son.'"

"You don't say no to a deal like that when you're half dead."

"I reached for him and promised I would follow the Word forever. The bleeding stopped immediately."

"Very interesting," Izzy said. "My friend wasn't as lucky as you. No one offered to help him."

The man thrust his shirt in his pants. "Was your friend a true believer?"

"After what he lived through, you don't believe in anything—but that's another story."

"We could pray together for his soul."

"I prayed at his funeral. That's enough."

"And what about your soul?" the man asked tenderly.

"What about it?" Izzy said. "Why should there be a problem?"

"Everybody needs forgiving. Everybody's done things they're not very proud of."

"Is that so? Speak for yourself!" Izzy pushed the door hard against the man's body but it didn't budge. "I want you to go now. I don't want to talk anymore."

He shoved a thin pamphlet into Izzy's hand. *The Lord Loves You Perfectly* it said in big letters on the top page. "Read it," the man said. "You can call the number on the back when you're ready." Then he turned and walked away.

Izzy stood in the doorway and watched the man cross the street and climb into a white car. His neighbor Pat, weeding her lawn from under a broad conical hat, stood up and stared at the car as it rolled away. She looked like the clapper of a bell, he thought, as she rushed across her stiff grass and stopped on Izzy's front walk beyond the shade of a palm tree. "Anything wrong?" she asked.

"Everything's fine."

Her hat wavered like a mirage. "Who was that man?" she said. "A government official? You're not in any trouble with the tax department, are you?"

"The man's an evangelist. He knocked on my door and we had a chat."

"He came to my place too. I saw him through the window, but I never open my door to strangers." A vein appeared between her brows. "You can't be too careful when you live alone."

"I can take care of myself." Izzy flexed his biceps. "Anybody steps out of line, I'll give him a good *klop.*"

Despite the heat, her forearms were prickly with goosebumps. She glanced at the muscles under the sleeves of his polo shirt, and Izzy was glad that he still did arm-pull exercises and lifted weights. "You certainly look strong enough to take on anyone. Rudy used to say a man is only as good as his right hook."

"Rudy was a big talker. The man had something to say about everything."

"You know, I was thinking . . . if you'd like to use my swimming pool . . ."—her eyes flitting from one of Izzy's arms to the other. "Lessons are a good idea, a nice way to stay cool. And wouldn't my children be surprised to see me in the water!" She covered her mouth to stop a giggle. "So, if you want to, if your offer still stands . . . we could start in tomorrow."

He watched a pair of geckos climb the front wall of his bungalow. "Well, I'll have to let you know. I have to check my schedule." Now that he had the upper hand he was no longer interested in teaching her anything.

He left his neighbor standing on the walkway beyond his porch, squinting in the glare of the sweltering afternoon. Even as he turned away he felt her expectation lapping against his back like agitated water. Good. Let her sit and wait—like she made Izzy wait to use her *farshtinkener* pool.

Inside the bungalow he walked across the living room, opened a sliding door, and entered the screened-in porch at the rear. Here he chose a chaise longue with a vinyl-covered pillow as a headrest and lay down. He was tired and wanted to have a nap, but couldn't get comfortable. He was altogether restless, his legs cramped and twitching and his brain thick with dialogue: lines remembered from the past; words from the born-again goy.

He still had the rolled-up booklet in his pocket. He pulled it out and stared at the title, *The Lord Loves You Perfectly*, then gave up on the chaise longue and headed for the bedroom.

He sat on the edge of the bed, arms hanging between his knees, and heard Eva as a child: "If God loves us so much, why does it hurt when I fall down? Why is there chicken pox?"

Years later Sam would ask, "Why are people starving if God's looking after us and wants us to be happy?"

Then Phil shouting, waving a fist: "Where was God when babies were thrown into burning pits? When millions were slaughtered?"

Where was God when this happened, where was He when that happened?: everyone had the same complaint. Maybe He was watching over us, maybe He couldn't care less. It's possible whatever set the universe in motion isn't a conscious thing at all, never gave the Ten Commandments, parted the Red Sea, decides who will live or die. That everything he learned and believes simply isn't so.

"It's not for us to question his ways," Hilda used to shake a finger whenever Izzy did as much. "It's not for us to understand."

Sometimes Izzy speaks to God and is sure He is listening: a being not unlike his own father, wise and patient. But hearing him is one thing; to love and forgive a worm of a man is something else entirely.

He scanned the pamphlet, not reading, seeing that the print was large, ranging from bold to faint. He could have thrown it out but didn't; put it under his pillow instead. At night—every night—he would know it was there.

Now he straightened and got to his feet, no longer sleepy. Too much thinking, too much talk! Bits and pieces filling his brain, spinning and dissolving like sugar stirred in a cup of tea. Conversations from long ago—or only this morning—repeating like onions.

Neighbors corner you on the street and strangers come to your front door, there's no getting away from it. And now he can't quiet down, he wants even more of it. More people, more stories. Someone to tell them to. All at once he's lonely.

It wasn't the right day of the week for him to eat out, but he made up his mind to spend the rest of the afternoon in the Bay View Mall, then go to Mallory's for the Early Bird Special. There were shoppers he could talk to and salespeople in the stores, and he always managed to find a friendly soul in the cafeteria to sit with while he ate.

Izzy changed his polo shirt for something a little dressier, a short-sleeved textured cotton he tucked into his trousers, then unlocked the heavy door between his kitchen and garage. Sometimes he walked to the mall, which wasn't very far, but he hated crossing U.S. 19 on foot because the light changed so fast he'd wind up stuck between the divider and the other side, cars honking, swerving, or screaming to a stop as he hurried across the last lane. Anyway, it was too hot, you could hardly breathe. He got in his car, pushed the remote to open the garage door, started the engine, and turned on the air conditioner, which blew warm air in his face. He opened his window.

Pat waved to him as he backed down his driveway. She was sitting in a square of shade under the roof of her front porch, exactly the same as his. In fact, all the porches on the block were more or less alike, with flat roofs, metal poles, and concrete floors. They were nothing much to look at. If you wanted wide verandas, wooden beams, and balustrades, you had to go to a more expensive neighborhood like Phil's, away from the highway and closer to the water. Something Izzy couldn't afford.

A horn blared and he hit the brake. "Wake up!" the driver yelled. He'd almost backed into a car coming along the street. A small silver car, it was hard to see in bright light. Anyone might have missed it. Still, his hands were shaking as he readjusted his glasses. "You be careful!" Pat called. He rolled up his window.

At the end of the street he had to make a difficult left turn across a busy road with traffic moving both ways. He waited for an opening, but you could sit forever and no one would let you in. Finally he shot across a stream of oncoming cars and made room in the far lane by cutting off an Oldsmobile. More honking. He honked back. "*Lig in drerd!*" Izzy turned to shout at the driver—he should only go bury himself! As an afterthought he added, "May a trolley grow in your stomach and may you shit transfers! May your bones be drained of marrow!"

That made him feel better. But then he had to brake again, flopping against the steering wheel, because a light had turned red, cars were stopped in front of him, and he didn't notice soon enough. By the time he reached the Bay View Mall his clean shirt was soaking.

Parking was a problem. The lot was so crowded it was difficult to find a space. He circled the area several times, then, in a distant corner, nosed into a narrow slot, but could barely open his door without banging the next car. He had to get out on the passenger side and even that was a tight squeeze. And while he was making his way to the plaza—sun in his eyes and heat like fur in his nose and throat—a car backing out of a spot almost ran into him, the driver so short Izzy could only see a white cap of hair above the steering wheel. He banged on the trunk with his fist and hollered another curse: "May you stick to the wall like a calendar and every day one more piece should be torn from you!"

When at last he entered the mall, Izzy had to sit down on the nearest bench to compose himself. He waited for his eyes to adjust to the strange light, the artificial brightness of the stores and corridors, the dusty gloom in corners. Phil never went to malls, he said they were unnatural and were ruining the state. But Phil had enough money to shop in exclusive boutiques and never lacked companions.

He pulled a cloth from his pocket and wiped his glasses, which were dirty with thumbprints. Naturally there was no view to soothe a shopper's senses, not of the bay or much else having to do with nature. Close to the entrance was a trio of potted plants (palm, rubber, and philodendron) whose leaves had such a waxy sheen he doubted if they were real. An upbeat song from a hidden speaker filled his ears, a popular jingle altered beyond recognition. But he wasn't here for the view or for musical entertainment. He was looking for pleasant company, no more, no less.

A large woman sat beside him, shopping bags on her lap and spilling over onto the bench. She kicked off her sandals and rubbed her feet. "Well, I've had it," she said. Izzy didn't answer. He didn't like bare legs, especially with stubble and veins. Hilda always wore stockings. At home she rolled them down to her knees, but not when they were out somewhere. And naturally she wouldn't dream of touching her feet in public. What kind of person does that? He got up and walked away. He wasn't going to talk to just anyone: he was choosy.

At the end of the corridor he entered a department store and went directly to Menswear. Karen, his favorite salesgirl, was standing behind the register ringing up sales. She was young, very shapely, and liked to chat with him about her problems with her boyfriend. Izzy gave her good advice (call him, don't call; leave him, don't leave), depending on the circumstance. Now he stood at the end of the line that stretched beyond the counter, and when he came up to her he said, "So how's everything?"

"Sorry, can't talk now, my boss is watching."

Just a few yards away a short man in a good suit was indeed eyeing them. "How does he know what we're talking about? Maybe you're telling me what kind of socks to get. Maybe I need a new shirt."

"He's seen you hanging around before. He knows you don't buy anything. He says I'm not getting paid to entertain old men."

"The *momzer*," Izzy muttered as he walked up to the bastard. "Your shoes are dirty," he told him. "Your tie's too loud and there's dandruff on your collar. A fine example you are!"

"Excuse me?" the man said. Izzy grinned and kept going.

He headed for the atrium, where there was a nice coffee shop, tables and comfortable chairs. He bought a coffee but no dessert, so he'd be good and hungry for the Early Bird Special, and found a seat in a corner. But no sooner did he lift the Styrofoam cup than a man in a belted coat, carrying a briefcase, stopped at his table. "Do me a favor?" the man said.

Clearly there was something wrong. The man's speech was slurred and his eyes were unfocused; he swayed a little as he spoke. And who wears a raincoat on a day like this? "What's the matter?" Izzy said. "What kind of favor?"

"Can't drink," the man said. "Alcohol is poison . . . my body is poisoned. Got to go to a hospital. Help me . . . a hospital." Then he stumbled into the table, knocking over Izzy's cup.

Coffee streamed onto the floor, splashing Izzy's shoes and pants. "Look what you did!" he said. The man was leaning over the table, holding himself up with his palms. Once again he asked for help, his voice more insistent now—but why should Izzy help a *shikker*? Let him sleep it off somewhere. It wasn't his business.

Besides, what could Izzy do? Drag him to an exit and phone for a taxi? Probably the man was broke and Izzy would have to pay his fare, money he'd never see again. Or maybe he'd get violent, shouting curses, throwing punches, then puke his guts up. And what if he wasn't even drunk, but on drugs? What if he was carrying a briefcase of heroin? Could be it was all a setup: once they were alone in an out-of-the-way spot the man would stick a knife in his back and steal Izzy's wallet. He'd heard worse stories than that.

Izzy was shivering. Every nerve was telling him the situation was dangerous, stay out of it, don't get involved, let him ask someone else, don't be a hero. If Phil were here, he wouldn't think twice, Izzy imagined: he'd carry the man to a taxi or put him in his own car and drive him to a hospital; give him money, offer him a job if he needed one. Never a thought for his safety. How marvelous it must be to live your life without fear.

But people were watching now, he had to do something. How would it look if he did nothing? Like that time someone leaped in front of a train in Toronto and Izzy didn't help out—how much it bothered him after! Like all the other times in his life he might have done something and didn't, or times he didn't do enough. He was no Phil Lewis . . . but the last thing he needed was another face to haunt him at night.

So he got up suddenly, tiptoed through spilled coffee, and tried to straighten the man up. Pulling, pushing, lifting, he finally got the drunk's arm fixed across his shoulders, the dead weight of him almost more than he could manage. Together they took a step, tottered and zigzagged, then Izzy's knees buckled and he struggled to stay erect. "Someone help!" he cried out. "Somebody help me!"

A man appeared from nowhere, ducked under the drunk's arm attached to his briefcase, and easily supported him. Izzy was grateful and relieved. Now there were two of them to deal with whatever came next—Izzy and someone who was younger and stronger than he was.

The man spoke with an accent. "Where are you taking him?"

"He has to get to a hospital. We have to find a taxi."

They half dragged the drunk to the main entrance of the mall and out to the curb, where a cab was already waiting. The driver waved them off, he was on another call, but Izzy opened the rear door and they laid the man across the seat. "This is an emergency. Take him to a hospital."

"Who's gonna pay?" the driver said. His passenger rose onto an elbow, opened his briefcase, and pulled out a roll of bills. "Don't worry, I'll pay"—whereupon he collapsed on the seat. The driver swore and sped off toward the steaming asphalt of U.S. 19.

"Looks like he robbed a bank," said the man who had helped out.

"Probably a drug deal. We're lucky he didn't kill us both."

Izzy looked at the man closely. About sixty, he guessed, with a lantern jaw, a nice smile; bald except for a fringe at the back. Black

T-shirt, gray pants, sneakers white as egrets. A European accent. "*Sprechen Sie Deutsch?*" he asked him.

The man pumped Izzy's hand and began speaking German at once. His name was Klaus Hauptmann, he had married an American and moved with her to Florida but never really fit in. Now he was a widower without many friends—and not one of them German! He was thinking of going back to Berlin.

"*Sind Sie ein Berliner?*" Izzy was excited: a landsman in the Bay View Mall!

He was eager to talk about Berlin in the twenties and thirties, but his German was clumsy. Over and over he would stop, stutter, click his teeth, then he'd have to start again. He could almost remember certain words, his fingers curling as he spoke, trying to pluck them from the air, but in the end the words were lost, like snowflakes melting on your skin. Klaus encouraged him, circling his hands rapidly as if he could bring the phrases forth, but still Izzy was mortified. An old man whose memory was shot. A German no longer German. Where was his place in the world and what was his proper tongue?

Izzy reverted to English, which he'd spoken now for fifty years—thought in, dreamed in—and yet it would never be as weighty or expressive as the language of his childhood. "Did you have dinner yet?" he asked. "I know a good place in the mall, Mallory's Cafeteria, all you can eat for $4.99 if we get there right away."

Klaus slapped him on the back—"Sure, let's go"—and together they walked through busy corridors, past white-haired men and women and noisy packs of teenagers until they reached the restaurant a few minutes before five.

Izzy had his usual, roast beef, mashed potatoes, a few peas on the side of his plate, though Klaus had only salad and a large glass of water. He led him to a booth at the back with long vinyl banquettes and immediately told him the story of his escape from Berlin by train and boat. When talking to Germans (even nice, friendly ones), Izzy let it be known as soon as possible that he was a

Jew. Get it out of the way quickly, that was his rule. Why waste time on a man who could turn out to be an anti-Semite by the end of the night?

Klaus looked at his salad. "*Ja*, the Nazis. *Ja, die Juden . . .*"

He waited for him to go on, but Klaus only shook his head. So Izzy said, "Tell me something, where were you in 1939? Where was your father?"

The man coughed and sipped water, his cheeks blooming. Then he said, "I was a child—just a little boy—when Germany attacked Poland. Please understand that. Sure I joined the *Hitler Jugend*—we had to in those days—but that didn't make me a Nazi. I liked the sports, the camping and hiking, but not the rest." He drank more water. "My father was a Luftwaffe pilot who was lucky to survive the Battle of Britain. He knew nothing about Jews and what was happening on the ground."

Izzy chose to believe this. Klaus seemed an honest sort, a decent man who helped others and listened to their stories. And clearly he wasn't old enough to have worn a Nazi uniform. Besides which, there had to be Germans who didn't know what was going on, and even some who hid Jews—along with those who turned away or actively participated in torture and murder.

As a Jew, he was wary of Germans. As a German, he wanted to be welcomed back to his homeland, returned to the culture of his birth. Has he not been getting a pension from Bonn since 1976, allowing for when he couldn't work because of persecution? Is it not an act of forgiveness to accept this restitution?

Klaus was good company, a link to Izzy's boyhood, and though he might be careful at first, Izzy wanted to be his friend. Later in his bed he would deal with the complaints of the dead. *No matter what*, he'd say, *I am also a German.*

But they didn't just discuss the war. He and Klaus spoke about things they had done in Berlin (swimming, skating, soccer games, movies, and concerts), and by the time they got dessert they'd already told each other about their wives and children. ("A daughter in Miami and a son in Key West I'm afraid is homosexual"; "My wife Hilda was a jewel . . .") By the time Izzy had his pie and they were drinking coffee, he was already talking about Phil. Phil-the-Jewish-partisan, Phil-the-famous-hero (okay, the war again), but also his employer and friend, Eva's one-time father-in-law, a man who knew him longer and better than anyone, except for Hilda naturally (who knew him differently, you could say): shot dead at close range outside his factory in a sleepy Toronto neighborhood.

"What, murdered?" Klaus was shocked.

"He had a girlfriend, Selma Gold, who had a jealous boy-friend . . ." Izzy turned his palms up. "Who goes after a girl like that?"

"Maybe she was a knockout."

"I'll know when I visit her."

"You're going to see his girlfriend? You think that's a good idea?"

"It's important to know what's what, to try and figure things out. Otherwise you might as well spend your time in a seniors club playing bingo and drinking tea."

"I like bingo," Klaus said. "It's not good to stay home and be alone so much."

"My daughter thinks my life is dull, she thinks I should get a dog." Izzy pushed his cup aside. "But today I spoke to a holy roller, helped a poor drunk in the mall, and ate with you, a lands-man. Tomorrow I'll look up Selma Gold. Does that sound boring to you?"

"Certainly not."

"All right, I'm an old man, my life isn't what it was—but that doesn't mean I should be measured for a coffin."

"Not at all."

"I used to be something," Izzy said. He crossed his arms, tipped his head. "Tell me, have you ever done anything bold and fearless?"

Klaus nodded slowly. "Small things, like helping drunks . . . and once I pulled a dog out of the path of a speeding bus."

Izzy locked eyes with him and spoke in a solemn tone: "I saved a man from drowning in the Grunewaldsee at dusk. He threw up his hands and started to shout and I saw him go under once, twice, so I jumped in and got him out. Later he presented me with a silver cigarette case—which I gave to my grandson—a little tarnished now but you can still read the inscription, '*In Dankbarkeit meinem Lebensretter Isidor Schneider.*'"

"You *were* something," Klaus said.

"But that was many years ago. I was nineteen, still a boy. Since then, nothing. During the war, nothing. My daughter thinks I'm a jellyfish. She probably would've liked it more if Phil was her father, not me."

"Because he was something too?"

"Because he was something better—Phil-the-avenger!"

Klaus tugged his fringe of hair. "Here is what I think: the mighty are never as strong as we imagine, the weak aren't helpless. I'm sure you're a good man, a kind and loving father. You should tell your daughter that people aren't this or that. Most of us are in between."

Izzy pushed his chair back, squinting at the distance. "You're right!"—jumping to his feet as if he were going to wave a flag. "You're right, she should know that." He leaned across the table and spoke in a whisper. "I'm going to talk to her and this is what I'm going to say: 'Eva, listen carefully, I have to tell you something. We're all more or less alike. Do you hear me? We're all the same.'"

6

THIS WAS IN THE MORNING PAPER: a Polish cardinal opposed an agreement to relocate a Catholic convent in Auschwitz outside the camp grounds. The Vatican would not interfere; Jewish leaders were offended ... Izzy dropped the paper and threw up his hands. A convent in Auschwitz—of course they were offended! Where Nazis murdered two million, including his own family. Sure others died too, but mostly Jews—they targeted *Jews*. Auschwitz today should be a Jewish memorial, not to be shared with nuns and a twenty-four-foot cross. How could the Church not understand?

When the phone rang he thought it was Pope John Paul calling to ask his opinion: should the cardinal be silenced and the convent moved according to plan? So okay, it wasn't the Pope, but the voice on the line was surprising anyway—Irene, calling from Tampa.

She was here with Yvonne, they were visiting Yvonne's mom and driving all over the place—to islands and aquariums, gardens, historical sites, wildlife sanctuaries, and roadside attractions. Already they'd seen alligators, manatees, and sea turtles, spoonbills, pelicans, a two-headed snake, and a sponge-diver mannequin; they'd eaten catfish, snapper, and crab, cruised on an airboat, found shells and sharks' teeth; waded in water where you had to shuffle your feet in the sand so you wouldn't step on a stingray. Now they were on their way to the Gulf and thought they'd visit Izzy too, maybe he could show them around.

When he hung up the phone he was all *farmisht*. What was he supposed to do with two women he hardly knew? Should he take them to a park, a beach, or maybe fishing and boating? Did they play golf or tennis? Did they like museums, arts and crafts, flea markets, concerts? Would they rather shop in the Bay View Mall? And what more was there to say they hadn't already talked about?

He changed from pajamas into beige pants and loafers and a blue piqué-cotton polo that brought out the color of his eyes. Two buttons he left undone to show a curl of chest hair, gray but still springy. Then he went to the sun porch and paced around the concrete floor. It was still early morning and the sun hadn't yet turned the porch into a *shvitzbud*. He picked up a watering can and sprinkled his potted plants—the jade with its rubbery leaves, the aloes and cacti—then rearranged three patio chairs in a circle. Maybe the ladies would just like to sit and relax first. There were cans of ginger ale in the fridge and a bottle of orange juice: he could serve everyone cold drinks and Ritz crackers with cream cheese. Once they were rested they could tell him where they wanted to go: he wouldn't have to decide alone and maybe choose the wrong thing, then be blamed for ruining the day.

They arrived an hour later. When Izzy opened the front door Irene squeezed him in a hug, her breasts spread across his chest like jelly on toast. He drew back, wrinkling his nose, getting a whiff of too-sweet honeysuckle perfume and also the stink of sweat. He looked the women over. Irene's eyelids were ocean-blue, her mouth as red as the blossom of a flame tree. Because of the humidity her hair was a wiry bush, but Yvonne's was pulled away from her face, as tight as guitar strings. She stood in the open doorway, her fair skin flushed with sun, heat, or excitement.

"Please come in. Follow me."

Izzy ushered them onto the porch and seated them in patio chairs. They were dressed alike in stretchy shorts and scoop-necked T-shirts spotted with perspiration. He brought in a tray of crackers and cheese which neither of them touched, but the cold drinks were a big hit. He watched them drinking juice and pop, chins up, heads back, their pink, fleshy necks arched, and found himself staring at the *V* between their collarbones that ended at the start of each one's cleavage. Irene pressed her ice-filled glass on that very spot, turning it slowly round and round, like the mesmerizing globe in the ceiling of a dance hall. He had to pull his eyes away so that they wouldn't call him a *zhlub*.

"Oh my God, the heat," said Irene, "that awful humidity. How can you stand it?"

"You get used to it," Izzy said. "Besides, everything's air-conditioned. Some days I go from my house to the car, car to the mall, I don't take more than two gulps of fresh air."

"I used to come with Phil when he had the condo," Yvonne said. "You could fry an egg on the balcony."

Izzy raised an eyebrow. "That's where you met Selma Gold?"

"Oh no!" Yvonne blushed. "I never actually met her. I saw them together once and found out later who she was."

"Phil told you?"

"Not at first. Somebody sent me a note, I never figured out who."

Irene asked for more pop. Then she turned the conversation to tourist spots, accommodations, the price of this, the price of that. Izzy tried but couldn't bring it back to Phil and Selma. "That's enough about them," Irene kept saying. "We're here to have a good time." Finally she stood up. "We brought a cooler of food along so we could have a picnic. Izzy, how does that sound? All you have to do is direct us to a nice spot."

"Park or beach?"

"Your choice. But you have to bring a bathing suit, we're going somewhere after. I won't tell you where, only that you're going to get wet."

They decided to take the rental car, Izzy up front, Yvonne in back, Irene driving. They went south on U.S. 19 for a short distance, then Izzy pointed right and they drove through a development of pricey-looking two-story homes: Mediterranean-style houses with wrought-iron gates and window grilles, arches and balconies, stuccoed walls and red-tile roofs. Nice, if you could afford it.

Beyond this a narrow road with sand and shrubs on either side led to a parking lot. From there they went on foot along a raised boardwalk that wound through a marsh of stunted trees, frogs and turtles, bushes and reeds. A duck quacked, a dove cooed, a woodpecker rat-a-tatted: a quaint bit of wilderness, unusual for Bay Point. The women walked behind Izzy, swinging the cooler between them.

The trail meandered for a while, then wound up at a lookout tower that gave them a sweeping view of the Gulf, glassy and buoyantly blue under a peach-colored sky. Weathered stairs zigzagged from the tower to a strip of beach alive with the eruptions of crabs scooting across the sand. Back from the water in a grassy area were two empty picnic tables stained with bird droppings. Yvonne shook a paper cloth over one of the tables while Irene unloaded the cooler. "A park *and* a beach," she said. "How clever of you, Izzy."

His face burned with pleasure. He turned away so they wouldn't see.

They ate tuna sandwiches and drank tepid lemonade from plastic cups. For dessert there were oranges and Sara Lee frozen brownies, nearly thawed. Irene ate with gusto, taking large bites of everything, but Yvonne was more hesitant, a nibble of this, a nibble of that, her lips barely moving.

One bold, the other not, yet Phil had been attracted to both, had wed Irene, then Yvonne, had rubbed his face in their blonde hair, between their breasts and plump thighs, had known the smell of their breath and skin, the sounds they made while sleeping. Even his experience of sex and marriage, like his experience of war and death, was greater than Izzy's. In every way he was outsized. Izzy could only imagine what it was like to kiss so many mouths, taste so many dark nipples, lick so many round bellies, *shtup* so many beauties. Phil, you greedy *chozzer*! If the man were alive today, he'd be in bed with Selma Gold.

After lunch the women waded in knee-high breakers hissing across the shore. The water was luminous, blue-green. "It's like a bathtub!" Irene called. Izzy watched from the picnic bench, especially when they wandered back to shore and bent to look for shells. A long time since he squeezed a round bulging *tochis*. Not that he'd lost interest, only opportunity. In addition to which he was choosy. The thought of touching his neighbor Pat's skinny rear end, for instance, made him shake with revulsion. He liked fullness, meatiness. Even Hilda, small as she was, was gifted in that way.

In their matching red-and-white shorts, doubled over, inspecting shells, Irene and Yvonne were shiny beach balls bouncing across the sand. Watching them, he felt alive. But it wasn't just that they made him think of himself and Hilda at Coney Island, Jones Beach, and Orchard Beach, sand in their swimsuits, sand in their mouths, sand burning the soles of their feet . . . or certain girls at the factory who wore such flimsy, tight skirts you couldn't keep your mind on your work. No, there was more to it than that. Hanging around the ex-wives, he felt he had entered Phil's world. For just a moment he was younger, taller, stronger, more assured.

For just a moment he was Phil.

Then it was over. The sky darkened without warning and suddenly it began to pour. A cold, drenching shower: you could feel the temperature dropping. The girls ran back to the table, waving their arms and squealing. They grabbed the cooler and tore off in the direction of the parking lot, Izzy hurrying in their wake. Three car doors opened; three doors slammed shut.

Rain pelted metal and glass with a hiss and chink as they squirmed in their respective seats, shaking beads of water from their arms and heads. The car windows fogged and the interior smelled like a jungle, a mix of mud and mustiness. "Look at me," Yvonne said, plucking at her soggy shirt. A drop clung to the tip of her nose. "Look how I'm shivering. My hair's like a wet rug."

Irene shook her damp tangle of hair and snickered, "Look at *you*?"

Izzy started laughing too, as easy as if he were spending the afternoon with his buddy Phil.

Minutes later the rain stopped as abruptly as it began. Soon after, the sun was out, the asphalt steaming like a smoldering fire; the car stuffy. Irene started the engine and buzzed down her window. "To our next destination."

"We have to go back and change," said Yvonne. "I can't spend the whole day feeling like a wet frog."

"You'll dry," Irene said. "Open your window." She was already driving out of the park. "We're going to the springs next. The water's eighty-seven degrees"—this said to Izzy—"and we'll all have a good soak. Did you remember to pack your trunks?"

Yes he did, though he wasn't looking forward to exposing his soft chest and belly to the ladies. He couldn't hold a candle to Phil in a bathing suit.

"The water's curative," said Irene. "A high mineral content. You can drink it or swim in the lake. It gets rid of aches and pains, gives you energy, smoothes wrinkles. A regular fountain of youth, they say, what Ponce de Leon was after."

"We can all use some of that," he said.

"There's something I want to see first," Yvonne said quietly. "It's on the way."

Irene glanced at the rearview mirror. "You'll only make yourself miserable. And me, too."

They were talking about the big house in Port Chase, naturally. Selma Gold's expensive house. Thirty-one fifty-seven Waterview Crescent, with an unlisted phone number. Irene had given Izzy the address several weeks ago and right away he drove there and knocked on the front door, but no one was home. He came back a second time and still no one answered: it was such a disappointment. Through the windows he'd seen only dark halls and big rooms messy with building materials; here and there the ghostly hump of a piece of furniture under a sheet. The place looked abandoned.

"Sometimes we have to do what *I* want," Yvonne said. "It's my vacation too, and if I want to spend it being miserable, that's my business."

"You have to think about your health. It's no good to get upset. If Phil was alive, he'd forbid you to do this—and then you wouldn't go because you listened to him, he knew best. You won't listen to me but you always did what he said, even if you disagreed."

"I just want to see the house."

"Let's do it," Izzy said. Maybe this time Selma would be there and they could have a chat. "Nobody has to go inside, you can wait in the car."

"Two against one," Yvonne said.

Irene sighed loudly. Nevertheless, she crossed the highway and followed the signs to Port Chase.

The town was just another collection of strip malls, trailer parks, ranch homes, gas stations, fast-food outlets, drive-through banks, and a hangar-like supermarket. Not unlike Bay Point. Nowhere Izzy ever pictured Phil buying property. But just beyond the sprawl was a sudden spurt of trees and the faintest smell of salt air riding the odor of gasoline. They drove through the open gate of a brick-walled community and then along a winding road that dead-ended at Waterview Crescent. All the houses on the street did indeed have a view of the Gulf, and Selma's was the largest.

Izzy had never been inside. Phil had never shown him the house—it was undergoing repairs, he said, come see it when it's done. He expected to move in in March, but of course that never happened. Life is so unpredictable, how can you plan anything?

They parked beside two stone lions on vine-covered posts and stared out the car windows. At the end of a brick path the house was one story high with a low-pitched white roof, pale yellow stuccoed walls and green-shuttered windows. All very nice. There were palms in the front yard, boxwood hedges, and a wide-reaching carpet of lawn. Cost a fortune, Izzy guessed—a million or more.

Irene got out of the car, though she wouldn't step beyond the lions. Yvonne stayed hunched down in the rear seat. But Izzy didn't hesitate, he walked up to the entrance and rang the bell. When no one answered, he circled the building and entered the yard for the first time. The view was astounding: an empty pool flanked by a red-roofed gazebo held up by concrete pillars; swaying palms, a strip of grass, the beach, and a private dock; the turquoise sea with its lip of foam; the sky a cerulean cap. He sat down on the rim of the pool, his legs swinging freely over the rectangular dugout, and gazed at the tableau. This too was part of what he'd missed in his lifetime, some of the pleasures he couldn't afford—or hadn't gone after because he's not a playboy.

What kind of man would he be, Izzy wondered, if he lived here in this house and not in his bungalow? If he enjoyed a panoramic view of the Gulf every day instead of his neighbors' mowed yards. If he never lacked for boats and cars and female companionship. It was hard not to envy Phil, even though the man had met an early and violent death. He had packed more living into sixty-six years, it seemed, than Izzy had in seventy-eight.

Not that he regretted leading a quiet but decent life. Not that he was complaining.

But he was kvetching, wasn't he? There was something to be said for a bad reputation.

His mouth tasted sour. As he got up and turned to go, he saw a woman staring at him over the hedge. Her arms were crossed, her expression grim. She peered at him intently as he walked to the edge of the yard, no doubt memorizing his features for a police report. "I'm looking for Selma Gold," he said, "the lady who lives here. Maybe you've seen her recently?"

"You've been here already," the neighbor said. "I saw you snooping around before."

"Do you know where she is?"

"Someone comes to cut the grass. Otherwise there's no one around. Men came by, just like you, to ask if I'd seen anything. I told them what I'm telling you—there's nobody home."

"What men? Policemen?"

"They said the owner was killed in Toronto." She cupped her mouth and lowered her voice. "Shot in the head in broad daylight."

"I know that already, it was in the papers, old news. Tell me about Selma Gold."

"You think she had something to do with it?"

"What do I know?" Izzy said. "I'm not a policeman."

"Looks fishy to me that she's never home."

"You think she's hiding?"

"Why ask me?"

"Because you seem to know things."

The woman waved her hands in front of her face and stepped away from the hedge. "Not my business," she said, then she disappeared.

Izzy walked back to the car and climbed into the passenger seat. Irene was waiting behind the wheel. "Did you find Selma?" she asked as she sped away from the carved lions. "You were gone a long time."

"Selma's not here but I sat in the backyard, overlooking the water. I was daydreaming, watching the Gulf, thinking Phil was lucky to have had such a fine view."

"The poor man," Irene said. "He owned lots of things but they didn't make him happy. He was always restless, always dreaming, coming up with new schemes. One day he wanted a cottage in Bermuda, the next day a private plane. I used to listen to him for hours and tried to be enthusiastic, even though I knew he'd be tired of whatever he was after in a few months."

"Including women," Izzy said. "He got tired of them too, though it took a little longer."

Irene stopped talking.

From the rear seat Yvonne said, "He would've dropped Selma before long, I'm sure of it."

Izzy turned to look at her. "So how did they meet in the first place?"

"She lived with her boyfriend in a condo apartment in the same building Phil was in. She met him at the swimming pool . . . or maybe the gym." Yvonne's eyes were shiny and he thought she was going to cry. "She left Vic to be with Phil, who left me to be with her—and now she's got no one!"

"She got the house," Izzy said.

"Well, I hope she likes it, after all the trouble she went to. I hope—" Yvonne's voice cracked.

"Phil's house, Selma's house . . ." Irene hit the gas and drove the car onto the highway. "Can't we talk about anything else?" She was passing other vehicles, exceeding the speed limit, but didn't seem to notice. Cars honked loudly as she tore in and out of lanes.

"Maybe you should slow down a little," Izzy told her.

"I want to get to the springs before they close," she answered curtly.

From the rear seat he heard snuffling. He offered Yvonne his handkerchief, but she already had a tissue. "I knew this would happen," Irene said. "Just ignore her, okay? She wants to be miserable, let her."

"I can't forget him one-two-three"—Yvonne snapped her fingers—"just because you say so. He was good to me, a good husband. Treated me like a princess. For the first time in my life I felt safe . . . I was safe with him. I really believed he loved me."

"He *did* love you," Irene said. "He loved us all the best he could."

Or nobody, Izzy thought.

"But now it's time to move on."

For how could a man like that, who ran from one girl to the next, get close to anyone? How could a wife feel safe with a husband who couldn't be trusted? Irene was just fooling herself, fooling Yvonne, fooling him. Phil loved neither of them: both women had been betrayed.

Izzy was the good husband. If either one had married him, she'd still be his wife today.

At the mineral springs they parked the car, then paid and entered the change house, men to the right, ladies left. Izzy put his clothes in a locker, pulled on his bathing suit, and met the women again at the side of a cloudy lake. They overflowed their swimsuits, with handfuls of spongy flesh above and below the expanse of the material. Their faces were in shadow under the wide brims of straw hats. Izzy had forgotten a hat. His sunglasses slipped to the end of his nose while the sun singed his bare head and seared his back and shoulders.

He imagined one of the ex-wives rubbing lotion over his skin, worried that he might burn: the plump, oily tips of her fingers soothing his red flesh.

First Irene, then Yvonne walked into the water. Izzy followed close behind, arms crossed to hide his chest and show off his biceps. Finally the three of them stood waist-deep in a row, digging their toes into mud, waiting to be transformed. The lake stank of sulphur.

Irene splashed her bosom. "I came here with Phil once."

"You did?" said Yvonne. "Me too."

"Really? I didn't know. We don't have to stay..."

"But I want to! It was wonderful." Yvonne turned to Izzy. "Phil tried to teach me to swim but I was hopeless. I kicked and screamed and couldn't float, so he put me on his shoulders and carried me out piggyback."

"I used to carry my wife the same way, in the Atlantic. We also had a good time."

"Then I'd hold my nose and he'd *throw* me off, fish me out— and do it all over again! I laughed so hard I nearly drowned." She squeezed Izzy's biceps. "He was powerful, his arms like yours... only bigger."

"I had lots of fun too." Irene ducked suddenly, up to her neck in water. "Phil swam like a champion, but I wasn't bad myself. I kept up with him, neck and neck. He said we were a good match—he liked having a strong wife."

"He carried me back to shore like I was a treasure he'd found in the lake. I was slippery in his arms, and Phil was wet and shining."

"He'd always wanted a wife, he said, who wasn't afraid of water."

"I'm a good swimmer too—not exactly a fish, but I'm no rookie either." Izzy pushed his glasses up, stepped forward into a deeper part of the lake, and began treading water. But right away the hot, smelly spring made him itchy and tired. The women ignored him as he swam back.

Irene stood up. "Let's go."

"I don't feel any different yet." Yvonne dipped her arms in the lake. "Aren't you supposed to feel young?"

"It's not working," Irene said.

"If you really want to feel young"—Izzy scratched his wet skin—"don't think about the past."

"But that's all I ever do!" Yvonne shook herself dry and trudged out of the murky lake. "It's no life."

No one said much on the ride back to Bay Point. Yvonne grumbled about her shorts and T-shirt, still damp; Irene complained that wading in the springs had only worn her out. Then they were silent. Though Phil wasn't mentioned again, Izzy felt his presence in the speeding car.

He was thinking about an afternoon they swam together in the Gulf; how later they lay down on towels on the hot sand, their skin baking, crusty with salt, exhausted but comfortable in one another's company. "My father didn't want me to swim," Izzy had remembered aloud. "He thought it was dangerous. Because of that I've always been uneasy in the water, even though I swim well."

Phil rolled over to face him. "*My* father"—slapping the sand—"threw me in a pond and said, 'Swim, *tateleh*, swim for your life!'

As it happened, that was good training for what was to come. I learned how to stay afloat before I could tie my shoes."

Izzy turned his back to Phil and wriggled deeper into the sand. In such a manner heroes are made, he decided.

Later still, they went to Phil's apartment for coffee. In all the years he owned it, Izzy had been to the condo only a few times, mostly to pick up Phil before they went out somewhere. He was never invited to stay overnight in the guest room like Eva did the time she visited Phil and it was too late to drive back. How ordinary the bungalow must have looked to her after that.

The condo was luxurious: a large, sunny kitchen and a view of the Gulf from the living room; a fireplace used only rarely when the temperature dropped. "Here's the bedroom," Phil had said, showing off a brass headboard, giant mattress, satin sheets. "This is Yvonne's favorite room. She likes to stay in bed till noon." The window was open and a breeze shook the curtains. The room smelled of suntan oil and salt air. Phil was standing beside the bed, a towel around his shoulders, grinning down as if his wife were still there.

Izzy could picture her clearly now, languorous and naked on an oversized mattress: those heavy breasts with watermelon-colored nipples to play with; legs and hips to stroke and squeeze; the wide-open sea-scented cavern between her thighs . . .

Something stirred in Izzy's pants. He crossed his hands over his crotch and smiled a little to himself: the equipment was rusty, but it still worked.

The late afternoon sky was viscous and white when they turned into the driveway and stopped in front of Izzy's garage. The air was thick with humidity and his glasses steamed up as he left the car. He wiped the lenses on his shirt, then poked his head through a rolled-down window to say goodbye. Irene said, "Be seeing you," and Yvonne waved and blew him a kiss.

The car inched back and he stepped away, looking down. Behind his dark glasses his eyes were wet. He was sorry to see them go. The wives were his fountain of youth; they made him forget all the long years gone by. It was true what Phil used to say: a man is always happiest in the company of women.

He raised his head and waggled his fingers at Phil's wives. As the car scooted out of sight, it was like he was losing his friend for the second time.

Izzy walked to his front door, turned, and peered at the empty street. His breathing was labored, the air heavy in his lungs. Suddenly he was old again—an old man on his front porch—with no one to talk to, nothing to do.

He woke at dawn and showered (ignoring the mold around the tub he kept meaning to clean up), dressed casually, ate something. The early morning sky was dotted with clouds the color of apricots. Later, the day was sticky and warm. Lawn mowers were clamoring and air conditioners humming when he opened his garage door, got in his car, pulled out, and drove back to Port Chase.

The highway was crowded with fast cars. Every town he drove through resembled the one before. He passed by tiny homes of cinder block or concrete, each exactly like the next. When he reached the walled development at the north end of Port Chase, it looked like a movie set built in a wasteland. He turned east and went as far as possible along the road that stopped at Waterview Crescent.

The stone lions guarding the place scowled at him as he walked by. He banged on the door to no avail, rang the bell till his finger ached, nodded at the suspicious neighbor watching from across the lawn, standing by her house that was half as big as this one. "Why don't you give up?" she called.

He sauntered up to the low hedge between the two properties as she did the same thing. "Maybe you met Phil Lewis, the owner who was murdered? He was tall with a round face, curly hair, muscular build, in his middle sixties?"

The woman squinted, concentrating. "I must've seen him once or twice after the house was sold. Mr. Barry used to own it, he lived in Jersey most of the year. Never saw much of him either."

"Maybe you spoke to him one time?"

"I must've said, 'Hello, I'm your neighbor'—something like that."

"Did he ever talk about Selma Gold?"

"'Glad to meet you,' that's what he said. He wasn't too interested in sharing information."

"Did he mention Selma's boyfriend?"

"He never told me anything. Well, maybe one thing... He said he wanted to let the hedge grow between our properties. He said he liked his privacy."

"Who do you think he was hiding from?"

"Not my business."

Izzy pulled a pen and bit of paper from his pocket. "Do me a favor, will you?"—writing down his name and number. "If you should see anything, like someone coming back to the house... I'd be grateful if you called." He passed the paper over the hedge.

"Are you a private detective?"

"Just a friend of the family who needs to talk to Selma Gold."

His phone didn't ring for days and when it did it was Eva, making her once-a-week duty call Friday night. Seven was her usual time, after his dinner, but if she was working the evening shift, he'd hear from her later on. Sometimes Izzy phoned her, but not as often or regularly because after all he was living on a fixed income, vulnerable to inflation and rising costs. Besides, it shows respect when a daughter calls her father and not the other way around.

After they exchanged hellos, he told her about Irene and Yvonne taking him out for a picnic and she said that was nice of them. He told her about the springs and she thought that was nice too. But when he mentioned Port Chase, something changed in Eva's voice.

"You drove out to Port Chase?"

"First I went there with the wives, then I went alone, but I couldn't find Selma. Where do you think she is?"

"I have no idea."

"Maybe she didn't like the house and moved back to the condo." Silence on the other end.

"She used to live in his building, in a condo apartment like Phil's. You saw him there, you stayed overnight—maybe you ran into them, Selma and her boyfriend?"

"No, I don't think so."

Again he heard something strange, a vibration in the line, as if she were trembling with the effort of holding words back.

"Ach, I don't believe it! I can hear something in your voice. What aren't you telling me?"

Eva made a sharp sound as if she were choking on a crumb. Then she said quietly, "I do remember Selma. I did meet her once. At the condo... by the pool, I think. Phil introduced us."

"You told me before you never met her, now you're saying something else." Izzy winced. "I don't like it when you lie. When you were a girl you lied plenty, but now that you're a grownup I expect you to tell the truth."

"I forgot about her—no big deal. People forget things all the time. I met her a long time ago. Why should I remember?"

"And the boyfriend? Did you meet him too?"

"I'm sure I didn't."

"Think hard. Maybe you just forgot. Maybe you're lying again."

"I met Selma, not him. I'm absolutely certain."

"Tell me what she looks like."

"I saw her only briefly."

"Tall, short? Fat, thin?"

"Medium height. Slim, I think."

"Pretty?"

"I suppose so."

"How did Phil introduce her?"

"A neighbor who watered his plants."

"Did you think there was more to it than that?"

"I didn't think anything. Just what he told me."

"A neighbor with a boyfriend who turns around and murders Phil!"

"I didn't think—" There was a sudden catch in her voice, then she said firmly, "Promise me you won't get involved."

"I'm already involved," he said.

"Then say you won't get *more* involved. You're too old to be tearing around."

"Sure, sure, good night now. We'll talk again."

Izzy put the phone down, fell back in his La-Z-Boy, and clenched his hands. What did it mean that his daughter met Selma but wouldn't admit it till today? Why lie about that? A pain in his chest like heartburn: he poked his fingers between his ribs. Who was left to trust in the world if not his own flesh and blood?

She never should've been at the condo in the first place. She was seeing too much of Phil; was much too fond of him. She loved him like a father—that's the bitter truth.

He slept badly that night, waking every couple of hours to dreams of swimmers pulled underwater by hungry sharks; of children thrashing in deep pools, their mouths filled with water. Everyone was drowning—and *gevalt*, he had to save them! He jumped in after them, sweeping aside floating debris, but no matter how hard he swam, they drew farther away. Sometimes it was difficult to breathe and he woke gasping. Sometimes he could no longer move and woke quivering. Once he shouted Eva's name, which startled him awake too. When he opened his eyes at sunrise he was lying in sweat: no one was saved.

Izzy got out of bed slowly, washed his face with cold water, turned the air conditioning up, and drank coffee to clear his head. His skull was sore and throbbing, as if he'd banged it on a log.

The phone rang at six-thirty. The shrill sound at such an early hour was alarming: it could only be an emergency, bad news about his daughter, bad news about Sam. His hand shook when he grabbed the phone.

"Figured you'd be up by now." He recognized the testy voice of Selma's nosy neighbor. "I figured you'd want to know the minute I saw something."

He sucked in his breath, breathed out: everything was okay. "Well, what did you see?" he said.

"A taxi stopped next door and the driver carried half a dozen suitcases up the walk. Then a lady followed him and dragged everything inside."

"You think that was Selma?"

"How should I know who it was? All I'm saying is there's someone in the house now."

"I'm on my way."

Izzy put on a white shirt, pleated plants, and oxfords and smoothed his hair across his scalp: first impressions were important. What should he ask her? he wondered as he got in his car. There were so many things he wanted to know. Was Phil in love with Selma? Was she in love with him—or was real estate her main concern? Why did she leave, where did she go, why was she suddenly back? Naturally, he'd have to pose his questions delicately and win her trust.

Traffic was light at this hour and Izzy arrived at Port Chase in less than fifty minutes. He drove to Waterview Crescent and parked in front of Selma's house. Nodding at the fierce lions, he followed the path to the main door. He knocked softly, then loudly; then he rang the doorbell. A curtain moved in the house next door: the yenta was watching him. He stepped to a window and peered in, seeing a table and two chairs he hadn't noticed previously, behind which were boards and brushes, ladders and paint cans. The walls were patched in several places, the floor spotted with white dust. He heard a noise and swung his head.

"Who's there?" A woman in a bathrobe was slouched in the doorway, her short hair on end. Her face was unnaturally white—with powder, illness, or tiredness, he couldn't tell.

He shuffled toward her, arms at his sides, the way you'd approach a strange dog. When he got close he saw that she was only in her thirties, with the smooth skin, button eyes, and small bud mouth of a child. "Are you Selma Gold?" he asked.

"Who wants to know?" she said.

"My name is Izzy—Izzy Schneider. Phil was my best friend. I've been trying to reach Selma Gold."

"Yeah, well, that's me."

"I was hoping we could have a talk."

"You woke me up. I was sleeping."

"Sorry to bother you, but since you're up already . . ."

She looked down, chewing her lip. Tightly wrapped in a thin robe, her body was as straight as a pipe. Not exactly Phil's type. But if she was half his age, no doubt that was compensation for missing curves. "I know your name"—a weak smile. "He told me about you."

"Phil and I were very close, he talked about you too and only said nice things, I want you to know that. Now can I come inside and maybe we can have a chat? I've been trying to get in touch with you for a long time."

"I just got back and the place is, like, a total mess. They're doing renovations."

"I won't look," Izzy said. But he peeked past her head at the cavernous room behind her, the beamed ceiling, wood paneling, wrought-iron chandelier; the tiled floor littered with tools and dusty with footprints. It spoke of Phil, of Phil's taste: the more costly and ornate the decorations, the better.

"I know what—we'll sit out back. Give me a minute, I'll get dressed and meet you on the patio." She pointed to show the way and Izzy smiled agreement, though he'd rather have wandered through the house and checked out the interior.

Something was different in the yard, though he couldn't put his finger on it right away. All at once it came to him: the pool was filled with water. It glinted bluer than the sky, brighter than the lapping Gulf. There were pads on the patio chairs too, he noticed as he pulled one to the side of the pool and sat down—thick and expensive pads.

When Selma reappeared she was wearing cut-off jeans and a loose-fitting shirt with the sleeves rolled up to her elbows, her long, thin legs tanned. She looked to him like a sapling. She sat at the edge of the pool, kicking her bare feet in the water, eyeing the Gulf through dark glasses. Izzy dragged his chair up close. "So where have you been—Canada? Every time I dropped by there was nobody home."

"I don't like Canada, it's too cold in winter. Only been there a few times and the last time I almost froze." She straightened her legs, wiggled her toes, leaned back on her elbows. "I was visiting friends out West. Didn't want to stay here, there were all these cops and reporters."

"You mean after Phil died?"

She yawned and didn't cover her mouth. "Yeah, after all that."

"You just locked the door and went? Who was looking after the place?"

She turned her head from side to side, appraising the yard. "I got a friend to cut the grass and come by to check on things."

"The police didn't care that you left?"

"They already talked to me and said I was in the clear, I had nothing to do with Phil's death. Vic was the criminal, not me."

"Tell me about Vic. How long did you know him?"

"We lived together three years, but I knew him before that. I knew him like forever."

"But you dropped him and ran off with Phil..."

"It just happened."

"What did your boyfriend think of that?"

"He didn't want me to move out, he was still crazy in love with me. But Phil said I had to choose, he wouldn't share me with anyone. *He* was crazy in love with me too." She threw back her head. "It was all so romantic."

"Your boyfriend didn't think so."

"He didn't understand it. Because Phil was so old." She straightened up and circled her feet in the water. "He wasn't even real cute—I mean, not like Vic is. His skin was all moley."

"Your boyfriend has nice skin?"

"Wait, I'll show you a picture." She dashed inside and came back with a camera in one hand, a framed shot in the other. She put the camera on a chair and gave Izzy the photo.

The boyfriend was a full-lipped, heavy-browed, muscular man in tight jeans and an open shirt. "Good-looking guy," he said. "It's hard to believe you picked Phil."

"Vic says I'm impulsive."

"Not as impulsive as he was."

"Yeah, well . . . I never thought he'd do a crazy thing like that. I never thought he was *violent*. He wouldn't even step on an ant."

"Jealousy can make a man act like a lunatic."

"Poor Vic. I never thought it would end like this." She pressed the picture to her breast. "He'll be in jail forever. That is *so* sad."

"He's still better off than Phil."

"No kidding! Poor Phil. Every time I enter the house I think I'm going to find him there."

She put the photo to one side and reached for the camera. "You can take a picture of me." She took off her sunglasses. "I want to send it to my mom. She's real worried about me—you know, since the murder. Make sure you get the pool and gazebo and a few trees. I want her to know I'm okay."

He centered her in the viewfinder along with some of the eye-popping scenery and clicked the shutter. Selma was smiling, her arms wide as if she were carrying the sea and sky, and looked very much at home. "Your mother's going to be impressed."

"Thanks"—taking the camera. "I wish she got to know Phil, she really would of liked him. They had a lot in common."

Their age, he thought, for one thing.

"She loves having a good time, just like he did. We were always going places, he was always buying me pretty things . . ." She flopped down on the patio stones. "He really had something, you know. He made me think I was special. Vic wasn't like that. Half the time he wasn't home. He traveled for his business and left me alone too much."

"Phil had something else too"—Izzy smiled genially—"a great deal of money. 'With money you get honey,' as my dear mother liked to say. 'All locks can be opened with a golden key.'"

"Hey, I'm no gold-digging bitch if that's what you're thinking! The house was a present, a place I could move to and get away from Vic. It was Phil's idea to put my name on the deed, I never asked him."

"Now that he's gone I suppose his half will be transferring to his son."

"It goes to me, a hundred percent. I'm the beneficiary, that's what he put in his will."

"He must have loved you very much."

"He wanted to take care of me. He wanted us to live together happily ever after."

"Naturally. What else would he want?"

She lay back on the flagstones and covered her eyes with her glasses. "He said I reminded him of a girl he loved during the war—someone who died back then. He didn't say much but I think she meant a lot to him."

Ach! he thought, was that it—the girl in the forest again? Was that all that mattered to him, how much the women he met were like his darling Rivke?

Years ago, Izzy recalled, Phil had been smitten by an operator in the plant. Things weren't going well with him and Irene by then: he said she was bossy and they got on each other's nerves. So naturally he was vulnerable to the charms of a pretty girl who sat in line with his office window day in, day out. They were all susceptible, to a man (even "Uncle Izzy," who the girls confided in), but Phil more than usual. This one was different, he assured Izzy over drinks one night in the warehouse. If only she would sleep with him, he'd get her out of his system, but she brushed him off repeatedly. She paid no attention to his threats ("Fire me if you want," she'd said), refused a raise and fancy gifts, and spurned his advances, which only strengthened his desire.

The sewer's name was Inez. A girl really, still in her teens. She was dark-haired and dark-skinned with liquid eyes, a wide mouth, curves on the bottom, curves on top in all the proper places. Despite her immaturity, Inez knew her own mind and cared not a whit for Phil. No wonder he was half mad.

He cried that night in the warehouse. Izzy said, "You're overworked, go home and get a good night's sleep," but Phil kept blubbering. She reminded him of someone he knew during the war, he said, someone from the Jewish camp he'd once been in love with, a young, beautiful girl who was brutally killed. "Sure, sure," he answered, then he poured Phil another schnapps and told him to drink up. There were prettier girls in the factory, he said, and more willing too. "Leave this one alone," he begged. "You're making yourself sick."

Three months later she was gone. She'd said goodbye to no one and simply didn't show up at her sewing machine one morning. Some said because of Phil, who wouldn't stop bothering her; some said another man had broken Inez's heart and now she was going back to her parents in Lisbon. There were rumors she was pregnant, though no one pointed a finger. Phil cried again that night. He swore he'd never get over her as he bumped against Izzy's shoulder, swaying like a dangling rope. "I've done terrible things," he said. "Now I'm paying for my sins." And Izzy had tried to comfort him, had fed him booze and rubbed his back and told him he was a good man at heart, he was a hero. For who hasn't done terrible things in his lifetime? Who doesn't have regrets?

Now he stared at Selma on her back on the patio and tried to imagine her pregnant: like a road with a dangerous bump.

"Surely he didn't love you just because you looked like someone else..."

She sat up stiffly. "You don't fall in love with a person only because of who they are. Who they *remind* you of is just as important. I even grew my hair long so it was more like hers. I cut it again when Phil died, to show I was mourning."

"And if he was here today, you think he'd be happy with you?"

"What kind of question is that?" She glared at him over her glasses.

"I want to know if Phil finally found what he was looking for."

"I don't know why I'm talking to you anyway, okay? You're, like, this total stranger—this geezer who shows up and asks all these fucking things!"

A geezer! Is that what he was? The young have no respect today. *Kish meyn tochis*, Izzy thought, and he almost turned and bent over to give her an eyeful.

Instead he smiled with pursed lips, reached out, and cupped her knee. "I didn't mean to upset you, that's the last thing I want to do. We're just having a conversation, talking about a mutual friend. If you don't want to answer something, that's fine, I understand. I was only thinking about Phil, how sad that he didn't get to live with his dream girl in this"—sweeping his arm across the backyard—"his dream house. Work, women, and real estate, those were his passions. I think he would've liked it here with you, he would've liked it a lot."

Selma lay back again, cradling her head in her arms, regarding the polished sky. Gulls and terns were circling and plunging in the distance; sandpipers ran on the beach. Somewhere close a heron squawked, a marsh wren gurgled and trilled. Palm trees rustled, bent in the breeze: a tropical panorama. All this! Izzy thought. All this and a new lover young enough and pretty enough to take the place of Rivke. He might have been happy after all, if not with Selma, at least with the view.

"I don't know," she spoke to the sky, "how it would of worked out. Phil was pretty jumpy, you know, always zipping back and forth from Canada to Florida—even when he was married."

"You knew when you met him he had a wife?"

"Yeah, but he was tired of her. It wouldn't of lasted anyway. I even saw her one time. She was nothing much to look at."

"You met Yvonne?"

"She was wrapped around his arm like a sleeve. We looked at each other, me and her, and knew we were enemies. Someone must of told her about me, the way she stared."

"Yvonne said she saw you once but never actually met you."

"People tend to forget things they don't want to know about."

"She told me she got a note about you and Phil, but she doesn't know who sent it."

"How come you talked to his wife?"

"I'm talking to anyone who had anything to do with him."

Selma got up suddenly, took off her glasses, wiped her eyes. "I have to go inside now. I need some sleep."

"Can I come back and see you again?"

She bent down and picked up the camera, the portrait of Vic. "I'm a busy person."

"Then I won't keep you longer." He pushed himself out of his chair. "But if I'm in the neighborhood, I'll stop by and see how you're doing, how the house is coming along."

"Don't bother," Selma said. "I'm doing fine." Then she walked toward the house, moving as clumsily as a wind-up toy.

When he got to his car the nosy neighbor was leaning against the hood. She asked if that was Selma he was talking to on the patio and Izzy admitted that it was. She asked if she was going to keep the house and live there on her own and he answered that he thought so, but the woman snorted, shook her head: "That's not what I think." Then she strode away from his car.

What does she know, Izzy thought. An empty-headed yenta.

He hardly paid attention to the road on the drive home: his foot moved automatically, his hands did what they had to do. He recognized the sound of horns, the outlines of passing cars, but his mind was busy elsewhere. He was concentrating on Selma Gold—one lover dead and the other in prison, but she was doing fine, thanks, the solitary owner of a million-dollar mansion. Could it be that what happened to Phil was more than a crime of passion? That Selma was greedier and more cunning than she seemed? What if she seduced Phil and got him to change his will, then encouraged the boyfriend (already mad enough to kill) to shoot him for half a house and a share of the plunder?

Murders have been committed for less. A few dollars. Cruelty. Hatred, boredom, politics. Punks who were looking for kicks. Soldiers following orders. When you look at the possibilities, the wonder is that so many people die a natural death. You take a person like Phil, with ex-wives, ex-lovers, an angry son, and haunted old men bearing grudges . . . the wonder is the man lived as long as he did.

Some would say that Phil Lewis got what was coming to him. Some would say, Go home, Izzy, put your feet up, close your eyes, forget the whole *megillah* now, you already got enough crimes on your mind to keep you up at night.

And they would be right, too. What good was Izzy doing? What did he hope to find out? Why was he foolish enough to think he could figure out what made Phil tick? Who could say why he loved a *tsatske* with a fresh mouth and a *no-goodnik* boyfriend? Who can understand another's passions and secrets, no matter what they tell you?

If Selma was guilty of anything, let the police sort it out. It was their job, not his. Anyway, he was worn out. All he wanted was a nap. And after that, God willing, he shouldn't think about Phil anymore, he shouldn't think about murder: he should sleep quietly through the night.

7

ALL THROUGH OCTOBER and into November there was one thunderstorm after the next. It got so Izzy couldn't go outdoors for days on end. As if he were trapped in a bomb shelter, he lived on canned and dry foods and frozen TV dinners, excited at first, then bored, peering out his windows at the turbulent world behind the blinds.

Trees toppled in strong winds and power lines went down; roads flooded, cars stalled. One time the weatherman reported six inches of rain in just over two hours. Muddy Creek, at the end of his street, usually a dry ditch, filled in only one night, swelled and overflowed its banks for the first time in many years—though Izzy hadn't seen it himself but heard about it from Pat, who spoke to their neighbor Frank, who walked his dog beside the creek and saw it rising, saw it flood.

In December the riverbed was dry again. The sun shone often and the weather was surprisingly mild. Izzy resumed his routine of Tuesday banking, Thursday shopping, as well as frequent trips to the Bay View Mall.

One Friday evening, when he was feeling sociable, he phoned Klaus Hauptmann to meet for dinner at Mallory's. Klaus got there first, and when Izzy arrived, he grabbed him unexpectedly in a suffocating hug, as if they were long-lost brothers reunited. Or else a couple of *faygeles* swooning in each other's arms. *Feh!* How it must look! Everyone was watching as Izzy tore himself free.

After that they bought food and sat in a booth at the back, where no one could see them. Izzy's plate was piled high with fried chicken and vegetables, while Klaus nibbled a salad. He wasn't much of an eater. But his bald head was flushed and his smile broader than usual. Something was up. Maybe he's happy to see me again, Izzy thought. But that wasn't it at all.

"I'm going back to Berlin," he said. "I'm going for good this time."

"What? What are you talking about?"

"The Wall's coming down, Izzy. Don't tell me you haven't heard!"

"Naturally I saw something..."

"The border's wide open now and people are pouring across, the guards aren't stopping them. I saw it all on TV—East Berliners coming by the thousands to see the West; West Berliners greeting them with hugs and flowers, food and drink. Bells ringing, horns honking, everybody singing—it's a great big party."

"What's that got to do with you?"

"I want to be there. Don't you?"

"Why should I want to be in Berlin?"

"Because it's united again! People are chipping away at the Wall and I want a piece too, something with graffiti or a painting, something colorful. Don't you feel an urge to go home? A sense of adventure?"

"I feel nothing." Izzy sniffed. "In halves or in one piece, Berlin is the city that threw out my parents, that took away my citizenship, and sent my sister Rosa and her children to the gas chambers. Wall-shmall, it's nothing to me."

Klaus shook his head. "That was very long ago, Izzy. Can't you forget a little?"

"No! They won't let me." He gripped the edge of the table with both hands and leaned forward. "Every night I hear their cries, I ask their forgiveness and promise to remember."

"It's a new generation of Germans. How can you blame them?"

Izzy sank back in his chair. "In my heart I blame them all."

"Even me?"

"Every German . . . including me."

"Even you? Why you?"

"For what I did and didn't do."

Klaus looked down and picked at his salad. Izzy's food was cold by now and he pushed his plate to one side. Klaus got up and brought back coffee for each of them. He changed the drift of their conversation, first by talking about his daughter Lottie (expecting a child), then about the weather (all the rain they had last month), and finally about Phil. Did Izzy speak to his girlfriend?

He shook his head. "It came to nothing. I learned nothing new."

"Is she beautiful?" Klaus said.

"Some people would think so, but she's too skinny for my taste. To me, she looks half-starved."

"Did she love your friend?"

"She loves the house. That much I'm sure of."

"Did he love her?"

Izzy shrugged. "I knew Phil forty-two years—and you know what? I know nothing."

"It's hard to know what other people feel in their hearts," Klaus said. "We barely know our own hearts."

Wise or foolish, weak or strong? A crook, a *shnook*, a good man? What was he to make of Phil? "You never know the real story."

"Real or not, it's all we've got. That's what we're left with."

The men fell silent. Izzy got up to fetch a dish of rice pudding with whipped cream and Klaus had some Jell-O. They ate quickly, not looking up. A disk of shivering green Jell-O slipped off Klaus's spoon and landed between them. It reminded Izzy of something unpleasant, like a cesspool.

Finally he spoke up. "So when are you leaving for Berlin?"

"Soon. By the end of the month."

"You'll miss Lottie's baby."

"She'll send pictures. She'll visit me. You should come visit too. Maybe you'll change your mind about the city if you see it again."

"I'm an old man," Izzy said. "I was hoping you'd stay in Florida and come to my funeral. Now there won't be anyone there besides Sam and Eva."

"Why are you saying that? You're in a dark mood tonight."

"Go then. Goodbye and good luck."

"Come on, don't talk like that."

"We won't see each other again."

"I'll miss you," Klaus said.

Izzy stuck out his hand stiffly. "Have a good trip," he said. "Have a good life in Berlin."

Later that evening Izzy sat in his La-Z-Boy in front of the TV and watched the news. He saw pictures of men with axes, men with hammers and chisels, breaking pieces of the Wall. He saw a clip of grinning people climbing up onto the Wall, standing on a low wide section by the Brandenburg Gate, more and more of them clambering up and crowding close together; they were cheering, drinking, dancing. How can they be happy? he wondered. Can't they hear the cries of the dead—the hundreds who were shot while trying to escape the East, the millions slaughtered in the war? Why does a guilty nation rejoice while he, Izzy, huddles in shame?

He turned off the TV and took off his glasses. Squinting at the blank screen with unfocused eyes, he could almost see Klaus laughing, hugging a colorful piece of the Wall, while fellow Berliners slapped his back. Could almost hear him hollering, *Izzy, you should be here too!*

Instead of where he was, in his dark, airless living room, doing nothing, all alone. It wasn't fair that people he liked should move somewhere else. He was always losing someone.

Klaus slowly faded as another face took shape on the dappled screen of Izzy's mind. Phil. It was Phil's turn. A close-up in black and white: his round cheeks and heavy chin; every hair in focus. "What have you got to say for yourself?" Izzy wagged a finger, but his friend only stared back, grinning so hard that his childlike teeth were visible, his eyes pinched to nothing.

"You hurt as many as you helped. No wonder you were murdered!"

Phil moved back on the screen so that he appeared head to toe, wearing a good gray suit and a white shirt and knotted tie. He stretched out on his back from the left border to the right and floated rigidly, halfway up, as if he were in a magic show. "Stand up!" Izzy cried, but he grew thinner, flat and pale—a flickering image, barely there. He crossed his arms, closed his eyes: Phil was dying. Phil dead. A big, black, vacant screen.

Izzy swiped at his wet cheeks. *Get up, get up, it's not right! It never should've happened!*

It was one thing to pay for your sins with nightmares and guilt, but another thing to pay with your life. Only a few deserved that—like Hitler and his generals. Certainly not the hero of the Rudniki Forest, who did the best he could in extraordinary circumstances. Given the same opportunity, would Izzy have been as brave? Or would he have been another starving panic-stricken victim who escaped death by running away, who looked to a leader like Phil for protection?

That's what the war did: it simplified people's lives, shrank them to heroes or not, victims and villains, the dead, the survivors. Afterwards the labels stuck: Phil was one thing, Izzy another. But the whole truth of who they were and what they became was in fact unknowable—neither this nor that one but always shifting, always skewed, depending on who told the story and what was said. Sometimes they behaved well and sometimes they didn't. That was all it came to.

Yet Phil was shot and he wasn't. Where was the sense in that?

He cupped his hands over his face and tried to imagine Phil's death. Was it sudden and startling, like the unexpected sting of a wasp? Or did he glimpse his executioner standing on the factory steps in the thin light of morning? Did Phil confront him squarely, did he plant his feet, wave his arms, shout at him, stare him down? Or—was it possible—that Phil behaved badly, that he trembled and staggered with fear? Fumbled the keys to the locked door, trying in vain to get inside. Cried out in disbelief. Cringed in the face of death. Turned on his heel, tried to run . . . and was blasted in the back of the head. Died, in fact, in the usual way, as Izzy would've in his place: shitting his pants and desperate.

They were not so different after all.

Izzy put his glasses on. He got out of his chair and circled the empty rooms of the bungalow, his footsteps falling softly, as if he were treading on grass. The air conditioning puffed like a child blowing candles. He stopped by the glass door facing his back porch and gazed out at his mowed lawn. Somewhere children called out and the bell of a bicycle tinkled. He heard the whack of a bat and ball.

And suddenly he was wishing he had known Phil as a young boy. He closed his eyes and tried to picture him climbing fences, kicking cans, skipping stones on water. Neither big nor small . . . with a dark complexion, large ears, loose buttons, scabby knees, knickers, and suspenders. A rowdy boy, but kind-hearted: anything he caught in a jar he'd let go before long. He played with other children but had no one to confide in. A boy very much like the boy Izzy once was. Whose world was new, unfolding, hinting at adventures to come. Who didn't know his life would never again be as easy as this.

Fields and flowers, sky and sun. The brown, rubbery skin of boys; their arms and legs like pistons . . .

Behind his eyelids Izzy saw them flitting like a pair of moths through waist-high whispering grass, as light and transparent as wings. Barefoot, with dirty heels and scratches on their ankles, panting secrets as they ran. "Listen—listen," Izzy sputtered. *Listen, listen,* echoed back. They were blood brothers, best friends. Forever spinning in the wind.

The phone rang piercingly, so that he gasped and slapped his chest and his eyes fluttered open. For a moment he was frozen in place, caught in another time, but then he turned on a table lamp and reached for the receiver.

"It's me," he heard.

Eva. She said she tried him earlier but he didn't pick up.

"I was out with Klaus Hauptmann," he said. "He's going back to Germany. Now that the Wall's coming down he wants to live in Berlin."

"That's too bad. You liked him."

"But what can I do."

"You'll have to make new friends, join a club or something. Have you thought more about getting a dog?"

"Don't start with your clubs and pets."

"You can't just sit home by yourself."

"It's not so terrible on your own. You go over what's in your mind, you're never really alone. You hear voices, see faces, try to remember how it was."

"You can't live only in the past."

"Before you called, as a matter of fact, I was thinking about Phil . . . wondering what he was like as a boy."

"You didn't know him back then."

"But I can imagine it, can't I? A good-looking boy, I thought, but always fidgeting, out of breath. Like Sam was when he was that age. Like a puppy with a stick."

"He's a lot quieter nowadays. He watches too much TV."

"In my time there was no TV. I played outdoors, I was never still. Just like Phil, I thought."

"All boys are like that."

"That's my point!" Izzy said. "We're all more or less the same. Sometimes a little braver, sometimes a little scared . . . but not so different finally. We play, we fight, we fall in love. Our lives turn unexpectedly, we wind up here or else there, then fortune decides our fate. If I had gone to the Rudniki Forest instead of France, I might've been a hero too. If Phil didn't buy a condominium, he'd be alive today."

A pause; then the quick slight huff of Eva's breathing. "We make certain choices. It's not just a matter of luck."

"Bad luck killed him in the end as much as anything."

"You think about him too much," Eva said tersely. "It's time to forget about it, put his death behind you. It's over—no one cares anymore. Get back to your own life and let him rest in peace already. Honor him with a little silence. Stop going on and on!"

One hero's enough for her, he thought. Even a dead one. There's no room in her heart for an unremarkable father, because her heart is full of Phil.

A stone was blocking Izzy's throat; his chest was tight and hurting. He said, "I have to go now." He tried saying more but the words lodged behind his tongue.

Eva said, "I'm glad I called. I'm glad we had this little talk and now we can move on."

After Izzy hung up he stared at the receiver. It was slender and smooth as a snake, ready to bite if he touched it again—which wasn't going to happen. Enough pain for one night.

But she was right: it was over. Soon people would no longer mention Phil's brutal death; soon enough they'd stop mentioning him altogether. Even Izzy. Even him. One day he'd remember Phil as seldom as he put on a wool coat or winter suit. And Izzy was sure the same thing would happen after he died. Eva would miss him for a while and think about him often, then less and less and not at all. Like Phil, he would cease to exist. And it wouldn't matter what they did or hadn't done in their lifetimes: they'd live on in the minds of others only for a short time.

There was some comfort in that.

It was still too early to go to bed. If Izzy went to sleep now, he'd wake at five in the morning and the day would be too long. He could turn on the late news and maybe see an actual clip of Klaus Hauptmann on the Wall . . . but wasn't interested anymore. Why should he care about a man he'd never see again? Who left behind family and friends. Who wouldn't be at his funeral.

There was nothing much he felt like doing. Nothing he could picture doing tonight, tomorrow, the day after that. But he was too worn out to worry about it right now: a small blessing. He climbed into his La-Z-Boy, adjusting the chair so it straightened out and Izzy was on his back.

He must have dozed. Because when he heard a sharp knock and opened his eyes, he was tunneling out of a sweaty dream. He was thinking, *Gestapo!* He got up slowly, his side aching as if he'd been kicked. The rapping was harder now: *bang-bang, bang-bang!* Someone hitting the door or the beat of his heavy pulse.

He checked the lock on the front door and also tried the bolt on the sliding door to the back porch. Then he drew the curtains, hurried into the kitchen, shut the blind. He didn't want to see anyone, it was too late for visitors. No one with any sense would bother him now anyway, when people were getting ready for bed.

He was panting and shaky and propped his arms against the sink in an effort to steady himself. Who could it be then? What was so important that it couldn't wait till tomorrow?

He heard footsteps out back, then persistent tapping on the screen door that led to the yard. Someone could put his shoulder to the door and easily break the latch, enter the porch, smash the glass door, and be in the living room. It wouldn't take long for him to find Izzy in the kitchen, shivering like a wet dog. If he were young, he'd put up a fight—but what could he do at his age?

Maybe the prowler had a knife. Or else he had a billy club to *klop* Izzy on the head. But if he said the wrong thing or didn't have enough cash, maybe the man would strangle him or shoot him in the back of his skull. And he would die like Phil did, with two bullets in his brain. In a way this pleased him: a film of satisfaction resting on his oily fear.

He heard a shout—"Open up! Izzy, I know you're there!"—and peeked through the kitchen blind. His neighbor Pat was standing at the back door, holding a pie. He raised the blind and opened the window, heart drumming. *It's only Pat, no one else. Don't be nervous. Just Pat.*

She spotted him and rushed over, lifting the pie as high as the ledge. "I know it's late but I saw a light, I knew you weren't in bed yet. I thought you'd like some company so I brought dessert—lemon meringue."

He shook his head and shooed her away—"Sorry, sorry, no thanks, I already brushed my teeth and can't eat another thing"—flicking his wrists to hide that his hands were still quivering.

She offered to come in anyway for a minute, if he didn't mind—"A person gets hungry for a little conversation"—and said she'd even leave the pie for him to eat in the morning. But he *did* mind, he told her. He wanted to go to bed now and wasn't in the mood for talk.

She lowered the pie. "I wanted to ask about our swimming lessons," Pat said. "I was hoping we could finally start, before it gets too cold."

"It's too cold already," he said. "We'll talk about it next spring."

Her face was pinched and worried-looking. She gazed at the pie in her arms as if it were a foundling, then backed up and started home. He knew he'd hurt her feelings—but look what she did to him! He could hardly stand up anymore, his legs wiry, vibrating. Who pounds on someone's door at night like a maniac, scaring him for no reason! Good riddance to her, he thought.

His heart was hot and galloping. He only wanted to get back to his La-Z-Boy and lie down.

In the living room he turned on another lamp beside the couch, which just seemed to deepen the dark shadows crossing the floor like thick ropes unwinding. They moved quickly, startling him. They reached his ankles suddenly, circled, toughened, held him fast. They coiled up his left leg and squeezed so hard it went numb. *No feeling in my leg!* He stamped his foot: nothing.

They stretched into his eyes and ears, so that he saw black lines and heard only the static of cords rubbing against cloth.

Gottenyu! What's happening?

His head ached: they were in his brain. The ropes tightened, pulling him down, and he struggled to stay on his feet. He screamed for help—though who would hear?—and didn't even recognize the garbled sound of his own words, only the pitch of his panic. Balls of twine were in his throat. He opened his mouth to shout again... but what was the word he was looking for?

A table lamp loomed large. It was rising, tilting like a cannon, firing at his forehead. The cannonball struck hard and he fell for a long time... through carpet and underlay and a thick slab of concrete, through gravel and the soil beyond. Falling through water and bedrock, through softer matter, solid rock, a wet layer of molten metal.

At last he was thrust into the densest, blackest shadow of all—the iron heart of the earth's core.

He was wedged in place, squeezed still. There was no danger, no feeling, no possibility of wiggling out and fleeing: there was nothing here to run from. He would lie like this forever, in a silent metal berth where there was no future, no past.

For the very first time in his life, Izzy Schneider was unafraid.

Part Two

EVA

8

SHE DIDN'T KNOW WHAT TO EXPECT.

All the way from Toronto her stomach had been hard and clenched and Eva was light-headed. She couldn't even eat peanuts; only sipped water. The woman in the window seat slept through most of the flight but then woke up suddenly, wanting to talk. "Unusually warm for December," she said. "Every day in the eighties. Where are you from? Canada? You should be grateful."

The plane landed and Eva got out. The heat was like a punch in the face. Her sunglasses fogged up and she stood on the tarmac, blinded, not knowing where to turn.

Will he recognize me? she was thinking. How will I know if he does?

Moments later she followed the other passengers into the terminal and picked up her luggage. It was cool and dry in the building. She liked that, the unnatural arctic cold. Back home she liked being indoors, her nose in a book, or gazing out the window at a shake of snow: to watch the giddy dance of a single spinning snowflake. What she didn't like was stickiness. Florida humidity. She didn't like raising her arm outside the terminal to summon a taxi, only to feel her skin wet and to smell her own nervous sweat.

In the cab from the airport the driver asked, "Where to?" and she had to pause. Stop at the nursing home first, of course, and see him, but the address she gave was 720 Muddy Creek Road. Better to unwind a little before that, she told herself. Calm down. Have a shower. Wash away the perspiration dribbling between her breasts, down her back, from under her arms.

The cabbie had the windows open. She asked him to roll them up and turn on the air conditioner. "Wind messing your hair?" he said.

"I don't like the heat much."

"That's what people come here for. I'm from New York myself. Couldn't stand the winters. Everyone I know's like that—they came here to get away from somewhere cold."

She pulled off her suit jacket and leaned back in the vinyl seat. The car smelled like a stagnant pool. She was wearing loose linen pants and a short-sleeved cotton blouse but was still too warm. At last she felt cool air blowing over her arms, which erupted in goosebumps. Good, she thought. That's better.

"On vacation?"

The driver again. She didn't feel like talking, but who knew when she'd get another chance. "I came to see my father. He had a stroke."

"Real common around here. I drove a couple to Tampa this morning, they were here for the same thing. The old guy was ninety so you can't feel too bad. It's not like if it was a kid."

"My dad's seventy-eight." Old enough for things to go wrong.

"Some of these guys they bounce back a few months later good as new, walking, talking, everything. You'd never know they had a stroke. Miracles happen all the time. I have a good friend, George, he works in a funeral home. A while ago he totalled his car and after the crash he couldn't move, couldn't speak or think straight. They told his wife he'd never survive so she made plans to bury him. Except that he wouldn't die. One day he got up and now he's back at work arranging other people's funerals."

Eva stared out the window. Palm trees and pelicans. Flashes of oily blue water. Bright sails here and there. Identical little white homes with screened-in porches and scrubby lawns, shiny cars in the driveway. Was Izzy going to sit up, swing out of his hospital bed—*Glad that's over with!*—and jog back to his bungalow? Cruise the Gulf in a speedboat?

Aphasia, the doctor said on the phone. And hemiplegia, right side. She'd had to look the words up before she understood completely. Can't speak. One half of him can't move. No extraordinary measures to keep him alive, she'd said. That's how he'd want it. What all guilty relatives say: *We did what he would've wanted.*

"Speaking of miracles, look at me. My fourth kidney transplant. My wife's got cirrhosis, she's waiting for a new liver. My brother's getting an eye operation in a few weeks. That's the way it goes here. Everyone I know has something wrong that needs fixing."

Fix his tongue, an arm, a leg, the right side of his body. And how much of her father's brain? *Will he understand a word I say?*

"But at least we're still breathing, right? No matter what, we're still alive. My wife lost her mother two years ago, it was terrible. At least she went quickly though, she suffered a heart attack. One-two-three."

The way it was for Phil too: over fast, one-two. Immediate loss of consciousness. No lingering, half paralyzed; no pain. No need for anyone to see him in a reduced state and struggle to remember him as he once was.

Better than dying bit by bit, little by little, drips and drabs. Hanging IV sacs, oxygen tanks, feeding tubes. Would Izzy smooth his hospital gown and sit up? Would he nod, look her squarely in the eye, make contact? Take her shaky fingers in his left hand, the good one, and let her know through strokes and squeezes he was still there?

". . . except we were in New York at the time. She was looking after our place. We came home and found her on the sofa, she was five days dead. I knew by the smell before I opened the door."

Smell? Yes, that too. His useless body will smell bad. Rotting flesh, urine, feces—odors she has always known. Not in fact, but in her mind: what she has imagined. The stench of a cattle car, sniff of gas. The choking stink of corpses. All of it vividly recreated from hidden photos found in a drawer; a film clip on TV; history books with pictures; a stray word or grim look exchanged between her parents—none of this meant for Eva to see or hear or fret about, because she was supposed to grow up happy and carefree. She wasn't supposed to know about the war till she was older. She wasn't supposed to feel the twanging stillness in the room when she interrupted her parents' talk. But she did see and hear and feel. She did know. Her eyes would sting, her nose run at unexpected moments, and sometimes she would gag on her food. "Eat your supper," Hilda scolded. "Why aren't you eating?" *Because*, she never told her mother. *Because of what I see and smell—what I am thinking.*

"It was pretty awful," the driver said. "She was bloated so bad that her face stuck to her glasses and her hair was glued to the sofa. After they took her away we went to throw the couch out, but when we picked it up, it was so full of fluids that it dripped all over the rug and we had to toss that too."

She dropped her head back on the seat. The roof of the cab was turning slowly, like a ceiling fan, and she felt a little queasy. Who knew what she'd find in the health care center, what swollen, leaky bodies?

"You okay?" the driver asked, glancing in the rearview mirror.

"Tired," she said, "and carsick." Two possibilities were better than one.

Suddenly he was pointing at an intersection—"Look at that!" The car swerved and her seat belt tightened across her chest. She imagined the taxi veering into a ditch and rolling over, finally landing on its roof, wheels turning in the air, a fatally wounded animal. She imagined herself wedged between twisted metal and split vinyl, feeling pain, wetness, heat. Broken bones, torn flesh. Blood on her white blouse, crisp and fresh just hours ago.

"Glass all over the road," said the cabbie. "Had to avoid it. Sorry if I scared you."

"No," she said. "I'm just fine."

"There must of been an accident. This highway's famous for that. People go drinking Friday nights, they get in their cars and slam into each other at three in the morning. Every weekend the count goes up but nothing ever changes."

"I'm fine," said Eva. "Really I am. Maybe just a little sick."

The first thing she noticed when she entered the bungalow was the gray gloom. Particles of darkness, like dust motes, throughout the rooms. Blinds were closed, curtains drawn, as if night had permanently moved in. As if she were a girl again, eating dinner with her parents, the kitchen window blacked out by drapes and a venetian blind. So the neighbors couldn't see in and envy them their good food. To keep away the evil eye, *kayn aynhoreh*. Staring down at her plate, where a fried egg stared back, the demon eye turning the morsels in her mouth sour.

"Eat already," Hilda would nag. "Children in Europe are starving." And Eva would automatically think, Camps ghettos gas chambers: children in Europe are dying.

Her throat was dry, her eyes wide open. Eva didn't like being alone in the bungalow. That childhood fear of unspeakable things happening in the dark. "Daddy!" she used to cry out when she woke from a bad dream of chase scenes and monsters. "Daddy, hurry, save me!" And he would sit at the side of her bed, holding her small hand until she fell asleep again, safe and protected.

Nightmares happened, or even worse. Suffocation. Sudden death. People got out of bed groping, clutched their chests, or had strokes, they fell hard against the floor and lay there gasping for breath, their limbs going rubbery-numb, shouting until they lost words, shutting down, their brains shrinking, cell by cell, hour by hour, till someone found them near-dead or already gone.

She felt it, his withering—what her father would've gone through: his disengagement from the world. Weakness in her arms and legs, her mind unfocused and her heart thudding against her ribs. She felt his panic rising, circling the coils of her brain. *I'm dying!* he would've thought as he lay on the floor choking, no one there to save him. For several minutes—maybe hours—he would've known.

Get out of here! she told herself. No use staying. It'll only make you feel worse.

But she didn't leave. The plan was to stay in the house, drive his car, tidy up, pack some of her father's things, and go through his papers. She paced around the living room, breathing deliberately, counting out loud as she inhaled and exhaled, her mind stitched to numbers . . . And soon she was quieter. She thought, I can handle this. Her legs felt strong again. She marched through the bungalow yanking back heavy curtains, snapping open dusty blinds.

She carried her bags to the guest room. The master bedroom was bigger, with a bathroom ensuite, but how could she sleep in her father's bed? His thoughts and dreams and murmurings still locked in the pillows. His scent on the sheets and his shape impressed on the mattress. Footprints forever stamped in the thick beige carpet.

A room too noisy to sleep in. The echo of goose steps, clatter of trains. The cries, screams, pleading, and prayers of the victims. "*Shah!*" Izzy would silence his wife. "She shouldn't hear us talking. A child shouldn't know these things." But Eva, hiding behind the sofa, heard it all.

The guest room the only choice. It doubled as her father's study, furnished with a metal chair and large, stern, wooden desk; a portable TV on a rickety-looking cabinet; a black vinyl chesterfield; an end table and jumbo lamp. She spied a key ring on the desk and put it in her pocket.

Everything was covered with dust. As soon as Eva opened her luggage and put on a T-shirt and shorts, she started sneezing. Not just dust but mildew was tickling her nasal passages; it was settled on the furniture and blowing through the house in the stale air-conditioned air, not a whiff of anything fresh from outside for weeks now. Who knew what germs were proliferating in the filter, which probably hadn't been changed in years. She thought of Legionnaire's disease as she sniffed and sneezed and wrinkled her nose against the smell of something plastic, chemical, and moldy.

The bathroom between the bedrooms was tiled and apparently clean, except for woolly streaks of fungi around the tub. Eva found a bucket, a rag, a bottle of liquid cleanser, and set about scrubbing the guest room. After washing the chesterfield, she removed the cushions and pulled out a thin, curved mattress she knew well from previous visits. Restless, uncomfortable nights: springs poking her back and the drone of traffic outside; the pendulum clock in the dining room that bonged the hour every hour; the air conditioning off at night, regardless of the weather and Eva's preference, so Izzy could save a few cents. "It's too stuffy," she'd pleaded. "I can't sleep. Turn it on low at least. I came all this way to see you..."

But he wasn't moved. He said he got chilly at night. "Then use a blanket!" Eva cried, but he answered no. A pouty no. Their eyes locked and glaring. Izzy's house, Izzy's rules. He wasn't going to change his ways for her or for anyone else. Well, except for Hilda, if she were alive and asked nicely, something Eva could never do. Why give in to him when he was acting like a rude child?

He would've turned the furnace on in a heat wave to please his wife, but not for his daughter.

There was a Hoover in the closet. While vacuuming under the bed she spotted a dead gecko in the threads of the carpet. Dried up and skeletal, it startled her and she cried out. Like finding bones in a dungeon; a body dead from starvation or some horrible wasting disease. Quickly she aimed the nozzle and sucked the carcass into the hose. There were more ghosts in these rooms than even she could imagine.

Holding her rag, she pushed the vacuum forward, like a sentry, into the master bedroom and left it standing by the door. She circled Izzy's king-size bed and wiped the headboard clean. Phil had a bed like this in his condo apartment. Firm mattress because of his back, which flared up now and then despite the fact that he worked out and swam laps regularly. If you stood by his bedroom window, opened the shutter and craned your neck, you could glimpse a blue wedge of the Gulf. Cool blue water, the color of possibility. Her body filled with blue light, her fingers shooting blue rays. Sometimes he would put his hand on the back of her neck as she stood there, massaging with his large fingers, writing a message of devotion on her neon skin.

You're very special to me, do you know that?

Say it again.

She sat down on her father's bed and bounced. It was also firm. A dust ball shivered near her foot. When she looked up and through his window, the view was of a chain-link fence and a yellow lawn, the grass thick and too high. She would have to see about getting it cut.

Which side of the bed had he slept on, she wondered, the one nearest the door or the half that was closest to his ensuite bathroom? The bathroom side, she decided. She walked into the tiny room, the counters covered with pill bottles and toiletries, all in rows. A wooden rack for drying clothes was open in the shower stall, a single pair of unmatched socks hanging over a bar. The grout between the tiles of the stall was green and furry. The room spoke of solitude, age, and infirmity. A man without a woman looking after his home and laundry. Eva's eyes were suddenly wet. Looking around his dirty bathroom, she could forgive him anything.

Back in the bedroom she dusted the blond dresser, the wardrobe, and end tables. Her father had been proud of his five-piece bedroom set, which he'd bought with Hilda years ago and shipped to Florida after her death. Once he told Eva that when he ran his hand over the smooth, polished wood he would think of his wife's perfect skin.

She had her mother's thick wavy hair and appealing mouth, but not her pale, flawless skin. Here and there her face bore the faint acne scars of her youth, a time when she'd kept to herself, festering in the cell of her room, because it was easier than being snubbed by her schoolmates, who dressed better, were outgoing, had boyfriends and dates for the prom. Not that a passerby would notice the scars today. You had to look closely. Phil had touched them gently once and said that her imperfections made her beauty more profound. Like Rivke, his first love, who had a mark across her jaw where someone slashed her with a knife.

She turned on the Hoover and pushed it over the carpet. It bumped against something hard when she poked the nozzle under the bed. She got on her knees to investigate and pulled out a billy club. So this is where her father slept—on the door side of the wide bed, a nightstick close at hand to protect him from who knows what. Robbers, vandals, or his own phantom visitors.

At home in her own bedroom Eva dreamed of burglars too. They smashed through the apartment windows, wearing masks and black boots, carrying knives and pistols; her mattress dotted with shards of glass, pearls of blood. Sometimes she would lie still, hoping they would just take the TV and jewelry and leave her be. Sometimes she would try to escape, race for the door or dive through a window, hide in a closet, under the bed. If Sam was in the dream, they would run together, holding hands. But sooner or later they'd be caught, their arms wrenched behind their backs, hands and feet tied to chairs. Then maybe she would act boldly and snap the ropes that bound her, free her son and lead them away—flush with the strength of a mother whose child is in danger.

Once, when she woke yelling because the ropes wouldn't give, Phil was there beside her. He held her, kissed her, stroked her hair. "Shush," he said, "it's okay, I'm right here, you're safe now." And she was. The dream faded: it rose and thinned to nothing, like steam from a cup of hot tea.

There was something under her father's pillow when she fluffed it—a thin white pamphlet. *The Lord Loves You Perfectly* it shouted in bold print. She flipped through the pages, put it back: it was all about salvation through Jesus Christ. What was Izzy doing with that? An unlikely candidate for an eleventh-hour conversion. Did he use it like a rabbit's foot—trying to increase his chances of dying with dignity in his sleep? If so, he wasn't loved as perfectly as he had hoped.

Eva left her father's room. She dusted and vacuumed the rest of the house, saving the kitchen for last. Here the only window was broken and boarded up, probably from a recent storm. When she turned on the overhead light the room was a stark square of white planes, skewed shadows. The cupboards were mostly bare: a few cans of heat-and-serve soup, a box of crackers. The fridge had frozen TV dinners, cans of pop, a bottle of juice, two English muffins, and a wedge of cheese gone bad. She poured the juice down the sink, then tossed the bottle, muffins, and cheese into a garbage can beside the kitchen table, a small formica-and-chrome stand with one plastic placemat and a cut-glass shaker of coagulated salt on top.

A calendar above the table was still turned to December, showing a curling picture of a green-eyed girl in pigtails hugging a golden-haired dog. Eva had always wanted a dog—and who needed one more than a lonely, timid only child?—but Hilda wouldn't allow it. She insisted pets were too much trouble, they ruined the furniture, soiled the rugs, demanded attention. Izzy might've gotten her one—he argued that a dog would teach her to be more responsible—but in the end he bowed to the will of his wife.

She tore off the final sheet from the calendar, so that there were no more days and months, as if time had run out. Overhead, the young blonde was heedless of the blank square, her lips still pointed at the dog's ear. Had Izzy talked to her daily as he ate his solitary meals? Did he wish he'd fathered a child like that instead of the one he got, a serious girl with brown eyes? Why wouldn't he? Eva thought. Didn't everyone want a family of easygoing children and a simple life?

What we went through, your mother and I . . . the hardship and persecution. You should never know a life like that—only a good one—and God willing, you never will.

And hadn't Eva wanted as much—joyful parents and a happy-go-lucky girlhood?

A locked door stood firmly between the kitchen and garage. Eva found the proper key from the ring in her pocket and opened the door. His car, a fairly new Buick, took up most of the space, but she also saw a washer and dryer, storage shelves, an unused freezer, cardboard boxes, and a hill of plastic bags from a supermarket. She pressed a button on the wall to open the garage door. Heat and sunlight poured in, making her flinch.

She picked out the car keys, opened the door on the driver's side, got in, and started the Buick. The engine turned over at once, which was lucky, and she backed the car onto the drive. She sat there, letting it idle, and turned on the air conditioner. A hot burst of rancid air came through the vents as she buzzed open the car windows, letting it out. When the air cooled she closed the windows, crossed her arms, and gazed at the gaping mouth of the empty garage.

She should drive to the health center. Get it over with. Do it now. Fretting about it had to be worse than actually going there. She would stay only a short time for this, her first visit: it was such a busy, tiring day. Stop somewhere for a quick lunch. Buy a map, a tank of gas. Pick up milk and bread and other groceries on the way back.

She went inside to get her purse, then out through the front door, locking it behind her. Back in the car she found a remote and closed the garage door. Someone tapped on the side window. Eva jumped in her seat and turned.

An old woman wearing a preposterous coolie hat was grinning at her through the glass. She rapped again and Eva opened her window partway. "I'm Pat," the woman said, "Izzy's next-door neighbor. You must be his daughter."

"Nice to meet you," Eva said.

"How's the poor man doing?"

"I'm on my way to see him now."

"I was the one who phoned the cops. When I didn't see his blinds go up and he didn't take out his garbage, I guessed something wasn't right. They came in a jiffy too. Everything was locked up so they had to break the kitchen window to get inside. They found him on the living-room floor, a big bruise on his forehead. Some furniture was knocked over, a lamp and a table. They think he must of hit his head hard on the way down."

"How long...?"

"At least overnight, I'd say, but maybe since the morning before. A day and night and then some, is my guess. Lying there in his own filth, the poor thing. He shouldn't of been alone like that. If someone was there, they could of called an ambulance right away and he'd be better off today."

"He liked being independent. His health was fine, as far as we knew."

"He promised to give me swimming lessons but never did, I don't know why. Once or twice I brought him a pie—I thought he'd appreciate a bit of home baking—but he didn't want my company on a regular basis. Mostly he kept to himself, that's the way he liked it. A real shame, if you ask me—a widow and widower living next door to each other, two lonely people and all. He told such interesting stories too—about growing up in Berlin, before the Nazis came to power, and what it was like after..."

"I have to go now," Eva said, buzzing up her window. She gave the neighbor a slight wave, then backed up the car and turned it onto the road.

"Have a good visit!" Pat called. "Tell him I said hello."

The health care center was a thirty-five-minute drive north on U.S. 19, then east on a side road. It appeared quite suddenly in a treeless, grassy area, a collection of long, low buildings with pointy roofs. The sky was pale and seemed close, like a palm pressing the squat structures into the ground. Eva circled the complex, half inclined to turn back, but finally drove through the main gates.

The parking lot was crowded and she had to search awhile before finding a spot by the red-carpeted entrance. She got out, locked the car, walked under a portico, past a discreet sign announcing "Reception," and into the building. She stopped in the air-conditioned lobby and looked around. The walls were freshly papered in a bold design of leaves and flowers, a floral border at the top. In the middle of the hall was a circular reception desk, no one there. Close by, a bulletin board announced various entertainments: bingo at three p.m.; Peter Piper's Piano at noon; Magic Tricks with Marty and Mindy after breakfast.

If her father truly knew where he was, and if he could talk, he'd be yelling, "Get me out of here! Peter Piper, Marty and Mindy— what kind of joke is this?"

There were glass-enclosed rooms on all sides, each identified by a plaque beside the doorway. The one with striped wallpaper and dark mahogany furniture was labeled DINING ROOM. The EXERCISE ROOM had weights and mats, a stationary bicycle and parallel bars, and was painted cheery yellow. ARTS AND CRAFTS, a green room, had a long table and plastic chairs. A room with puffy sofa cushions covered in flowered chintz was called LOUNGE. A few slumped and shriveled men were sitting in wheelchairs in a row outside the lounge, but the room itself was empty, as were all the others, like abandoned movie sets.

She strode past the crippled men to a room at the end of the hall that was actually full: TV ROOM. Lopsided men and women in wheelchairs or armchairs stared at a TV, out the picture windows, or at nothing at all. No two were close together. No one spoke to anyone else. Only the chipper voice of a TV forecaster announcing the weather: "Unseasonably mild today, tomorrow, and Wednesday . . ." She peered through the glass wall at the old slack faces, expecting to find Izzy, but he wasn't there.

His room was in A Wing, number 132, the rehab part of the center. But instead of going directly there, she followed the signs to B, C, and D wings, the chronic-care sections. The walls were papered here too, though the pattern was faded. A faint smell of feces. Patients lay in tiny rooms, mumbling or groaning. A few were standing, rounded like question marks, or shuffling about in disposable slippers. Skinny arms and skinny legs, their bones showing through papery skin. Attendants were busily mopping floors, but still the corridor stank of urine and antiseptic. He could wind up here, she thought, staring at cracks in the ceiling, shitting in his pajamas. She would have to visit Izzy here, in B, C, or D Wing, breathing the stench of decay, smiling encouragingly, and making pleasant small talk. But not yet. *Not yet.* Miracles happened. She hurried down the aisle in the direction of A Wing.

Here the rooms were larger and the air seemed perfumed, as if the bright corridor had been recently sprayed with "Rosebud" or "Apple Blossom" freshener. Flowers. She should've brought flowers. A big sweet-smelling bouquet to make her entrance easier. *Look what I got for you. Don't they smell wonderful?*

She paused outside her father's room, tweaking her mouth into a grin. Her legs were unsteady, her breathing quick. *You look fine,* she'll say, whether he does or not. Kiss his cheek. A quick hug. *Are you comfortable? Do you like it here?* Yes or no questions only. Maybe he can nod his head. Maybe he can shake her hand, at least with the left one. *You still have a good grip. Strong as ever. Yessiree!*

She entered room 132, her heart beating so hard she thought he would hear it. There were two dressers, two chairs, two TVs, and two beds, both dismayingly empty. Had he made a miraculous recovery and walked out? The room had a large window next to one of the narrow beds: had he slipped out that way? Knotted sheets and blankets and dropped onto the lawn below?

Her father was in no shape for a getaway.

It was a well-lit, clean room, but spartan nevertheless. Impersonal. Blandly beige. Flowers would have helped a lot, as well as an assortment of family photographs. Framed pictures of her and Sam, of Izzy and Hilda, could be seen on nearly every flat surface in the bungalow. Everyone posed and smiling, their eyes and mouths turned up in counterfeit cheeriness. She should've brought a handful of those.

She sat down on a gray metal chair by the window. Maybe he went to the bathroom or something. Maybe he'd be right back. Any minute now, she thought, he'll walk in and scold her: *What are you doing sitting here? Why didn't you look for me or ask a nurse?—she'd know.* Not her post-stroke father, not the one who couldn't talk, but a stronger, healthier Izzy who was flush with annoyance. The way he was the last time she saw him in Toronto, when they argued about everything. Before the police phoned. Before she spoke to his neighbor Pat. Before he spent a day and night or longer on the living-room floor.

So where were you when I needed you? If someone got to me sooner, I wouldn't be like this now.

"I came here as soon as I heard!"

She realized she'd spoken aloud. Embarrassed, she glanced around, then got to her feet and paced back and forth between the two beds.

As soon as I knew—the next flight! Would you have done that for me?

Eva walked out of the room and headed to Reception. A nurse was behind the desk. "I'm looking for Isidor Schneider," she said. "A Wing, 132. He's not in his room. Do you know where I can find him?"

"Izzy? Right behind you."

She turned slowly: the row of decrepit men in wheelchairs in front of the lounge. She passed right by before and didn't even notice him—barely recognized him now. The man on the end was her father. A twitching half-collapsed gnome. She walked up to his chair and stared.

Daddy, is that you?

His hair was uncombed, standing straight out in white tufts. He didn't have his teeth in so the lower part of his face was sunken, the rest gaunt and bony. His nose a large, sharp shelf thrusting forward like a figurehead on the prow of a ship. His thin, useless right arm propped on a pillow. With his good hand he plucked at his loosely tied hospital gown, so that it rose up to reveal part of his diaper. His belly was bloated and his legs were sticks. His right foot was purple-tinged, the toenails of both feet yellow and hooked like talons. But his eyes were still familiar, sky blue and gleaming. You'd think he was happy with his fate.

She bent way over so that her gaze met his. There was light in his eyes, intelligence—Eva was almost sure of it. He shrugged and pointed a finger as if he were about to speak. But didn't speak. Couldn't speak. Then he smirked, aimed his finger, moved his jaw from side to side, and half smiled: a jumble of ordinary motions she couldn't read. "Hello, Dad. It's Eva."

Teeth out. Lips cracked. Mouth a hole. No words. *Where oh where has my daddy gone?*

The long humiliation of a slow death.

He ran through his gestures another time. He'd always been an expressive man who moved his hands and face when he talked. What was he trying to tell her now? She took his left hand, squeezing gently, and he squeezed back. He stroked her fingers over and over with his working thumb.

"Remember that game where we hooked our fingers together and you tried to catch my thumb and pin it down with your thumb—then I tried to capture yours?"

His face moved as if he were grinding his teeth. Guttural sounds rose from his throat and softened to purring.

"Remember?" she pleaded. "The times we played and had fun? At the zoo? In the park?" Though it seemed as if she'd be the only one remembering from now on.

He held onto her hand as his eyes shifted to one side. What was he gazing at? A bright light? An attendant? "Look at me, over here"—trying to win his attention. "It's Eva."

A young woman came by to push Izzy back to his room. "I'm his daughter," Eva said. "I just flew in from Canada."

The nurse wore a name tag, MELODY, and spoke robustly. "Well, he's having a good day. We got him to sit up. Thought I'd wheel him out of his room for a change of scenery."

A good day? Is that what she said? This was what her father was like on a *good* day?

Eva followed Izzy and the young attendant slowly, from a distance, back to A Wing. When she entered his room again Izzy was on the bed by the window, rolled onto his left side. Melody, wearing rubber gloves, was tugging at his diaper. "Let's have a peek," she said, and Eva felt her stomach rise. She looked away immediately but couldn't keep from picturing the flat, dirty cheeks of his bum, his limp and shriveled penis.

Can't even wipe his own ass.

"All clean," said Melody. When she set him on his back again he raised his good hand toward the window and pawed the air, his eyes looking past his fingers. An indefinite gesture. "He was doing that this morning," said Melody.

"What does it mean?"

"I've seen other patients do it. The ones who can still speak tell me what they're doing is they're talking to angels. Three of them bunched together. They all see the same thing, three floating angels, and they reach out to touch them. That's what your dad's doing, talking to the angels."

When Melody finally left them alone, Eva pulled a chair close and leaned over the bed rail. "No you're not," she told Izzy. "You don't believe in angels and devils or the Son of God. You're too caught up in this world to worry about the next one. You only care about what was, not what's going to happen."

She picked up his hand again, but his eyes stayed fixed on the window behind her head. Her father's strong, dry hand. She pressed it; he pressed back. He was always proud of the strength of his grip. When introduced to a man or boy, he'd say, "Go on, squeeze my hand. Squeeze it as hard as you can." Then he'd wince in mock pain. "Now let me squeeze yours . . ." At one time he'd squeeze so hard a youngster would cry for him to stop and even a grown man might say, "Jeez, cut it out already, I've had enough—let go." In his old age, men and boys alike would simply humor him: "Hey, that's some grip you've got," then smirk when his back was turned. It would tear her heart to see that. As though they were destroying the pride she'd felt for him as a girl. Ruining her memories of a strong and fearless daddy who'd protect her from bad men.

"You've still got a strong grip," she said to him now. He glanced at her and smiled and she believed he had understood. That he could remember a few things. Speechless, immobile, he could still play fragments of the films of his life on the blank, white screen of his mind.

They weren't alone for long before a speech therapist walked in. The tag on her smock said BRENDA. She sat across from Eva and close to Izzy's right side, arranging equipment on a tray. Eva introduced herself as Brenda swabbed Izzy's lips and the toothless cavity of his mouth. "His palette collapsed onto his tongue," Brenda said buoyantly, as if this were a good thing, "but we're going to work with that. We're going to try to teach him to swallow again, using ice, and get him off that feeding tube. Then we want to teach him to nod his head yes or no"—saying the words loudly and moving Izzy's head firmly up and down, side to side.

Can't swallow his own food. Can't answer yes or no.

"When you talk to him," Brenda said, "ask simple questions and move his head like I did, yes or no."

No, she wouldn't be part of this. She wouldn't feed him, shake his head, or change his dirty diapers, humiliate him further in any

way. She was not here to teach him to swallow or speak his mind.
She was here because she had to be, for his sake and her own. To
say whatever she had to say.

But not today. She was tired now, half stunned. "I have to go,"
Eva said. The therapist paused and stepped back while Eva lowered her face in the direction of her father's head, the pale, freckled, flaky skin. Her intention was to kiss his lips, but her nose
touched his forehead instead and she settled for that. "Goodbye
for now. See you tomorrow."

He gurgled something in reply. "Love you too," she whispered,
though he hadn't said those words. Has never said he loves her.
Has always been too busy loving the dead.

She hurried down the corridor, through the lobby and outside.
She stood under the portico, in the only block of visible shade,
breathing the syrupy air. Waiting for her breath to slow; her face
crinkled, itchy and wet. She was sweating again. Hot and sweaty.
No, she was crying.

———————

She drove to a gas station, filled the tank, bought a map. Her intention was to head back to Bay Point immediately, but instead she
found herself going in the opposite direction, toward Phil's condo.
Phil's *former* condo. All of a sudden she needed to see those windows and stuccoed walls. To look up at his balcony, where they
sometimes ate breakfast if they got out of bed at a decent hour and
it wasn't yet too hot, the sun still tiptoeing on the horizon. Where
they fed each other strawberries and slices of tangerine and laughed
at the stains on their matching silk kimonos. His eyes the purple-
blue of grapes; his cheeks cherry-red with the flush of delight. With
pleasure. What she wasn't used to seeing in a man's face.

"When did you fall in love with me?" she asked one morning
over coffee and croissants, and Phil recalled one of the afternoons

she spoke to him about her problems with Roger. They were eating fish and chips, he said, in a diner near the factory. Her lips were trembling, shiny with grease. Her hair flopped over her face and she flicked it away again and again in a nervous, delicate gesture. When she glanced up, her eyes were sad and hopeful at the same time. "That was the moment," he said. "My heart blew up, I couldn't breathe. Because"—shaking his head—"I was shamefully in love with my friend's daughter, my son's wife."

"That was the first time you told me you loved me."

But she had loved him before that—oh, years and years before!—when she was still unmarried, a teenager fervently wishing Phil had been her father instead of the one she got. Because he was taller than Izzy, muscular and sexy. Because he was the boss and not an ass-licking worker. Because he laughed heartily, with lightness and joy, and he spoke without an accent. Because if she was Phil's daughter, no one at school would've dared push Eva around, say mean things to her, or whisper behind her back. Because he was a hero, untroubled by self-reproach—who paid attention to Eva because she was *like herself*, not the incarnation of someone martyred in the war.

Sometimes when he came to the house to drive Izzy somewhere, she'd gaze at him from the across the hall—his handsome face and merry eyes, his big hands with delicate wrists—and could almost feel his mouth on hers, his fingers on her bare skin. "Hi there!" he'd call to her, Izzy's *shayne maidel*, such a pretty girl you got there, she's going to drive the boys crazy one day, wait and see. "Look how nice she's growing," he'd say, or "Such lovely hair she has," reaching out to pat her head. Never imagining those hot heaving nights when she shoved her pillow between her thighs, pretending he was in her bed. Never guessing how much she longed for him, even then.

Eva shook her head clear and drove quickly along the Gulf, one huge apartment building crowding the next. Here and there a palm tree, a patch of thick, weedless lawn, unnaturally green. The sky and water pale blue, one running into the next, as if the sea had risen or the heavens collapsed.

An hour later she parked her car in front of Phil's building and followed someone inside before the security door clicked shut. She walked down a flight of stairs to the basement gym, which was empty. Machines for building arm muscles, leg muscles, back muscles, abs, pecs, glutes—he had used them all. The first time she'd seen him in the nude he was fifty-seven (she nearly twenty years younger than he was), but still he looked better than his son, who was thirty-two, small, slight, and flabby.

Phil was always well built, proud of his body, proud of hers. He loved it when they lay close, her breasts flattened against his chest. He loved her hips and plump *tochis*, strong thighs, round knees, her small ankles and long toes, the mole on her shoulder. Describing every part of her as he moved his hands here and there. Flaming under his touch as if he were dropping lit matches on her naked flesh.

Eva sat down on a stationary bicycle and pedaled hard. Round and round, with difficulty, that's how their affair went. Start, stop, start again. *We should—We can't—We have to!*

That time in the diner when he put his hand over hers and said that he loved her, her hand on the table like a turtle shivering under its shell: that was the true beginning, what she'd been waiting nearly twenty-five years for. Through Rachel and Irene and other women in between . . . all the years she thought he never noticed she had grown up and become a passionate woman—no longer Izzy's little daughter to smile at and ask at a Christmas party if she was having a good time. He never guessed she finally agreed to marry Roger because she couldn't have him. Never guessed that one day the young lady he admired but didn't want his son to wed would bobble his own heart and stop his breath.

"You remind me of someone," Phil had said, his eyes filmy, turned back; her knuckles burrowing into his palm. "A girl I knew who died in the Rudniki Forest." Her fish and chips, cold by then, had darkened and flattened. There were coins on the diner table, crumpled dirty napkins, and a thin trail of glistening oil.

The war! Eva understood. Someone he lost in the war. Someone important to him. Camp ghetto corpses: the unruly ghosts of the dead were living in him too. *He's thinking of somebody else when he looks at me—just like Izzy!*

"What about me?" she said, pulling her hand back. "If you don't love me for who I am, you don't really love me at all."

"I do"—grabbing her hand again and squeezing till she cried out. "It's you I want. Only you."

"Why should I believe that?"

"Because it's true—I love you. Let me show you how much."

Wild beating in her ears as he pulled her suddenly to her feet, his fingers on her elbow leading her, steadying her, and drove to the nearest motel. "You," he insisted. "Just you."

Fully dressed, they lay on a bed and he kissed and rubbed her through her clothes. Minutes, hours—who could tell? It went on for so long. *What do you like? Do you like this?* Until the floor bucked and the ceiling spun like a whirligig. Until she was whimpering, grabbing his zipper. Until she threw her skirt up and hooked her legs around his waist, every nerve humming.

And still he waited, unhurried, one button at a time. He licked, pinched, bit, squeezed: *Beautiful, you're beautiful . . .* His warm breath, kinky hair; her pink, wet, sweaty skin. One nipple, then the other. This thigh and that thigh. A crease, a fold, a knob of flesh. *Like satin . . . like velvet.* Until she rolled her eyes up and years of hoarded fantasies exploded behind the lids. And when he finally entered her she had already slipped to another place: half conscious, dumb with joy.

But later she was sick with guilt. "Oh, Phil! What did we do?"

He pushed the heels of his hands up his face, chin to forehead. "What if Roger finds out? He'll ruin me just to get even."

Roger, Izzy, Sam! They would call them monsters, criminals, and never speak to them again. They'd rail and swear and smash things: God in heaven, look what they did! It's sinful—incestuous! A wife, mother, and daughter! A father and grandfather, business-man, trusted friend!

"We can't let this happen again."

And yet it did. It happened. Father-in-law and daughter-in-law, they'd see each other now and then—it couldn't be avoided—at business functions, get-togethers, holidays, and birthday parties. Like, for example, the one for Sam when he turned nine: a tumble of children playing Telephone and Treasure Hunt and Pin the Tail on the Donkey.

Roger was doing the blindfolding, urgently spinning boys and girls while Eva served pizza, and Phil, with his arms crossed, standing to one side, watched her every movement. Sometimes they would accidentally brush against each other, their clothes touching, or maybe their hands, or else they'd exchange a look, a half-heard muttered word, and suddenly she would feel sparks—a burning stinging fierce current—whatever it is that flits and twists between two thwarted lovers caught in the same room. The passion and frenzy she had never known with Roger. A rush and bubbling of her blood. A prickly memory of rapture and stillness, of tenderness and safety that made her want to cry out. So that when it was time for Sam to blow out the candles on his cake, she sang "Happy birthday to you" loudly and plaintively, with unex-pected feeling.

And then they'd have to meet again. Dear God, forgive us! Impossible not to hold each other and breathe into each other's mouths one more time. Just once! To join bodies, roar with pleas-ure. One more time. A last time. Oh please, another time! And once more after that. And again, yet again . . .

Always sneaking, secretive. Driving for hours to dine in an out-of-the-way restaurant, listen to music, slow dance. Plotting to share a sleeper on a train, a suite in a hotel. Lying to Roger so often that finally she never flinched, her face as smooth as a starched shirt—though her stomach knotted every time and she learned to avert her eyes. "Sorry, I'll be home late, another meeting," she would say. Or else that she was staying overnight at Allison's cottage.

"But what if Roger finds out?" Phil would ask again and again.

"He won't. He doesn't have a clue."

He didn't know about them, but Roger knew something. He sensed something wasn't right. His wife was cooler, absent-minded, irritable with Sam, and away from home too many nights. And all of a sudden nervous in bed—embarrassed and impatient. "Don't touch me," Eva would say. "I don't feel like being touched. Just do it, hurry up." Where once upon a time she would coax him to take it easy, go slow, enjoy the ride; wait for her to catch up.

"What's wrong?" Roger finally asked. "Are you tired of me?"

"No."

"What is it?"

"Nothing's wrong."

But Roger wasn't easily fooled. He must have been watching her carefully—the way her eyes unfocused and her cheeks suddenly turned red for no apparent reason. The way she smiled and spoke to herself in an empty room. "You're cheating on me," Roger said. "You're screwing around."

"I'm not," she lied.

"I know what I know."

"There's nothing to know."

"Stupid bitch, slut, cunt!"—punching the air with his fists. "Who is it? Tell me who!"

"There's nothing to tell."

And then he screamed the names of men she scarcely knew or cared about, never once mentioning the only name that mattered.

"It's no one. You're dead wrong."

At first he threatened to talk to Izzy, then he swore he'd tell Sam his mother was a lying whore. She begged him not to involve their son, only a ten-year-old who couldn't possibly understand, and in the end Roger simply filed for divorce, nothing more. No one confided in Izzy, and Sam was told that Mommy and Daddy couldn't get along anymore but still loved him dearly. Then from out of nowhere Loreen appeared to comfort Roger, lend an ear, calm him down. She must have been waiting in the wings all along, encouraging him to ditch his wife. He must've been looking for any excuse.

Phil was away at the time, spending several months at his condo apartment. So Eva flew to Florida for her own consolation. "Roger and I are getting divorced"—throwing herself against him.

"Does he know about us?"

"He knows nothing. Now we can marry at last."

"Marry?" said Phil, shaking loose. "How would that look? My grandchild becomes my son—my son becomes my enemy? I know Roger, he'd fix us both. And what about Izzy? Think what it would do to him, his daughter and her father-in-law—supposedly his best friend—standing under the *chuppah* exchanging vows!"

What about Izzy, indeed? For a man obsessed with evil, he was surprisingly innocent. She truly believed that he never suspected anything. Even when she went to Bay Point to see her father but insisted on meeting Phil. Even when she invited him to join them for dinner or a day at the beach. Or stayed at his condo overnight. Izzy didn't like sharing Eva with his friend, but there wasn't more to it than that as far as she could determine. He always treated Phil the same, with love and resentment; always wished his daughter had been more like his dead sister, gifted and cheerful. He was too busy looking back to see what was going on under his nose.

Eva was shivering, as if Phil had taken all her body heat with him when he pulled out of her embrace. "You won't be my father-in-law when Roger and I divorce."

"It's too soon to talk about marrying. It's shameful."

But Roger didn't hesitate to marry Loreen. They bought a large, expensive house, while Sam and Eva moved into a two-bedroom apartment. Phil stayed in Florida for weeks on end, then suddenly traveled overseas to look at mills and factories.

Eva was desolate. Where was he? Why was he gone at a time like this? She'd call in sick, fall into bed and tunnel under the covers, or pace crooked furrows in the living-room rug. She served suppers of cold pizza, corn flakes, or canned beans till Sam threatened to move out. Painted her kitchen cabinets the same glossy plum-blue as Phil's eyes. Left messages on his phone: *Miss you like crazy. Come home!* Wrote his name with a ballpoint on the underside of her arms and the tender flesh of her inner thighs. Why wasn't he here when she needed him most?

Finally he came back and, after waiting several days, went to see her one night—but things had changed. He felt wooden, smelled sour, wouldn't look her in the eye. His droopy face was deeply lined. He didn't ask how she was doing, didn't talk about his trip; in fact, he hardly spoke at all. "Tell me about Rivke," she prompted. "Tell me about the partisans." Because it was safer there, locked in the past with Phil, as familiar by now as the tangled bits and pieces of her own father's history. To live in the present day was so much riskier—like stepping among booby traps or tripping through a minefield.

So he told her once again in a tired voice, a monotone, about the girl he loved when he thought he'd love no one else because of the family he left behind in the ghetto to be starved or gassed—and when he found her dead after a raid on the Jewish camp, he went after her killers and he caught one and cut him down, burned his house and barn, but it didn't help to ease his grief, nothing helped, it just went on.

"Tell me how I remind you of her—touch my hair, feel my skin. I know you love me for myself but also because of her . . . and I don't mind that anymore, I'll share you if I have to. Tell me again how you found something good with me you once thought was long gone."

He shook his head: that's enough. And each time she saw him after that he was quieter still.

"Tell me about the roundup and life in the ghetto. Tell me how many you saved..."

But there was little left to say: she knew all his stories. How he escaped the ghetto through a sewer pipe and reached the woods; how he stole a rifle and fought with Russian partisans, sabotaged rail lines, defended Jewish fugitives, and rode around on a stallion. There was nothing she hadn't already heard.

So he would sit silently, hands in his lap, head lowered, his hunched body a half-moon waning a slice at a time. Until he almost wasn't there, fading into darkness. Until he was no more than an echo's thin echo or a memory of love.

When he told her he was marrying Yvonne, she only nodded, startled by the sound of words. She stopped hearing the rest of it—his reasons and apologies, *she needs me* and so forth. Instead she thought about herself, trying to imagine what she ought to be feeling right now. Shock, pain, desperation? In fact, she was hollowed out, an empty pocket, flimsy as lint. The wind could carry her away.

Her mind wandered, lit on this: something her father once said when Phil left his second wife. "He gets close to no one. He loves them and leaves them first so no one can leave him, and this way he thinks he won't lose anybody special again. That's what the war did, that's what it did to Phil."

But that's how he dealt with others, she decided back then, not how he would treat her. For doesn't every woman think that she's the one to change a man? Wasted effort, she learned in the end. Foolishness that leads to disappointment and heartache. He is who he is, does what he does, over and over again.

She avoided him for more than a year after he married Yvonne: Eva was determined not to see him again. No messages, chance encounters, visits to the factory; no family get-togethers. If he wanted to see Sam, he would have to speak to Roger. If he saw Izzy in Florida, that wasn't her concern. If Izzy phoned to talk about Phil—or if he even mentioned Yvonne—she'd say she had to call back: there was always someone at the door or something burning on her stove.

But her resoluteness didn't last. She'd wake up cold and shaky, her head aching, elbows locked. Her hand would move of its own accord and grab the phone, dial his number, wait a moment, hang up. She'd fall out of bed and stare in the mirror, feeling old and used up even though she was forty-three—seeing pouches under her eyes, frown lines, crepey skin. Or leave the apartment to go for a drive, only to wind up parked in front of his big house on Riversee Lane, gazing at his bedroom window with wet eyes and clenched teeth. Her life was nothing without Phil, she finally understood, a march of meaningless days and nights, a parched field of loneliness. No other man would do. If she couldn't be his wife, she would be his lover, as before.

She won't know. We'll be careful. Please, if you still have any feelings for me . . . just once. I won't bother you again.

Because she wouldn't let up, he came to see her once more. And that's how it started again: one time, another time. Slowly at first, sporadically, but soon it was like it was in the days when she was Roger's wife and Phil loved her dearly. As if he'd never turned away. As if Eva were his bride and they were eager newlyweds. Whole afternoons together, dopey with lovemaking, breathless with foreboding. Because he was a married man. Because something so intense could not continue very long.

Yvonne mustn't find out.

She'll never know. I promise . . .

On the bicycle in the basement gym, Eva was tired of pedaling. Stop, start, stop, start, desire frenzy fury grief: she was tired of remembering. It was nothing less than a curse to recall so exactly every word that was spoken, every missed beat of her clobbered heart. She swung off the bicycle and left the silent, haunted room.

She rode an elevator up, got off at Phil's floor, knocked on his apartment door. Phil's *former* apartment. Someone looked through the peephole. "Who's there?" A woman's voice.

"I'm looking for Mr. Lewis," she said. "I was told this is where he lives."

"He doesn't live here anymore."

"Can I speak to you face to face? I won't be long."

The woman opened the door a crack. She was white-haired, stooped, and small. "What do you want?"

Eva looked past her. The living room was brushed yellow with long strokes of sunlight. Through the picture window you could see the blue lip of the Gulf, a brow of sky. Often they had stood together right there, looking out, arm in arm and hip to hip, and sometimes she would break away and do a little fluttery dance, her arms dipping and soaring. Once he lifted her over his head like a ballet partner and they spiraled across the room. "You make me happy," Phil had said, and she had answered, "Me too."

"Well?" the old woman asked.

"Please let me come inside. I knew Mr. Lewis well. It would mean a lot to me to see the place once more."

"It's my apartment, not his," the woman said sharply. "There's nothing here for you to see." With that she started to close the door, but Eva stopped it with her foot.

"One look and then I'll go. Please, I'm not asking much." To see the kitchen, where they ate. The master bedroom where they slept spoon-like, his breath on her neck.

"Move your foot," the woman said, and when Eva didn't, she jabbed her shoe with the end of a cane.

Eva's foot shot back and the door slammed hard in her face. "I'm phoning the super!" the woman hollered through the door. "He's coming up to throw you out. You don't belong in the building!"

"I'm going now. Save your breath."

Eva took an elevator down to the lobby and hurried out. Only one more thing to do. One more scene to replay.

The swimming pool was around back, facing the Gulf. She followed a path of pink stones and slowly approached the deck, the slap of water in her ears. A few bathers lay on chairs: older women in one-piece suits with crossed straps and pleated skirts, and younger ones in bikinis; pasty-looking men in trunks watching the prettiest girls from behind dark glasses. Eva found an empty chair at a table under a wide umbrella and sat right next to the pool. Bubbles floated in unison like synchronized swimmers and the surface was brilliant with strings of light, but no one was in the water.

Why doesn't anyone swim? It seemed unnatural not to be watching someone doing laps.

Phil used to swim daily, even when she was visiting. She'd sit like this, in a slip of shade, reading a book beside the pool until he was finished. Sometimes if he slept in, she'd come down here alone, a nice place to wait until he got up later and joined her. Eva wasn't much of a swimmer but liked the muttering sound of water, the geometrical view of the beach beyond. With her raised book as a cover, she enjoyed watching the passing scene. She would study faces, notice clothes, listen to chatter and laughter, and imagine different people's lives. Were those two newly in love? Was that pair incredibly bored? Which was how one morning in the winter of 1988, quite accidentally, she overheard Selma and Vic.

The umbrella at her table had been sharply tilted against the sun, her face well hidden. Anyway, she was wearing dark glasses and a sun hat: they certainly wouldn't have recognized her even if they looked up. Vic had never met her, in any case, and Selma only one time the previous year when she knocked on Phil's door and he was forced to introduce them.

Selma, this is Eva. Eva . . . Selma.

She knew at once they were lovers. The woman's scowl told her so; the scratch in her voice when she said hello; the way she slit her eyes at Phil, nailing him, claiming him. Without thinking, Eva reached out and grappled Phil's arm as if to pull him back, though she feared she'd already lost him. Still finding some small comfort in the feel of his sleeve . . . although she was crumbling, weak with pain. Stuck to his body like a wet leaf.

Selma lives in the building and waters my plants when I'm away. She's already got a boyfriend. What are you carrying on about?

Selma and Vic by the swimming pool: a handsome couple, young and fit. Early thirties, she supposed, though Selma, thin and boyish, could be taken for sixteen. They were speaking loudly that morning, overly excited, and it wasn't hard to hear their conversation as she slouched in her chair. Not that she intended to spy. She was there first, after all, minding her own business, skimming a novel, and didn't even notice them until she heard Selma's voice. Hoping, for a dangling moment, that Phil had been telling the truth and nothing much was going on. Why would a girl like that be interested in a man like him?

"Of course I love you, nothing's changed. I just want to live with Phil. He's going to sell his apartment and buy us a big house."

And Vic had said, "I'll kill him. I'll kill the old motherfucker!" Said it like he meant it.

Eva could have warned Phil: *The boyfriend of that whore you're seeing says he's going to get you.* But she said nothing, did nothing. Vic was just talking, she figured. Vic was just a wronged lover letting off a little steam. And even if he knew, Phil would never have taken it seriously. *An idle threat*, he might've said, or *What do you expect me to do, hire a bodyguard? I can take care of myself.* At worst, he might even have accused her of making it up, of trying to scare him away from Selma. *You want me to give her up and I won't!*

And she had thought this too: that Phil deserved to die after betraying her a second time. First Yvonne, then this—this juvenile, built like a stick, who could be his granddaughter. Who scowled and snapped and stared at passersby with small, angry eyes. Why wasn't Eva enough? She loved him absolutely. She needed him like a plant needs roots.

But even his wives weren't enough: how well Eva knew that. No one was enough for Phil. *He gets close to no one.* He was unfaithful, ungrateful, greedy, and heartless. If someone hadn't gotten to him first, she might have killed him herself.

But now that he's dead, what guilt! As if she had indeed done him in with her own hands. A word in Phil's ear and he might be alive today.

She bore the weight of her weakness and indecision like a hump . . . as Izzy carried the burden of his uselessness during the war. Perhaps he should be grateful for his present semi-consciousness—a state she half wished for herself to spare her this endless regret. Like her father before her, she had let someone she once loved—*loves now, will love forever*—die a pointless, brutal death.

Eva stood up suddenly—could not stand to spend another moment at the edge of the pool. She walked through an opening in a low stone wall to a narrow strip of raked beach, kicked off her sneakers, and buried her feet in hot sand. She sat down in the shade of a tree and leaned back on her elbows.

It was lovely here. Quieting. A horizontal vista: the earth curving before her eyes in blue-green striations. Children ran and splashed in the Gulf, laughing and hooting, and she wanted to join them; to feel cool water and vanilla ice-cream foam. And then a strong image of another sea, unlike this, pushed forward, filled her eyes . . . the booming waves of Jones Beach. Where Izzy used to carry her out just past the breakers, the ocean rolling under them like a humpbacked dragon, and try to teach her how to float. Slapping the water, kicking her feet, giddy, wet, and salt-sprayed, she lay on his outstretched arms, fearing nothing. Long ago this was, when she was still young enough to think her daddy would keep her safe.

Much more recently—after Yvonne but before she'd met Selma—Eva brought a pail and shovel to this very beach, close to this very spot, and built a tall sand castle. Around that a high wall. Around that a deep moat. She set two hand-shaped figures on the castle roof: they were happy there, contented. Phil, sitting cross-legged, elbows on his knees and his hands folded under his chin, peered at her sand people as prominent as flags in the tranquil turquoise afternoon. "They look like the bride and groom on a wedding cake," he said, and her ears were suddenly burning. Later he went for a swim and Eva lay on a blanket and dozed. She dreamed she was swimming on her back while, underneath her, cupped and disembodied hands were ready to catch her if she sank.

She woke up to shouting and the ping of sand on her ankles: there were boys racing along the beach. The castle, when she sat up and stared, was horribly flattened; it was branded with footprints. She got up and ran around, calling and searching for Phil, but he wasn't there.

She should have understood then that nothing good lasts forever. No one is happy for long.

9

IT WAS PAST NOON by the time she got to the health care center. She carried in a suitcase of clothes for her father, so he wouldn't have to wear hospital gowns, and the morning paper under her arm. He was lying in bed this time, not propped in a wheelchair. Tubes in his arm and a plastic breathing apparatus up his nose. Eyes shut.

She put his clothes in a dresser, the suitcase beside it, and two framed photos on a nightstand beside his bed. One of Izzy and Hilda, one of Eva and Sam. Both taken years ago when her mother was still rosy with health, her son was a toddler, and Eva, busy being a mom, forgot for a while that she and Roger were a poor match.

She pulled a chair close to his bed and sat down. "Hi, Dad. Eva again. Are you awake? How are you doing?" She spoke slowly, loudly, enunciating every word.

He opened his eyes. The light had gone out of them. With his good hand he plucked at his sheet, plucked at his blue gown. His fingernails were purple. He blinked at a TV mounted to the ceiling at the foot of his bed, playing silently. Eva reached through the bed rail and touched his hand. As if she had pushed a button, he ran through his cycle of gestures—shrugging, pointing, grimacing—but listlessly this time. He rubbed her knuckles with his thumb, squinting at her, watching her: a still, aching moment.

I have always loved you, she thought, but said something else.

"I brought some of your clothes and a couple of snapshots." She pointed to the nightstand and his eyes followed her finger.

"I put them over there, okay? Look a little to your left. Here's one of you and Hilda, another one of me and Sam. Your wife, daughter, and grandson." Never mind that Hilda was dead. If he remembered her at all, he probably thought she was home right now cooking dinner.

Izzy turned his head slightly, glanced at the photographs, the beige wall, the window. Eva's hand was hot and damp. She tried to slide it away but he looked down, tightened his grip. Had he seen her bitten fingernails? He'd always hated her ragged nails and tried to break her habit by scaring her with stories of how, when she chewed a finger, deadly invasive germs goose-stepped through her mouth like Hitler's Brownshirts. She would worry about the bad men marching in her mouth, but she couldn't stop. Most of the time she bit her nails she wasn't aware she was doing it.

A tall man with a vacant face entered the room in a walker and switched on a TV on the dresser closest to the door. He turned the sound way up, put his face against the screen, and ran his arms over the box, seemingly caressing it. He pushed aside a supper trolley, rolled his walker up to the empty bed, and lay down. Izzy's roommate, Eva thought. When she said hello, he didn't reply. Not good company, but at least he could get around.

A nurse bounded into the room and turned down the volume: a loping man with gelled hair and black tattoos on one arm— writhing snakes and a death's head. He nodded at Eva and paused at Izzy's bedside. His name tag said LYMAN. Haltingly, she asked about the tubes in her father's nose, which weren't there yesterday.

"His breathing's been a little rough. That's why the oxygen." He played with the fingers of his patient's useless hand, then put his face close to his and said, "How you doing?" Izzy smiled, pointed, shrugged. "Circulation's not good," he told Eva quietly. "He's got a low fever and his blood pressure's gone up."

"What's that mean?"

"That he's got a slight infection. We put him on an antibiotic drip for a few days."

"Will he get better?"

"He's weak," said Lyman, "but antibiotics will do the trick."

She didn't believe him. Lie-man.

But did she really want her father to conquer his infection, to live out his days immobile and dumb, half-dead in a hospital bed? Did she want a physiotherapist to teach him to walk again so he could stumble across the room and hug the portable TV? She pulled her sweaty hand back and let it drop.

The nurse took Izzy's temperature while Eva stared at the death's head insignia on his arm. Pictures of the SS sprang up behind her eyes. She blinked hard, turned away. She was queasy and needed a Gravol. "I brought some of my father's clothes"— pointing at the dresser. "I put them in the top drawer."

Lyman said, "That's good," and loomed over Izzy again. "We'll dress you up real nice," he spoke sweetly in his ear. Then he turned and hurried off and Eva was alone again with her insensible father.

"I had a busy morning," she said. "I met with your lawyer, Mr. Grant, so I could get power of attorney and pay your bills. Then I went to the post office to get your mail forwarded. I even phoned a realtor who's coming later to look at the house. When you feel well again"—her voice dropping, hesitant—"we'll set you up in a nice apartment, somewhere you won't have to cook or clean. Assisted living, they call it." Though she knew, to look at him, he'd never be getting out of here.

Izzy made a gargling sound and closed his eyes. Eva touched his forehead, which was quite warm. She went to the bathroom and soaked a cloth in cold water, wrung it out, walked back, and dabbed it around his face. The way he did for her when she was little and had a fever. *Is that better? Does that help?* Deep gurgles from his throat: maybe he was saying thanks.

She put the cloth on his nightstand. "I brought the morning paper. Would you like me to read it to you?"

His eyes fluttered open and shut, which she took as a yes.

She spread the paper on his bed and leaned over to scan it. There were local reports of car crashes, break-ins and robberies, a stabbing and shooting, none of which was appropriate read-aloud material. The weather and stock reports, unemployment statistics . . . Why would he care about any of that? Finally, under International News, an interesting item. "Listen to this," said Eva. "Two hundred thousand East Germans are calling for a united country. And here's something else," she said. "East and West Germany are stepping up air traffic between the two German states . . . What do you think of that?"—glancing up at him quickly. "Looks like reunification's going to happen soon." She paused to hear his raspy breath. His hand was moving slightly.

"It gets better," she went on. "Helmut Kohl met with the East German Premier. They agreed to open a crossing point at the Brandenburg Gate and to lift travel restrictions on West Germans heading east. The West Germans are going to help East German industries and everyone will cooperate on economic, transport, and social issues."

She raised her eyes. "Everybody's friends again, like the past doesn't matter. They're putting their differences behind them and starting fresh."

He turned his head to one side, as if showing disapproval.

"That's good!" Eva said. "We have to remember what was, but have to move forward too. History should teach us, but it should-n't be a torment that keeps us from enjoying our lives." She looked down at the paper again and read a final item: "Later on Kohl addressed a big crowd in Dresden and said that his goal was to unify the nation. 'God bless our German fatherland,' he told them."

Eva stopped once more to monitor her listener. Izzy was com-pletely still, his breathing noisy but regular, and seemed to be sleeping. She quit reading and sat back. "Remember your friend Klaus? The one who went back to Berlin? He must be so excited." Her voice became softer. "I wish we had gone too. Not to live—to visit. I wanted to ride the U-Bahn and see where you grew up, where your father had his shop, the park where you flew your kite, the street where Aunt Rosa lived. It would've meant a lot to have you show me those places. To see some of your old life. It would've made the stories that you used to tell me come alive."

This is where the synagogue stood. And here's the canal where the whole family liked to walk. Over there, your grandfather ran a tailoring business, it was next door to a pharmacy...

"But you never wanted to go back. You said maybe one day when your memories weren't so sharp... and now of course it's too late."

It was hard growing up missing one half of a family, especially when the part that remained was so meager. Other children had family dinners at birthdays and Thanksgiving and summer reunions at resorts with lots of cousins to play with, but Eva had none of that. She vaguely remembered her mother's parents, Latvian immigrants who died in the Bronx when she was small, and an aunt and uncle in Brooklyn they hardly ever saw because her father thought they were loudmouths. Nor did he like their two sons no one spoke to anyway after they moved out West.

If only she'd known Izzy's parents, her Aunt Rosa and Uncle Arnold, her cousins Kurt and Martin. She imagined they were smart and cultured, generous and warm-hearted, everything the other side of Eva's family wasn't. Sometimes, in her younger years, she'd talk to people about them as if they were still alive and living in Germany. They fooled the Nazis, she would say, and worked as farmhands during the war, pretending they were Christians. After, they rebuilt their lives. Arnold got his job back as a history professor. Rosa became a widely known concert pianist. Kurt played the violin and Martin was a composer. They wrote to Eva frequently, inviting her to visit, and in fact she was planning a trip soon...

Once Izzy said that she resembled Rosa so much it was hard for him to watch her without getting choked up; hard not to think that Rosa lived again in his daughter. Hard not to see his own childhood reflected in the wet mirrors of her eyes. Though sometimes she wished he would look at her and see only *Eva*, no one else, she liked being a link to his past. Liked how he stared when she entered a room and he thought she didn't notice. In this way at least she could hold his attention; she was more remarkable than his wife.

But it wasn't enough to look like Rosa, she had to be brilliant and talented too. Refined, expressive, selfless: a happy person who hummed along as she practiced tunes on the piano. Above all else, a happy girl. Though surely Rosa was miserable! Hounded by the Nazis and her husband gone to Poland; slaving in a factory while her children starved.

That part Eva learned by eavesdropping late at night, which is how she learned a lot of things, crouched behind a wall while her parents huddled in the kitchen, muttering over cups of tea. They would never tell her things like that—they meant to protect her from evil. And yet she absorbed it anyway by some kind of osmosis: their melancholy and distrust, sadness and nervousness, anger and shame.

Sometimes Hilda might forget and speak as if she were talking to herself and not her daughter: "What your father suffered! What the Nazis did to his family! I was lucky to live in New York, but they weren't as lucky as me . . . While the world watched and did nothing. No one cares about the Jews."

And Eva would feel her legs fold. She'd fall headfirst into the pit of her mother's woe. *What they did to our family! No one cares.*

"That's enough!" Izzy would snap at Hilda if he overheard. "She doesn't need to know that, she's just a child."

She only wanted to please them and ease their pain a little, but she always seemed to fall short. When she was still a girl they complained that she was long-faced, shy, and unsociable. "Cheer up," Izzy would say. "Life's not so terrible."

Though she knew he didn't believe that, she tried to be sunny anyway. She smiled often in his presence and sang popular show tunes. She performed pliés and pirouettes she'd learned in ballet school before her mother pulled her out because she thought it wasn't right that twelve- and thirteen-year-olds should prance about in leotards. For her father's sake she banged away at the piano in the living room, years and years of useless lessons till even her teacher had to admit she had no aptitude.

But sometimes she would puff up, red-faced with anger— because it wasn't fair that she couldn't do what she wanted to and had to be what she wasn't! Because she wasn't loved for herself but had to be a stand-in for her murdered aunt.

She tried not to let it show. Her parents were weak and miserable—how could she make them feel worse? What did her little grievances amount to anyway next to their big ones? So Eva gnawed her fingernails, endured headaches, withdrew to her room. Secretly she danced in front of the mirror on her closet door, turning on pointe like the tiny perfect spinning ballerina on the music box she got for her seventh birthday.

Or else she would sneak outside to capture insects in a jar— caterpillars, grasshoppers, beetles, and fighter ants—and watch them kill each other if she didn't do them in herself. Sometimes she would snatch a thing lying around the apartment that belonged to her parents—a piece of jewelry or small garment—and break it, tear it, throw it away. Sometimes she would hide it in a drawer or under her mattress, to pull out on awful days and rub over her face like a charm: *Stop the bad feelings, make the bad feelings go away.*

Regardless of what she did she was never happy, carefree, and never stopped letting them down. Sullen child, rebellious teen; late to marry, quick to divorce; a run-of-the-mill librarian: she was no match for Rosa.

Izzy grunted, moved his head. She turned to him and made herself stop thinking about the past. When she touched his hand his fingers twitched, surely a good sign. "Get better," she told him. She *did* want him to get well, to hang in there, beat this. Be strong at last. Beat death.

But what if he didn't want to live? What if he got well enough to weigh the possibilities and decided against them? What could he look forward to even if he recovered except the usual solitude, sleeplessness, and nightmares—with probably some paralysis and other disabilities thrown in. A cute and perky home-care nurse who'd visit twice a week? A call from his daughter?

So what's new?

I'm constipated.

Are you getting out?

I can hardly walk. What are you talking about?

A life of dozing and TV. No more snooping, driving around, asking people about Phil. Why bother getting well?

"So I went to Phil's condo," she said as if he'd followed her thoughts. "Yesterday, to look around. Right after I left here. An old woman lives in his apartment now, but she wouldn't let me inside. So then I went and sat by the pool."

He opened his eyes, gripped her hand. "I'm sure you think about him too." If he thinks about anything. If he understands any of this.

"I have to say something," she said, feeling a ball in her throat like a lump of unswallowed food. "About Selma's boyfriend. Remember that time we spoke on the phone, maybe three months ago . . . you talked about Irene and Yvonne? You asked me if I knew him? I didn't tell you the whole truth." Her stomach tight; her eyes on his hand. "I never actually met the guy—I didn't lie about that—but I did see him one time. He was by the pool with Selma and I heard some of what they said. They were talking about Phil, in fact . . . Vic threatened to kill him."

Izzy let go of her hand and plucked at his hospital gown, which moved slowly up his thigh, exposing his diaper. Eva pulled the fabric down and flattened his hand with her own. "I should've told you everything. And Phil—I should've warned him. I thought it didn't mean anything, that Vic was just talking . . ."

Izzy gasped, sniffed, and gurgled, as if startled by what she'd said.

"So I did nothing—nothing at all. Not before and not after. There were reasons, believe me . . . I had my reasons. But that doesn't make it right. Doesn't help me sleep at night."

Her father's eyes were shut again, and his hand softened under hers. Finally he was able to fall asleep easily, day or night. From now on she'd be the only one to lie awake tossing and turning, seeing Phil. Phil staggering. Phil slumping. Blood pooling on the stairs.

"Our feelings get in the way and we don't do the right thing, we're not as good as we should be. You know what I'm saying, don't you?" She glanced at Izzy's roommate, snoring fitfully on his bed, then leaned forward, whispering, smoothing her father's hand in her palms. "Remember Inez, the girl from the plant? The sewer who quit unexpectedly and no one heard from her again? You said Phil was hounding her, but Roger told me something else—that you were the one who slept with her, that you took advantage. 'Uncle Izzy' did it, he said. Isn't that what they called you? 'Uncle Izzy knocked her up and paid her to leave her job.'" She was rubbing his hand so hard she thought she would flay it. "You let Phil take the blame when really it was you all along. It *was* you, wasn't it?"

Izzy made a sound like a snort, his eyelids quivering.

"But I forgive you anyway. I want you to know that. I understand about feelings, I know what they can make you do. It doesn't mean you're a bad person, just not as good as you thought." She raised his hand and kissed it. "And Phil—we have to forgive him too, for doing things he shouldn't have. Just like you . . . and like me."

Izzy half opened his eyes.

"Are you surprised? Don't be. I'm no better than you or Phil. We're alike, the three of us. You have to forgive *me* too. It doesn't matter what for . . . just let me know you do."

But his face was impassive, his hand a dead weight in hers.

"Say it," she pleaded. "One word. Do something. Nod your head."

He looked past her, turning toward the dust-colored window. Eva lay his hand on the bed. "Maybe another time."

She stood up, her legs rubbery, and took a few steps back. Swaying, fighting an urge to weep. Giving in and crying briefly, cupping a hand over her mouth, trying not to disturb Izzy or his snoring roommate. A tear ran into her collar. "See you tomorrow then," she said when she could speak again.

———

Izzy's skinny neighbor and a man with an ugly dog were standing on Pat's porch when Eva parked in the driveway and opened the garage door. Pat called and waved her over. Eva walked carefully across the woman's cropped lawn, thick, stiff blades of grass crunching and flattening underfoot.

"Come join us, get out of the sun. It's a hot one today," Pat said. She introduced the man with the dog. "This is Frank. He lives in the house behind Izzy's, they share a fence between their yards."

The man nodded. He was short, with beady eyes; his features blunt, his face long. He looked like his bull terrier, pulling wildly on its leash, a white dog with black markings. "This here is Snowball." He rubbed and patted the animal's head.

A dumb name, Eva thought. Rex was better. Even Spot.

She had wanted Izzy to get a dog, for companionship and something to do. At the very least it would've gotten him out of the bungalow every day to buy kibble, walk his pet. But he didn't like the idea, and there was no changing his mind once he decided against something. Eva blamed Hilda for turning him against dogs, for making him think they were dirty and smelly, more trouble than they were worth.

Who's going to stop it from peeing on the carpet? Who's going to clean up the hair?

At least get a goldfish.

Who's going to change the water? Who's going to feed it?

"So how's your dad?" Pat said.

"Oh, well . . ." Well what? "As well as can be expected." Wasn't that the right expression?

"When's he coming home again?"

"He can't live alone anymore. He won't be coming back here."

"What about the bungalow?"

"I'm going to sell it as soon as I can."

"We'll all miss him," Pat said. Discreetly she elbowed Frank, who nodded agreement. "A loner," she went on, "but a good neighbor anyhow. You can't complain about a man who minds his own business. He was going to teach me how to swim—I already bought a new suit—but I guess it wasn't meant to be."

Frank stroked the dog's head, his eyes fixed on the distance. "Soon, Snowball, soon," he said.

Eva said abruptly that she needed someone to cut the grass until she got the house sold. Did either of them know anyone?

She was hoping Frank would volunteer, but instead he offered the name of the guy who mowed his own lawn. "Come on home with me," he said. "My wife's got the number." With that he strode away from the porch, Snowball leading, Eva behind.

"If you get too hot," Pat hollered, "come over for a swim. No one uses the pool anymore. You can have it all to yourself."

Frank lived on the next block, but it took a while to get there, what with Snowball stopping to pee on every hydrant and mature tree. His wife was crouched in the small front yard when they finally arrived, planting pots of grim-faced pansies in even rows. Frank let go of the leash and the terrier ran up to her, pushing his snout into her crotch. She lifted the dog's head and kissed him between the eyes.

"This here is Izzy Schneider's daughter Eva," Frank said. "She needs to phone Al Stock and get him to cut her daddy's grass."

The woman stood, smiling broadly, showing her teeth. She was tall, slim, and white-haired, wearing a yellow tracksuit and matching sweatband. Not young, but not as old and crinkled as Pat. "I'm

Frieda. Nice to meet you." She stuck out her hand and Eva shook it. Firm handshake. Warm skin. "I bet you'd like a cup of tea."

"That would be very nice"—holding the woman's hand longer than she meant to.

She followed Frieda into the house, the same size and shape as Izzy's, but breezy and tropical with warm air and natural light. They sat down on an overstuffed couch in the living room, the blades of a ceiling fan sibilating overhead. Frank sat in a padded rocker, gently creaking back and forth, Snowball dozing at his feet. All the doors and windows in the bungalow were opened wide. Eva looked out at the yard of grapefruit trees and a tidy lawn through a mesh of screens. She sank into the white cushions, her limbs heavy, softening.

Frieda went to the kitchen and came back carrying a tray of cups and saucers, cookies, and a teapot, and set it down on a low table in front of the couch. Still smiling, she poured and served. She seemed pleased when Eva ate a cookie and asked for more tea. "Your father told us all about you"—glancing at Frank—"his daughter in Canada. You know, he's very proud of you. A good job, a fine son."

Was that true? she wondered. Frieda could be making it up, by way of giving comfort.

"It's terrible what happened to him—and you living so far away. You must be heartsick." She leaned over and hugged Eva, her first hug in eight days, since she said goodbye to Sam. According to an article she'd read at the library, people need twelve hugs a day in order to flourish. Fat chance of getting that.

Frieda sat back and said, "You know, I used to listen to your father for hours on end. He'd see me in the backyard and call me over to the fence. Oh, how that man could talk! About the war and his family, his time in France, his life in New York. I listened, I suppose, because I felt sorry for him, he had no one else to talk to. And certainly his stories were interesting at first—when you hadn't heard them too many times."

Frank stopped rocking. "I used to listen too. I'd be out with Snowball and I think he knew my routine, he'd be waiting every morning when I turned down his street, and he'd just go on and on till I couldn't stand it no more." He chuckled, shaking his bald head, as red and cratered as Mars. "Snowball here would pull on his leash and I'd say, 'Got to go now, I have to finish walking the dog,' but there was no getting away, he'd follow you right out on the road. Finally I changed my route and never went down his street again."

Eva looked from one to the other and her belly jumped. "He was lonely after my mother died. That's why he talked so much— he was lonely."

"I think he got mad at me," Frieda said, "when I told him one day that I couldn't stand by the fence any longer as much as he liked, I was too darn busy. After that I almost never saw him in the yard again, and when I did he wouldn't look up. If I said hello, he'd answer with a single word and no more. I guess you could say he dropped me, he didn't need me anymore. After all that time I spent listening to him, day after day! Maybe he found someone else to talk to, I don't know."

"He had a buddy, Klaus, but he went back to Germany. And then there was his friend Phil, shot in Toronto. That was a terrible blow."

"We heard all about it." Frank and his wife exchanged a look.

"Phil, Klaus, you, your son, a stranger he met, a neighbor . . . He was always going on about someone," Frieda said. "You couldn't get a word in." She raised her teacup, set it down. "He used to go to the mall and talk to the girls working in the stores. I know one of them, Karen Downey, daughter of a friend of mine. She said he'd come in so much and yak for so long that her boss used to glare at them, she thought she was going to lose her job."

"He was a character, all right." Frank shook his head slowly, grinning like a numbskull.

Eva squirmed and sat up, her stomach squeezing tight and puffing out like a bellows. She wanted to get the hell out of there.

"About the lawn," she said. "You were going to give me the number of a man who could cut the grass."

"That's right. I'll get it." Frieda disappeared in the kitchen, then she came back with a note she handed to Eva. "Al's very reliable. He does Pat's lawn too. Have you met Pat from next door?"

"She has," said Frank. "We were just chatting on her porch."

"Nice person. A widow too. She used to bring your father pies straight from the oven, but he wouldn't spend any time with her. I can't imagine why not."

"He liked his ladies young and blonde." Frank winked at Eva, his bald crown darkening. "*Shiksas*. Isn't that the word?"

Eva thanked them, checked her watch, and stood up. It occurred to her that maybe they were anti-Semitic as well as mean-spirited; that Izzy had reason not to be friendly with his neighbors. That his grim, dismal view of the world was more or less accurate. "I have to be going now. A realtor's coming to see the house."

"You want to sell it?"

"That's right."

"Poor Izzy. What a shame! To survive the war—then this." Frieda gave her a final hug. "If there's anything more we can do for you, let us know."

From the doorway, Eva looked back. Frank and Frieda were waving hard, their mouths curved into sickles.

She walked out, turned the corner, and hurried back to Muddy Creek Road. Scrambling across the straw-like grass that was Izzy's yard, she let herself into the bungalow. She was hot and wanted a shower but there wasn't time: the realtor was due at three. Instead she phoned Al Stock, who agreed to come by with his mower the next day.

The real estate agent was punctual. When Eva let her in she saw a tall, middle-aged woman carrying a briefcase, wearing a light-weight suit and little makeup, much less dazzling than her photo in the ad she had found in Izzy's mailbox. "Lucy Lyon knows how to roar!" is what the ad said. What that had to do with selling houses was anyone's guess, but why not go for an agent who valued puns?

The first thing Lucy said was, "Gotta do something about the lawn."

"I already called someone. He's going to cut it tomorrow."

"Maybe he could water it too. Looks like a haystack." She put down her briefcase and strode into the living room, her heels punching indentations in the carpet. She paused under the stationary blades of the ceiling fan scraping the top of her bouffant. "Never turn this on," she said. "Anyone over five-eight would get their head chopped off. Your dad must be pretty short."

He never used to be, Eva thought. But she was remembering when she was small, holding his hand, craning her neck, and he was as tall as a lamppost. Or when he swung her onto his shoulders, up and up and up, where clouds were blowing through her hair.

Lucy quickly checked out the other rooms and came back. "You know what this place needs? Industrial-strength cleaning. Get rid of the cobwebs, the fingerprints, and green mold. I know someone to do the job, it'll cost maybe two hundred. What do you say?" Eva agreed and Lucy went on. "I assume you'll be selling the furniture too. If I find a buyer who wants it, great. If not, we'll get an auctioneer to pick up the whole lot."

"What do you think the house is worth?"

"You want to move it fast, we can list it at forty-three. If you're not in a hurry, we can ask a couple of thousand more."

"I'm in a hurry," Eva said. "I can't keep an eye on things from Toronto."

Lucy pulled some papers out of her briefcase for Eva to sign. Then the women shook hands. "We'll be in touch," Lucy said. "Here's to a quick sale."

Eva thanked her, saw her out. After the realtor left, she wandered around the bungalow wondering what she ought to pack and ship to Toronto before it was too late. Glassware, kitchenware, silver-plated candlesticks? LPs of Lawrence Welk, polkas, and show tunes? Yiddish and German folk songs and an album of Opera's Greatest Hits? Maybe a couple of wall ornaments dating back to her childhood: the life-size ship's wheel with a functioning barometer glued to its center; a pair of plaques from Israel with stylized figures in bas-relief. Or maybe Hilda's needlepoints, framed and hanging over the couch. Her life measured in stitches.

Gold threads, green threads, orange and blue threads: Hilda sitting on the sofa, sewing little chains and crosses, running stitches, backstitches, double, French, and coral knots until she squinted through reddened eyes; while Izzy in an armchair, his feet on an embroidered stool, read the evening paper. While Eva, restless on the rug, dressed and undressed a pair of boring paper cut-out dolls. It was too quiet. No one spoke.

Your father had a hard day, he doesn't want to talk now. He wants to relax. She was not allowed to sit on his lap, play with his slippers, pirouette. *Later, Eva, not now. He doesn't want to watch you dance. He's tired. Can't you see that?*

What she saw was this: Hilda kept them apart. With her silence and her sewing and her *go-to-your-room-if-you-can't-sit-still*, she kept Izzy for herself. At night, when Eva crept out of her bedroom to eavesdrop, sure enough they'd be side by side, nodding and whispering, their arms touching, fingers linked.

Her mother's world: curtains, cushions, needles, cloth. A hushed world of ticking clocks, softly singing radios, beeswax, and chicken soup; the dimness of indoors. She didn't work, didn't drive, didn't like to go outside if Izzy wasn't with her. A dull, circumscribed world. Eva wanted none of that. So she dyed her hair, learned to smoke, wore tight sweaters and pointy bras, and looked enough like a teenage tramp to make Hilda weep. Which is just what Eva wanted. If the price of independence was her mother's love and approval—well, she never had that anyway, so what was the problem? All those years of being good had gotten her nowhere.

Once, after Hilda's death, Izzy shook a finger and said, "I never saw you crying. It's not right, the way you act. Don't you miss her? Don't you care? She was your mother, for God's sake." And Eva answered quietly, "I have always missed her. I have always cried."

She stared at the needlepoints above her father's sofa. Did she like them or not? Should she pack them or leave them? All she decided was to think about it later. For now, she turned her back on them and moved on.

There were cardboard boxes in the garage and all those white plastic bags. She dropped a load of them into a box and dragged in a couple of boxes, one for the guest room and one for her father's room. Then slowly, gingerly, she began going through his things.

In the cabinet under the TV she found a collection of tools from his days as a jewelry worker in Manhattan: a long tapered steel rod and set of metal measuring rings, each with its circumference engraved, six-and-a-quarter, six-and-a-half . . . ; a monocle-like magnifying eyepiece and headband; wristwatches, watchbands, and tiny-headed screwdrivers for making repairs. Nothing interesting in the closet—pillows, towels, blankets, and a rusty bike. In his desk were expired passports, old bankbooks, canceled checks, bills, and receipts dating back more than ten years, everything in labeled envelopes held together with rubber bands. Loose coins and a handful of Phil Lewis and Sons pens. A pair of binoculars. Old maps, travel brochures, dozens of black-and-white or hand-tinted postcards from the twenties and thirties: snapshots of Brussels, Zurich, Dresden, Le Havre, and other cities he'd been to, a few inscribed but most blank. She partly filled the cardboard box with tools, pens, documents, and all of the postcards, but left the binoculars on the desk.

In the master bedroom she went through her father's walk-in closet, his fine collection of shoes and suits, and then through his wardrobe, the dresser and end tables filled with socks and underwear, bedclothes, cardigans, fancy and casual shirts. Nothing here she wanted to keep except for a set of handkerchiefs, delicately initialed "I.S." When she was little and lost a tooth, he'd put it in one of those handkerchiefs and slide it under her pillow. The tooth fairy would leave a dime, but more important was the hankie Eva hid away to hold at night like a teddy bear. When she pressed it against her nose, she'd smell her father's Old Spice and feel as warm and safe as if she were sleeping in his pocket.

In a bottom drawer she found his album. Izzy's photo album. What he took when he left Berlin: the album, a few marks, a gold ring. A book with a hard cover severed at one edge of the spine and pasted back together again with dry, curled, transparent tape, the whole thing tied with string. She'd seen it many times before, had looked through it while Izzy spoke, explaining the pictures. Had heard the story of how it dropped when his suitcase was roughly searched in 1936 on the train from Berlin to Paris—the front cover torn off and snapshots scattered everywhere; Izzy on his hands and knees desperately scooping them up.

She untied the album and opened it on her father's bed. It gave off a musty smell—the odor of fear and loss and many years gone by. Soft black pages. Every picture held in place by four triangular pockets that were stuck to the paper like postage stamps. A few of them were missing, leaving dark silhouettes in the shape of three-sided hats.

She flipped through the photos of her father as a young man: Izzy hiking, skating, skiing; Izzy on the beach in a one-piece getup, his arm around a pretty blonde with small elliptical breasts and a scoop-necked swimsuit. He used to stand over Eva's shoulder, pointing and naming his friends. *Wilma, my first girlfriend, and that one is Charlotte, who wouldn't see me after the Nuremberg Laws, it was dangerous to date a Jew* . . . But when he came to the photos of his family, he'd become still.

The ones she wanted to see now.

All the missing relatives were glued to the middle pages. There were pictures of her grandparents sitting on a park bench: Grandma in a fur-collared coat, her face soft and fleshy, with thick eyebrows, small mouth; Grampa in an open jacket and waistcoat, a fob-watch, a cigarette in his left hand, his mouth turned down under a short mustache. A portrait of Rosa and her family posing in front of a tree: Arnold in a double-breasted suit and fedora, calmly gazing straight ahead; the boys wearing knickers and bright, wide suspenders, their knees slightly turned in, their grinning expressions alike. And Rosa—dear Aunt Rosa! Slender but hourglass-shapely in a fitted blouse and ankle-length pleated skirt. Her nose long, chin strong—so much like her brother. And yes, like her niece too. If she had lived, she might have been someone to talk to. She might've been a second mother to Eva, a better one. Loving. Understanding.

She touched Rosa's picture, then closed the album, tied it up, wrapped it in plastic, and put it in the cardboard box.

There was something else in the dresser drawer, something unexpected—a large kraft envelope, stained and creased, with a rusty clasp. Labeled in red ink, "Letters from Germany." Carefully she slid them out. The envelopes were frayed and torn as if they'd been chewed, addressed to Isidor Schneider, Union Avenue, Bronx, New York, and stamped with the Nazi emblem, a swastika and eagle, and "*Oberkommando der Wehrmacht*." Some were sealed on one end with a white strip: "Opened by Examiner 4103"—or else by Examiner 4333, 5336, 5442. Most came from Poland, the *Generalgouvernement*. A few of the letters were from *Berlin, Deutschland*.

Some were written on paper as thin and transparent as skin, words on the back of a page clearly showing through the front. Often the ink was faint or smudged, and sometimes lines were heavily blacked out by the censors. Letters signed by Arnold, by Mutti or Rosa, each one's handwriting distinctly recognizable. Arnold's was the straightest and Mutti's slanted; Rosa's loopy with flourishes. The first was from Mutti, dated February 13, 1941. The last was sent from Rosa in October of the same year. Two letters mailed from the Bronx in November, one from Izzy to his mother, one to his sister, had been returned. Everything was written in German, naturally, which Eva didn't understand. Back in Toronto, when the letters were translated, she'd get to know these people better, not just through Izzy's eyes. She'd hear them speak their own words.

She put the letters back in the big brown envelope and left it on the dresser. Not to be shipped or even jammed into her suitcase, but carried safely in her purse. Then she went to the living room to phone Sam at Roger's. Surely he'd be interested in family history, World War II, and what she'd discovered. In any case, they hadn't talked to each other in a few days.

Loreen picked up. "Oh yes," she said in her farfetched, whispery voice, "he's right here, I'll get him. But tell me, how's your father?"

"As well as can be expected."

"I'm so sorry," Loreen said.

Eva made a humph-like sound through her nose, then finally Sam was on the line. "Hi," she said to him. "How's it going?"

"Okay," Sam replied.

"They treating you well?"

"Yeah, sure."

"You miss me?"

"Yeah," he said.

"I miss you a whole lot." When he didn't answer she went on. "I found something interesting here, letters from 1941 written by Grampa's family. Swastikas on the envelopes and everything."

"What do they say?"

"Well, they're in German. I'll have to get them translated."

A brief silence, then he said, "How's he doing?"

"No change."

"So when are you coming home?"

"The end of the week. Saturday. I have to go back to work Monday."

"Okay. See you then."

"Love you, Sam."

"Yeah," he said.

After she hung up she sat in her father's La-Z-Boy, suddenly exhausted, and stared at the needlepoints over the couch. Three scenes of Florida like sentimental postcards: candy-pink sunsets; pelicans and spoonbills; mangroves and palm trees; water blue as sapphires, as flat as liquid in a pan. If only she could climb into one of the pictures and stay there! Sunning in a striped bikini, listening to the radio, and sipping frozen daiquiris. No memories. No thoughts.

If only she were small again, sitting on her mother's lap. If only she could rest there among the needles, yarn, and thread, the tangle of half-knitted scarves. Hilda would tell her there's no use worrying about the dead and dying, whatever happens is God's will. Then, with clever fingers, she'd play with the buttons on Eva's blouse to make sure nothing was loose; that Eva wasn't coming apart.

She had an eye for loose buttons. When Eva was still a girl her mother would inspect her dresses, the long-sleeved white shirts she wore to school for assembly, her sweaters, jackets, and winter coats. She'd pluck a button from its berth and promptly sew it back on. If Eva was actually wearing the garment at that moment, Hilda would make her suck on a thread, the ends hanging from her mouth like cooked vermicelli. "So I don't sew up your brains," she'd say. And Eva would be touched by her mother's superstition. It made her seem kinder, whimsical. But more than that— most of all—it proved that she really cared. She wouldn't risk harming whatever filled her daughter's head. Better to protect her with a chewed thread.

Eva got up and took the needlepoints off the wall. She touched the cloth and raised stitches, feeling a trace of her mother through her fingertips. Later she would pack the hangings carefully and send them home.

It was late afternoon. Sun came in at a low slope from the back porch, bleaching the rug. Despite the air conditioning she was sticky and warm. Hair stuck to the back of her neck; her feet were slippery in her shoes. She needed to cool off.

She changed into a bathing suit, pulled on a long shirt, grabbed one of Izzy's towels, and walked out the front door. Across a strip of scratchy grass, the asphalt driveway, and over to Pat's house. She knocked sharply on the door and Pat opened it at once. When Eva asked to use the pool, the woman practically yanked her in. "I keep it clean in case the kids show up unexpectedly, but they never come. It's such a waste."

The rooms were unnaturally dark. Chilly, damp, and cave-like. It took a minute to figure out that every window she could see, except for the one facing the street, was boarded up from the outside. Pat followed Eva's gaze. "There was so much bad weather in October," she said, "that my son Stevie came by and nailed those boards on the windows. 'Better safe than sorry,' as my husband Rudy liked to say. Stevie hasn't got around to taking them down yet." She took Eva by the hand and led her past a sliding door. "Come out here where you can see. There's lots of light back here."

The pool was inviting—kidney-shaped with blue-white clear water, perfectly still. Floor-to-ceiling screens all around softened the sunlight, making the air seem hazy. Along the edges of the porch were large, thriving potted plants: begonias, gardenias, geraniums, and orchids. "Your plants are lovely," Eva said, dropping her towel on a webbed chair. "Maybe you'd like some more? The ones on my father's porch really need a good home."

The woman clapped her blue-veined hands and crinkled her eyes up. Apparently she didn't get gifts very often.

"I'll bring them over after my swim."

Pat sat down to watch as Eva slipped her shirt off and stepped into the water. She wasn't a good swimmer and had hoped she would be alone.

"That's a nice suit you got, it looks real good on you. One-pieces are the best. Rudy used to hate bikinis. He said a girl should hide her flesh and leave a little something to a man's imagination."

She walked in up to her waist, flopped forward, and dog-paddled slowly to the deep end. With one hand gripping the ledge, she held her breath, put her face in the water, and opened her eyes. She was momentarily clear-headed, sizing up her life so far as if it were written in point form in waterproof ink on the bright bottom of the pool.

Forty-seven. Grown son. Ex-husband. Dead mother. Murdered lover. Dying dad. A more-or-less suitable job and a circle of casual friends, but no one she was close to. No one left to laugh with, confide in, rely on: her world shrinking day by day.

She snapped her head up, gulping air. The first thing she saw was Pat leaning over the side of the pool, her long reflection jagged and wiggly in the water. "You were under so long I was starting to get worried."

Eva's eyes were stinging, but it could've been the chlorine. "Move away from the edge," she said. "You don't want to fall in."

Pat inched backward. "You're right," she said, "I can't swim. Your father promised to teach me, but now of course it's too late."

Eva got out and toweled dry. She went back to Izzy's house and re-emerged from the sun porch carrying a cactus. Pat held her screen door open for Eva as she traveled between the bungalows, conveying pots: Pat applauding every plant, proclaiming its loveliness, as if it were a green-suited model on a runway.

When she was finished and the plants were clustered around the pool, Eva was pleased. She had managed to save something.

"Now come inside," Pat said. "Have a cup of tea and a slice of lemon meringue pie. I made it myself this morning."

The sudden chill and murkiness inside the bungalow surprised Eva yet again. Pat drew her into the kitchen and pressed her into a chair at the table, facing a boarded-up window with limp curtains. The air smelled of baking and mold and swirled with dancing gray specks. She felt as if she were underwater again, bobbing breathless. When the ceiling light was flipped on she jumped in her seat.

There were framed snapshots on the table, one in front of every chair and several grouped together in the middle like a center-piece. "Those are my children and grandchildren," Pat explained. "Stevie, Bertie, Melanie—the whole brood. I keep them on the table so I don't have to eat alone."

"And Rudy?"

"In the living room. You never get a word in edgewise with him around." Pat moved the chair-facing photos to the center. "Now that I got some company, we can give the kids a rest."

She served tea with bags in the cups, hardened sugar in a bowl, a can of Carnation milk, and slices of pie on chipped plates. The crust wasn't well cooked and the filling made her teeth ache, but still Eva gobbled her piece and asked for more. She was hungry.

Pat brought the pie to the table. "Go on now, help yourself. I bet you haven't eaten anything all day. I know how it is. You run and run, trying to get a million things done, but forget to take care of yourself. Lord, you must be starving! Why don't I make you a sandwich. There's still a little roast beef, it's good with lettuce and mayonnaise."

The lettuce was brown at the edges and the bread turning stale, but Eva ate her sandwich greedily, thanking Pat between bites.

The woman sat across the table, watching her eat. "'Hunger is the best sauce,' Rudy used to tell the kids."

Overhead the light fixture buzzed like a mosquito. Light shone on the framed pictures, bouncing off the glass to the floor and the doorway and into the gloom of the next room. Pat turned the snap-shots in the middle of the table to face Eva: Stevie, Bertie, Melanie, their spouses and children; a smartly dressed, attractive clan. Eva smiled at the photos as if she knew these people well. As if they were her own siblings, nieces, nephews, in-laws, and she was part of the family. She imagined herself among them at a backyard bar-becue . . . Stevie grilling hamburgers while Bertie wiped the picnic table, Melanie counted plastic spoons, and Eva played games with the kids. Later they would talk about diaper rash and thunderstorms, sitcoms and speedboats. No one would know a thing about European history.

How easy to fill a life, she thought, with Frisbees and paper plates; to live in the moment of a warm, lazy afternoon. She picked up a group portrait and put her finger on the glass, front-row center. If she had gone to the barbecue, that's where she would have sat, between Bertie and Melanie.

Pat said, "They like you. I can tell."

And though it was silly notion, Eva hoped that it was true.

10

IN EVA'S DREAM the Luftwaffe was buzzing the neighborhood. A plane landed in the yard with a loud rattling roar and she jerked up in bed, gasping. The engine cut out suddenly and she heard the pilot whistling; the thud of his boots as he approached. A rap on the back door. She dropped to her hands and knees on the floor, intending to roll under the bed, but then, becoming fully awake, she stood up, pulled on a robe, and went to see who was knocking.

She peered through the screen door. A deeply tanned young man in a cap and grimy T-shirt was leaning against the U-shaped handle of a lawn mower. Like Sam, he was dark-haired and lanky. Utterly harmless. "You owe me twelve-fifty," he said. "I'm Al. I mowed your lawn."

"What time is it?" Eva yawned.

"Seven-thirty."

"You start early."

"Lots of grass to cut yet."

She got her purse and paid him, watched him leave. The spring in his step; the whistling. Someone glad to be alive, who didn't mind mowing lawns. Who looked no further than the end of every sunny day. The kind of busy happy fellow Izzy probably would've liked. He might've liked him better than his shy and moody grandson.

He hardly talks to me—just like you.

She talked to him plenty these days.

She turned on the TV and listened to the forecast. Another warm and cloudless day, a peppy woman in a bright dress reported. It was starting to get monotonous. She missed Toronto's gray skies and bone-cracking temperatures: weather you didn't have to live up to.

Eva dressed in a white shirt, white sneakers, white shorts—looking trim and healthy—and ate a hearty breakfast of eggs and toast. Even if she didn't feel perky, she would play the part.

She drove to a florist for an armful of daisies and lilies and a glass vase, then on to the health center. Despite the early morning hour the parking lot was nearly full. She found a spot, got out, went directly to A Wing, 132. His roommate was not around but Izzy was lying on his bed, squinting at the ceiling. She looked up, saw a crack in the plaster in the shape of a sleeve. Maybe he was thinking of shirts—the good old days when he made shirts. Days when he could dress himself. Living a movie of your life was better than nothing.

"Look what I brought," she greeted him. She held out the flowers and he turned his eyes toward them. "Aren't they beautiful? I'll get some water for the vase." She filled it in the washroom, arranged the stems carefully, and put the bouquet on his nightstand.

His eyes followed her movements, his jaw working. He pursed his lips and puffed out his cheeks. "Fff," he said.

She bent over him. "That's right! Flowers, *flowers*. Say it again—try again. Flow-errs."

He stared at her, silent now.

"Never mind. When you're ready. Anyway, it's a good start. I know you're going to get well."

He does look better, she thought. The oxygen tubes were gone, he was breathing on his own, and his skin had lost its purple tinge. His eyes were bright, his forehead cool when she touched it. And now this, trying to speak—a definite improvement. She could leave on Saturday as she planned without feeling guilty.

"I'm flying home soon. Because I have to get back to work."

His mouth opened, stayed loose. A toothless hole. A puzzled gaze.

"I work in a library finding things that people want, books and information. You remember, don't you?"

He shrugged twice, smiled at nothing, pointed at the window.

"It's not the most exciting job, but that didn't matter till recently. Phil was enough excitement for me."

She caught her breath, covered her mouth. Why did she say that? He didn't need to know *that*. If Eva wasn't careful, she'd reveal too much in a spasm of confession—enough to make his eyes roll, to stop his breathing, stall his heart. Another death to answer for.

She leaned closer, studying his face for signs of comprehension. Saw nothing, no response. No reason to worry. And so she added, "Yes, Phil. Your buddy Phil. Do you know how much he meant to me? How much I miss him?"

It felt good to say that. Like steam released from a jiggling valve. She wanted to shake her father's shoulders and say it again, but didn't.

Izzy shuddered, closed his eyes and mouth, put his hand down. Eva pressed her lips together, hardly breathing, waiting. What if he sat up any moment now and scolded her: *What are you saying, that you two—? My daughter and my old friend? You think I don't understand? You think I know nothing?*

"I mean," she said, relenting, "that Phil and I were very close. That he was fun to be with. I miss his company very much, that's all I'm saying."

Lyman came in to check his patient's pulse and blood pressure. Eva stepped away from the bed, turned up her mouth, widened her eyes, and tried to look cheerful. His gelled hair was in spikes like the pointed bars of an iron fence. His snake tattoo wriggled when he moved his arm up and down her father's shriveled body. "Good morning, Izzy. How you doing?"

"He tried to speak," she told him. "He tried to say 'flowers.'"

"Your father rallied last night. The infection finally cleared up."

"That's wonderful," Eva said.

"The flowers look good in here."

"Well, I was just leaving." She touched Izzy's cold foot poking out from under the sheet. "See you again tomorrow."

Eva backed out of the room and hurried down the corridor. She knew where she was going next: one more thing to see.

———————

The sun had already heated the car when she got in, opened the windows, and looked at a road map. The crispness was gone from her shirt and her skin seemed molten. Finally she closed the windows, turned on the air conditioner, and drove out of the parking lot, heading toward Port Chase. First the condo, now the house. Like a dogged tourist checking out roadside attractions.

Her father would've understood her need to visit Phil's house, to see the places where he'd been—as Izzy had to go to the factory and Riversee Lane. Izzy would've known that remembering a person was a way to keep him with you, though looking back was a tricky thing. Her father's memories, however unreliable, had kept him stuck like a phonograph needle in a damaged track . . . and if she wasn't careful, her own recollections might do the same to her.

And yet she had to go there.

She was not going to visit Selma—hoped never to meet her again—but simply to see Port Chase, to wonder how things might have been. If Phil had bought the house with her. If he had lived a long life. She wanted to remember the whole affair, good and bad, his promises, endearments, lies. Maybe then she could fly home, think of him occasionally and casually. Get on with her life.

The trip was uninteresting, a monotonous drive through suburban sprawl: a smear of malls and burger joints, shiny aluminum mobile homes, and oversized billboards advertising everything from plastic surgeons to pet food. But then a sprouting of oaks and pines, a walled-in community of pink-and-white stucco houses, stone or board-and-batten ones. A creek with small boats and yachts. A road that led to Selma's street and thirty-one fifty-seven.

Eva parked beside a pair of fierce-looking stone lions but stayed in the car. She buzzed down the window and stared so hard her eyes stung. A low-spreading beautiful home. A heart-stopping fairy-tale house with yellow walls, a white roof, and moss-colored shutters; with palm trees, hedges, and a lawn like a coat of green felt.

It should've been hers, not Selma's. By all rights hers and Phil's. He should've left Yvonne for her—and never should've taken up with Selma in the first place!

I have something with you, Eva, I didn't think could happen again . . .

Tears pushed at the back of her eyes, which only made her angrier. She was shaking, her face pinched . . . rubbing her arms to calm down, contain herself, be still. Liar! she thought. Bastard! You said you'd take care of me, you said you'd never hurt me. But look at me now. Look what you did!

She backed up the car until she could see around the side of the house and into the backyard. She glimpsed a pool and lounge chairs, a tile-roofed gazebo, a row of tall palms that resembled dusters with their slender trunks and bushy heads. Beyond that a ribbon of beach, an arc of bright water like the grin of a Cheshire cat. For just a moment she closed her eyes and sagged against the car door.

In another dimension, another world, she would've sailed with Phil on the Gulf first thing in the morning. They would have jogged across the sand, then eaten breakfast in the yard, under the gazebo: warm croissants, coffee, and fruit; the news on the radio. She imagined him doing laps in the pool. Imagined him dripping, blocking the sun as she stretched out on a webbed chair, oiling her tanned legs. Lowering his wet, brown body slowly onto hers, the two of them like buttered sandwich slices pressed together.

Beautiful hair, beautiful eyes . . . Sometimes it breaks my heart just to look at you.

Someone entered the backyard and sat down beside the pool. Eva opened the glove compartment and fumbled for the binoculars she'd put there this morning. She held them against her face, adjusting the focus, and Selma zoomed into view. Eva's eyes were burning as she stared at Selma's enormous shades, her puckered lips and thin neck. A teeny string bikini and a shape like a broomstick. Why did Phil want that? Why did he throw her over for *that*?

Another person turned up—a man smoking a cigarette. Fair and slight, with a high forehead, long fingers, and tousled hair, he could pass for Selma's brother. Or a pianist. A painter. He kept his eyes fixed on his knees, ignoring the splendid view.

Neither one of them moved nor spoke. They slouched in their respective chairs as if they were exhausted. Maybe they were. Maybe they'd been screwing like bunnies all night and morning and only came outside for a quick breath of fresh air. Though Selma didn't look like she could bear the weight of a man's body for more than an instant. Well, maybe *this* man, but not a brawny guy like Phil. Unless he swung her on top. Unless they did it on their sides, back to front, as he often did with Eva.

What else did he do with Selma? Did he cuddle her, kiss her eyes, whisper silly words of love—"*pitseleh*" and "moonbeam," "*bubeleh*" and "buttercup"? Thumb her skin like a sculptor with a block of clay—did he do *that*? Or did he just screw her with his eyes bulging, mouth shut, twisted like a thorny vine?

"*Oy-oy-oy!*" he would cry out at the end, with his eyes squeezed into folds, and Eva had to laugh because it was such an *alter-kocker* thing to say in a moment of rapture. Something Izzy might've said while humping her stoic mother spread-eagled on the bed. Who lay there as still as a board, Eva imagined, never experiencing the noisy, sweaty passion that happened between her daughter and Phil.

Suddenly someone was blocking her view, knuckling the car door. She put her binoculars on the floor, stuck her head out the window, and glared. A sour-looking woman with a grim mouth and peaked eyebrows crossed her arms and stared back. "Peeping Tom?" she said. "Don't you know that's illegal?"

"I certainly wasn't peeping. I was birdwatching," Eva said.

The woman glanced into the yard. "I bet you were."

"I spotted a belted kingfisher sitting on a phone wire. I recognized the band on his chest. A very suspicious bird, you know—downright paranoid. He raises the feathers on his head, beats his wings, and makes a fuss whenever someone comes near."

"That was no kingfisher you were zooming in on."

"Who are you anyway? Do you live here?"

"Next door. And I don't like people nosing around, there's too much of that already. A person gets fed up."

"Actually, if you must know, I'm interested in the property."

"It's not for sale."

"It will be. The owner just died, I hear."

"You were staring at the new owner a minute ago."

"I'm sure you're wrong."

"Tell your story to the cops." The neighbor strode to the front of the car, pulled a pen from behind her ear, and wrote down the license-plate number on the palm of her hand.

Eva stumbled out of the car. "No, listen, you made a mistake. I'm not a snoop. Honestly. I knew the man who bought this place— Phil Lewis—he died in March. I only wanted to see his house, out of curiosity."

The woman didn't look up. "I know this car . . . saw it before. What'd you say your name was?"

"Eva. Eva Schneider. I'm visiting my father, Izzy, who had a stroke."

"Sure, I remember him. Chasing down Selma Gold. So now you want to stir things up again, is that it?"

"I'm not here to cause trouble. I told you, I was just looking."

The neighbor turned and squinted at her. "It's bad for property values." She looked Eva up and down. "No one wants to live near murderers, detectives, and Peeping Toms."

"I'm leaving now and won't be back. Let's forget the whole thing."

"If I ever see you here again"—spreading her hands on her hips—"pointing those binoculars at people minding their own business, sitting in their own yard . . ."

"You're never going to see me again."

The woman shrugged. "Go on then. Get moving."

Eva climbed into the car, made a jerky U-turn, and drove back the way she'd come, past the gate and brick wall, the startling eruption of trees. Her throat was dry, her hands slippery on the wheel. She turned up the air conditioner. A useless trip. A foolish idea. Whatever she had hoped to accomplish seemed ridiculous now.

She glanced at her watch—it was after twelve—pulled into a strip mall, and entered a halfway decent-looking diner. The place was nearly empty, so she chose a large booth for herself and slid onto a high-backed banquette. When a waitress came by she ordered a tuna sandwich and salad and a cup of coffee to clear her head, though it wouldn't do much for her nerves.

What if the neighbor phoned the police anyway to report her? Would they wonder what she was doing here, spying with binoculars? Would they think she was threatening Selma? Who might remember having seen her hugging Phil's arm in his condo apartment . . .

She was crazy in love with him, I could tell. And now she wants to get even. You'd better keep an eye on her. I don't feel safe in my own home.

I went there for personal reasons, Eva would tell the detectives. To remember Phil, nothing more. Selma doesn't interest me.

Whoever heard of going back to your former lover's house— which is now solely occupied by his last known mistress, who you have every reason to hate—with no other intention than to walk down memory lane?

Ridiculous, she'd say. I'm a law-abiding citizen! But how can Eva know for sure what she might have done if the neighbor hadn't interfered? What she might've been driven to by overflowing feelings. A scene perhaps—or something worse?

I don't know what got into me. I wasn't myself!

When the coffee arrived at her table it was strong and hot. She drank it a sip at a time, her throat relaxing, opening. Surely the neighbor wouldn't phone and nothing more would happen. Or if she did, the cops would shrug it off—they had more important business to attend to.

Steam rose, washing her face. By force of habit she flicked it away, her thoughts shifting, rewinding: face, steam, water, soup. Like bending over a scalding bowl of chicken soup, Eva thought, your cheeks wet, eyes full, your stomach closed tighter than an oyster's shell.

Whoever heard of a person not liking chicken soup?

Hilda had been a good cook. "Your mother makes the best soup," Izzy liked to announce at the dinner table Friday nights. "Her secret is to boil the chicken's feet too."

Foot soup! Even though she tried hard, Eva couldn't get it down. She'd smell the hen's sacrifice; could hear her squawks and flapping wings; could see her final headless sprint and toeless carcass in the fatty globules on her spoon.

Whoever heard of a child who sides with a dead hen?

That's how her mother spoke, like a criminal investigator. What kind of human being spends all day in her room? Whoever heard of a girl not doing housework? Why do you want to dress like a slut? What kind of person doesn't care what people think of her?

The waitress set her food down and Eva ate her salad first, pushing the coffee aside to cool. Behind her, in the next booth, someone was coughing. No, she was crying. A man was speaking

slowly and gravely, deliberately, as if trying to make himself understood by an idiot: "Well, I'm not saying that. I'm not saying that
at all."

"What—?" The woman choked up.

"Listen to me. I'll try again."

The same deep, buttery voice, the same repeated phrases: it
could've been Phil talking. It could have been Eva weeping. Phil
saying, "It's over now," and Eva sputtering, "Over?"

I'm not saying I don't love you. That's not what I'm saying.

What then? What do you mean?

*Seven years is a long time. We were good together seven years.
How can I forget that?*

*Twice you were free to marry me—twice you married someone
else! Why didn't you pick me?*

*I could never have married you. Not while Roger is my son and
Izzy is your father.*

But you didn't mind fucking me!

You know there was more to it than that.

I only know this—that you dropped me for Lolita.

She's thirty-three.

Half your age.

*I didn't want this to happen. I thought you'd always be in my life.
But you know what kind of man I am—the things I saw, what I lost.
I'm not like ordinary men, there's something wrong inside me.
That's all I can say for myself. I keep looking for someone . . . For a
long time I thought it was you. Now I think it's Selma.*

*You told me I was special! You felt things with me that you couldn't
feel with anyone else.*

*I thought I could love just you but it didn't work. I still love you,
as I can.*

And then she'd started sobbing, making blubbery noises as
loud and pathetic as the sounds from the next booth. Phil gave her
a handkerchief which she still has, unwashed, hidden in a drawer
when she got home that very evening, slipped under a silk teddy

she hasn't had reason to wear since. Sometimes when she's feeling blue she pulls the hankie out again and rubs it all over her face, catching a whiff of his cologne.

I never meant to hurt you.

What am I supposed to do now? How can I go on?

She signaled the waitress for her check and left some bills on the table. When she stood up she didn't turn around to see the couple in the next booth. The man was still explaining, "I'm going to say it one more time..."

Save your pride and walk out! she wanted to tell the woman. He's not worth the trouble. But of course she said nothing at all. No one likes to be overheard and offered advice at such a time—a moment when you shrink in the glare of your lover's gaze like an actor who's forgotten her lines.

"It's over?" she had asked Phil stupidly, her eyes wet, hands shaking in her lap. When she should've stamped her foot and screamed, "It's over! This is the last straw!" Tears stuttering down her cheeks... and even then he reached out to dry her face with his fingers.

Eva hurried outside, squeezing her head between her hands. Phil was everywhere she turned. Phil was tramping her brain to mud.

In front of the diner she saw someone in a skimpy dress, a colorful scarf around her head, leaning over the open trunk of a silver convertible with the top down and leather seats. Someone who reminded her a little of Selma. Who got in the car and drove off.

No, it couldn't possibly...

As if by reflex, Eva started her own car and followed the convertible onto the road. Surely she was wrong and the woman was a stranger who only looked like Selma because she was on her mind—but Eva tailed her anyway, speeding up to change lanes, even running a yellow light. Smacking the wheel and muttering, "Watch it, buddy! Move aside!" at anyone who got in her way, though the chase hardly made sense. Not knowing what she'd do if she pulled up alongside and it really was Selma in her sporty car.

The convertible finally slowed down and turned into a supermarket on the edge of Port Chase, a barn-like building she had noticed on the drive in. The car stopped at the front of the lot and Eva parked a few aisles back. She didn't actually see the woman go inside.

Eva rushed into the store, immediately dazed by the lights and jittery Muzak, the traffic of shopping carts, the narrow, darting eyes of shoppers focused on the looming shelves. She picked up a basket and carried it through the crowded aisles like Little Red Riding Hood, adrift in a forest of groceries. The woman in the scarf and sundress wasn't anywhere in sight and seemed to have vanished. Maybe she was still in her car. Maybe she was out behind the supermarket having a smoke. Just as well, thought Eva. What could she possibly have said to her anyway?

As long as she was here she decided to pick up a few things—milk, apples, bread, cheese, a can of soup, tomato juice. Wednesday already. She was leaving on Saturday. Another meeting with the lawyer, a couple of phone calls: there wasn't much left to do.

Eva read the overhead signs and wandered up and down the aisles, finding neither Selma's twin nor the groceries she was after. Then, when she found something, not knowing what to choose. One-percent or two-percent? Colby, marble, Monterey Jack? There were too many products. Why not just one brand of butter or toilet paper, one row of canned beans? How could she be expected to make important life decisions when she was battered with trifles?

Finally she filled her basket and went up front to pay for her food. The lines went on forever, curling and waving like tentacles, but the Selma look-alike wasn't here either. She waited at the Express checkout, tapping her foot behind a man in a raincoat and fedora with too many things in his basket. Anxious to leave the store, Eva said, "Excuse me, but you have more than eight items. You should be in another line."

The man turned slowly and looked down his nose at her. Sharp nose, thin mouth, jutting cheekbones, fierce eyes. He could pass for a commandant, an agent of the Gestapo. What did he care about fairness or propriety? He stood where he liked.

"Who do you think you're talking to!" the man said.

She drooped like a leaf in the sun. Like boiled cabbage, wet hair, the tail of a beaten dog. Like Izzy slumped in a wheelchair. Or long before his stroke, when he hunched in an armchair and told her the one about the Nazi and his papers . . .

"They took away my citizenship," he said when he thought she was old enough to hear it. "They called me to the police station, I had to sit in an office with a *farshtinkener* Nazi bureaucrat—Horst, a former schoolmate—and he stole from me my passport, my papers, and everything. He left me stateless, empty-handed, walking home like a whipped dog."

But what could her father have done? When Eva was younger she believed he should've grabbed the Nazi bastard by his collar and slapped him till he gave back the passport and papers, but now she knew better: that sometimes speaking out isn't the best strategy.

For instance, in this case, face to face with a crackpot capable of anything—of pummeling her with his basket or attacking her in the parking lot. Why risk so much when so little is at stake? Better to save your bravery for something that matters. So Eva switched to another line, her eyes downcast and her tongue still.

Outside, she couldn't remember where she had parked the car. Couldn't remember the plate number, only that she was looking for a light blue Buick. She heaved her bag of groceries and staggered from car to car. Somewhere in the middle, she thought, or maybe toward the back of the lot . . . this side or that side. The sun reflecting off the pavement, the smell of oil and gas and tar, were giving her a headache. She pulled her sunglasses from her purse and covered her eyes. A picture of Selma flashed in her mind—not in a sundress but relaxing in her splendid yard in a next-to-nothing bikini, staring at the ocean through her stylish shades.

Someone was following her. A shopping cart clattered behind, stopping when Eva stopped, moving again when she dashed ahead. What if the commandant had come after her anyway, determined to teach her a lesson? *If you ever speak to me like that again, here's what I will do . . .* But surely she was imagining it. Her nerves were really twangy today. When she got back to the bungalow she'd visit Pat next door, have a nice cup of tea, a slice of pie. Talk to her and her happy children on the kitchen table.

The car! Eva found it at last, nosed into a spot by a pole at the side of the lot. She opened the trunk, leaned over, dropped in her plastic bag. Shot back, thinking someone was going to shove her into the trunk. Heard a squeal and clickety-clack just over her shoulder. Felt something bump her heel. Jerked around: it was Selma. Incredible as it seemed, it was Selma Gold.

Her sundress had a tight bodice and thin straps tied at the neck, the sort of thing a child would wear. Her knees were showing, but her eyes were barely visible behind dark glasses. A paisley scarf around her head; long legs, sandals, and purple-painted toenails. No taller than Eva, which wasn't very big at all.

The shopping cart was between them, filled with bulging plastic bags that showed the tops and corners of things: a cereal box, container of milk, bottle of Pepsi, a carton of cigarettes. "I thought it was you!" Selma said. She sounded squeaky, out of breath. "It's been so long I wasn't sure, and I only saw you one time, but you get a feeling about things. I said to myself, 'That's her.'"

"I'm visiting my father."

"I'm Selma Gold," she said, "in case you don't remember. I used to live in Phil's condo. That's where I saw you, when I knocked on his door and he opened it and there you were."

"I remember," Eva said.

"I always wanted to tell you something . . . like, about me and him."

"You don't have to say anything."

"Yeah, but it's been bothering me. I know you knew about us and I don't want you thinking that I stole him away or anything. I mean, I'm not a home wrecker. Phil was on the make. He was already looking for someone else when he met me."

"Why do you care what I think?" Eva grabbed the front of the cart. "Am I supposed to forgive you?"

"It's no big deal. But I saw you here and I was, like, given this *opportunity*." A horn honked somewhere close and she glanced over her shoulder. "I got this friend Denny who tells me these spiritual things. He says we get second chances—*holy opportunities*—to help whoever we hurt in the past, to fix things up a little. That's how you wipe the slate clean. Then you just start again, trying to be holier."

"How are you helping me by saying Phil was chasing someone else when he was still with me?"

"Now you know it wasn't my fault, you'll stop hating me, and that'll, like, *free* you. You'll be a happier person."

"And how do I stop hating Phil?"

"Yeah, well, that's a problem, him being dead and all. When I heard about what Vic did, I was a mess too. I had all these feelings I didn't know what to do with." She pushed her glasses up her nose. "So what I did, I went to the dock and threw petals in the Gulf. Denny was there with me and we said some words, sang songs, remembered all the good times I had with Phil. We talked about Vic too, the nice things I did with him, the way it used to be with us. I really loved him once and I'm sorry that he's locked up . . . even knowing what he did." She chewed a corner of her lip. "So then my head cleared and I didn't resent him so much."

"But he shot Phil!"

"I *know* that."

"You throw a few petals in the water and everything's fine?"

"The murder was a big shock, but it didn't happen yesterday. I been, like, adjusting."

"There's always the house if you need consolation. The pool and gazebo, a priceless view of sand and sea . . ."

Selma looked at Eva over her glasses. "So you saw it. Yeah, it's a beaut, all right. Nine rooms, private beach. Worth a small fortune—and it's all mine."

Eva flinched. "What do you mean all yours? What about Roger?"

"One hundred percent mine. That's what it said in the will."

Eva chewed a thumbnail, her pulse ticking quickly. Then she drew a breath and said, "Maybe you were less shocked by Phil's death than you're letting on."

"What the fuck does that mean?"

"You knew Vic was angry at Phil and threatened to kill him. Maybe you encouraged him. It wouldn't have taken very much."

Selma swung the cart aside so the women were closer. "You got a suspicious mind, which isn't very holy." She pointed a finger at Eva's nose. "Denny would say you need to go home and concentrate on nice things. Denny would say you better clear your head for your own good."

Eva slammed the trunk of her car and felt for her keys in her pocket. She took a few steps back. In another lane someone leaned on his horn again, long and hard.

"Bye. Gotta go now." Selma turned on her heel, aiming her cart at the noise. "Good to see you, Yvonne. It was such an *opportunity*."

"It's *Eva*—not Yvonne."

"Whatever. *Mrs. Lewis*."

"I'm Eva Schneider. I was his lover, not his wife."

"Huh?" Selma spun around. "You mean he wasn't married?"

"He married Yvonne in 1984 but kept seeing me."

"A wife and a mistress? A wife, a lover, and, like, *me*?"

"I told her about you. I sent her a note."

"*You* did?"

Eva nodded.

"That wasn't very nice." Selma shook her head. "But it all worked out in the end. He dumped her, he dumped you, then he gave me a great big house for us to live in happily ever after."

"You didn't know him very well. He would've tired of you too in a few years, maybe less."

"He was tired of *you*, not me! Phil was in love with me and bought whatever I wanted—a house, diamonds, anything. Because I excited him like nobody else did—not you and not his wife."

"Understand one thing—he loved me more than anyone. I was very special to him."

"Yeah, right. Whatever." The horn again: two longs and three shorts. "Look, someone's waiting for me."

Eva turned around without another word and got in the car. For good measure she locked the doors and started the engine. In the rearview mirror she saw Selma trotting away, pushing the cart with one hand, and pulling at the bodice of her sundress with the other as if it were scratchy or too tight. Like a child, Eva thought again. A bad child with a big mouth. Phil must've been losing it.

Losing his head? Losing his heart? For an ordinary gold-digging tramp? No, it wasn't possible: his heart belonged to Eva. *With you I feel alive again.* Whatever he felt for Selma had been fleeting, unimportant. She flattered him, amused him, and Phil was infatuated. An old man's infatuation. How could it have been anything more? How could he go on without the lifeblood of Eva's love?

I loved you even in high school. Boys my age didn't interest me, I only wanted to be with you.

But I was married to Rachel.

I hung around the factory, smiled at you at parties, dyed my hair honey blonde, wore my sweaters skin-tight—and still you looked right through me!

I saw you, all right.

I was twenty-three when Rachel died. Why didn't you chase me then?

I was mourning the loss of my wife.

And after?

*There were others . . . though I don't know their names anymore.
I kept my mind on the business and worked till I couldn't see straight.*

When you married Irene, I lost hope.

*Irene is a strong woman. She got me through a bad time. Rachel's
death was hard on me, it made me remember what I try not to think
about.*

You mean about Rivke?

*And even before that. My mother, my brother and sister in the
ghetto . . . all the ones I couldn't take with me when I escaped. The
ones who died, like Rivke, because I couldn't save them.*

*You couldn't help what happened to them. The ghetto wasn't
your doing. The raid wasn't your fault. My God, you sound like Izzy!*

We're not so different, me and him.

*Except that many people owe their lives to your bravery. Except
that you're a hero!*

*Is that why you were in love with me? Your knight in rusty
armor? How disappointed you must be now.*

The truth is that Eva loved him longer and better than Phil ever
loved her. The truth is that two people never love each other in
absolutely equal amounts, no matter how much they try.

Or else he didn't love her at all and lied to her from the start. At
first he would've been flattered by her stubborn adoration. He
might've even gotten off on sleeping with his son's wife—in one-
upping the boy who competed with him daily for control of the
business. Years later she might have been an extra, like a spare tire
to use when Yvonne wore thin.

But can love be so easily faked? Was Eva such an eager fool she
overlooked his half-truths?

And yet the body doesn't lie: it tells you what your brain can't.
Her blood and bones, heart and cunt, sang out with pleasure.

Except that it didn't last. Maybe Selma was right and he had
simply grown tired of her, as he grew tired of Yvonne. Maybe it was
true that Selma thrilled him like no one else. With someone young
and energetic on his arm, in his bed, Eva was superfluous. *I tried to*

love just you . . . But didn't—or couldn't. Either way it comes to this: he dropped her for a young bitch!

Was she supposed to feel better now? Her mind clear? Instead she felt she wanted to scream. The windows were up, the car idling, the air conditioner hissing like a punctured blimp, so who would hear? She opened her mouth, her lips moving, her shoulders lifted to her ears, but made only the weakest sound, a mewl like a kitten's cry. She tried again; a third time. Again, nothing more than a squeak. She doubled over as if she'd been stabbed with a bayonet.

Finally she sat up and gripped the wheel stiffly. She backed out of the parking lot and drove without direction at first, through the rest of the town, and then along U.S. 19. The highway moved gently, like a banner swaying in a breeze. Malls and stores and billboards undulated, eerie and huge, as if they were part of a dream. And then she saw the turnoff for the health care center and made a sudden left turn.

Where else but here? she thought. Who else to talk to but her half-conscious father?

She parked the car clumsily, not quite fitting it between the allotted lines. Someone glanced her way when she slid out and Eva said, "It's too damn narrow!" Then she hurried inside.

He wasn't in the lobby, so she went straight to Izzy's room. A young man in a white coat that looked too big for him was standing over her father. She peered at the back of his neck, his cinnamon-colored cowlick, and thought he ought to be outside playing with marbles.

When Eva stepped closer he turned and introduced himself. "I'm Dr. Willard," he said. "You must be Mr. Schneider's daughter."

She stared at his snub nose, his wholesome pink, freckled cheeks. "Do we look that much alike?"

His cheeks darkened slightly and he cleared his throat before he spoke. "Your father's been trying to talk again today. That's a good sign."

"You think he'll recover?"

"We can't say at this point."

"Will he ever get out of bed again?"

"We'll just have to wait and see. But trying to speak is an indication of increased awareness." The doctor turned back to Izzy and said very distinctly, "Are you feeling better, Mr. Schneider?"

Her father pressed his lips together and moved his jaw and lower face as if he were chewing. Then he opened his mouth a bit and rounded it to form an *O*, exhaling softly. "You see?" said Dr. Willard.

"He's been making sounds all along. I heard him trying to say 'flowers.'"

"I believe he just said 'no.'"

Eva sat down in the chair next to Izzy's bed, across from Dr. Willard. "Is there anything else you can tell me about his condition?"

"Only that he's stable. Of course, if there's any change, we'll be in touch." Then the doctor excused himself, he had to continue his rounds. He left the room abruptly, his white coat flapping like a sail in a gust, and nearly collided with Izzy's roommate just coming through the door. He pushed the man's walker aside as if it were a stage prop.

The roommate rolled his walker up to the TV. He turned it on, turned it up, and flattened his cheek against the screen. A crackle of static. Eva glanced at the tall, stooped figure: he looked content.

She reached for her father's hand. "Are you trying to say something again?"

Izzy pursed his dry lips, his sunken cheeks like craters, and rubbed the back of her hand with his thumb. His touch was insubstantial, a strip of paper brushing her skin. He turned his eyes toward the closed window and a wedge of sky.

"I'll do the talking then."

He pointed at the window and clawed in the direction of the glass as if reaching for clouds . . . or maybe a trio of angels. She pressed his hand between hers. Was he thinking about the next world? Finally tuned to the future instead of the noisy past? She drew a breath and spoke fast.

"Remember when I was small," she said, "those Sunday mornings you stayed in bed while Mama was cooking breakfast—and I'd sneak into your room so you could give me a pony ride? Sitting on your raised knees, my feet on your chest, squeezing your hands, and you bounced me till my teeth chattered—'Giddy-up, giddy-up!' Remember how we laughed so hard I almost fell off? Then Mama always came in waving a spatula. 'That's enough already, Izzy. She's too old for bouncy-bouncy.' And after she walked out I'd slide down into your arms. With my nose in your neck I could smell soap and Old Spice and something sort of leafy. You were more important than anyone—king of the universe. And I was your princess. I never loved you more than I loved you Sunday morning."

He turned away from the window, his eyes sweeping over her and lighting on the ceiling, his mouth shaped like an *O* again. *No,* he remembered nothing? *No,* he wasn't so important, not the king of anything—or *no,* she wasn't a princess?

"When did I know I'd let you down, your true love was Hilda? When did I understand your heart was too full of her, too full of grieving and a family of dead souls to leave any room for me?

"About the same time, I guess, I figured out you weren't half as powerful as I once thought." Her shoulders humped forward and she lowered her eyes.

"Even in grade school I knew the world was a scary place, I knew you couldn't protect me. Kids would shove me, call me names, and you would talk to their parents, but it just went on or got worse. They made fun of how you spoke, they goose-stepped in the schoolyard. They raised their arms—'Heil Hitler!'—and shouted 'Kraut!' and 'Fascist!' When I cried that we were Jews, that my father fled the Nazis and his family was killed in the war, they called me 'kike' and 'Christ-killer.'

"I blamed you. Because you weren't Canadian. Because you had an accent and a family dead in Europe. Because we weren't fair-haired Gentiles who went to church and got together on Sundays.

"Years later Phil told me worse things, about your guilt. The relatives you left behind and how you never forgave yourself." She paused. "I have to say this: I haven't forgiven you either. Phil had his own regrets—but in fact he acted bravely, he risked his life to save others. While you . . . you just ran away."

She looked at their flattened hands sandwiched together. "'You weren't there, you don't know,' Phil used to tell me. 'You can't possibly understand.'

"I want to understand, I do. I want to know what's in the letters you got from Europe. But also . . . I don't want to think about all that. I want to forget everything that happened before I was born. I don't want to carry the past—your past, not mine—like an old swollen suitcase I can't put down."

She lifted her eyes. Izzy's lips were stretched thin and curled under, barely visible, closing and opening like a puppet's wooden mouth. He kept making a sound like a plop or a pop of air. "What is it?" Eva said. "The letter *B*? The word 'but'?"

But it *is* your past—our past! But you're never going to understand! Is that what he was trying to say?

"Phil would say, 'The war's over, nobody cares anymore, what's done is done. It doesn't help to look back, it only makes you crazy. You have to live in the here and now.'"

She let go of Izzy's hand, pushed her chair a few inches back toward the window. "He only told a few of us anything about his past, yet everyone knew how much he suffered, how he finally triumphed. People admired him, they said he had the right stuff—a man you could count on. I remember company picnics when I was a teenager . . . how I'd blush and stutter when he asked if I was having fun. My legs would go soft and I couldn't move."

She cleared her throat to steady her voice. "I was already in love with him then. I even loved Phil when I was married to Roger—

unhappily, as you know. He married me for his mother's sake, not because he wanted me. If not for Sam, we would've divorced years sooner than we did. I used to cry to Phil about it, ask him to explain his son and tell me what I should do. I let him know I was miserable . . . and finally got his attention. He felt the same as I did—that Roger was moody and weak. 'He doesn't deserve you,' Phil said."

She stood up, stepped back, and Izzy followed her with his eyes. Eva turned and faced the window, pleading her case to the angels. "One day he looked twice and saw me in a different way. He stared at me across a table and found his beloved Rivke. From then on I was always in his thoughts, I was in his heart." And in his arms, in his bed, she couldn't say out loud.

"Phil was confident, passionate, the only hero left to me. A man who wouldn't let me down."

She rested her forehead against a cool pane of glass. "But I was wrong about him. Whatever he might've been in the past, he wasn't like that anymore."

She came back to the side of the bed. "There's something else you should know . . . I ran into Selma Gold today when I was shopping. She owns Phil's house and is very happy about it." She leaned over and lowered her voice. "I think she played a bigger part in his death than anyone ever guessed. I think it's quite possible she took advantage of Vic's rage and instigated the murder. Maybe she even planned it."

Her father shrugged and wrinkled his nose.

"But of course I can't prove anything."

Izzy looked past her, his jaw moving up and down, making a sound like bubbles breaking, pop-pop-pop-pop . . .

"She told me something else too . . . that Phil didn't love me." She grabbed hold of the bed rail. "But he did love me—I know he did! Even if it didn't last." She paused, breathing too fast, then inhaled and spoke again. "He never would've settled down, not with me or anyone else. I see that now, I understand—a part of him was broken. No one could've given him enough or stopped his suffering."

Izzy's eyes were wide open, gazing into hers as she said very softly, "He loved me the best he could. He did try. He tried hard."

A sudden loud puffing noise and Eva stopped talking. Izzy's lips were moving again, the top one protruding. He was huffing as if he meant to blow out a candle. A sound like *V*. For "Eva"? Was he saying her name?

Or was it the letter *F* again? She dropped the rail and moved closer; heard yet another sound—a sound like *L*. *F* first, then *L*. "Flowers? Is it that again?" But he wasn't looking at the vase on his nightstand, only at her.

Not "flowers." *Full*, she thought. That's what he's trying to say. Full of sadness, full of pain. Because of what she told him. Because of what he already knew.

She bent low and put her head against his chest. "I shouldn't have said as much as I did. I'm sorry if I upset you."

He plucked at her sleeve with his left hand. "Ff... lll. Ff... lll..."

Not "flowers." Not "full." The word was "Phil"—he was saying "Phil." Obviously he meant Phil. She should have known the first time. His friend and enemy, Phil, *Phil!* He wasn't calling Eva: he was calling Phil.

11

ON THE STREETS OF TORONTO snow was piled high, turning dirty brown. The sky was a gray sponge of clouds and flurries were predicted. The roads were wet and slippery, traffic slow and heavy on the drive north. Still, Eva was glad to be in her car, on her way to work; in the close woolly embrace of routine.

A busy day at the library, every chair in sight filled. A crowd at the information desk, all the phones ringing. She raised a finger—"One moment"—and picked up a receiver. "Language, Literature and Fine Arts . . . Yes, second floor, yes . . . till eight-thirty, that's right. Five o'clock on weekends. That's right . . . that's right." Then she turned back to the lineup in front of the desk. "How can I help you?" she asked the nearest person.

Someone wanted change for the photocopier; someone was looking for videos. Two people asked for directions to the washrooms. Where's the foreign language collection? Where's art and music? Eva pointed this way and that, feeling like a traffic cop. Is this what she's paid for?

Finally, along came a student doing research who had to be shown how to use the microfilm machine (which gave her a welcome chance to get up and stretch her legs). Then there was a slight woman with rapidly blinking eyes looking for criticism of Jane Austen's novels. After that an old man with egg-white false teeth and an interest in idioms. ("Did you know that minding your p's and q's has to do with pints and quarts?") And all the while the phones kept ringing like bleating goats.

Her job, as she saw it, was to meet the needs of strangers; to give them whatever they asked for: citations, abstracts, or full text articles; catalogues, magazines, and, most of all, books. All this regardless of how understaffed they were, how exhausted Eva was from increasing evening and weekend hours.

On her break she entered the mall attached to the library, sat in a coffee shop, and looked through the paper. Plans were in the works, she read, to make the West German mark the single currency for East and West Germany, accelerating the move toward reunification... expected to happen by the end of the year.

Her father would be wary, she thought, of the economic power of a reunited Germany. He'd ask if such a country would remain democratic, aware of its obligations to Jews because of Nazi crimes. He'd brood about skinheads and other neo-fascists. Then it would all come back to him—the war, the taunts and violence. He'd wake at night in a jittery sweat, trying to shake visions of storm troopers from his head. By day, he would cross the street to avoid a man in uniform. As Eva did at the library, giving wide berth to the stuttering security guard.

If only she could phone Izzy and talk to him about the news. Tell him that she understood; that she too had nightmares: bombs going off, buildings falling, people wounded on the streets. Was it possible, she'd ask him, to let go of history—what she knew of him and Phil, the strings of her life tied to theirs—and start again?

We must remember, he'd reply. This is how we keep them alive, Rosa, Mutti, Martin, Kurt...

Alive and writhing in her, too, though she didn't even know them.

She checked her watch, finished her coffee, picked up another piece of the paper, the business news. Expecting nothing remarkable here. But there, on the second page, a photo of Roger in the shop, his legs wide and arms spread as if he meant to hug the machines and all their operators in one mighty gesture. He was grinning at the camera, his tiny teeth visible between his slightly parted lips, his eyes squeezed to nothing. There was joy in his expression, as she'd rarely seen in their marriage, and then only when he was with Sam. She skimmed the article, inhaled deeply, and read it again, more carefully this time.

Diversifying, modernizing, expanding into new markets, attracting younger customers, sourcing from Asia: Roger was doing all that. Working at fever pitch and changing the company dramatically, the story claimed. Roger Lewis, sources said, was focused and passionate, tireless and bold. Known as a modern thinker, aggressive, entrepreneurial. Relentless too, the article said. Gets an idea and runs with it. Makes it happen. Never quits. Someone was even quoted as saying that Phil Lewis and Sons was only the success it was because of Roger, who'd been secretly running the business for years while his father followed "other pursuits" in Florida.

Eva folded the paper and put it down. Yes, it was probably true that Roger worked behind the scenes to keep the company going while his father shopped for real estate and copulated in Florida. He was diligent, if nothing else. Throughout the years of their marriage he would be at the plant by six—whether Phil was in town or not—returning in the evening. She was left to drop off and pick up Sam from daycare and rush to and from her job at the library in between. Often he would be at the factory on weekends too. You had to wonder when he managed to meet Loreen for a quickie. He only bothered *shtupping* his wife once in a blue moon—which angered her at first but suited her perfectly after she started seeing Phil.

Now he had what he'd always wanted: the business, praise, Loreen—even his picture in the paper. Roger had more of everything, while she had less.

Eva returned to work. She spent time in the staff room reading publishers' catalogues, then she was back in the open, sitting at the info desk answering questions. "Cassettes are in the second aisle . . . Get change on the main floor . . . The washroom is behind you and to the right." Her brain eventually slowing down. A dull

ache in her forehead as she stared at her computer screen, hunched
to shield her eyes from the too-bright ceiling lights.

Dinner soon, she thought as she fielded endless questions.
Dinner break in half an hour.

At five she went to supper with another librarian, Allison Dill,
someone she'd been working with for nearly a decade, though
they'd never met for a drink or movie or gone to each other's apartments. Eva never invited her. She was tired at the end of the day,
her only thought to get home and see Sam. On her days off she did
chores and anything else she'd avoided doing during the week.
Saturday nights she watched TV—with Sam if he was home—or
read a book. It didn't take much to fill the little free time she had.

Allison had never asked Eva anywhere either. Maybe she was
too busy doing things with her husband or shy, afraid of rejection.
Nevertheless, Eva considered her to be a friend. If neo-fascists ever
rose to power in Canada and started rounding up Jews, Eva would
ask her to hide her under the floorboards: the litmus test of friendship according to the Schneiders.

*You think so much of your goyishe friend, why don't you ask her if
she'll hide you when the Nazis come!*

"So what do you feel like?" Allison said. "Chinese? Italian?"

"Somewhere we can eat in peace."

They chose a small bistro on the ground floor of a hotel that
bordered the north side of the mall, mainly because it was dimly lit
and nearly empty at this hour, unlike the library adjoining the
south side. It was possible, Eva realized as she sat down in a plush
chair, to spend days, even weeks, without breathing natural air:
to drive from the underground parking in her building to the lot
below the library and ride a poky elevator to Language, Literature
and Fine Arts; to work in the mall, eat in the mall, shop, stroll,
lounge in the mall. If she took the subway to and fro—one station in
the concourse under her apartment complex, the other at the end
of the mall's lower level—she might never see the light of day. If she
cared to, she could stay overnight, here in this very hotel, and never

leave the mall at all. Sam would visit her now and then, fretting that she was red-eyed and winter-pale the whole year round.

The boy was a worrier. He worried that she didn't get enough sleep or fresh air. He worried that she was lonely and sad without a husband, never guessing that Roger was a stand-in for Phil; that Roger didn't excite her, had never made her heart stutter, her innards boil. That she was glad to lose him. If Phil hadn't proposed to Irene in 1971, Roger would've been out of the question.

"What are you having?" Allison said.

They ordered the same thing, grilled chicken on greens with a low-cal dressing, then squinted at their food in the dusky light. Allison had a puckered mouth with grooves over her top lip and ate as though she were sipping morsels through a straw. With her ropy hair and long neck she resembled a mop. When she spoke again her voice dropped as if she were afraid of the dark or feared waking someone up, and Eva had to lean across the table to hear her.

"Tell me about your trip. How is your father?"

"Oh, more or less the same. Good days, bad days, but no improvement overall. Well, maybe just a little. He said the name of his friend Phil."

"You mean your ex-father-in-law? The man who was shot?"

"Same guy." Eva poked her salad with a fork and stared down at the plate. Here was an opportunity to tell Allison everything, about the affair, Selma and Vic; to clear her mind a little. To talk about the burden of the memories she carried—worse since she's been back.

"The trip was hard," she began, but said no more than that. Because a woman like Allison, married and faithful for thirty years, couldn't possibly understand Eva's attraction to Phil—an obviously off-limits man with a dark past. There was nothing to be gained by exposing herself to Allison. Someone as wary as that would probably look the other way when the Nazis came calling.

"You had to go," said Allison. "It was the right thing to do."

"I couldn't stay away."

"Well, at least it was warm. Did you go to the beach?"

"I stayed in his bungalow and had to drive a long way to see anything interesting. But when I went through his papers I found a pack of old letters . . ."

"Love letters?" Her voice rose.

"Letters from his mother and sister written during the war . . . before they were murdered."

"What do they say?"

"They're in German. I have to get them translated."

"You must be dying to find out."

"I'm looking for a translator who doesn't charge a fortune."

Allison sucked a shred of chicken. "I have a German friend," she said, "who runs her own business. Medical equipment, I think. She's perfectly bilingual and her office isn't far from here." She tugged on a string of hair. "Let me have a word with her. I think she'll want to help you. She might even do it for free."

"Medical equipment?" Josef Mengele came to mind: medical experiments. "What's your friend like?"

"She's not anti-Semitic, if that's what you're asking. Not every-one sees the world in terms of 'us' and 'them.' Not everyone blames their misfortunes on others."

"I just thought . . ."

"Some people are generous with no ulterior motives. They act decently just because."

"Well, I'm sure there must be . . ."

"Her name is Olga Bauer. I'll phone her today."

Saturday morning the buzzer sounded. Eva spoke to the intercom: "Who's there?"

"Roger." His voice crackled. He said more but she didn't catch it.

"Sam's not here yet. You're too early."

"What?" she heard. "What—?"

"Oh, come on up." She buzzed him in.

Moments later he stood in the doorway, brushing snow from a cashmere coat Eva hadn't seen before, the collar rakishly turned up. Dark blue textured shirt, buttons hidden under a placket—the sort of thing his father would wear. He looked wealthy. Powerful. Sure of himself, she thought.

He had not been so confident at twenty-three, she remembered, when they were newly married and he worried about pleasing his bride. Because she was older and had already lost her virginity to a married policeman, he was nervous in bed. She expected him to ravish her (as she imagined Phil would've done), but Roger was hesitant. She had to whisper sweet-nothings, guide his fingers, lips, tongue; encourage him to slow down. Remind him to remove his socks. And though he improved over time, Eva wouldn't be swept away until she landed in the arms of his father.

She tightened the belt and clutched the top of her loose terry bathrobe. There was nothing underneath except for white bikini panties.

"Sam's playing volleyball this morning. I told you."

"Shit! I forgot." Roger ran his fingers through his hair, as thick and curly as Phil's. He rolled his eyes, nut-sized, as small as Phil's. "What now?" he said, and his little pointy teeth showed—also like his father's.

"You might as well come inside. I just made coffee."

He shifted his weight from leg to leg, unused to hospitality from his ex.

"It's really okay," she said. "Sam will be back soon."

She stroked a sleeve of his velvety coat as she hung it in the closet. Phil had a coat like that. She used to love to rub her chin and cheeks on his woolly lapels, as soft as cotton candy. Once they made love standing up, while he was still in his coat. He said she drove him crazy. He hiked her skirt above her hips and clawed the crotch of her pantyhose till it tore free.

But Roger swore she didn't turn him on—it was her fault! Her tits were small, her hips wide; he didn't like the texture of her hair, the smell and feel of her skin. Even worse than that, she was bossy and aggressive. In order to get it up, he said he had to close his eyes and pretend she was someone else.

While she was doing the same thing.

Now he glanced around her apartment, wondering where to sit. "The living room," she pointed. "I'll bring the coffee in there."

She didn't have to ask how he liked it—no sugar, a splash of milk. Some things you never forget, no matter how trivial. Silly things, like what a person reads in the toilet, the kind of pasta he prefers, the way he wears his shoes without socks, weather permitting. Today he wore expensive socks with a chevron pattern as he entered her living room and started pacing up and down.

He never could stay still: one of the things that nearly drove her mad when they were married. Drumming his fingers, jiggling a leg, walking round and round in tight circles like a windup toy—and never really listening. You could talk for minutes, talk for hours; he'd nod and mutter but wouldn't hear. Ask him to repeat a single sentence, a phrase even—*two words I just said!*—and he'd frown, trying to place you, as if you were an unwelcome guest who crashed his party.

Unlike Phil, who used to pull her onto his lap and say, "Tell me. Tell me everything." Laughing at the right places, tugging her hair, clucking his tongue: "They did *what*? You said *that*?"

In the kitchen she got the coffeepot, two mugs, milk, and spoons, and carried everything back in her arms. "Sit already," she told him, and Roger plopped down on the couch. She sat in a chair facing him, a glass table between them, and poured coffee, a little milk. When she bent forward to pass him the cup he glanced at her partly open robe, then turned his eyes elsewhere.

"You gave me this robe for my thirty-eighth birthday."

"It suits you."

"A compliment?"

He shrugged and drank his coffee.

He was never one for compliments. Rather, he would tell her what was wrong with the way she dressed, the way she spoke, what she cooked, how she loaded the dishwasher—even her expression. *That hangdog face again! The world's still spinning, Eva. Why don't you cheer up?* If he had a bad day at the plant, he'd spill things and break things and lumber around the house, grumbling that she didn't understand how hard it was to work with his father— the put-downs and rivalry—and anyway she didn't care, she was too wrapped up in herself. Tired after spending the day doing next to nothing! Dressed in an ugly tracksuit! Serving spaghetti with canned sauce! Why didn't she ever welcome him home with a brilliant smile, wearing something sexy, his favorite supper of pot roast and gravy bubbling on the stove?

Then he would say—or she would say—"Why did I ever marry you?" Once they even said it together at the same time.

Eva sipped her coffee. She was forty-seven and several months, older than Roger by six years. Loreen was only twenty-nine, pretty, sweet, and obliging. Was he happy at last?

"How's married life?" she asked.

He spread his arms on the back of the sofa, rubbing the material. "Oh, you know . . ."

"I don't know."

He crossed his legs right over left, then crossed them the other way. "Loreen says I work too much, she never sees me anymore. When I'm not in Europe or Asia, I get to the plant at sunrise and don't leave till suppertime. You used to give me grief about the same thing."

"It's not a healthy way to live."

"I love what I'm doing now—running the show, calling the shots. I work harder and get more done than my dad did. You want to know how much I accomplished in the past year? A thirty percent increase in sales—and I've just begun."

"I saw your face in the paper and read all about it."

"You have no idea how easy it's been..."

"Now that Phil's out of the way?"

Roger pulled his sleeve up and ostentatiously checked his watch. "Still no sign of Sam. I should come back later."

"He won't be much longer."

"I don't have all day," he said.

She picked up the coffeepot and refilled Roger's mug. She didn't want him to go yet. She liked seeing his clothes and face and hearing his familiar voice; the Phil-ish way he turned his hands when he spoke, as if stirring the air.

"How was Sam while I was in Florida?" Eva said.

"You think we beat him or something?"

"He didn't say much when I got back, that's all."

"He asked about you, worried about you. Sam's a big worrier. He asked if Izzy's going to live, if you'll be okay if he doesn't. Things like that."

"What did you say?"

"I told him not to worry so much."

"He's a good boy," Eva said.

"At least we did something right."

"Maybe we don't deserve any credit. Maybe Sam turned out all right in spite of us."

"We took him places, read to him. We were always hugging and kissing him. What more were we supposed to do?"

"But you and me... our marriage..."

"We had some good times together. He didn't know about the rest."

Good times with Roger were really good times with Sam: pushing the baby in his stroller through a park, beside the lake, or along the streets of the Annex where they lived in a big house; teaching Sam to throw a ball, fly a kite, ride a trike; singing him to sleep at night; swinging him by the arms as they walked together, three abreast, the boy like a sparkling pendant on a necklace. There was a truce between Roger and Eva during those years. With Sam in their lives they were busier and merrier, more willing to overlook the holes in their relationship. Though they knew this happy interlude would end as he grew—and by then even a second child wouldn't save their marriage.

When Sam started grade school in 1979 (the same year, as it turned out, that Irene and Phil divorced), old enough to have his own friends and a separate life, and she saw how he was leaving her bit by bit, year by year, Eva was desolate. She started phoning her father-in-law, asking him to stop by for a drink on an evening when her husband was out late so they could speak in private. When Roger worked on a Saturday she'd leave Sam with a neighbor and rush to meet Phil for lunch. Breathless and fidgety, she'd talk about her failed marriage and tell him with lowered eyes how much she admired him. If only Roger were more like Phil!

Just divorced, Phil knew the importance of being loved—the awfulness of living with the wrong mate. When she whimpered that her husband was indifferent, he nodded. When she cried that he was heartless, he gave her his handkerchief. Roger had been devoted to his mother (may she rest in peace) and was hard-working from the start—but also (Phil shook his head) self-centered and stubborn. He didn't deserve a wife like Eva, whose needs he couldn't understand. All in all, an unhappy situation, Phil agreed.

Then one day a year later he took her hand across a dirty table and everything changed.

Sam was ten when Roger and Eva finally broke up, old enough to sense that something serious was happening: his mommy and daddy didn't love each other anymore.

"He would've felt it," Eva said, "the tension, the anger . . . I feel awful about that."

Roger finished his coffee. "We all have things to feel bad about. It doesn't help to dwell on them—you have to live in the moment."

"Your father used to say that."

"My father said a lot of things." He squinted at his watch again and stood up.

"One more thing," she spoke quickly, "about when I was in Florida."

He turned toward the doorway and stroked a crease in his pantleg until it was flattened.

"One day when I was there I ran into Selma Gold. She told me things that made me think some smart detective ought to bring her in for more questioning."

"What are you saying?"

"You know how Phil's share of the house went to Selma, not you?"

"I got the company, she got the house. That's what he decided."

"Suppose she was greedy enough to have wanted your father dead. Suppose she'd been talking to Vic . . ."

"The cops say she's innocent."

"I have a feeling about her."

"It's almost a year now and nothing new has turned up. For my part it's over with—he's dead and buried, case closed. Why don't you leave it alone already? Selma doesn't matter."

Eva covered her face in her hands: everything mattered too much; her mind always working. In the dark of her palms she saw Phil through the moon-eyes of a teenager—hunky, hairy, steam-roller-strong. Phil-the-mighty. Phil-the-first. Who would actually love her one day; who'd meet a sudden bloody end but live on within her, chewing her heart as if it were a meaty bone.

Roger had the right idea: leave it be; case closed. Why stay yoked to a ghost? The only thing that matters is this: Phil's gone. Gone for good. Eva will never see him again.

She dropped her hands and said, "You're right. It's not important, nothing would change. There's no proof anyway."

"What's done is done. Forget about it."

"Nothing can bring him back."

But when she looked at Roger and blinked twice . . . there he was! Phil Lewis in the flesh! Standing before her one more time.

Turning his watch on his slender wrist. His hair and teeth and blue shirt; his accidental gestures.

Oh dear God, he was just like his father!

The light in the window dimmed. The air flickered with neon lines. Her breath quickened, her heart skipped, and she flushed under her bathrobe. Here was an unexpected *holy opportunity* to say goodbye to Phil at last. Now. In her own way.

She got to her feet, stepped forward, touched Roger's elbow. He jerked his face to one side as if she had slapped him. She grabbed his hand and slipped it under the top of her bathrobe, which opened like a cracked egg from collar to cinched waist. She spread his fingers over her breast and the poor man was shocked still.

His hand was smaller, softer than Phil's—but warm and fleshy like Phil's. A spark—a prickle—ran from her nipple through her body. It was almost painful.

Roger yanked his hand back. He scooped up a throw that was bunched on the sofa and dropped it over her shoulders. Like a paramedic on a call, responding to an emergency.

"I'm not cold"—shrugging it off. The robe parted, fell to her waist, her bare breasts heaving.

He was standing somewhere close behind. She felt the heat of his breathing on her naked back. The hairs on her nape were upright. His tension made the air jell; she inhaled in small sips. And thought she heard the beat of adrenalin pulsing in his veins, loud, louder, loudest: Roger was excited.

Now he put his hands on her shoulders, fingers moving, sticky-damp. When she closed her eyes they were Phil's hands, Phil's fingers on her skin. She turned around to face his son, her lips parted, eyes fluttering, thinking, Touch me . . . touch me *there*.

Roger stammered, "Some—sometimes when I'm with Loreen . . . it's you I'm seeing, not her."

She put a finger to her lips.

"I just wanted you to know."

She kissed him to stop his voice. Didn't know if he'd kiss her back, but he did—hard—biting her lip. Grabbed her arms as if to shake her, pulling her against his chest. He let go with one hand and untied her bathrobe, which fell heavily to the floor.

He stepped back to look at her. To see her nipples tighten and jump, her thighs quiver, knees touch. He stared at her with Phil's eyes, small, dark, and sparkling. When he didn't move she reached out and drew his head toward hers.

"We can't—" he started.

"Kiss me again."

Phil's lips on her mouth and throat, her left breast, right breast, the dip of her navel, belly bulge; the white flag of her panties. "Here," she whispered, "down there." The mound below: that wet gift.

Now she was tilting, the room turning upside down. Now she was in his arms—one of them across her back, the other arm under her knees. Carrying her as if she weighed next to nothing, a bit of fluff. Her head rolling side to side as if she were in a boat. The air like water on her skin: cold, tickling, slippery.

His eyes never left her. He seemed to know that if he looked elsewhere, he would lose her, she would slip away entirely.

"Sam!" His sudden startled voice. "What if—what about Sam?"

"He didn't take his key so he'll have to ring from downstairs."

He swung her onto her bed and paused, head tipped as if he were waiting for the sound of a bell. He combed his fingers through his hair. "I don't..."

"But I want you to. Just this once."

She sat up to open his buckle, the hidden buttons of his shirt, the bulging zipper of his fly. Leaned back on her elbows to slide his jeans down with her toes. Plucked at his underpants. Rubbed the swollen fabric over his crotch with the ball of her foot.

He sat on the bed and took off his socks. Then he was all over her, sucking her chin, kissing her neck. Arms and legs flung apart.

Her white panties swept away. His hot breath and curious fingers: lips, teeth, spittle, tongue.

He grunted and sweated with his eyes narrowed, mouth set as he pumped urgently in and out, steady as a metronome. "Slower," she whispered. "Wait for me."

And then she was moving in the ocean behind her eyes. Phil was swimming toward her, coming closer and closer. They were rubbing, sliding, twisting together like seaweed. She was holding her breath; focusing.

Now—do it. Love me. Now!

Phil's body. Phil's scent. Her breathing hoarse, her breath exploding. *Oh, Phil!*

Then she was still again, her brain collapsed. She only wanted to turn over and sleep for days.

But someone was pinning her down. Fallen over her, squishing her chest. She opened her heavy-lidded eyes and saw that it was Roger.

He rolled off. Flushed pink and panting, he swung his legs abruptly over the side of the bed and sat up. "That never should've happened," he said. "We can't let it happen again."

"Never again," she promised, a laugh in her throat she held back. As if she'd ever want to!

His arms dangled between his knees. "Loreen and I, we made a pact."

She stared at his rounded back, at a splash of bold freckles in the shape of Orion's Belt. Once she played connect-the-dots with lipstick on Roger's back, drawing constellations. Forever ago, it seemed now. On the distant star of history.

He stood up. He bent over from the waist as if trying to touch his toes but only picked his things up: pretty socks, bikini underpants, tight jeans. His pale, fleshy buttocks like a ball of risen bread dough.

She drew the covers up to her chin and watched him put his clothes on. He dressed with his eyes on the door. "Forget about it," Eva said. "What's done is done."

He slid his feet into his shoes and left the room quietly. The hall closet squealed open. Now he was putting on his cashmere coat, she imagined. Then she heard the buzzer sound; she heard him speaking loudly to the intercom, "I'm coming down!" Right after that, the apartment door thumped closed.

She got out of bed, grabbed her robe, pulled on her panties, wet her lips. Smoothed her hair in the dresser mirror. Pinched her cheeks rosy again. So Sam wouldn't notice anything wrong.

She ran to the foyer, opened the door, and looked down the hall-way. Sam was just getting off an elevator, waving, a sprinkle of snow on his jacket. She grinned so hard her mouth hurt. When he got inside she hugged him, inhaling his sweat. "How was the match?"

"We won the best of three," he said. "We're first in the league."

"That's great." She kissed his cheek.

"Have to hurry"—already moving. "Dad's waiting downstairs."

He went to his room to change and pack some things for the weekend. Eva followed close behind, waiting outside while he got ready. Minutes later he opened his door and handed her his dirty clothes. "Would you mind? I'm in a rush."

Instead she strode into his room and stopped at the end of his bed, bunching his uniform in her arms—the rubbery-smelling white socks; the shorts and damp T-shirt that were fresh and sour at the same time. "I'm proud of you," she told him.

"Thanks, Mom"—stuffing socks and underwear and a sweater into his knapsack.

"Not just about the game."

"I know." He didn't look up.

"Proud of the kind of person you are." She dropped his uniform on the bed, spread and rounded her arms as if hugging a red-wood. "I love you this much, Sam."

He finished packing, zipped the bag, and slung it over his shoulder. He walked up to her, head lowered, clutching something in his hand. "This is for you," he said.

He opened his palm and she looked down: a yellow badge with black letters, something like the Star of David Jews used to wear on their coats in Nazi Germany.

But no, this was altogether different—a gift from Sam. "'House League Volleyball Champions,'" she read aloud.

In the center of the round badge was a black felt volleyball with yellow seams—one straight across the middle, one curved above that, and one below, like closed lips; the top seam crosscut by five lines. "Sam, it's yours, you earned it. I really shouldn't take it."

He pulled a safety pin out of his jeans and stuck the badge to the front of her robe. Like a coronation, Eva thought: Queen Mum in her trailing robe. She swallowed hard to keep from crying. Tears would only embarrass him.

"You can wear it all weekend and give it back Sunday night."

"I will," she answered. "That's what I'll do. I won't even take my robe off."

He smiled at his shoes and was gone, unaware of what had taken place in Eva's bedroom only minutes before; of what was behind her now. What had been put to rest. The apartment door banged shut.

She tossed his clothes in the hamper and walked into the living room, a certain quickness in her step, as if she were skating.

Over and done with. History!

She stopped by a window and looked out at the falling snow. Across the street, in other buildings, other people were doing the same. A community of watchers, she thought, under a ceiling of clouds round and close and heaped together like apples in a basket. All eyes were on the snow, playful and unchecked, sliding on currents of air.

She swung around, her robe lifting. Like when she was an eager girl practicing ballet in tights and a leotard: pirouette and fouetté, jeté and chaîné... In a time before Roger. Before Phil.

She danced because it felt good; no one there to stop her. She danced until she was dizzy and hot. Then she loosened her robe and let it slip apart at the center, fanning herself with her hands.

She circled back to the window and stared at the blowing snow—those quick flakes that seemed more important than anything. Movement and *snowness*: more important than her life so far.

She spread her arms, touching the glass, leaning toward the gap between one building and the next, and felt that she was falling gently, gliding on a huff of wind . . . What matters most, she decided, is the moment you're swirling in. What matters is lightness and grace.

12

ONE EVENING AFTER WORK she drove to Olga Bauer's office somewhere north in a deserted industrial area. She parked the car and felt nervous getting out on an empty road, not for herself but for the letters in her briefcase. What if someone leaped out of the dark and made off with them? She hurried to the proper building, leaned on the bell, and was buzzed in.

On the second floor, Olga was alone in her office. She shook Eva's hand, then led her through a waiting room and into a back room crowded with papers and boxes. They sat kitty-corner at a long metal table. Olga folded her hands and said, "So. Let me see what you've brought."

Eva pulled a folder from her briefcase and opened it. She'd made copies of all the letters, even though there were some that were too faint or transparent to reproduce very well. She passed Olga the first one, a letter from Mutti, and the woman put on reading glasses and bent low over the page. "Let me have them all," she said. Hesitating just a moment, Eva gave Olga the rest.

A dark-eyed woman, forty-something, with brown hair, blotchy skin, the start of a double chin. A bun on her head was half undone as if she'd been out jogging. Her blouse was pulled tight across the breadth of her bosom, a gap between two buttons revealing some of the bra below. Eva glanced under the table: a run in Olga's stocking. She found the woman's imperfections reassuring. It was easier to trust someone whose humanness was apparent.

She'd been expecting something else, she was embarrassed to admit. Someone older, shipshape, with fair hair and blue eyes; brusque and impatient or icily disapproving. Whose father had been a soldier or a minor Nazi bureaucrat just following orders.

Olga finished skimming the pages and looked up. "My father was from Düsseldorf"—as if responding to Eva's thoughts. "He worked for the railroad. During the war he saw things . . . awful things he talked about. And so I'm very interested to read your letters. We can start right away," she said. "Did you bring a tape recorder?"

Eva emptied her briefcase. She pushed the recorder across the table and turned it on. A faint hum.

"The writing is clear enough, except in a few spots. I'll read what I can out loud, translating as I go."

Eva leaned forward with her elbows on the table, rolling a pen in her fingers. She nodded at Olga to start.

Olga read the letters from Mutti and Arnold, all from Poland in 1941, into the recorder, her voice surprisingly high-pitched. "My dear Izzy," they all began. In February, Mutti wrote that Papa passed away on the tenth from a heart attack. A month later she complained that she was run down, weighing only fifty kilograms, and so depressed she doubted she could go on much longer . . . Arnold said it was necessary to leave his job in Kraków and come live with Mutti because her doctor insisted she couldn't be alone anymore—and so, God help them, Rosa and the children were still on their own in Berlin. His shoes were worn out from his endless worried pacing.

In June, Mutti asked for money for a headstone for Papa's grave. She wrote that he was lying in an unmarked pile of sand and couldn't possibly rest like that. She dreamt of him every night and couldn't sleep.

"'Otherwise, one day passes like the next one, very monotonous. Going to the cemetery every Sunday is my only change of routine. The boredom and constant mulling are driving me crazy.'"

A few weeks later she pleaded for money again, explaining that she was penniless now that Arnold was out of work, completely dependent on whatever Izzy sent her. She'd already sold what belongings were left to pay for Papa's funeral—there was nothing else to live on.

"'I am feeling lonely and hopeless. They won't let us leave this place, but staying is impossible. What is to become of me? You are my only support and consolation, Izzy. You are my whole life now.'"

Olga turned the recorder off and went to another room, while Eva doodled on a pad. She was drawing a stick figure, its head in a noose, like a body on a gallows in that word game, Hangman. She was thinking of Mutti's shrinking world, her looming and brutal fate. She was thinking of Izzy, severed from his mother when she needed him most: his longing to save her; his drilling shame. And yet if he had been in Brzesko like Arnold, dejected and unemployed, how could he have helped her more?

Olga returned with a glass of water, glancing at Eva. "Ready," she said, half questioning; then she picked up another sheet, flicked on the recorder, and spoke into the microphone. July. A letter from Rosa.

"'Don't be angry, Izzy, that I'm only just answering your letter now, but I've had a small breakdown and couldn't write. Coping with everything by myself for almost three years now has been a heavy burden. I've been working very long hours at Siemens for several months and am dead tired in the evenings. Nevertheless, I am not earning nearly enough.

"'The death of our father was a hard blow. His picture hangs over my bed and he still lives on for me. I miss him so very much. I miss Arnold, Mother, and you. Everything is desolate. When will we see each other again?

"'Martin will be ten soon. He cries every night for his father. Kurt will have his bar mitzvah July 26 in the rabbi's apartment. With no one here to celebrate, it will be a solemn occasion, though

I will try my best to look happy for his sake. Arnold is in Brzesko, as you probably know. He said it was his duty to stay with Mother in her loneliness and poor health, even though he had to quit his job in Kraków and knew it would be difficult to get work elsewhere. In fact, he has found nothing. His emotional state is bad and getting worse daily.'"

Olga stopped and looked up. "Your father's sister?"

"We never met. Aunt Rosa died there."

"Her letter is full of despair."

Eva nodded, breathing fast. She was scrawling figures on her pad, pressing down too hard, the pen scratching the paper.

"I'll continue," Olga said.

"'My heartfelt thanks for the money you have sent till now and for what you might spare again. I understand that you have been unable so far to raise enough for ship's passage for me and the children, but please try harder. There must be something else you can do! Though I know that you have urgent obligations toward Mother as well, you *must* get the tickets, Izzy, at least for the two boys. Arnold cannot help us and I've already sold everything I could possibly do without. Surely there is someone or another group you can call on! My situation is very grave. I will have to leave my apartment soon. You must do anything possible and make every sacrifice. We are quickly running out of time.'"

In September, she said, "Dear God! I would never have dreamt our efforts would fail because there is not enough money for the passages. Izzy, I am sick with grief. Is there nothing more to be done? Is there no one else you can turn to? I am so afraid."

Eva cringed to hear that and felt as if her heart had been flattened under the heel of a boot. She was Rosa, begging her brother for help. She was Izzy, scrounging for dollars, increasingly desperate. Who else could he talk to? What should he do?

"He was making peanuts," Eva said, "working in a factory. He gave her every cent he could!"

"It's clear that he tried his best," Olga said quietly. "Your father was a good person living in bad times."

He did try! Eva spoke to Rosa silently. He loved you very much and he did what he could to save you. There was no opportunity for him to be a hero.

She wrote again in October, but the note had been heavily censored. It started out with lines about the cold weather approaching and her fruitless search for a stove; the harshness of winter that would only make her circumstances utterly unbearable . . . All the rest was blacked out.

Izzy sent a letter to Brzesko in November, and one to Berlin. To Mutti and Arnold he said, "With Hilda's blessing I have raised a large sum of money, but can't say more than this. I know you cannot emigrate, and new regulations have blocked all transfers, but I will get something to you, as God is my witness. I have already sent enough to Rosa for the passages."

To his sister he simply said, "The money for the tickets will arrive very shortly, though not in the usual way. I expect to see you soon."

"He got it—he got the money!" Eva half rose in her seat. "But why didn't he tell me?"

"We don't know what he had to do, or if the money got through . . . or if it would've helped her by that time anyway."

"I don't care what he did to get it, only that he sent it—that he came through after all."

"He acted bravely," Olga said, "even though it was too late." She put the envelopes mailed from the Bronx on the table. "Both his letters came back, as you can see."

Eva looked them over. The letters had been opened, examined by censors, sealed, and stamped "Return to Sender, Service Suspended." One was returned in March, the other in August 1942— by which time his relatives were dying in a camp or a ghetto or already killed.

But that didn't keep him from speaking to them in his mind, their new place of residence; from seeing the dead when he stared at the living. Part of him would be forever absent, Eva knew, squeezed in the palm of history.

An old anger burned her cheeks: there was no spot in his heart for her because it was filled with the bones and ashes of Auschwitz.

Yet how could she fault *them*, the unlucky victims, for stealing her father's soul? They were no more to blame for suffering than he was for surviving.

And how could she fault *him* for brooding over loved ones he wasn't able to rescue despite his every effort?

No, he is not to blame.

Olga put the papers down, arranging them neatly, and turned off the recorder. She pulled off her reading glasses and lay them close beside the letters, as if to watch over them. Then she leaned back in her chair, pinching the bridge of her nose.

Eva put the tape recorder back in her briefcase and reached for her checkbook. "I'd like to pay you something, for your time and trouble."

"No, nothing. Put that away. I wanted to do this, please understand. It was such an evil time."

Eva put the letters away. She stood up, extended a hand to Olga, and thanked her. The woman took Eva's hand and held it a moment. "It's all so sad," she said. "So awful for everyone."

Eva hugged her briefcase in her arms and left the office. Crossing the road to her car, she thought about Rosa again. Imagined her aunt's voice, deeper than Olga's and heavy with misery. The words she'd heard were Rosa's; the life glimpsed also hers: a world cracked, convulsing. Rosa's pain in *her* words—not explained by Izzy but experienced by Eva.

She has never felt more caught up in the war than this. Never felt more apart.

Her face was wet when she got in the car. Now her father was on her mind—*Izzy's* pain, Izzy's shame . . . always there, that hot wound. Like having barbs or razor blades or broken glass under your skin. He was always hurting, ready to burst; always looking backward. A half-life, not his own. A life of loss; a lost life.

You *almost* saved them, Daddy, she thought. Everybody understands.

Now let go. It's over.

For a long while she didn't move. Finally she wiped her face and started the car. She threw her briefcase in the back, and this is what she was thinking: just like her father, she would always hear the murmuring, insistent voices of the dead . . . but maybe not as loudly now. Regardless of the weight she carried, she would move on.

The phone rang early the next day. Eva was still in bed. Still another hour before she had to wake Sam for school. She picked up on the fourth ring. Long distance. "Yes?" she said.

Dr. Willard calling from the health care center. "Yes, yes?"—standing barefoot. "What's the matter? What's wrong?"

Dr. Willard cleared his throat. "Your father had another stroke last night, during the night. We lost him. I'm afraid he's gone. There was nothing we could do."

The receiver wobbled in her hand. Her feet were cold on the wood floor. She turned toward the bedroom window, seeing her father's face in the glass. Not the way Izzy was the last time she saw him, but as he had once been, young and spry and handsome. So! he might've said to the angels. What are you doing after work?

Dr. Willard was waiting. She could hear his expectant breath. He wanted her to cry out or stammer, No, it can't be! He was doing so much better—he was trying to speak! But she felt too tired for that and wasn't even sure those were the right words. Maybe she should ask if there was anyone with him in the end—but no, he would've died alone, as he had lived his last years. His mind shrinking quickly to a single tiny point of light.

They would have found him pale and still, no longer breathing. They would've checked his pulse, called the doctor with the cowlick, disconnected various tubes, and rolled her father out the door and straight to the morgue on a squeaky-wheeled gurney. Gone back and stripped the bed. *Well, that's over with.*

Surely those were the proper words: Thank God it's over.

"Thanks for letting me know," Eva said to the doctor. "Thank you for trying."

She hung up and stood by the window for a moment, seeing Izzy's face again. She pressed her palms against the glass, level with her shoulders, and felt a draft on her hot, shaky fingers like a cool breath. Kissed a spot above her hands about where his cheek should be.

When she was steadier, she woke Sam to tell him the news. Sitting on the side of his bed, she reached out and cupped his head. "Grampa died last night. I just heard. In his sleep. Quietly, without pain."

He rolled over, folded his arms, and nestled against her thigh. "Are you very sad?"

"Yes," she said.

"Will you be okay?"

"Yes, I will."

"What will you do?" he asked.

"Miss him. Remember him. That's all we can do."

13

TORONTO IS UGLY IN MARCH, cold, damp, and overcast. Snow is melting, trees are bare; everywhere the grass is brown and littered with wet paper, candy wrappers, dog shit. Rain, flurries, sleet, hail: all this is possible. People turn their collars up, duck their heads, and lurch forward, hair swirling in the wind, their faces as gray-white as the threatening sky. But on the morning Izzy was buried the sun broke through for a short while, so that his poplar casket, positioned on a cloth-covered rack over his dug grave, shimmered briefly with pale light.

The site was on a low hill, fairly close to Hilda's—not right beside it because he hadn't reserved in advance and the next plot was taken, but two rows back and a few spaces to the left. Four people showed up for the graveside service, not including the grim-looking employees of the funeral home or the nasal-voiced rabbi—who had never actually met the deceased but talked to his daughter earlier and was able to give a short speech about the finer attributes of one Isidor Schneider.

"The war—the Shoah—marked his life," the rabbi said in part. "It separated Izzy from his beloved parents and sister and their deaths forever wounded him. But though he suffered, he survived and managed to make a new life here in North America. Some would call it an ordinary, unremarkable life since nothing like his flight from Berlin or the devastating murder of his family in Europe ever happened to him again.

"But is this not a blessing? Should we not be thankful that men like Izzy Schneider overcame their losses and were able to live fruitful lives? We celebrate his ordinary love for his wife Hilda, his love for his daughter Eva, here now before us, and his grandson"—nodding at Sam. "For his one-time son-in-law and business associate, Roger, also here today. For his many friends"—a glance at Loreen—"and all those unable to be with us this morning."

The rabbi peered at the four mourners, trying to catch each one's eye before he continued. "We celebrate a man today who lived wholeheartedly despite many obstacles. A generous and loving man who worked hard, was kind to others, lived a simple, decent life—and in so doing celebrated the Almighty, his Creator..."

Eva looked past him and down the rows of headstones, uniform in height, width, color, and style. How easy it was, she thought, to sum up an entire life in a handful of sentences: to tell a simple story. To smooth over the rough spots—the contradictions, ironies, and tiers of complexity—with a few well-practiced words. To draw a recognizable outline of a person, but omit the telling details—that he *didn't* surmount his losses; that he lived half-heartedly, his love unreliable.

This then is what we leave behind when we pass on—this crude impression, like a stamp on a bill of exchange. Like how she has already begun to remember Phil: a war hero, once loved. We live on in the minds of others, but more and more vaguely.

Unless we're very lucky. Unless there is someone we knew in our lifetime who cares enough, is sensitive enough, to remember us in all our particulars. A person who chooses to act as a kind of librarian, a keeper of nuances as well as information; a guardian of intricate memories, both good and bad. If we are not recalled in exactly the right way, it's as if we didn't live at all. In that way, at least, her father was a fortunate man: Eva will remember him well.

Using a razor blade, the rabbi cut the black ribbons on Eva's and Sam's lapels to show that their lives had been rent. Then he began chanting prayers. He davened on one side of the grave while the rest stood on the other side in a short, uneven line with Roger and Eva on either end, Loreen and Sam in the middle. The service was brief. Finally, in unison, they all recited Kaddish: "*Yisgadal v'yiskadash sh'may rabbo...*"

After that, one by one they threw dirt on the coffin, not yet lowered into the grave. One by one they washed their hands in water poured from a pitcher by a frowning attendant, and then the service was over.

Everybody started back along the soggy crest of the hill. It was cloudy again, the sky dark; cold enough and damp enough for freezing rain, even snow. Everybody buttoned his coat. As they filed past her mother's grave, Eva stopped briefly to put a rock on the tombstone. "He's here now," she whispered. "You can rest in peace." Then she rushed ahead to catch up to the others, who were already partway down the slope of brown grass and dirty snow.

Loreen was having trouble walking. One of her shoes had got stuck in mud and the heel snapped off, so that she hopped and hobbled, hanging onto Roger's arm, waving the heel in her hand as if it were a pointer. He looped his arm around her waist and made a show of almost carrying her the rest of the way.

They passed through a row of pines and went to their respective vehicles parked at the side of the road. The hearse drove away first, followed by the rabbi in his own car. Roger opened the door of his BMW and sat in the driver's seat, adjusting a lever, while Loreen approached Sam and Eva, kissed Sam on both cheeks, touched Eva's hand and murmured something appropriate. Neither mentioned going back to Eva's apartment for coffee, cake, and sandwiches. It wasn't that sort of funeral. Loreen turned, limped away, and motioned Roger out of the car.

He walked over, head down, and gave Sam a quick hug. He kicked a rock with the tip of his shoe. Then he looked up and said quietly, "I'm sorry."

She raised her eyes and stared at a soft, blurry, distant point. Yes, he was, she felt it: his hard regret. She kept her eyes fixed on the scenery and nodded.

He shoved his hands in his coat pockets, turned, and went back to his car. Loreen stuck her arm out the window and waved at them, then the engine raced and the BMW sped off in a plume of smoke and gravel.

Sam was standing on the road, half covered in gray exhaust. He wagged his arms like a semaphore until the air cleared again. Then he opened the passenger door of Eva's car: "Let's go."

"What's your hurry?"

"I'm hungry."

Eva took him by the hand and led him round the car instead, up a small rise to a weather-stained wooden bench set between tree trunks. "Sit a minute," she said, and he flopped down beside her.

The sky was even gloomier now, the sun submerged in a sea of clouds; the air as wet as it was cold. They stared ahead at the empty road, the bent trees and hill beyond, the even rows of tombstones. Eva lifted her eyes and looked further into the distance. In another part of the cemetery where the headstones were higher and the grounds dotted with evergreens, Phil was lying in his grave. She thought for a moment of going there, but didn't move. He would rest uneasily regardless of whether she saw him or not. And so she decided to do herself a favor and let him be.

"Anyone special buried here?" Sam asked.

"Your grandparents."

"I don't mean like them."

"Don't know." Eva shrugged. "Anyway, whatever a person might've been in his lifetime, he's just like everybody else when he gets here."

"Bones and dust?"

"History."

Sam picked up some pine cones and tossed them around his lap. "What about Grampa—you think he's gonna like it here?"

"He's close to Grandma, where he belongs."

Sam threw a pine cone that bounced off the roof of the car. "It wasn't much of a funeral."

"What do you mean?"

"There shoulda been more people. It shoulda been in Florida. Then his friends and neighbors coulda come too."

"I don't think it mattered to him, so long as you and I were there."

"At least Dad and Loreen showed up."

"Yes, that was good of them."

"She's really nice. I told you."

A squirrel stopped in front of them and stood up on its hind legs. Sam held out a pine cone, but the squirrel only sniffed it and ran away. He threw the cone in a wide arc and it landed somewhere out of sight. Then he turned to Eva. "I have something for you," he said.

"You do? What?"

He reached into his jacket pocket and carefully pulled out a flat and shiny object. He opened his palm and showed it to her: the silver cigarette case.

"Here. Take it."

"Sam, I can't. He gave it to you."

He put the case into her hand. "You should have it, not me."

She paused. "But I don't think..."

"I made up my mind. You have to."

"Well then." She smiled at him.

"You don't have to give it back. It's yours for keeps."

She looked down, opened the case. A little bit tarnished, but the writing inside was perfectly clear. "Did Grampa tell you the story—?"

"He saved a guy from drowning."

"He was only nineteen at the time . . . a summer evening in Berlin. He'd gone for a swim in a lake in the forest and was resting by the shore when he heard someone shouting, so he looked out across the water and saw a head, a pair of arms—a man going under..."

"You don't have to say everything. I get the idea."

"He didn't even stop to think! He dove in, swam to him, and grabbed him from behind, then he yanked him to the surface. The man was so frightened that he swung his arms and kicked his legs and threw himself at your grandfather, pulling him under too, but Grampa was strong enough to pin the man's arms back and slap him hard across the face, and in this way he dragged him ashore. His name was Jakob Abrahamsohn, and he was so grateful that your grandpa—your *zayde*—jumped in and saved him that he gave him this cigarette case. '... to my lifesaver Isidor Schneider...' it says inside."

"I know that already," Sam said.

"Not all of it," Eva said. "I want you to know the whole story."

"What for?"

"To get it right."

"I didn't need to hear it again."

"But listen to me. Are you listening?"

"Yeah, if it's so important."

"It is important."

"Okay."

She took his smooth, slender hand and pressed it between her own. "You have to remember everything, to pay attention and not forget. Watch, learn, memorize *everything*, from now on. Do you hear me, Sam?"

"I do," he said.